CATRIONA TROTH :::::::::::

*To Michelle,
from
Catriona Troth*

TRISKELE BOOKS

Copyright © 2013 Catriona Troth

The moral rights of the author have been asserted.

All rights Reserved. No part of this publication may be reproduced, distributed or transmitted in any form or by any means, including photocopying, recording or other electronic or mechanical methods, without prior permission of the publisher, except in the case of brief quotation embedded in critical reviews and certain other non-commercial uses permitted by copyright law. For permission requests, write to the publisher, addressed "Attention: Permissions Coordinator," at the email address below.

Ghost Town is based on real events and many of its locations described can be found on a map. However, the people involved in those events, and the way they conducted themselves, are unrelated to the characters in this book—all of whom sprang entirely from the author's imagination. Any resemblance to any persons, living or dead, is purely coincidental.

Published by Piebald Publishing

piebald.publishing@gmail.com

ISBN: 978-0-9576180-4-6

To Phillip, who thinks his wife is weird but gives her space to get on with it anyway.

And to the patience and incisive minds of the members of the Writers' Asylum—especially Jill Marsh, Amanda Hodgkinson and Sharon Hutt, who were at once the book's greatest champions and its harshest critics.

This is for you.

CONTENTS

Author's Note	vii
GHOST TOWN	1
Acknowledgements	457
Glossary	459
Also From Triskele Books	471

Author's Note

Coventry has a reputation as a concrete monstrosity—blighted first by WWII bombs and then by ill-judged post-war planning. Some of that is undoubtedly true. But in the seven years I lived there (from 1976 to 1983) I came to know a different Coventry. Hidden away behind all that concrete are survivors of the old medieval city—the little pot-bellied houses on Spon Street, the Guild Hall with its extraordinary angel ceilings, the 'Doom' painting on the walls of Holy Trinity Church. One of the most beautiful places on earth to stand is on the steps between the old and new cathedrals, seeing the ruins of one reflected in the great West Window of the other.

Contained within the old city walls until the end of the 19th Century, Coventry's city centre is surrounded by satellite villages that have characters of their own. But some things bring the whole city together. One of them is Coventry City FC—the Sky Blues. And when I was living there, the other was Two Tone Records. Ska bands like The Specials and The Selecter were the sound of Coventry, and for a few years they reigned supreme.

Even in my comfortable, insulated student existence, I couldn't miss the fact that by 1981, Coventry was also deeply troubled. Tension between skinheads and Asian youths was escalating into violence. Two racially motivated murders—one of a student and one of a young doctor—took place in the early summer of 1981, as did the bombing of a Hindu temple. The murder of the student led to a series of protest marches which were met by furious counter-demonstrations by the skinheads, culminating in the Battle of Poole Meadow. The Specials, known for their anti-racist stance, responded by organising a Concert for Racial Harmony.

To my shame, I knew less about these events as they were happening than I should have done. But I do remember the sense of growing tension. I also remember that after that concert the mood changed. The city stepped back from the brink.

This book is my attempt to explore what happened that summer. It is also my love letter to Coventry—a wonderful and much misunderstood city.

Catriona Troth, September 2013

Chapter 1

The night before Ossie returned to South Africa, he and I camped on the window seat in the chaplaincy, half hidden behind its dusty curtains, and watched his farewell party gyrate past. The Selecter played on a tinny cassette player. A first year skanked by, plastic beer mug in hand, splashing lager in his wake. I leaned over to share the joke and caught sight of the lines of exhaustion scoring Ossie's face. The laughter died in my throat.

Ever since he made his decision, I'd heard him prowling round the house at night. By my reckoning, he hadn't slept in weeks.

"I can't just watch things happening. I need to go back."

"You know what it's like out there, Ossie. Look what they did to Biko."

In South Africa, you didn't have to use guns and bombs to be defined as a terrorist. Words could get you locked up. Words could get you killed.

"I plan to stay alive. I promise you that, Maia."

But plans go wrong. Every day, every hour.

Damn it, I wasn't going to cry. I dashed away the threatened tears, conjured up a smile and jogged him with my shoulder.

"How am I supposed to manage without you, hey?"

He took my hand, pale against the rosy pink of his palms. The lines on his hands were the colour of sun-faded Indian ink.

The backs like baked earth.

"You know what they say. Strike a woman, strike a rock."

"Right now, this woman's like talc."

"Pure quartz. She doesn't always know it, that's all." Ossie tugged my fingers. "Someone has to carry on here, *nosisi*."

If I had any stone in my body, it was lodged in my stomach. "All my life, I've been going on marches. Attending meetings. Boycotting sodding grapes. If any of it worked, you wouldn't have to go play the big hero, would you?"

"You can't win a war on just one front."

"This isn't a front, though, is it? We're back behind the lines with the catering corps and bloody ENSA. Doing a song and dance act while the bombs fall."

The corners of Ossie's mouth quirked into a smile. "You? Doing a song and dance act? That would bring the South African government to its knees."

"Sod off!"

"I think you have invented a whole new weapon of war."

I threw a punch and he held up his arms to protect himself, overplaying it. "You get yourself killed and I'll bloody murder you."

"Then if I get myself killed, I must remember to stay out of your way."

When things were bad, we teased each other. It's what we did, Ossie and I.

Tonight, we were dancing on knives.

Towards the end of the evening, Shona and Philly found us behind the curtain and informed us they would stay the night at our place and drive Ossie to Coventry station in the morning. I scowled. You're only here, I thought, because if anything happens to him, if he becomes another headline, you'll say, 'I was there, you know, the night before he went back.' It'll become one of the stories you tell about yourselves.

But Ossie was too much of a gentleman to tell them we wanted this last night to ourselves. I let myself be bundled into the back of their 2CV with Philly, while Shona sat in the front with Ossie, talking loudly over the rattle of the engine. At the flat, Ossie got out a quarter bottle of supermarket whisky and poured measures into an assortment of glasses.

"Cheers," Shona said, from Ossie's favourite chair. "May you be forty years in heaven before the devil knows you're dead."

I took a gulp of whisky.

"Freedom in our lifetime," I said, my voice too loud for the room.

Just before the whisky ran out, Ossie got to his feet. "*Mayibuye iAfrika*," he said. Come back, Africa. We echoed him and downed the last dregs. A moment of silence followed, during which, I swear, Ossie seemed to grow taller.

"Time for me to go to bed," he said.

"Me too."

Outside his room at the top of the stairs, I held up my hand and his palm touched mine.

"I have something for you," he said. "Go. Go. I will follow you."

I sat on my bed, feeling drunk and wretched. I hadn't thought to buy anything for him. I'd spent the last of my dole money chipping in for the booze at the party. All I had left was my bus fare to the station. And I didn't even need that any more.

He came in holding his battered, dog-eared copy of Steve Biko's *I Write What I Like*. The one he'd bought in the University bookshop the week we met, and carried with him everywhere since. He put it in my hands.

"Oh, Oz. Not your Biko—"

"You take it, *nosisi*. I can't risk being caught with it."

After a while, we got under the quilt to keep warm. I could smell the clean scent of Lifebuoy soap on his skin. The smell of minibus rides, the two of us squashed together on the back seat on the way to another demo. Of long nights in the bar. Of snatched breakfasts in the flat and fights over the hot water.

We'd shared a bed before, staying over after a march in some crowded bedsit, or falling asleep in the midst of an all-night argument. For all that, we'd never been particularly physical. Friends, not lovers. It felt strange to have his arms round me. Stranger still when we kissed.

It was a desperate kiss, more sadness than sex. But it led on to fumblings with buttons and zips. To fingers gliding over my skin. To a tender fuck that fizzled but never flamed.

Before I switched the light off, I let my gaze rest on Ossie's face. Maybe I had found a gift for him. For the first time in weeks, he was asleep.

I watched over him all night, while my head stopped spinning in slow circles and started to throb. Sometime before dawn, he rolled over in his sleep, dragging the quilt with him. I saw our legs, uncovered and scissored together. Dark entwined with light.

In the recesses of my mind, an image stirred. My mom and me, newly arrived in yet another African village. My nine-year-old self, peeking through the cracks in the wall the mud hut that was to be our temporary home. Outside, a small boy playing in the dust. I wanted to stay hidden, watching him through the walls, but my mother shooed me outside.

"This time, try to blend in, Maia."

The boy was squatting. I copied him, balancing awkwardly on the balls of my feet, but he tugged at my blond pigtails and I tumbled over. He thrust his arm against mine—dusty mahogany against pale pearwood—and ran off, giggling.

Mom took me on her study trips to Africa every summer through my school years. Blonde hair and fair skin pretty much ruled out my 'blending in;' so I mostly chose to stay watching from the shadows.

Ossie changed that. He and I fitted together like two halves of the same whole. With him, I stopped being an observer and started being a participant.

God, I was going to miss him.

The street lamp winked out and the light of a winter dawn began to bleed though the thin curtains. My hangover was coming on nicely. Nausea had arrived to accompany the throbbing head, and my arms and legs trembled as if I'd just finished a workout. I shivered for a few minutes under our miserly trickle of a shower, then stole downstairs to find aspirin.

Shona and Philly were making themselves at home in our kitchen. Shona thrust a cup of coffee at me. Her bandana pulled her features tight and made her eyes bulge like a gecko's.

"You've no milk," she said.

You invited yourself here, I thought. Get your own bloody milk. I took the coffee from her and swallowed a scalding sip. Philly had burnt the toast and was scraping it in the sink. The noise was like sandpaper on my brain.

Ossie came down, rucksack on his shoulder. His knee brushed mine as he sat down and the shock reverberated through my body. A hot flood of embarrassment first, tinged with the recollection of desire. A sudden need to laugh. And then, as if someone had reached inside me and pulled something out, an unravelling. A sense of loss, like an intimation of mortality. Oh, God, how was it possible to feel so much in such a short time and not fall apart?

Tonight, Ossie would fly from Heathrow to Zimbabwe. From there, he would go by train to a town close to the South African border. He'd be met by sympathisers who would take him to a safe house to plan when and how to smuggle him across. Once in South Africa, he planned to travel around the townships, carrying Biko's subversive message. If he was caught by Pik Botha's security police, he could be detained without trial. He could disappear, like hundreds before him, lost in the system or murdered in detention.

It was real. It was about to happen. Time was running out.

I could hear Shona asking questions and Ossie answering. Another voice, on the radio, said something about a fire … A house fire in London … Children dead … But it was just noise.

Shona clicked off the radio.

"Ossie needs to get to the station."

The yellow front of the locomotive appeared, slowing as it approached the platform. Ossie put his arms around me, pulling me close enough to feel his heart.

"Look at me, *nosisi*."

"I can't. If I do, I'll cry."

"So you going to let me go without a look, hey?"

I tilted my head up and when he kissed me, I tasted salt on our lips.

Then he was on the train, waving from the open window of the carriage door, moving his arm in wide, slow arcs until a twist of the track took him out of sight. As the last carriage cleared the end of the platform, my blurred eyes turned it into a coffin, borne through a crowd of mourners.

It was a shock to tumble back into the here and now and find two pairs of eyes staring at me.

"Want a lift?" Shona said. I never noticed Philly speak, except in whispered comments in Shona's ear. I shook my head and they walked away, arms brushing against each other as they went.

As they disappeared onto the main concourse, the platform

seemed to buckle under my feet. My stomach heaved and I just made it to the toilet before Philly's toast came back up. I waited for the floor to stop undulating, then splashed cold water on my face. I wanted to rinse my mouth out, but a notice behind the taps warned that the water was not for drinking. I ran my tongue over my teeth, spat twice, and rinsed the sour saliva from the sink.

On the benches out in the waiting room, two old biddies were muttering, their whispers pitched in audible range.

"It was her. Snogging that nignog. Did you see?"

"Big rubbery lips … I couldn't fancy it."

"Makes you feel quite sick."

They saw me staring and went quiet, their lips disappearing into a set line, their chins puckering into their necks like a pair of old turtles. When I was sure they'd taken a good look, I stalked past them and shouldered open the door.

Chapter 2

Baz huddled his coat around him. Holding his camera at waist level, he tracked a young black boy dawdling along Coldharbour Lane, one foot on the kerb, one in the gutter. Just as a frozen puddle caught the reflection of the kid's trainers, he pressed the shutter release. The boy wheeled round, his stance mimicking the bad bwais on the Frontline.

"Wha' you doin', raas claat?"

"Just taking pictures, man. It's cool." Baz pointed the camera again and took another shot, smiling. The boy's body unwound. He screwed up his face, stuck out his tongue and ambled off.

Baz twisted the lens on the front of the camera, zooming out to view the bleak frontage of a block of flats. The early morning light made jagged shadows under the zigzag window ledges. A play of dark on light.

You had to play it cautious, taking photographs round here. Some days he'd see a gang of youths limin' on the street, hold up his camera and they would strut and pose for him. Another day, the same gang were as likely to try and grab the camera from round his neck and smash it.

He took a step to one side, framing another shot, and the pint of milk in the pocket of his greatcoat bumped against his leg, reminding him he was supposed to be taking it back to Abena. She wouldn't thank him if he wandered off to take photographs. He slipped the camera back inside his coat and retraced his steps.

Abena's bedsit was on the top floor of a Victorian mansion house, in what must once have been servants' quarters. On the last flight of stairs, his feet echoed on the narrow wooden treads.

Inside the tiny room, Abena pressed herself against him, her fingers tugging at his long hair. The red and gold kente cloth from her bed was knotted under her arms like a sarong, leaving her shoulders bare. Her skin was the same coffee brown as his—hers a shade less milky, her face and arms freckled with darker spots. 'My Milk and Honey,' he called her in tender moments.

Not so many of those lately.

"What we going to do today?" she asked. "I thought I'd cook us a real Ghanaian meal. And tonight, what you say, maybe we check out that new sound system at the Bali Hai?"

Before he could answer, a knock sounded at the door. Abena veered away and flung the door wide. The young black woman on the landing was smartly dressed, her hair neat in cornrow plaits. Yet her eyes were wide with shock and she looked as if she were about to topple over. Abena grabbed her arm and steered her to a chair by the gateleg table.

"Denise, wh'appen, girl?"

It always came as a surprise that Abena—so loud and authoritative—could make herself gentle when needed. She lowered her voice, resting an arm near Denise's. The other woman's voice was almost a whisper.

"You hear the radio?"

"Not this morning."

"There's been a fire over at New Cross. People say some National Front type threw a firebomb into a house where they have a birthday party."

Baz, pouring water into the washing up bowl, had to put the

kettle down to avoid splashing himself with scalding water.

"I went as soon as I heard," Denise said. "Man and man were coming to see if they could help." He saw her hand grope for Abena's and squeeze it hard. "Girl, you can't imagine the smell of that house."

No need to imagine. Baz knew the smell of charred wood and melted plastic, of singed fabric doused in gallons of water. And that other smell, the one that would stay with you the rest of your life. The smell of seared human flesh.

A plate slipped from his grip and fell into the sink with a clatter. Abena threw him an irritable glance.

"People are trying to find out who's dead, who's alive," Denise said. "Some of the bodies so burnt up, no one knows how they will be identified."

Baz put his hands flat on the draining board, steadying himself, breathing slow.

A piece of charred driftwood, that was what someone looked like when they'd been burnt to death.

"They were children, Abena. Children enjoying a party. Who could do such a thing?" Denise asked.

Abena snorted. "How many murders have there been in the past few years and you ask me that?"

The bad times were on their way back. They all knew it.

The boy he'd photographed that morning came loafing into Baz's mind. How old were the children at the party? Older than that, surely? He tried to swallow. Found he couldn't breathe.

"I want you to come with me," Denise told Abena. "Talk to people. See what you can do to help."

"Anything I can do. You know that, girl."

They arranged to meet later and Abena went to see Denise out. When she came back, Baz was bundling his camera into his kitbag. She stood in the doorway, rocking on the balls of her feet.

"What you doing?"

"No point my hanging around if you're going over to New Cross."

She came in, banging the door shut behind her. "You could make a difference, Baz. You and your camera."

"You expect me to take pictures of the injured? The bereaved …?"

In his head, flames licked the scar tissue on his shoulder. Abena had that look on her face, the one she used in public meetings—the one that said, 'if only you will listen, you will see how reasonable I am being.'

"Fuck my days, this is not just some family tragedy, cha?"

"I know—"

"If some racist has done this thing, the whole black community is under attack."

He knew. He knew it in his bones. And it changed nothing. He took a step towards the door and she planted herself in front of him, arms akimbo.

"How many times has this happened and whitey has turned his back on us? Your pictures can make people see what they don't want to admit."

"Abena—" He struggled for a way to explain. Not for the first time, the words refused to come. "I have to go."

Abena planted a hand in the middle of his chest. "You and me, we're the same, cha? Mixed race. Half caste. Yellow. Bounty. That's what they call us. But there's one big difference. When I see the way black people are treated in this country, I say I am black. All black. And I fight to change things for all of us."

He'd heard this speech before, in public and in private. "And you think I don't? Abena, it's different for—"

She sucked her lips back, kissing her teeth. "You bet it's different. Because the white man, he looks at me and he says, 'you're black.' But when he looks at you, he's not so sure, is he? And I guess that gives you a get-out clause."

The unfairness silenced him. Part of him wanted to strip off, expose the scars on his back, tell her the truth about how he came by them. But the habit of silence burnt too deep.

Abena dropped her arm and stepped aside.

"Fuck off back to Coventry, then. Pretend it couldn't happen to you."

Not far from Abena's building, a couple of black bwais in Adidas jackets and trainers slouched in a doorway. As Baz neared, they passed something between them, sleeves dropped low to mask the transaction. A few moments later, two policemen came into view and the youths melted away into the Somerleyton Estate. Baz turned the other way, into Atlantic Road, heading for the Tube. The streets were quiet, but you couldn't let that fool you. This was still a war zone built on a rift.

A paper bag blew across his path, dragging his attention down the long curve of Electric Avenue. Sunday morning had reduced the market to a scattering of debris. Leaves cut from a cauliflower, the bruised remains of some plantain, blue paper from a crate of oranges, scrunched and wet. Even in the cold, the air smelt of vegetables and salt fish.

A shout rang out from somewhere along the terraced road. Looking up, he saw, as plainly as he could see the ochre-coloured bricks, flames spurting from an upstairs window. Someone screamed, the noise filling his ears.

Flashbacks. This was the first one in months. They came, not when he was asleep, but always when he was wide awake. He forced himself to walk on, focusing on what was in front of him. The pavement half sheltered by the overhanging edge of the railway platform. Shuttered shops in the arches. Words sprayed in yellow paint: 'This Year Bristol: Next Year Brixton.'

Flames flashed again, this time from behind a shutter. He screwed his eyes tight and pressed on. A few paces further, he had to stop, leaning against a graffiti-covered door, sweating despite the cold. The smell of smoke was in his nostrils and his nerve endings were telling him the metal shutter was burning hot. Someone switched on a stereo—the Gong's 'Redemption Song' turned up loud.

He started to laugh then realised, too late, that he'd attracted attention. Two uniformed police officers were walking his way. Baz hauled himself upright and started to walk in the direction of the Tube station, doing what Abena had taught him to avoid being stopped: don't hurry, don't idle, don't stare, but don't look away; keep moving and maybe they'll decide you're not worth bothering with. But within a few paces, they'd swung into step alongside him.

"Excuse me, sir. Do you mind if we take a look in your bag?"

"Is there a problem, officer?"

The voice of middle-class professional

"Just let us see in the bag, sir."

They were on the small side for policemen. Baz was eye level with the badge on of the front of their helmets. They were young and they both looked tense. He held the bag out, the webbing strap across his palm.

"Open it, please."

Baz undid the catch. The jumble of shoved-in possessions struggled to escape.

"In a hurry, were we, sir?"

The officer with a shaving rash picked through the dirty clothes. A youth of about twenty, wearing a baker boy hat, crossed the road to pass by. Someone shouted, "Beast!" from the safety of an upstairs window. With a grimace of distaste the officer extracted the underwear in which Baz had wrapped the camera. A hint of a smirk appeared across his freckled face.

"Nice camera, sir."

"A Canon A-1 SLR," Baz answered.

"Expensive?"

"It wasn't cheap."

"And of course you'd be able to prove that, because you have the receipt on you?"

Of course he could: he'd been through this before. Baz reached for his inside pocket, and at once both policemen braced themselves. The one who had been watching the proceedings took a step nearer.

"The receipt? It's in my wallet."

Moving slowly, he extracted the wallet from his coat and passed them a thin slip of folded paper.

"Know about cameras, do you, sir?" The policeman unfolded it.

"I should do. I'm a photographer."

The policeman coloured, making his rash startle from his pale face. "Press?"

"Freelance."

He nodded uneasily and went back to studying the receipt.

"Coventry? That's a long way to go for a camera, sir."

"It's where I live."

"What you doing in Brixton, then?"

Baz's patience snapped. "Taking photographs of police harassment," he said. Before the words were past his lips, he regretted them. The officer thrust bag and camera at his colleague and barked, "Open your coat." He began patting Baz down, over his body, along his arms, between his thighs. A middle-aged black woman dressed for church tutted as she passed them.

The policeman switched his attention to Baz's coat and began fishing film, lenses and filters from the pockets. Baz thought of the stories the kids told at Abena's community centre. *The Beastman, they plant de herb on you, man.* In response, Abena's voice mocked him. *You better hope they treat you like a white man and not like a bad bwai from Brixton.* He wiped his face on his sleeve.

"You always carry this stuff around with you?" Shaving-rash demanded. They'd dropped the 'sir' now.

"Pretty much. Tools of the trade."

"Got any identification on you?"

"Driving licence. In my wallet."

They scrutinised the folded green paper with the same care they had given to the receipt.

"Bhajan Singh Lister," the policeman read aloud. He showed it to his colleague. "Singh, that's a Paki name, isn't it?"

"Sikh, actually," said Baz.

"Lister, on the other hand. That don't sound Paki, do it?"

Baz said nothing. The policeman appeared to be thinking something over. Maybe weighing up the amount of time he'd have to spend back at the station doing paperwork, the chances that someone would come and make a fuss if he arrested Baz.

"Well, Mr Paki Lister. Let me give you a piece of advice. A lot of young thugs around here would be happy to relieve you of a nice camera like that. So next time you come, I suggest you leave it at home. Along with the big mouth."

They thrust bag, camera and the jumble of things they'd removed from his pockets into his arms and were gone, two pairs of black-booted feet beating time on the pavement. Baz shoved his belongings back in the bag and steeled himself to negotiate the ragged army of beggars and crackpots that patrolled the entrance to the Tube station.

Chapter 3

I pushed open the plate glass door of the concourse and walked outside. For a few paces, the bulk of the station sheltered me, before the wind pierced the fabric of my jeans.

Nowhere to go and all day to get there. For want of anything better, I cut under the ring road and headed towards the city. A quarter of an hour later, I was trailing through the concrete canyon of Coventry city centre. The shops were shut—even the newsagents had closed at midday. But half a dozen kids had congregated round the fountain where the four arms of the Precinct crossed. Pulling on cigarettes, trying out a few dance steps. An undersized ghetto blaster balanced on the rim of the fountain. The wind caught a thin stream of Ska and snatched it away. I was shivering inside my quilted coat, but most of them wore denim jackets. One small figure huddled in a parka, his face barely visible inside its snorkel hood. The only thing to distinguish them from bored teenagers everywhere was that four of them wore turbans.

As I came close, Snorkel Parka glared at me. I gave him a 'don't mind me' smile and veered away towards the upper Precinct. As I rounded the corner, fine rain lashed my face and I heard a sound like thunder. But the noise rolled on, growing louder. Behind me, the kids' voices rose in alarm.

At the top of the Precinct, a line of youths fanned out. Donkey jackets and Abercrombies. Heads shaved. Jeans rolled up to show off their Doc Martens. I barely had time to take it in before they began to run, boots pounding against the pavement, gathering speed like an avalanche. Those at the edges had heavy sticks and clanged them against the iron shutters of the shops as they ran.

The charge swept past me, close enough to see faces tattooed with spiders' webs and swastikas. I knew I should do something, but my legs refused to move. One of the skinheads crashed into my shoulder and I was spun round, eyes stinging.

Below me, the Asian kids scattered, some into the Lower Precinct, some south towards the market. Snorkel Parka stayed to grab his ghetto blaster from the fountain. I felt a wrench of fear as one of the skinheads made a flying tackle and almost caught him, but the kid dodged away under the Wimpy rotunda. The skins' advance continued until they occupied the crossing unchallenged, then the charge petered out. Smirking, thumbs tucked in their belts, they swaggered back towards Broadgate.

I pressed back into the doorway of M&S, hearing laughter and the swish of their heavy sticks. When someone spoke my name, my knees buckled.

"Maia? You okay?"

A lanky figure hovered a few feet away, stubble on his chin and hair scragged into a stubby ponytail. Last seen the day we graduated.

"Sodding hell, Tom. You scared the life out of me."

"Sorry. I saw that skinhead use you for a pinball. Thought I'd better see you were all right."

"I'm fine, I think. What the hell was all that, anyway?"

A furrow appeared between his thick brows. "Skinheads v Pakis? Happens every weekend, lately."

"Jesus." It wasn't like I'd never seen skinheads. You could pretty much guarantee a few of them would show up at every anti-apartheid march to shout abuse and pick fights. I always figured we were fair game. A bunch of young guys mucking about with a ghetto blaster, though, that was different …

"How bad has it got?"

Tom shrugged. "So far it's been one group charging the other. British Bulldog with a bad attitude." The undertone of concern in his voice didn't escape me.

"You think it's going to get worse?"

Tom ran his fingers under his collar to flip out his ponytail and shrugged as if the question no longer interested him.

"Fancy a brew? I've got a job to do over by Spon Street, but I can put a kettle on while I'm at it. You can fill me in on what you've been up to."

Spon Street was a short row of pot-bellied Tudor houses that hung off the bottom of Corporation Street, severed by the concrete barrier of the ring road. About two thirds of the way along, Tom jinked right onto a narrow lane. A concrete prefab squatted at the end, its walls spotted with damp and graffiti. A crudely painted sign over the door read, *The Safe Skipper*.

Tom unlocked a rusty padlock and pushed the door open. I went to follow and was hit by a stench that nearly made me throw up again.

"Bloody hell, Tom. What is this place?"

"Night Shelter. Hard-core homeless and transients." Tom glanced back over his shoulder, apparently oblivious to the stink. "Shut the door, will you? I'll get the heaters on."

I stepped inside. The smell resolved itself into an unholy blend of cheap tobacco and unwashed bodies, alcohol, rotting cabbage and incontinence. Tom flipped a switch and two bare fluorescent tubes sputtered to life. The room was oblong and filled with rows of wooden benches and canteen tables. He flipped more switches and the heaters on the wall began to give off a stale, sluggish warmth. I couldn't help thinking heat was going to make the smell even worse.

"You're working here?"

"Last few months, yeah. I wanted a break from studying, so I deferred my PhD. Couldn't get a job, so I ended up volunteering."

He went through another door into the kitchen and started pouring water into an electric boiler. "So what are you doing in Cov?" he asked, through the wide serving hatch. "I thought you'd have been off on your travels again."

"I'm avoiding. The family thinks I've got a job, so I'm lying low in Leamington Spa."

Tom grinned. "And that is better than a mud hut in a jungle because …?"

"It doesn't have my mother in it."

"Fair point."

Doesn't have Ossie in it either, a voice in my head whispered, and my throat tightened.

"What's up, kiddo? You look like you're on another planet."

My thoughts were too close to the surface to stop them leaking past my lips. "Remember my flatmate, Ossie?"

"Your South African buddy? Yeah, I met him a few times."

I wrapped my hands around the mug of hot tea he held out and felt my fingers begin to ache as the warmth returned.

"He's gone back to South Africa. Left this morning."

Tom frowned. "I thought he was smuggled out? False papers, underground railroad, that sort of stuff?"

"Yeah. He was."

"So I take it he's not just walking back in through the front door?"

"Not exactly, no."

He let out a low, appreciative whistle. He busied himself opening cupboards and taking notes on a pad he pulled out of his back pocket. "You'll miss him," he said. "You two were kind of joined at the hip, weren't you?"

"It's important to him. You know, the struggle …"

"Doesn't change how you feel, though, does it?"

I couldn't handle sympathy. Sympathy was going to make

me cry. I thought of all those memories no one else shared. Ossie nursing me through chicken pox one Easter holiday when everyone else had gone home for the vacation. Ossie pacing up and down in my room as he practised his dissertation, in a sweat of nerves that vanished half an hour before he was due to go in. Ossie in bed last night, his fingertips circling my breasts.

"Flat's going to seem pretty empty now he's gone," I said, trying to ignore the quaver that crept into my voice. "Used to be a whole bunch of us sharing, but since September it's just been Ossie and me. And now—"

"You're on your own." Tom crouched down, taking inventory of some sacks of unsavoury looking vegetables stowed under the counter.

"Of course, I could go home …"

Tom shook his head. "No going home till we're out of shoe leather …" he said.

"… and we don't know where the next meal is coming from …"

"… Independent adults at last!" we finished together.

We'd made the pledge the night before graduation, all of us who had been on the course. Six months on the dole, though, and it had a hollow ring. I reached for my coat.

"I ought to go. I need to get a bus before they stop running."

"I'll walk you back to Poole Meadow."

He scribbled a few last notes on his pad and stuffed it in his pocket.

"Listen," he said, as he was padlocking the door again, "you don't have to go back to the flat tonight. We've got a place up in Hillfields where the volunteers live. Always a couple of spare beds. You could doss there."

"Oh, Tom, I don't know. I'm not sure the company of strangers is what I need right now."

"You think being in that flat on your own is what you need?"

Chapter 4

At Coventry station, Baz thought about going straight to Hillfields, decided against it, and headed instead for the makeshift studio he rented behind Rebeccah's big Victorian house.

Rebeccah's car was parked in the drive at the front but the house was dark. He made his way round the side and unlocked the door to the studio. The air in the converted conservatory was cold, despite underfloor heating. He clapped his hands on his arms a few times, then scrabbled around till he found an electric fan heater. A tortoiseshell cat sashayed through the cat flap. She had a fresh scratch across her nose and several missing tufts of fur.

"What have you been up to this time, Mrs Peel?"

He squatted down to stroke her and she arched her back, rubbing herself against his legs.

"I bet Rebeccah already fed you."

All the same, he opened a tin of cat food and set the dish on the floor. She turned her back on him, her tail raised, fastidiously selecting the bits she considered choice enough to eat. He went on with his routine, locking up his camera, cataloguing and storing the exposed film. Some prints for his upcoming exhibition were waiting to be framed. He made a note to buy mounting tissue. And he needed to call Vikram and confirm arrangements for the venue.

He was pouring water for tea when he heard a quiet knock and looked up to see Rebeccah in the doorway. It caught him off balance to see how grey she had grown these days. In his mind, her hair retained its original chestnut, her back was straight, the wrinkles filled out. When he stooped to kiss her on the cheek, the skin felt softer, less elastic. She had soil under her fingernails, as she always had, but her fingers were bent, their knuckles a little too prominent.

"You haven't been gardening in this weather?"

Her head tilted back to look up in his face. He'd always been taller than her. Even when he first came here as a foster child, he overtopped her by two fingers. Fifteen years on, she barely reached his chest.

"I was in the potting shed. Mrs Peel must have heard you. When she bolted from the shed, I thought she was after a blackbird, but then I saw your light."

She sat on a folding chair and accepted a cup of black tea. He could tell by the way she sat so quiet, waiting for him to speak, that she'd guessed he had something on his mind.

"I don't know if you've heard … I don't know how widely …" He cleared his throat, started again. "There's been a fire. In New Cross."

"It was on the radio this morning. Dreadful business."

He told her about Denise coming. He told her about the flashback. He found he was sweating again, his heart running too fast. There had been times when a flashback could make him scream out loud, when Rebeccah would have to hold him until he stopped thrashing with fear and it no longer felt as if his lungs were filling up with smoke. Once or twice he'd bolted, and she'd had to chase after him to stop him running blindly out into traffic. He'd come a long way, learning to control the panic. But not as far as he'd thought, apparently.

"Abena's gone to see if she can help," he told her. "She wanted me to go with her."

"And you said no?"

He flinched, remembering the look on Abena's face. "We had one of our rows about race and responsibility."

Rebeccah left a pause for him to say more. Mrs Peel jumped onto his lap, claws digging through his jeans. He buried his fingers deep in her fur.

"You've never told Abena what happened, have you?" she said.

"I can't. You know that."

"Ah, well. You can't keep your secrets and expect to be understood as well, my dear."

A smile teased at the corner of her mouth and Baz laughed in spite of himself. Mrs Peel, sensing a change of mood, settled down with her head on her front paws and began to purr. In the deep hush that followed he asked the question that had been in his head all day.

"Am I doing the right thing?"

"In what way?"

He thought about the black bwais in Brixton, dodging police harassment. The Punjabi-speaking kids on the streets of Coventry, dodging skinheads who thought they had a monopoly on being British.

"Some days it feels like the work we do at the Skipper is the most important thing in the world. But on days like this … Firebombs. National Front. All that crap. And I wonder if Abena isn't right. If I'm letting myself be diverted from the stuff that really matters."

"That's something you must decide for yourself."

Baz gave a short bark of laughter. "You couldn't once just give me a straight opinion?"

"If I did that, you might stop thinking for yourself."

When he was ready to leave, Rebeccah walked with him along the gravel path and under the bare branches of the ancient apple tree. At the end of the drive, she glanced towards the road.

"Gary was here again yesterday, standing in the road, staring up at the house. When I went out to speak to him, he disappeared." She pursed her lips. "It seems his new friends are having an effect."

"Skinheads getting to him?"

"His head was shaved."

"That figures."

"And he has a new tattoo."

His eyes widened. "Bloody hell, where's he found room?"

"On his scalp."

Baz laughed. Frigging hell. That must have hurt. Serve the little bastard right; maybe he'd think twice next time.

Rebeccah bent over a small patch of snowdrops that were pushing their way through the frozen soil. "You should watch yourself, Bhajan. I believe you are becoming the focus of something in his mind."

Baz shrugged. "He's a kid."

"He's nineteen, Bhajan. And he's being manipulated. They all are."

A green wooden gate covered the gap between the two houses occupied by the Skipper volunteers. Baz rested his hand on the latch. In the window to the left, he could make out Simon's faded poster of striking steel workers: 'If the Tories get up your nose, picket.' On the other side, an Art-Deco poster in pastel colours declared: 'A woman without a man is like a fish without a bicycle.'

The entry was already half dark. Concrete stumps of fence-posts poked from the gutter like broken teeth. Beyond, a jumble of ancient bicycles leant against a wall. The sound of bickering spilt from the kitchen on the left. The perpetual background hum of Paradise Road—the noise of a load of ill-assorted parts, cobbled together and working after their own fashion.

Home sweet fucking home.

He pushed open the door from the yard into the kitchen. Iain stopped with a knife poised over a large onion. Libby, a dusting of flour on her apron, looked about her, as if calculating whether the food could be stretched to feed an extra mouth.

"Hey, boss," Iain said. "Thought you weren't back till tomorrow."

Baz shrugged. "Everything okay here?"

As if he'd opened a tap, they both began speaking at once. Offloading. All the usual problems and niggles. Any one of them was capable of sorting them out, but he was the gaffer, the one who was paid to make decisions.

"Fine," he said, throwing up his hands. "Let me unpack. Have a wash. We can have a meeting after tea."

Turning to go out again, he almost collided with two people on their way in—Tom, the big lad from Lancashire, and a girl he'd never seen before. Tom looked taken aback but rallied. "Ah. Baz. I didn't think … I mean, you don't mind do you? I told Maia she could kip here tonight."

The girl stood about shoulder height to Tom, her hair cut short and spiky. Her skin was so pale it was almost translucent and her eyes were hollowed out with worry or exhaustion or maybe just lack of sleep. Tom followed his gaze. "She's had a bit of a day of it," he said.

Libby slammed a pie dish onto the counter. "I don't know how you expect me to feed everyone. First Baz comes home a day early, then you show up out of the blue with another mouth to feed."

The girl looked as if she'd just as soon walk straight back out the door. She glanced over her shoulder, as if clocking her escape route. It was true Tom was taking advantage. They had a basic allowance to feed the volunteers and never much to spare. But Libby's outburst, and something in the girl's face, decided him.

"Libby, you always do far more food than we need. It won't kill Tom if he has to do without second helpings tonight. Or me, if it comes to that." He smiled at the girl. "You come on in. It's cold out there."

Chapter 5

I followed Tom through a bead curtain into a room crammed with furniture and squeezed between a scuffed deal table and a couple of sofas leaking stuffing. A skinny, angular punk sprawled on one of the sofas—all leather trousers and bleached blonde hair. As I passed, he lowered a copy of the *News of the World* and looked from me to Tom.

"Fresh meat, is it?"

"Cheers, Simon. That's nice."

The punk shrugged. "Thought you might have brought us a new recruit, that's all." His voice sounded as if he was trying too hard to hang onto his Welsh lilt. "Don't suppose you fancy working here, do you? Could do with another pair of hands."

"Guess that'd depend on the company I'd have to keep," I said.

The punk grinned, showing a flash of gold tooth. "Fair play. Our Tom's not everyone's cup of tea, I'll grant you."

Tom knocked Simon's feet off the sofa. I lowered myself into an armchair whose springs were making a bid for freedom. Lack of sleep and the warmth from the fire made my eyelids heavy. They were all but closed when the rattle of the bead curtain startled them open again. Tom's boss took the chair on the other side of the hearth, his long legs filling the space between us. Now he had taken his coat off, I could see that his hair swung down his back in a sloe-black swag. He looked vaguely Greek and I wondered what Baz was short for. Barry? Basil?

My eyes drifted to where his hands rested on the arms of the chair. The fingers were stained brown, as though he had an especially noxious smoking habit. He followed my gaze.

"Dektol."

"I beg your pardon?"

He flexed his finger. "The stains? It's developing fluid. You always spill some, no matter how careful you are. And after a while it doesn't come out."

"You're a photographer?"

Tom leaned forward and pointed over the mantelpiece to a black and white photograph of an old man with a whisky nose. He was running his tongue along the edge of a fag paper to seal a roll-up not much thicker than a match. Blurred in the background was a billboard advertising tobacco, with the slogan 'Get the Economy Rolling'

"David Bailey here's got his first exhibition coming up in a few weeks time," he said.

"Impressive."

Baz smiled, enthusiasm lighting up his face. "Don't know about that. Personally, I'm terrified."

"So what are you doing working at a night shelter?"

He shrugged. "Gives me a roof over my head. Time for photography." His dark brown eyes rested on me. The lids were smoky grey, as if they had been brushed with kohl, the lashes thick and long for such a masculine face. Just below one eye, he had a teardrop-shaped mole. "And what about you? What are you doing here?" he asked.

"Me? I just got blown off course."

We moved the table to the centre of the room and ate sitting round it. Libby might have fussed over the extra mouths, but there was more than enough food to go round. I'd thought I might be too tired to eat, but I was suddenly very hungry indeed.

One other volunteer had come in for dinner. Robyn was a diminutive figure in oversized dungarees, with hair like a blonde dandelion clock. She talked so fast I wondered how she had time to breathe.

"So, boss," Iain said, when at last she fell quiet and began to eat, "why are you home a day early?"

Baz paused, a forkful of quiche halfway to his mouth. "Abena had stuff to do."

"How is Abena?" Libby asked. "Are things working out for her?"

Baz rocked back in his chair, but Robyn's floodgates were open again. "Things are pretty tense down there, aren't they? I heard she's been stopped and searched practically every day—"

"She's also been mugged," Libby said. "That is what the police are trying to stop, you know."

"You can be mugged in Coventry," Iain said. "But Abena could go about her business without the police treating her like a suspect."

Simon took an orange from the bowl in the middle of the table and began to peel it. "Don't kid yourself, butty. Scratch a policeman anywhere, and find a racist under the surface."

Libby's head swivelled round so fast you could almost hear her neck bones crack. But Baz got in first.

"For what it's worth, the Old Bill stopped and searched me this morning."

"What did I tell you? Fucking sus laws." Simon's flailing arm swept a glass off the table. Iain caught it with a practised hand.

"They still need probable cause, don't they?" he said. "What was it? Carrying a concealed camera? Loitering with intent to breathe?"

Baz shrugged. "I think the final consensus was possession of a big mouth."

Tom reached across the table and took an apple from the bowl. "Well, got that right, didn't they?"

I thought of a photograph I'd seen of one of Botha's security police, sjambok raised to beat a black protestor who had fallen to the ground. This lot didn't know how lucky they were.

"For God's sake," I said. "This isn't South Africa."

The silence was just long enough to remind me this was the first contribution I'd made to the conversation since the meal began.

"And what's that got to do with anything?" Baz said.

"I mean, it's not like you were in danger of being taken off to a cell and beaten."

Baz's eyes narrowed.

"It's been known. Especially if you're black."

"But you're not black, are you?"

His chair clattered down. The room went very quiet. Even Robyn had stopped talking.

"What do you know about South Africa?" he asked.

"I spent time out there. And I have a friend, a black South African, who's gone to join the dissidents."

"And that makes you an expert?"

"Not an expert, no, but—"

"What about Brixton? Know much about the problems there?"

Tiredness was making me feel as if I was watching myself through a spyglass. What was I doing, locking horns with this prat? One brush with the police and he thought he was some kind of great moral arbiter— "I know enough to realise that being stopped and searched doesn't qualify you for martyrdom!"

Baz's dark eyes widened. "I never claimed it did. What matters is, the kids my girlfriend works with get stopped three, four, five times a week. The police have turned hanging about on the streets with your friends into an offence."

Nobody's dead yet, though, are they? I thought. But before I could say anything, he dropped his voice, pitching his words as if they were just for me. "And Maia, trust me, if I was putting in for martyrdom, being stopped and searched is not the qualification

I'd use."

Something about the way he said it silenced me.

Chapter 6

Baz was almost always the first one up. The others liked to lie in when it wasn't their turn at the Skipper, but he enjoyed the early mornings, when the clamour of voices in the house was stilled. The snag at this time of year was having to light the fire in the sitting room.

When he first moved into Paradise Road, he'd been relieved to find gas fires. Rebeccah had open fires and burnt sweet-smelling wood from her fruit trees. When he was young, those fires both terrified and fascinated him. He'd begin at the far side of the room, flattened against the wall and creep nearer, until he was as close as Rebeccah's sturdy fireguard would permit. He'd crouch, staring, seeing nightmare shadows amongst the flames, till the wood turned to silvery ash. Later, a very young and messed-up Gary somehow divined Baz's fear and took to setting light to things in bins and ash trays, just to get a rise out of him. Once he stole a lighter and tried to set fire to Baz's hair.

Gas was okay. Electric would have been better, but he could cope with gas. Gas, once lit, was contained. Most days he could manage the knack of pressing the ignition as soon as the gas was turned on, so that the ensuing explosion was reduced to a small, manageable *pop*. Today, though, something distracted him. He hesitated a fraction too long, the gas ignited with a soft whoomph, and the flames leapt from their cage. He jumped backwards, almost falling over the sofa behind, and only just managed to stop himself from shouting out.

That was when he noticed Maia watching him.

She had come down the stairs and was standing in the doorway. She looked rumpled, as if she had slept in her clothes. She also looked as if she was struggling not to laugh.

"Are you okay?" she asked, with a passably straight face.

"I'm fine. Could have managed that better."

"Don't worry. I hate gas fires too."

An awkward silence ensued, before his manners kicked in. "You want some tea?"

"Coffee, please, if you've got it."

He brought a tray in and set it by the hearth. He watched her as they listened to the pop and fizzle of the now tame gas fire, noticing how fine boned she was, how the light fell on her skin. He imagined capturing her on film, just like that, with her knees drawn up to her chest, her arms wrapped around them. A lost sprite.

It galled him that she'd proved Abena right. Proved that someone seeing him for the first time could assume he was white. He really did have a get-out clause—if only a selective one. Of course, he could just tell her, put her on the spot. But some obstinacy inside him wanted to keep her around, see how long it would take her to figure it out for herself.

"Got anywhere you need to be this morning?" he asked.

Her gaze shifted from the fire to his face. "Not especially."

"No work to get back to?"

"I wish! Why? What did you have in mind?"

"The guys have been pretty much at full stretch since Abena left. They could do with a break. Fancy giving me a hand? Fair exchange for bed and board?"

She made a delicate movement of her shoulders. "Sure, I guess. Doing what?"

"I need to go to the wholesale market to pick up vegetables for the Skipper."

"Don't you have to go to places like that at the crack of dawn?"

"There's the thing." He sucked air over his teeth. "We go right at the end of the morning. Beg for stuff they've got left over."

Her eyes widened. "I'm not being given humble pie to eat, am I? Teach me not to argue with the boss?"

He laughed, trigger finger itching for a camera. She'd be a bugger to photograph, this one—a mass of contradictions. You'd have to try and capture the way her face changed as shadows of emotion flitted across it.

"Honestly," he said, "you'd be doing me a big favour."

For a beginner, Maia endured the ritual humiliation of the market well enough. She baulked a bit the first time a stall owner handed them a sack of cabbages, half of which were already rank.

"Don't," he warned. "Next time they might not give us anything."

She nodded. "Beggars can't be choosers, right? What do you do? Ditch it somewhere?"

"Not until we've picked it over."

She looked disgusted, but took the stinking sack and carried it to the car. After that she got the hang of fixing a smile and saying thank you, regardless.

While he had the loan of Rebeccah's car, he wanted to pick up supplies from the wholefood shop and an Indian grocer he liked. He drove back through Hillfields, passing halal butchers and shops selling Indian sweets. The further they went, the more shoppers were dressed in *shalwar kameez*.

"You have to admit, Britain's not so bad at this," Maia said.

"Not so bad at what?"

"Taking in new communities. Absorbing them. A few extremists aside, but on the whole—"

"Fuck me!" He put on the brakes, earning a hoot from the car behind. "Have you been walking around with blinkers on?" He glared at her startled face. "Do you know anything about being black in Britain today?"

"Why? Do you?"

Her chin snapped up and the answer came flinging back at him. Was she really that stupid? Furious, he let the driver behind pass and squeezed the car into a parking space down the road from the shops.

"You know what I think?" he said, climbing out of the Morris. "I think you're so wrapped up in anti-Apartheid protests can't see what's going on in your own country."

"Sod you. You have no right to assume—"

"I'd say you're the one making the assumptions here—"

"And anyway, if this is all so important to you, what are you doing looking after a bunch of white down and outs? Shouldn't you be out there doing something about it, instead of lecturing me?"

And there it was. The question he asked himself every morning when he looked in the mirror. The question Abena had flung at him before she left Coventry, and which she never failed to bring up whenever they met.

He was still struggling to frame an answer when, out of the corner of his eye, he spotted a figure skulking a few yards away.

Gary was perched on a low wall, his Doc Martens looking far too big on his scrawny frame. Rebeccah said he was nineteen now. He looked younger—a little kid trying to puff himself up to look big.

"What are you doing here, Gary?"

"None of your business."

Gary's stare slid away, morphing into a leer as it alighted on Maia. The two of them were about the same height, Baz saw, with the same ultra-pale skin—except that the kid's skinny neck and arms, where they stuck out from the donkey jacket, were marbled with tattoos. They had the same fair hair too, though Gary's scalp wore nothing now but the tattoo and a hint of bristle. *The sprite and the demon. Fuck me, but that would make a photograph.*

But Gary in this neck of the woods meant trouble.

"You know you're not supposed to be here, little brother."

Gary's head swung back and a dob of spittle landed on the sleeve of Baz's greatcoat.

"Don't you call me brother, Paki. You're not my fucking brother."

Chapter 7

I watched the skinhead strut along a garden wall, jeans rolled up to show off his high-laced boots, filthy donkey jacket worn over a button-down shirt and braces. An adolescent turkey vulture with a shaven head and so many tattoos his skin looked blue. Was this one of the bastards that charged those Asian kids? I didn't recognise him, but he had all the usual tribal markings—the shaved head, the faux Nazi symbolism.

And he called Baz a Paki.

Spat at him.

God, I must have been blind. Unless bastards like this just assumed anyone with dark skin had to be Asian? But no. Baz knew him. Even called him 'little brother', though that was surely ironic. Got the kid going, though. He looked as if Baz had twisted a handful of his guts.

He hopped down from the wall and thrust his face into mine, thumbs in his braces.

"Haven't I seen you somewhere?" he asked.

Sickening thought, that one of those creeps in the Precinct might have taken enough notice to recognise me again. I wanted to make a bolt for it, only I wouldn't give him the satisfaction.

"What they call you?" he said.

"Why? Want to introduce me to your folks?"

He grabbed my elbow and twisted me round. Fingers with HATE tattooed across the knuckles dug into my flesh.

"That's our shop, that is. The Paki tell you that, did he?" He jabbed his hand towards the name cut into the stone above the door of a small Indian corner shop. "Geo Treddle." That's how he said it. Geo. Not George. "That was my granddad. And his granddad before that."

My contempt must have leaked onto my face. He jerked my arm round again, pointing to an upstairs window.

"That was my room. Me and my little brother shared it. Before them Pakis stole it."

Baz gave a short bark of laughter. "If I had a pound for every time we've been round the houses on this, I could buy the sodding shop myself. I've told you. The Patels are Gujarati, not Pakistani. And they bought it off your family fair and square."

Gary twisted towards him, his face flushed. He had a tattoo like a distorted peace symbol on his scalp, the skin around it still red and angry.

"The sign's still there, isn't it? They know it's ours—"

"Face it, Gary," Baz said. "What your father didn't drink, he gambled away. You were lucky that the Patels bought it when they did."

"They bilked us!"

Baz reached out to grab the collar of his donkey jacket and Gary took a skip backwards.

"I know how I could get rid of them for good an' all," he said, in a voice that seemed to slide back through puberty. He pulled out a plastic lighter and brandished it towards Baz. "I could burn them out, like they did them niggers down in London."

Baz stared at him for a long moment. The hand holding the little red lighter began to shake. Baz reached out, took it from him and crushed it under his heel.

"The Patels so much as burn their toast, *little brother*, and I'm going to the police."

Chapter 8

Baz pushed open the door of Patel's. The shop bell jangled.

Gary's posturing didn't mean anything. Did it? Surely he got over his fire-starting phase years ago. He was just throwing his bantam weight around, making himself look hard. He'd be boasting about it to his new mates tonight. *Guess what I told them Pakis …*

Little shite.

The smell of the shop wrapped around him like a blanket. Once inside, he was a small child again, perched on a stool with Auntie Harjit's kids, breathing in the scent of spices and nibbling on *jalebi*, listening to conversations he could not understand. He had learnt his cooking from Auntie Harjit, listening to the ghee bubbling in the blackened cast-iron pan, watching her throw in the spices, smelling the scents that rose with the heat. He heard her now, naming the spices in her singsong voice: coriander, cardamom, cumin, cinnamon, nutmeg, cloves. Teaching him to recognise them by their smell and their colour. Auntie Harjit would buy her spices whole and grind them in a large stone pestle and mortar—a painstaking task she sometimes allowed him to share. It made his arm ache and Auntie Harjit would laugh. *Too slow. Too slow. We will be waiting here all day for our dinner. Here, give it to me.*

"Who the hell was that?" Maia asked. When he didn't answer,

she tried again. "You called him 'little brother.' Twice."

He closed his eyes, seeing a fair-haired kid with a gap between his front teeth, standing in the middle of Rebeccah's hall, an expression of mute defiance on his face. "He and I were fostered together for a while."

She looked as if she'd like to go on asking questions, but she backed off.

"So what did we come in here for?" she said.

He pulled himself together. "Spices. Ingredients for a *kofta*."

"Curry? I didn't realise Coventry's down and outs were so adventurous."

He looked up and caught her teasing smile.

"They're not. This is for Paradise Road."

She watched him scoop spices from the little wooden trays into the paper bags provided for the purpose. "Wow. The real deal. I haven't had a proper curry for ages."

He saw the shadow of another emotion cross her face, but he couldn't place what it was. "You could always stay," he said. "We really are short of a pair of hands."

She seemed about to answer. Then her eyes lighted on the peace badge he wore on the lapel of his greatcoat and she frowned.

"That tattoo. The one on that kid's head. It kind of looked like a peace symbol, but it wasn't, was it?"

"No. It's called Yggdrasil. The Norse Tree of Life. It's a white supremacist symbol."

She drew her breath sharply and turned to where Mrs Patel was sitting by the till, her bright yellow sari topped with a chunky knit cardigan in English beige. "Should we warn her, do you think?"

He shook his head. "Gary's like a kid swearing in front of the grown-ups. The less fuss you make, the sooner he'll leave off."

Did he really believe that? Gary went through phases like other people changed their clothes. Fire starting. Glue sniffing. The Bay City Rollers. Gary had done it all, and he usually did himself more harm than anyone else. This skinhead thing was just the latest in a long line.

At any rate, Maia didn't press him any further. They paid for the spices and went next door to buy oatmeal from the bulk wholefood store. When he was loading the sack into the boot, she leaned towards him, her hands on the roof of the car.

"Baz, I'm sorry."

"What for?"

"For being the biggest idiot on the planet. For opening my mouth without engaging my brain. For not realising …"

Her voice trailed away and this time he held out a lifeline to her.

"That's the thing with being neither one thing nor another. Gary looks at me and sees a Paki. Mrs Patel looks at me and sees another Englishman. And you look at me and see …?"

He left the words hanging while she studied his face. Her eyes were the blue-green of deep waters. Like her skin, they seemed to alter with the light, with her expression.

"I see a man carrying a lot of other people's problems on his shoulders," she said, and the unexpected words made his colour rise. She grinned at him. "You know what?" she said, facing forward again, "I think I do fancy curry for tea tonight after all."

It took him a moment to get it. When he did catch up her meaning, he laughed out loud. "You are going to be one very popular woman back at Paradise Road." He opened the car door and they both got in. "You sure about this? It's a big commitment."

Her finger traced a shape on the glass. "I've been sitting around on the dole for six months. You guys are doing something worthwhile. That's like gold dust." As if she'd revealed too much of herself and was keen to cover up, she ran her fingers through her hair so it stuck up in short spikes, and gave him a lopsided grin. "Anyway, the landlord's probably going to chuck me out of the flat, now I'm on my own. If I don't take the job, I could end up as one of your customers."

He grinned back. "Sorry. Can't help you there. Men only shelter."

"You see. Got no choice, have I?"

Chapter 9

When I woke, the borrowed t-shirt I wore had hitched up over my bum and the army surplus blanket was scratching my arm. A soft snuffling noise came from a few feet away, and it took me a while to work out that it was the sound of Robyn snoring.

Stupid of me not to have picked up my quilt when Baz drove me back to the flat. But it had lain on the bed, still moulded to the contours of Ossie's body, and I couldn't deal with it. I turned away, threw a few essentials into a backpack. Emptied the fridge, washed up, left a note for the milkman. And got the hell out.

02:40 by the illuminated dial on Robyn's alarm clock. I tugged Baz's t-shirt over my bum and tucked my knees inside. Where was Ossie now? On the night train from Bulawayo to Labotse, probably, travelling from Zimbabwe down through Botswana. Crossing the upper reaches of the Limpopo in the dark. I thought of him lying on the fold-out berth of a sleeping car, rocked by the motion of the train.

"Someone has to carry on here, *nosisi*," he'd said. What would he think about my choosing to work at some godforsaken night shelter? Would he understand that doing anything useful was better than sitting around waiting for the next dole cheque?

Or would he think I'd turned my back on him?

In the dim light of the single street lamp, a queue of men jostled for position in the lane outside the Skipper. Baz called a greeting and they shambled aside to let his bike pass. I followed, pushing my way through the smell of unwashed bodies and feeling a sudden need for a long, hot shower.

Baz reached the door and a security light came on, driving back the shadows and illuminating the men in the queue.

The man nearest to me wore a parka, secured round the waist by a rainbow-coloured luggage strap. Next to him was a big man in a greasy tweed overcoat several sizes too small, which he'd tried to fasten over his chest using a nappy pin, a length of string and a large bulldog clip. A smaller man, in a coat that swept the ground, had collected a train of rubbish behind him. Another clutched at his trousers as if he was afraid they would fall down. I heard the sound of running water and a dark stream of liquid trickled down the camber of the path. There was a collective groan and a shifting of bodies, and the ketone scent of urine filled the alleyway.

I was trying to shift my foot out of the way when the doors opened and the line of bodies pressed forward, carrying me with it. In moments, the room was swarming like an anthill. I tried to tell myself this was just like another of my mother's case studies. But this was different. This was like those villages we began to see towards the end of my school years. Places where a thousand years of tradition had been swept away in a couple of decades. Places that had been dragged half way into the twentieth century and dumped back into squalor. Even my mom hated those places.

Baz disappeared into an office off to the side of the main room. Iain took me into the kitchen and before long I was in an assembly line, spreading marge on sliced white bread and pouring cups of tea from an outsize aluminium pot. I hadn't figured out how to meet their eyes yet but I saw their hands. Hands taking chipped green mugs of tea. Hands folding slices of bread to carry away. Hands red with cold or yellow with nicotine or black with grime. Hands with scars. Hands with tattoos. Hands with fingerless gloves. Hands with open sores, with grubby plasters hanging off or bits of bandage twisted round them.

Okay, Maia, deep breath. Figure out the rules. You'll be okay when you've made sense of this place.

Iain was digging veg out of the bags we had collected the day before. The queue at the counter was dying down. Men came to the door in dribs and drabs.

"Why do some of the men go into the office when they arrive and others not?" I asked.

Iain glanced up, carrot peelings curled round his knuckles. "They'll register if they're going to spend the night. But even in the winter, a few will come in for the hot meal and go out again."

My mother could have written an entire book on a place like this. *A subculture within a larger ethnic grouping, sweetie. They are often the* most *fascinating.*

"So do those men have some sort of home to go to?"

Iain's eyebrows popped above the frames of his glasses and disappeared again. "Not exactly, no. They'll find a derry. Or maybe sleep on the streets."

"A derry?"

"Derelict building—like a squat without the amenities."

Bloody hell. It was a cold, wet, January night. Some of the men hunched over the tables were steaming as the damp in their clothes began to dry out. Some had lips that were nearly blue, and arms that shook as they lifted the mugs. What the hell was I missing here?

"Why would they go out again if they didn't have to?"

He tipped vegetables into a big soup kettle on the hob and began adding water. "Too independent, maybe? Or they don't fancy sharing a dorm with a bunch of lummed-up headbangers."

Headbangers? I shot him a sharp glance. "Is that what these guys are?"

Iain shook his head. He added a generous measure of salt to his brew and began to stir. "Not all of them. Not by a long chalk. There's always a few loonies, though, and if we don't look out, they take advantage of the rest." He pointed to the man who had urinated in the alley. Baz had taken him off and found him some more trousers, and now he sat by himself, clearly on some private voyage of his own. "Take Walter. He's a hopeless case, it has to be said. Drank away most of his marbles years ago and can't even keep himself clean most days. But he's gentle. And courteous. And if someone didn't look out for him, he'd get beaten up every other night."

"You're kidding. Why? He can't possibly have anything worth stealing."

Iain shrugged. "Someone will roll the poor bastard over for his dole money. Or give him a good kicking because he shouts in his sleep. Or just because they don't like the way he smells."

"Jesus."

As I stared at him, Walter got to his feet, clasped his hands and spoke above the hubbub. After a moment I recognised the words of the Evening Prayer. "We have left undone those things which we ought to have done; and we have done those things which we ought not to have done …"

For the first time in years, I remembered Loony Larry, who used to travel the Northern Line back when I still lived in Hampstead. At least once or twice a week, when I was coming home from school, he'd be in my carriage. He'd stand at one end, swearing at the empty air, his voice growing louder and louder till you could probably have heard him from the streets above. My mother, from her wood-panelled ivory tower at the top of our house, insisted that he simply lived in a world other people didn't see. But that never stopped me being terrified, convinced one day he would lunge at me, grab me, take me prisoner.

Now here I was, bang in the middle of Loony Larry Land.

Chapter 10

Baz flexed his fingers. He ran his eye down the list of names in the ruled notebook in front of him, slid the ribbon bookmark between the folded-back pages and snapped it shut. A lot of the men had booked in tonight. Even those who put up with the cold could be driven inside by the sort of rain that seeps in through every pore.

Through the thin partition wall, he heard a ruckus in the dormitory and went to see what was going on. Big Knoxie was stumbling between the beds, raging at demons only he could see. After a few minutes, he quietened down and slumped onto one of the beds. Almost at once he began to snore, an uneven gasping sound.

In the main room, Walter was at it again, reciting from the Book of Common Prayer. People said he'd once been a curate, before he'd discovered other uses for the communion wine.

He ought to check on Maia. But he was tired. Too frigging tired. Tired of standing in the dung heap, shovelling shit.

Maybe Abena was right. Maybe he had been doing this job too long. She'd certainly been ready to move on. And maybe not just from the job. It had crossed his mind since he came back from Brixton that she could have manufactured their quarrel, built it up into something more than it was, as an excuse to finish with him. If that was true, did he care?

The phone rang, pulling him out of himself. He pushed the

door shut to cut down the noise, expecting someone from the Sally Army, asking if they had any spare beds. Instead, as if she'd been eavesdropping on his thoughts, Abena's voice purred in his ear.

"Bwai, you make it hard to kiss and make up when you walk away from a fight like that."

Thrown off course, he traced the bevelled corners of the desk blotter and searched for a suitable response. Abena didn't wait.

"Police pretty quick to change their tune about the fire, you notice that? Can't have anyone think whitey had anything to do with it. Big fuckery that, to let slip about the firebomb. Bet someone was busted right down to traffic control. No, it had to be the kids at the party. Stupid jungle bunnies, they must have tried to have a barbecue right in the middle of the floor. Cos they're not used to living in houses, are they?"

Her voice shook with rage. An image flashed into his mind of her parents' immaculate terraced house in Haringey. Of the men and women who worked as cleaners or hospital porters during the day, and gathered there in the evenings for philosophical discussion and political debate. Abena's campaigning zeal had been kindled years ago by yobs calling these gentle, civilised people 'jungle bunnies'.

"C'mon, Abena. It's not that bad. The police have got to consider the possibility that it was an accident."

"Accident! With the beefheads marching through Lewisham every other week? 'There ain't no black in the Union Jack.' *Accident.*" She spat the word into the phone.

"Okay. I get the point."

"We're holding a vigil on Sunday. Outside the house." Her voice took on a different tone. More private. More personal. "I wish you'd come down, Baz, mon. Use that camera of yours."

He knew what she was asking was not unreasonable. This was a public event—one that deserved coverage the white press would never accord it. But one week on, outside the fire-gutted house? The air would still be bitter with smoke …

"Think what we can do if we link up," she said. "My big mouth and your clear eyes…"

"One hell of a combination," he finished for her, smiling in spite of himself. That was as close as she'd ever get to saying she couldn't do this on her own.

"I'll try and come soon."

"Raatid. When?"

"Soon—"

He heard the pips go. "Baz, I have to step out. Denise is waiting for me. You call and tell me when you're coming—"

He tried to say something, but the phone went dead. He sat for a moment, cradling it to his ear.

The National Front had marched through Leamington when he was a boy. He could remember the sound of their pounding feet. Drum beats. Union Jacks fluttering overhead. His mum pushing him behind the skirts of her coat. Men four or five abreast down the middle of the road, their macs beige, charcoal, black—the colour of clouds before a storm. Menace in the air like thunder …

What did Abena want? Was it him? Or just his camera?

And did he still want her?

He started to dial the number for the payphone in her house. But by now she'd be walking down the street with Denise. Getting into her car. Someone else would answer the phone …

He replaced the handset. When he opened the door, a tide of noise rose to meet him. A sea of clattering, clinking, slurping, masticating, coughing, grumbling, hectoring, shuffling, stomping, spitting. So familiar that most of the time he didn't even notice it, any more than he noticed the smell of the place. Something in his brain blanked it out, so that if it ever stopped, the silence would probably deafen him.

One or two pairs of eyes watched him, scaling him against the doorway. Some of the relative newcomers to the Skipper took his size as a challenge. "I could take you," they'd tell him. "I could take you easy."

He moved away from the door, crossing the room with a self-consciously idle stroll. The trick was to be as un-macho as possible. Smile. Shrug. "Yeah, I bet I'd go down like a ton of bricks." "And you wouldn't get up again, neither. Not in a hurry." They'd pull themselves up tall. Grin. Even offer to shake his hand. Like the fight had really happened and they were the victor.

"Cup of tea, boss?" Iain said as he reached the kitchen.

"Please." He turned to Maia. She'd walked in here tonight looking like she was facing a firing squad. She still looked like she was handling a bomb that might go off at any minute. So maybe it was time to remove the firing pin.

"Let's get you out from behind that counter."

Chapter 11

Just like back in Africa, someone always had to insist I leave the hut.

I took a half step into the room, feeling my trainers stick to the floor. Walter had finished his peroration and sat down again. Men shuffled between the rows, heading for the dorm or the washhouse or back towards the office. A few read newspapers. Almost all were smoking, and a pall of smog hung over the tables.

A few feet away, the nearest table was littered with dirty cups. Maybe if I rounded those up and made a bolt for the kitchen, they'd let me back in before I drew attention to myself. Except to reach those cups I had to lean across two of the men—

"All right, lovely girl?"

A grubby hand grabbed my arm and spittle sprayed my wrist. The man who had spoken stood up, one leg stiff and awkward. His nose was spread across most of this face and he had a half-healed gash on one cheek. He held onto the back of the bench with one hand and my shoulder with the other.

"Feck, but you've got a face on you like a ghost on washday."

His speech was thick and I struggled to understand him. He pushed me into the seat he had vacated, next to a bulky shape that appeared to be in suspended animation over a bowl of soup.

I began stacking the dirty dishes. "I'm supposed to be—"

"You sit yourself down and let Frank fetch you a cup of tea and some scran."

More nimbly than I'd have thought possible, he limped over to the counter, annexed a cup of tea and a slice of bread and was back. He gave the man next to him a poke.

"Shift your arse, ya bollocks."

The man hotched along the bench and Frank heaved himself into the vacated space.

"You get that inside you, now." He threw a scowl back at Baz. "I told your man he doesn't have to be working you so hard on your first night."

I was still finding him desperately hard to understand. When I asked him to repeat himself he frowned.

"You're thinking I've been on the lash. But I'm not drunk, darlin'. I lost part of my tongue, see? Same accident that did for my leg." He opened his mouth and showed me, behind a row of blackened teeth, a stump of tongue. "Fell off a scaffold on a building site. Couldn't work after that."

I took a sip of the tea. It was sweet—two sugars at least—and the bread and butter showed the imprint of a dirty thumb. I put the cup back down on the table.

"What do they call you?"

"Maia."

"Well, Maia, if any of these fellas here gives you any trouble, you tell Frank. Some of them, they can be a bit rough, see. A bit crude, if you know what I mean. But they don't mean anything by it. One or two are real trouble, but we'll sort them out for you."

"Thank you."

It was unsettling, being offered protection by what passed for the dregs of society. But touching too. Frank clearly wasn't about to let his disadvantages take the shine off his gallantry. I didn't drink any more of the sickly tea, or eat the bread, but I went on talking to him until I felt a tap on my shoulder. I looked round, expecting to see Baz asking why I was skiving. Simon stood there, arms shrugged into a black bondage coat, beanie flattening his gelled hair.

"All right, boss? Come to fetch her home, have you? Good man." Frank patted my arm, patently convinced I wasn't safe to be let out on my own. "Be seeing you again, will we, lovely girl?"

I glanced towards the kitchen. Baz was leaning against the counter, a broad grin on his face. Sod the bastard: he'd set me up with the Don Quixote of the Skipper.

Chapter 12

When Vik turned up, early as always, for their meeting at the community centre, Baz was stooped over the ironing board, feeling the heat on his fingers as he used the tip of the iron to fuse mounting tissue to the back a large print. His friend leaned against the glass wall of the conservatory, arms folded, hair slicked back like an Asian James Dean.

"Very domestic, *yaar*. Fancy ironing me a few shirts while you're at it?"

"Why? Your *ma-ji* finally got tired of wiping your arse for you?"

It was a routine he could have done in his sleep. The two of them had been sparring since, as lone *desis*, they'd gravitated together at art school.

"Not that you're a real *desi*," Vik would remind him from time to time. "You don't even speak Punjabi."

"Doesn't make any difference to the sodding racists, does it?"

"Too Paki to be White. Too *gora* to be *desi*. The true artist is always an outsider, *yaar*."

In the doorway of the studio, Vik tugged at the bottom of his denim jacket, his foot doing a restless shuffle across the floor.

"You gonna be much longer, man?"

Baz checked his watch. "There's plenty of time."

"Yeah, I know, but …"

Baz laid a piece of waxy release paper over his print and began ironing from the centre out to the edges, making first a cross and then a saltire, "I wouldn't hurry you when you're painting."

"I wouldn't try and paint when I am supposed to be going to a meeting," Vik grumbled.

"Maybe that's why you only paint a couple of canvases a year."

Vik gave him a wounded look. "You can't hurry genius, *yaar*."

"So stop trying to hurry me."

Baz took a last look at his work, laid another piece of mounting board over the top, weighted it down to stop the print curling, and unplugged the iron.

"Okay. We can go."

"*Rab da shukar hai.* Thank God for that."

The community centre was a small, brick-built box out by the canal. They had chosen it as a place that both *desi* and *gora* would be willing to come, and where *Desi Art* might get a broad airing.

They were met at the door by a small, plump man with wire-rimmed specs and a few sparse tufts of ginger hair. He ushered them into the office and introduced himself as Mr Waring, the centre manager.

"I have to tell you, gentlemen, we have received a few complaints."

Vik gave a brittle laugh. "How can there be complaints? The exhibition hasn't even opened yet."

Mr Waring straightened some papers on his desk.

"I regret to say that a number of people have expressed the view—quite forcibly expressed, I might say—that this exhibition of yours may not be the most appropriate use of the centre's facilities."

"Well, you can just tell them to go to hell, can't you?"

Baz put out a restraining hand. Vik's anger sparked and burned like a Roman candle. His was on a longer fuse, but it still burned.

"In what way is our exhibition 'inappropriate'?"

The manager cleared his throat again. "Gentlemen, I can assure you if it were up to me, I would be only too happy—"

"In what way 'inappropriate', Mr Waring?" Baz repeated.

"The trustees have decided that it would not serve anyone's best interests to stir up ill feeling—"

"And why would a few paintings and photographs and works of art stir up any ill feeling?"

The manager took out a large white handkerchief and wiped his mouth. "The fact is, people in this community feel that they are already rather swamped—"

Silence spread like a pool across the table. Vik leaned over the desk.

"Which community would that be, Mr Waring? The people from the mosque down the road? Or maybe the ones from the gurdwara round the corner?"

The manager's face turned the colour of tandoori chicken. The handkerchief came out again and dabbed at his mouth. "Two admirable institutions which I am sure would be happy to host your—"

"I live fifteen minutes away from this shit hole. Doesn't that make me part of this community? My family own a business that employs nearly thirty people—"

"But not English people, Mr Kalsi."

Baz saw Vik's hand close into a fist. He stood up, scraping his chair.

"Vik, we're leaving."

The manager looked from Vik to Baz. Unease seeped from his pores and glistened on his face. "Gentlemen, you have to understand. Unemployment around here is very high …"

Baz grabbed the sleeve of Vik's jacket and dragged him

backwards through the door. Outside the centre, he shoved him up against the wall.

"What were you going to do? Start a fist fight in there? How's that going to help?"

"And you're willing to let him get away with it?" He pushed Baz away. "You of all people, man. You know what happens if we don't stand up to these bastards."

Just for a second, Baz beat back smoke that wasn't there.

"I also know we don't get anywhere if we start behaving like mindless thugs."

"Sod you. You know what? You sound like my father."

He jerked away and strode off down the road. Baz caught up with him up and after a few strides, Vik slowed down.

"You know what my *pyo* thinks, *yaar*. He thinks he's indulged me enough, letting me go off to art school. Now it's time to be a good Punjabi boy and join the family firm. If I don't make a success of this exhibition, I'll be stuck doing cut and finish for the rest of my life!"

Baz took a deep breath. He could feel his own dreams collapsing under the weight of disappointment. But he wasn't going to give up yet.

"*Desi Art* is going to happen."

"How? We've got three weeks, *yaar*."

"We'll make it happen. We'll take it to every school, every church, every gurdwara and temple and mosque in the city—"

"Baz, if we put *Desi Art* in a gurdwara, who's going to see it apart from a load of old aunties in their *shalwar kameez*?"

"Fine. We'll think of something."

"It's not just you and me, man. There's Mohan we'd be letting down. And that friend of your doctor chum. We got them into this. We told them we could make the exhibition happen."

"And we will."

Though fuck knew how.

Chapter 13

The first time I was rostered for a proper night duty was Friday.

To begin with, the men trickled in. Baz spent time showing me the office routine—how to book people in, how to deal with the regulars (paid for by the DHSS) versus the casuals (beds paid for in cash each night). The Skipper locked its doors at ten, ("before pub closing time," Baz said) and no one, but NO ONE, was to be admitted after lock up.

The names of the regulars were already in the book, and we just ticked them off to show whether they'd been in. Casuals were added as they came in. One name had 'DNA' written alongside it, in large red letters.

"What's up with that?"

"Do Not Admit," Baz said. "We write it against anyone who's been barred, to make sure no one lets them in by mistake." He tapped the name with his finger. "You won't have to worry about this one for a while. He's banged up in Winson Green."

My mind flashed back to Loony Larry, to Iain's 'lummed up headbangers' and to Frank's 'real troublemakers.' "What do they do to get barred?" I asked.

Baz shrugged. "Keep breaking the rules, starting fights. Violence towards staff."

"What about this one?"

"Pulled a knife on me," he said, in the tone you might use to say, 'borrowed my pen'. He saw my face and seemed to realise he was scaring me. "Look, don't worry. It's very rare, and almost always bravado. But we can't ever let them get away with it."

The dormitory next to the main room was crammed with rows of what looked like ex-hospital beds, painted black and barely eighteen inches apart. Each one was made up with a mattress covered in tobacco-coloured plastic, with a couple of blankets folded at the foot. The smell was worse than in the main room.

The volunteers on night shift (always two) slept in the office. A pair of bunks, built of two-by-fours, was squeezed in down one wall. The mattresses were identical to the ones in the dorm, though we volunteers had the luxury of a pillow. The door was heavy and, like the one to the kitchen, could be bolted on the inside. I wasn't sure if that was reassuring or not.

Around nine, I heard singing in the alley, and a thunder of knocking on the door. I had a hand on the latch to let them in, when Baz stopped me.

"Always check the spyhole before you open the door. You never know when someone could be stood there with a broken bottle."

It seemed as though, after two shifts spent convincing me the Skipper was benign, he was now determined to turn all that on its head and scare the hell out of me. I wiped my damp palms on my jeans.

"What do you do if there is?" I asked.

"Call the police."

This time, though, it was just a busker with a guitar and a clutch of mates. I glanced for approval at Baz, and swung the door wide to let them in.

"Charlie Singer!" the busker announced, like a fairground showman introducing the top of the bill. "I've drunk all my money and it's been a fucking good night. You hear that everyone?" he shouted. "A fucking good night."

He climbed up onto one of the benches and struck a chord. One or two people cheered. Others shouted at him to shut up. Baz jerked his thumb for him to get down, and he clambered off and winked at me. I couldn't help smiling back.

The newcomers found a quiet corner and Charlie began to sing 'Danny Boy', interrupted by more knocking at the door. Men were arriving in a constant stream now, anxious to beat the ten o'clock curfew on this bitter, wet night. Robyn took a turn in the office, and Baz came to help me behind the counter.

"Who's that?" I pointed to a man with trouser creases sharp enough to slice bacon. His white shirt was clean and pressed, and his back was ramrod straight as he hung up his overcoat. As I watched, he unfolded the pages of his *Coventry Evening Telegraph* and spread them on the table.

"Must be a cold night if Pongo's booking in. He's usually had his soup and gone by now," said Baz.

"He's a *resident*?"

"Groups most likely to end up on the street," Baz said, ticking them off on his fingers, "ex-prisoners, ex-mental patients, kids out of care and ex-military. Pongo was a Lance Corporal."

"He doesn't exactly look like he can't cope."

"Institutionalised. He spent his entire adult life being told what to do. Then he came out and had to make decisions for himself. A lot of ex-squaddies can't hack it. Pongo coped by making his own Queen's Regulations. Up at the same time every morning. Spit and polish. Kit ready for inspection. He's got a son and daughter-in-law over Nuneaton way who would take him in like a shot. But he won't have it."

"Where does he stay? If he doesn't come in here?"

"Nobody knows. He's got a squat somewhere, we think. Or a derry. Comes in most evenings for his soup. And every morning for a shower and a shave."

"How does he keep his clothes like that?"

"Washes them in there." He jerks his thumb towards the washhouse. "He found an old iron in a skip one time. Asked us if he could plug it in. Now he irons his kit every day the way his sergeant taught him."

"You got to be kidding."

"You should talk to him sometime. He and Iain get on famously. They do maths puzzles together. And don't get him started on lateral thinking."

Shortly before lock up, there was more knocking, and this time we heard the telltale clink of bottles.

"One thing about the Skipper," Baz told me as he unbolted the door. "They come up here because the Sally Ann won't let them in if they've been drinking. We let them in, but they're not allowed to bring alcohol in here."

One young lad finished his can of Brew XI in the alley. Two others wandered off to share the last of a bottle of 'broon wine'. That left a bearded Scotsman, nearly as tall as Baz and twice as broad. The man swayed in the doorway, a cut on his nose still oozing blood and a bottle of cooking brandy clutched in his fist.

"You can't bring that in here, Knoxie. You know that," Baz told him.

"What time is it?" (Though it sounded more like 'wha'shimezit?')

"Five to ten."

"So I haven't got time to go somewhere else, have I? Cunt."

"So you dump it. Or you give it to me to keep safe till the morning."

The man's jumper was a collection of holes held together with patches of knitting. His clothes were already damp. In another hour, he'd be soaked through. It seemed to me that if he stayed out like that, big as he was, he'd be dead of hypothermia by morning. On the other hand, letting him in seemed like inviting a grizzly bear to join you in the tent.

"Come on, Knoxie." Baz said. "Hand it over and come inside to get warm."

The big man stayed rocking on the balls of his feet, his eyes fixed on a point somewhere inside Baz's skull. I watched him lift the bottle to shoulder height and contemplate the two inches of amber liquid still sloshing in the bottom. He raised it, as if to pour some more down his throat. Then he smashed the bottle on the concrete wall and held up the jagged shard

"Whoa!"

I leapt backwards. Baz pushed the door in front of him like a shield. But before he could shut it, I heard Knoxie drop the neck of the bottle into the alley with the rest. He shouldered the door aside as if Baz weighed no more than a bag of sugar.

"If I can't have it, there's no bugger else gonna touch it."

The skim of soup left in the big kettle was barely enough to fill a bowl. I served Knoxie and got a "what you looking at?" by way of thanks. He slumped over the table, head in his hands, eyes glassy. Charlie and his mates were singing again. They'd started on 'ninety-nine bottles of beer on the wall,' and each time they reached a new tally, they belted it out at the tops of their voices.

"Don't like tha' fucking noise. S'doing my fucking head in."

"Eat some of this soup, Knoxie. You'll feel better."

"No call to be singing. Fucking Charlie Singer."

"They'll have to stop soon. It's nearly bedtime."

Knoxie took a spoonful of soup. Most of it dribbled into his beard, but he seemed to get his eye in after that and managed two or three spoonfuls more or less straight into his mouth. Nearby, Walter crumbled the last of his bread onto the floor, muttering, "We are not worthy so much as to gather up the crumbs under thy table." Baz went outside to clear up the broken glass in the alley and Robyn put her coat on ready to leave. I started wiping down the tables.

"Are you going to shut your face, Charlie Singer, or am I going to have to do it for you?"

I spun round. Knoxie was on his feet, towering over Charlie. The busker stopped singing.

"You and whose army, gobshite?"

"I don't need no fucking army, pal."

Knoxie's head swung forward with the force of a club. Blood blossomed from Charlie's nose and he sat down with a bump on the floor. Knoxie swayed. "Christ, I feel sick," he mumbled. "Where's the fucking cludgie?" He stumbled towards the washhouse and vomited in the doorway.

A low-key rumbling of *Fight! Fight! Fight!* was swiftly quelled by Pongo and one or two others. Robyn's head popped out the door of the office, her white-blonde halo of hair rumpled, and disappeared again. By the time she reappeared, carrying a locked First Aid box, Knoxie had slid down the wall and was on the floor too. Baz came in from the alley, took in the scene, and swapped dustpan and brush for a mop.

The big Scotsman lapsed into silence. I remembered, rather late, that I wasn't just a bystander here. I had a job to do. I squatted on the floor and made a clumsy effort to check Knoxie's vital signs. To be on the safe side I moved him into the recovery position.

"Charlie, do keep still," Robyn said, as she attempted to staunch the blood still flowing from his nose.

"Singer by name and singer by nature."

"Yes, Charlie. I know."

I took the flannel Baz passed me and wiped Knoxie's face. The cloth came away grey and left a pale streak across his cheek. I was trying not to think about the pervading smell of Jeyes Fluid and vomit, nor the greasy touch of his skin and clothes. He was sleeping now. At least, I hoped he was sleeping.

"Oh my darling, oh my darling …" Charlie warbled.

Robyn groaned. "Are you going to let me clean you up or not?" she asked.

Baz leaned on the mop. He looked tired.

"You should get home," he told her. "It's late."

"Are you going to be able to get these guys to bed?"

"We'll manage. Someone will help."

From where I sat, on the lower bunk, I could see the soles of Baz's feet dangling down. Long and narrow, the toes clearly separate, like someone who was used to going barefoot. Kind of sexy.

"God, Baz, is it always like that on a Friday night?"

Most of the men had shuffled off to bed once the excitement was over. Pongo and one of the unemployed lads helped Baz to half carry, half drag Knoxie into the dorm. Charlie was coaxed through after them, still singing under his breath. Now we were in the office, with its heavy door bolted. And I started to shiver.

"Not that often. You had a baptism of bloody fire. Wouldn't blame you if you decided to piss off." The bed creaked as Baz lay back. Above me, the bands supporting the mattress flexed under his weight. "I hope you don't, though."

The shivering left my body. I had the sense of having put the worst behind me. Knoxie was terrifying, but he was outnumbered by the likes of Pongo and Charlie Singer and Frank. And even Knoxie had done me no harm, when all was said and done.

"Hey," I said, "I guess if you start at the bottom, the only way to go is up."

Baz chuckled. "You did well. Really well. Getting Knoxie into the recovery position, that was good thinking."

He reached out and pressed a switch. The light went off and I could see the glow from the infrared heater above the desk. I lay down on the bed and pulled the blankets up over me. We'd taken off our shoes but we were still dressed. "Never know when you might be needed in the night," Baz had said.

"You warm enough down there?"

"Sure."

"Only it gets pretty stuffy in here if you leave this on all night."

The faint fizzling of the heater element stopped. The red glow faded to a wavy line and went out. I could hear Baz's breathing in the darkness above me.

Six days ago, I'd lain awake, listening to the rhythm of Ossie's breathing. He'd be in the safe house in Botswana now. The border crossing wouldn't happen for days or weeks. He might even write to me, though I wouldn't be able to write back. He'd never risk sending the address.

Ossie, what would you think of your *nosisi* if you could see her now? Dealing with drunken, puking Scotsmen and ex-squaddies in razor-sharp trousers ... you wouldn't recognise her.

Chapter 14

Four days had passed since their disastrous meeting at the community centre. Almost a week since he came back from Brixton. Vik had called yesterday. No luck finding an alternative venue. If they didn't sort something soon, they might have to put the exhibition back weeks, or even months. The bugger of it was, there was so little he could do. Vik was the one with the contacts, the one who, if he chose, could blag and charm his way through locked doors.

He heard the bolts slide back in the Skipper's door. A moment later, the raw dank smell of fog pressed in through the half-open door of the office, and he heard milk bottles rattle in their crate. Maia was up and was getting on with things. Out of sheer lassitude, he lay a while longer, his eyes closed.

"Baz?" Maia stood in the doorway, her face still sleepy-looking. "Oh, good. You're awake. I thought I should make a start, only I wasn't sure about quantities for porridge and stuff."

He watched her through half-hooded eyes. Something about her fascinated him, something mutable as iridescent light. He had to get her to sit for him one day.

She cleared her throat and he became aware that she was waiting for a response.

"Sorry. I should have been up ages ago."

He let himself down from the bunk and into the morning routine. Tea. Porridge. Sending everyone out with something hot inside them. Bolstering them against the day ahead. In ones or twos, the men got up, ate, got ready to leave, until Knoxie was the only one left in the dormitory.

"I think you ought to take a look at him, gaffer," Pongo said, in the respectful tones of a lance corporal telling an officer how to do his job.

Knoxie was sitting on the edge of his bunk, reeling as though someone had punched him. When Baz called his name, he stared, his eyes refusing to focus.

Charlie Singer followed them back in. "He must have had a shitload to drink if he's still hammered in the morning," he said, in tones of admiration.

But there was more to this than another punter going a few pints over the limit. He'd had seen enough men emerging out of an alcoholic torpor to know this was way outside the normal range.

"Maia," he called, "there's a phone number over the desk in the office. Dr Kheraj. Can you get him to come down here? Urgently?"

Not many doctors would attend the Skipper, but Noordin Kheraj could be relied upon to turn out at all hours of the day or night. Baz led him through to the dormitory. The big Scotsman sat where they had left him, swaying as if on board ship, his eyes glassy.

Baz watched Dr Kheraj take the big man's head between his hands and tilt it.

"Well, well. Mr Knox, is it?"

"I don't think Knox is his real name. The men call him Knoxie because he thunders like John Knox."

The doctor pointed a light into each eye, gently raising the lids.

"You say he vomited last night? And he's not had any more

alcohol since?"

Baz shook his head, his mouth dry. Was this his fault? Was there something that should have alerted him to call the doctor last night?

"He chucked his last bottle away in the alley. So unless he had something hidden on him …"

"That's good." Noordin took Knoxie's pulse and put a stethoscope to his chest. "I don't think this is concussion. Nor is it alcohol poisoning, though it is certainly the effect of long-term alcohol abuse."

He took a disposable syringe from his bag and filled it from a small ampoule.

"Would you roll up his sleeve for me, Bhajan?"

As soon as Baz took hold of his arm, Knoxie began to flail about. Big as he was, he was too uncoordinated to struggle effectively and Baz managed to get him in a kind of arm lock and drag the tattered sleeve high enough to expose a vein. A stream of slurred swearwords spilt from Knoxie's mouth as the needle went in, then he went quiet. Baz let go his arm, and he slumped forward.

"He is a lucky man," Noordin said. "I have seen men die in police cells because the custody sergeant thought they were still drying out and did nothing."

Baz drew a ragged breath. "I thought I'd screwed up, not calling you last night."

Noordin shook his head. "I am not sure that last night I could have made the correct diagnosis. Intoxication would have obscured the signs." He began tidying his things back into the black leather bag. "I suspect that what we have here is Wernicke's Encephalopathy. A lack of thiamine in the brain, brought on, in this case, by prolonged alcohol abuse. If it's not treated promptly, the effects can be permanent, even fatal."

Baz looked at the big man seated on the bed. The rhythmic swaying of his body had stopped and his head had dropped to his chest. He looked like a giant rag doll, not dead, but lifeless.

"Will he be okay?"

"I have given him an injection of Vitamin B which should relieve the worst of his symptoms for now, but he needs to be admitted to hospital as soon as possible."

Baz wiped a hand over his face. He felt as if he'd woken up to find himself with his toes over the edge of a cliff.

"Lucky for us you had the right stuff with you."

Noordin gave a dismissive shake of the head. "Given the nature of your clientele, this was always a possibility. I've kept the remedy on me for a while now." He smiled at Baz. "But you, Bhajan, you may well have saved his life."

"Not me. Pongo. He was the one who spotted there was something wrong."

"But you listened. And you acted. That's more than many would have done, I assure you."

Baz sent Maia home, made some tea and took it in to Noordin. As always, an air of faded elegance clung to the doctor. Rumpled linen suit, wearing threadbare at the knees and elbows. Faded silk tie. A single antique silver ring set with a piece of amber. Immaculately trimmed beard disguising the smallpox scars that pitted his skin. Baz had photographed him once in his surgery, sitting at the elaborately carved desk he had salvaged from his life in Zanzibar. There, among all the framed photographs of his once-privileged life, he appeared diminished, and Baz threw away the print in disgust. Here, though, in the squalor of the dormitory, his dignity was unassailable.

The Ismaili took the tea and crossed one leg over the other. "So Bhajan, tell me about the plans for your exhibition?"

Baz's shoulders sagged. Noordin's friend, the dentist Paras Shah, was one of the exhibitors they'd be letting down. "To be honest, I think we've messed up. We had a venue sorted out, but it's all gone pear-shaped."

He told the doctor about their problems with the community centre.

"So now you're looking at temples, gurdwaras, that sort of place?" Noordin said.

"There aren't a whole lot of other options."

The doctor stroked his goatee. "What would you say to a venue a little more central? Somewhere that might draw a bit more attention?"

"What do you have in mind?"

Noordin shook his head. "Give me a day or two, Bhajan. I have an idea, but I need to see if it can be made to work." He looked down at his watch and clicked his tongue. "Perhaps the ambulance cannot find the entrance in the fog. I should walk down to Spon Street and see if I can guide them in."

Baz half stood up. "I'll go, shall I?"

Noordin patted his shoulder. "You stay and keep an eye on our patient. If he comes round, he should see a familiar face."

"Be careful. The fog's pretty dense."

When the doctor had left, Baz took a broom and began sweeping the dormitory floor. After a while he heard footsteps and two ambulance men followed Noordin into the dormitory. When they spoke to Knoxie, he was half-way lucid, and they managed to coax him to his feet. He stumbled along between them to where the ambulance was parked under a cone of jaundiced light from a single street light.

"Shall I go with him?" Baz asked.

"No, no. I can manage. I will pick up my car later."

"You sure?"

"Go on. Go home." Noordin shooed him away. "I will call you with any news. About our patient or about your venue."

Chapter 15

At the top of the Precinct, I paused to get my bearings. Somewhere on the other side of the road was Broadgate Square and the statue of Lady Godiva, but I might as well have been on the edge of the ocean. Buses moved through the fog like leviathans, diesel engines calling to one another.

I saw what I hoped was a gap in the traffic and pushed the bike out into the road. I'd almost reached the kerb on the far side when another bus came round, faster than most. It loomed out of the saturated air, headlights like angry eyes. I leapt out of the way and someone grabbed my arm.

"Oi! Watch where you're going, you stupid bint."

The hand clamped to my forearm had 'HATE' tattooed across the knuckles and more tattoos spilling down over his wrists. Not Gary, though. A beefier version. Gary on steroids. If this one didn't want me walking off, he wouldn't have much trouble stopping me.

"I'm sorry," I said, trying to sound reasonable. "That bus nearly—"

"Well, fuck me. Look who it isn't."

The voice behind me made me jump and the grip on my arm tightened. I glanced over my shoulder and saw Gary, strutting round me like he'd just spied fresh road kill.

"Know this one, do you?" Beefy asked him.

I swallowed hard and held myself still, as if by not moving I could make myself invisible. But Gary had seen me all right. He flicked his lighter and a flame appeared.

"Yeah, I know her. Paki-lover, she is."

"That right?" My captor gave my arm a painful twist. "White boys not good enough for you, eh? Like a bit of curry with your dick?"

More figures appeared out of the fog. Half a dozen of them milled around me now. Shadowy shapes in Doc Martens and rolled up Levis, their hair shaven or brush cut. More of the arseholes that I'd seen charge the Asian kids down by the fountain? Or were they breeding like cockroaches now?

"Give her some British banger," one of them called. "That'll teach her." Beefy yanked my arm behind my back and my bike clattered to the ground.

"You realise they'll ban all that, once we get this country back?"

My eyes were watering and I had to clench my jaw to stop my teeth from chattering. "Ban what?" I hissed back. "British sausages?"

Beefy tugged my arm harder and put his mouth to my ear.

"One race going with another. We'll make it illegal. Got that? We'll bang slags like you up and throw away the key."

He let go my arm and I spun round, looking for an escape. Gary shoved me back into the middle of the circle.

"Not natural, is it? Two species mixing. Wouldn't breed a dog with a cat, would you?"

Gary had his lighter up near my face now, close enough for me to feel the heat burn my skin. Each time I tried to back away, one of the bastards pushed me forward, as if I were a ball they had to keep in the air. Gary circled, holding the flame level with my eyes.

It was Saturday morning. The middle of the city. People must be within earshot, even if the fog was hiding them. If I screamed, someone would come. Wouldn't they?

Maybe the same thought occurred to Beefy. He grabbed my

coat and yanked me to one side.

"Fuck off out of here, bitch. I wouldn't dirty mine in the same hole as a filthy Paki anyway."

The circle loosened, as if he'd broken the force field that held them together. I stooped for the bike, not daring to drop my eyes. The moment a gap opened in the ring, I pushed through, not thinking about where I was going, just putting as much distance between me and those vermin as I could.

Despite the fog, I'd have taken my chances with the traffic and ridden the bike, but the fall had knocked the wheel out of alignment and I was finding it hard enough to push. I didn't dare stop to straighten it, so I stumbled along, cursing their filthy, racist minds. Cursing Baz for leaving me to come home alone.

I was almost at the turning for Paradise Road when I heard footsteps behind me. I stopped for a second and the sound ceased. Moved on, and it started again. It was a trick of the fog, it had to be. My own footsteps echoing. Nerves playing games with me.

I hurried along the road, the bike's pedal banging against my ankle. Half the houses were boarded up. Others had filthy windows and paint peeling in strips. But our green gate was just ahead now. I was reaching for the lock when I heard a voice behind me.

"That's where you do-gooders live, is it? S'good to know. Send you a postcard one day, maybe."

I gasped and looked over my shoulder. But Gary had gone, swaggering off down the street, hands in the pockets of his jeans so the back of his donkey jacket stuck out behind him like a rooster's tail.

"Maia, is that you? You're late. We were getting worried. Where's Baz?"

Robyn emerged from the bathroom with a folded drying

rack, radiating concentrated early morning energy. I fixed on the array of badges pinned to her dungarees. Spare Rib. Militant. 'Which of Us is the Opposite Sex?' Words were piling up inside me, pressing at my throat. If I could tell someone about Gary, about what happened in Broadgate

"Maia? You okay? You look a bit peaky. Do you need to put your head between your knees?"

But if I told, Robyn would make a drama out of it. People would fuss over me. I'd be the centre of attention when all I wanted to do was hide. I forced a smile.

"Just a problem with Knoxie, that's all. Baz had to call the doctor."

"Oh! Is he all right? He was pretty bad last night, wasn't he?" She went back into the bathroom and came back with a pile of wet knickers. "God knows what he'd been drinking. What's the matter with him? Do you know? You'd think you'd get used to it, working down there, but honestly—"

"I don't know. The doctor was still there when I left." I looked round for escape and saw the bathroom door still open. "Robyn, have you finished in there for now?"

Before she could answer, I pushed past her and locked the door behind me. I sat on the loo while the bath filled, feeling sick. When the water was deep enough, I stripped off my clothes, plunged in and scrubbed myself with a nail brush. Robyn must think last night at the Skipper had all been too much for me. That I was reacting to Knoxie, and the vomit and the blood and the dirt. But Knoxie's greasy clothes might have been snow white linen compared to how I felt now.

A wire rack across the bath held a slimy bar of Imperial Leather, its label just visible, some Pears, a piece of spicy smelling sandalwood. And a coral-coloured sliver of Lifebuoy. I cupped it to my face and breathed in its clean scent. The scent of Ossie.

My mind conjured an image of limbs tangled on a bed. Two species. *Christ.* I sank beneath the water, holding my breath until my lungs hurt and my pulse throbbed in my ears. Sodding ironic that those bastards had harassed me because I'd been seen with Baz. If they knew about Ossie, God …

My lungs about to burst, I surfaced, water streaming off my face. Drawing my knees up under my chin, I hugged my arms around them and sobbed, until the water grew cold and I was forced to get out.

One summer I was actually happy out in Africa. We were in Senegal and for a change we were living in a small house rather than a mud hut. And we had a cook-housekeeper called Pinda who spoke French and a bit of English, so I had someone to talk to when my mother wasn't around. If I ever moaned, Pinda used to take my hand in hers and say, 'It is better to walk than complain about the road.' And then she'd find me a job to do.

The rest of the Skipper volunteers must have figured it was new-girl keenness, the way I volunteered for every job going that weekend. But work kept Beefy's words from crawling out of the dark corners of my mind. Kept me from remembering Gary's lighter burning my face.

Sunday night at the Skipper passed peacefully enough. Monday morning, I went through the rooms with Baz, checking everyone had left. I'd been going to the loo constantly that weekend, and now on top of that I had cramps. The phone rang and while Baz answered it, I made another trip to the loo to check if my period had started. It hadn't.

"That was Dr Kheraj," Baz told me, as I emerged.

"How's Knoxie? Has he heard?"

"He's pulling through. Starting to detox. They've put him on diazepam, to stop the DTs." Baz puffed out his cheeks and blew air out, ran his hand over his hair. "Listen, I'm sorry to keep doing this to you, but do you think you could lock up here for me and make your own way home? I have to meet Noordin up in town."

Back through Broadgate, on my own, again? I had the phantom sense of a hand grabbing my arm. I swallowed hard.

"I was thinking of going back to Leamington." I hadn't known I was going to say it until it was out of my mouth, but now it seemed the obvious choice. "I still have to pack up the rest of my stuff."

"Are you going to need help to bring it back?" Baz glanced at his watch and I knew he was working out whether he had time to fit in a drive to Leamington on top of whatever else he had planned for today.

"Sometime, but it doesn't have to be today. The rent's paid for another week."

"Okay. We'll sort something out."

He was hustling now, eager to get out of the door. I checked it would be okay to leave the bike chained up outside, and let him go. I was about to make a last dash to the loo when I sensed someone behind me and wheeled round.

"Polish! You're not supposed to be here—"

Polish was one of our regulars. His hair was black, his clothes were black, and his face and hands were so ingrained with dirt that he might have been carved from a piece of Silesian coal. As if he hadn't heard me, he came on through the door and shuffled towards the desk. I took a step backwards.

"You don't understand. You have to leave now."

He sat down on the edge of the plastic chair, rested his fists on his knees and nodded towards the other chair. I tried standing for a bit longer, hoping to maintain some sort of authority, but I felt stupid.

No one knew much about Polish. The old die-hards seemed to tolerate him, even shared a bottle with him outside in the streets. But as far as I knew, he didn't speak much English. In fact he rarely spoke at all, in any language.

His real name was Jerzy... Jerzy something unpronounceable, though I'd never heard him called that, only read it in the register. He was just 'Polish'. Word was he might have been a navigator with the Polish Free Forces.

He began to speak, in a voice so rough it was like sandpaper rasping over concrete. But I made out the word 'please'. If he was a threat, he was a very polite one.

"What is it, Polish?"

More words spilt out. This time, the one word I managed to grasp was '*Solidarność*'. That meant 'Solidarity', didn't it? Like the Union? "I'm so sorry. I don't speak Polish."

He looked at me pityingly and repeated the words. I guess I'd had a bit of practice, what with listening to Frank. This time what I heard was heavily accented but intelligible English,

"I make my own strike. Like Lech Walesa. Like *Solidarność*."

Not that it made a whole lot more sense.

"I'm sorry, Polish. You're going to have to begin at the beginning. Why do you want to go on strike?"

The corners of his eyes creased and I saw for the first time how blue the irises were. To my chagrin, I realised he was happy that, out of everything he'd said, I'd managed to understand two words.

"Go on, P—. Go on, Jerzy."

"Social Services, they make me go every two days. They make me sign. They say I am No Fixed Abode. Like men that sleep on street. But this not true. I am resident here, no?"

"That's what it says on the register."

"The others here, they not go so often, I think?"

"No. I don't think so …"

"So I go on strike. Like Lech Walesa. I not sign until they treat me like others."

"But Jerzy, if you don't sign on, you won't get any money."

"I know this. You strike, you no get paid." Jerzy drew himself erect. "I suffer. Like *Solidarność*."

I didn't know whether to laugh or cry or just curl up with shame. Why had none of us taken the trouble to listen to him before?

"Listen, Jerzy, we're not going to let you suffer.'"

His eyes flashed blue again. "You help me?"

"Of course we'll help you. It must be some stupid mistake. Baz can call and—"

Jerzy gave a short, sharp jerk of his head. "No. You. You listen. You understand. You make call. You tell them, they no treat Jerzy right, he go on hunger strike, like Bobby Sands."

He saw my mouth drop open in shock, and he winked.

"I Polish Free Forces. I fly in Battle of Britain. I know how to fight, yes?"

I smiled back. "Yes, Jerzy, you know how to fight."

"You will help me?"

"I will help you."

He stood up. "You are good girl," he said, and he patted my arm. "I have much faith with you. Together we catch God by the arm, yes?"

As I turned the key in the big padlock on the Skipper's outer door, a dull ache nagged at my lower back and I wondered if this was my period starting or if I was going to have to see the doctor about a bladder infection. All the same, my encounter with Jerzy had cheered me up. I made a mental note to find out who I had to call to sort out his problem. Feeling almost equal to the task of clearing out the flat, I popped into Boots for tampons and paracetamol, and made my way to Pool Meadow to catch the bus.

The first thing I did when I got to the flat in Leamington was to pour a glass of water and swallow two paracetamol. Then I went upstairs to the bedrooms.

Ossie's door was ajar. I stopped outside, transfixed by the emptiness of it. He'd never been that big on possessions, apart from books. His room had always been a touch monastic. And what he didn't take with him, he'd given away. I knew that. But the room was so bare, it felt as if he'd been erased.

In my room, he was everywhere. On my dressing table, in the photograph, taken on a big march up in London. On the wall, in the black, green and gold ANC flag. On my bedside table, in the battered paperback copy of Steve Biko's 'I Write What I Like.'

This book—being able to read it in full, when even quoting from it was illegal in South Africa—was the most important thing in his life. It had shaped his thinking, given him a reason to go back.

Ubuntu. Ossie talked all the time about *Ubuntu.* The idea that every person is linked to everyone else. If one person is tortured or oppressed then so are we all. And a person becomes a human being through the way they choose to respond.

And he gave the book to me. Asked me to carry on.

Hugging it to me, I lay down and curved my body around the contours of the quilt that was still moulded to the shape of his body. Maybe all the sleeping in strange beds was catching up with me, or maybe it was the weight of expectation, but my eyelids were fighting a losing battle with gravity. I fell asleep with a whiff of Lifebuoy in my nostrils, and woke with my hands and feet freezing and a nagging sense I'd forgotten something. Weird, the way dreams could inflict that illogical sense of urgency on you.

Too cold to stay where I was, I began to go through cupboards and drawers, packing the stuff I meant to keep and filling black bin bags with the rest. All the time, I couldn't shake the feeling that I'd missed something important. I was going through the bathroom cabinet, when my mind flashed back to the queue at Boots.

I'd had to wait behind a woman buying Calpol and tissues for a snivelling child and a pensioner wanted something for her corns. Out of sheer boredom, I studied the shelves behind the head of the manicured assistant. I had barely registered it at the time, but there was a box. A plain, unpretentious, cellophane wrapped box.

Now, standing in the bathroom of our flat, I remembered

where I'd seen one like it before. A friend of mine at university, her period late, grateful to be able to find out the truth in the privacy of her own room rather than in the glare of the doctor's office. Asking for my help because I was used to handling experiments. The long wait. Genny's hand fumbling for mine. The two of us staring into the little mirror and seeing the brown ring that had formed in the bottom of the test tube …

Something tugged at my abdomen, as if the cord linking me to Ossie had spun out its full length and pulled taut. I walked back into the bedroom, pulled the quilt off the bed and wrapped it round me. For God's sake, this was stupid. My period wasn't even late yet. And I was on the Pill. You didn't get pregnant if you were on the Pill. Not if you …

But I'd been sick, the morning Ossie left. Really sick. And I'd taken the pill late the night before. I'd remembered after we got to the party, almost over the 12 hour limit …

All the fragments of Ossie that were scattered round the room seemed to coalesce and sit on the bed beside me. I counted back the nights to Ossie's party. Bang in the middle of my cycle, just at the time when I'd be ovulating.

How many errors—how many stupid human errors—could it take to create another life?

Chapter 16

"So," asked Noordin. "What do you think?"

Baz was standing with the doctor in the broad covered passage between Bull Yard and Shelton Square. A stream of Monday morning shoppers flowed round them, funnelled through on their way to the Retail Market or the shops in Market Way. But all Baz's focus was on the empty shop in front of him.

"The business closed down a few weeks ago," Noordin said. "The landlord is looking for a new tenant, but meanwhile it stands empty." He folded his hands over his gloves and looked up at Baz. "He and I play chess, once a week or so, on that giant chessboard in Smithford Way. Last time we played, he mentioned he was looking for a stop-gap tenant. When you told me of your predicament, I thought of him at once."

Baz looked round. No question, it was a hell of a location. Everyone in Coventry passed here sooner or later. But …

"Noordin, we couldn't possibly afford this."

The doctor shrugged. "You have a grant from the Council? To pay for the hire of the community centre?"

"Well, yes, but there's no way—"

"The landlord will accept the same payment for one month's rent of this shop."

"Why?" Their grant wouldn't even come close to covering a city centre rent. And landlords weren't given to unexplained acts of charity.

Noordin shrugged again. "Empty shops attract vandals. In his view, any tenant is better than none. And besides, he is interested in your project."

Through the whitewash-spattered windows, Baz could see the scars in the floor where the old counters had been ripped out. A small pile of junk mail lay inside the door.

"This was a butcher's, wasn't it?"

"I believe so, yes."

"We wouldn't need planning permission?"

"As I understand it, a shop is a shop, whether it sells paintings or pork."

"And Paras? He's a Jain, isn't he? How would he feel about us using a place that traded in slaughtered animals?"

"I asked him that before I called you. I believe he would take it in the spirit of swords into ploughshares."

Baz walked to the windows and peered inside. The space was large and well lit, painted or white tiled. It would need a bit of work but it was potentially the perfect, virgin space for a gallery.

"A location like this—we'd attract attention."

The doctor smiled. "I would hope so, Bhajan."

"And attention could mean trouble. Does your friend realise that?"

"He was in the East End of London in the 1930s, Bhajan. Believe me, he knows that sort of trouble."

Baz pressed his fingers to the windows, hardly daring to believe the glass was solid. This was way bigger than an exhibition in a community centre at the dog end of the city. This was taking the biggest dream he'd ever had, putting it in an enlarger and blowing it up so he could see all the details, all the light and shade …

"Noordin, I don't know what to say."

"Say thank you, my friend. And start organising your exhibition."

The morning they signed the lease, Vik cleaned some of the whitewash off the windows and put up a poster.

```
            Desi Art:
An Exhibition of Contemporary Asian
         Artists in Coventry
```

Today, they were going to transform the stripped-out butcher's shop into a clean white space to set off their exhibits. Baz strode past the abstract carvings on the front of the Three Tuns, swinging his paint can, feeling the excitement build in his chest. Charlie Singer, setting up his pitch outside the pub, gave him the thumbs-up. He grinned back stupidly.

A few yards from the shop, the jubilance drained from him.

Across the big window, someone had painted a swastika, blood red against the black and white of the poster. 'Pakis Out' sprawled in wobbly letters eighteen inches high across the other window. The initials 'NF' filled the doorway.

The blood in his head seemed to concentrate at a point behind his eyes. All at once, he was standing again on the crazy-paving path outside the house in Leamington. He was on the way to school, leather satchel over his shoulder. He could remember the feel of its rough stitching against his palm, and the wet-leaf smell of autumn. Looking back to see what was keeping his mother, he saw her framed against the peeling maroon paint of their front door. But the door looked all wrong. There was a spidery squiggle of black paint on it. And the words, 'Pakis Out.'

"We're not Pakis, are we, Mum?"

"Of course we're not." His mother's chin jutted; so he could see the knot of her headscarf. "They must have made a mistake, that's all." She took his hand in hers and squeezed. "That door needed painting anyway," she said. "We'll do it tonight, shall we, Baz? What colour would you like?"

He was gripping the handle of the paint can so hard his hand hurt. He took a step back and almost collided with the roll of dustsheets that Vik had slung over his shoulder.

"*Kiddan,* man? What's—" Vik saw what Baz was staring at, and whistled. "Fuck me. Didn't take them long, did it?"

Baz had to unknot the muscles in his face to speak. Even so, his voice came out like a snarl.

"I told you we had to be ready for trouble."

"Yeah but they could at least give us a chance to move in before they kicked off." Vik clapped him on the back and Baz jerked as if poked with a cattle prod. "Don't fret, *yaar*. We got more than enough paint stripper to deal with this lot."

Baz scoured away at the twisted limbs of the swastika, the smell of paint stripper filling his nose.

"How can you take it so calmly? You were ready to kill that pompous bigot at the community centre."

Vik spat at the N of the NF and carried on rubbing. "People like him turn my stomach. Hiding behind big words and pretending it's nothing to do with them. At least you know where you are with these bastards."

Expunging the graffiti took the best part of the morning. They still had to clear away the debris left from the stripped-out counters, spread the dustsheets, prepare the walls and paint them in pure white emulsion. At lunch time, Baz walked down to Fishy Moore's for a bag of chips.

"Just don't get any of that curry sauce," Vik shouted after him. "*Phenchod*, what were they thinking?"

"Cultural exchange, mate. India got the Civil Service; we got curry sauce."

Vik laughed. "Hard to know who to feel sorrier for."

Painting the walls at least proved straightforward. Vik blagged a couple of rollers from another uncle with a painting and decorating business, which speeded things up. All the same, by the time they finished, Baz's arms and shoulders ached. He had paint in his hair and on his clothes, and his eyes itched. But hard work had purged some of what he felt inside. And the shop, with its floor swept and its walls gleaming white, was beginning to look like somewhere to be proud of.

"Come on, man," Vik said. "There's nothing else we can do here tonight."

Outside, Baz turned and looked up at the windows, glinting now in the light from Bull Yard. Across the top, in place of the graffiti, Vik had painted 'Desi Art' in Punjabi and English.

Vik squinted up at it, his hands in his pockets. "Of course, strictly speaking, it ought to be 'Three and a half Desis and a Gora', seeing as you're only half desi."

Today, the joke was so near the knuckle he practically cut himself.

"They'll be back. You know that, don't you?"

"Then we clean it again." Vik slapped him on the back. "Lighten up, *yaar*. We won't let these *haramzadey* beat us."

Opening the door of the Gosford half an hour later, Baz was hit by the smell of beer and smoke and by the relentless bleat of the Galaxians machine. The Paradise Road crew were there, commandeering a table. He pointed Vik in their direction and pushed his way to the bar.

Vik took a seat next to Simon on the settle and bummed a cigarette. Maia was perched next to Tom, leaning towards him to catch what he was saying. Baz watched her through the smoke from Vik's fag. When she thought no one was looking, she seemed far away, and a little sad. He tried to remember when they had last talked, but the only conversation he could recall having with her for days was when she asked him for the number of the local DHSS.

She caught his stare and leant forward, pitching her voice to bypass Vik and Simon's squabble. "Do you know you have paint in your hair?"

He ran his hand over his hair. "Yeah, you can tell which one of us can handle a paint brush. Vik and I spend an afternoon painting—he looks immaculate and I end up looking at if I've gone three rounds with a clown and a bucket of whitewash."

"Hmmm." She gave him an appraising look. "Maybe two rounds."

They exchanged smiles. Not wanting to let her drift away again, he said, "You never told me what it was you wanted that DHSS number for."

"For Jerzy. You know? Polish." She picked up a beer mat and tapped the edge of it against the table. "Did you know they'd been making him sign on every other day, even though he was resident at the Skipper?"

"I didn't. How'd you find out?"

"He told me."

"You speak Polish?"

"Jerzy speaks English, if anyone bothered to listen."

Okay, that was a palpable hit. How come he hadn't known that?

She was flipping the beer mat between her fingers now, her face hard with anger. "I got hold of the DHSS yesterday, to try and sort it out for him. Do you know what the bastards told me? They knew perfectly well he only needed to come in once a week, but they thought he 'liked coming to see them.' Can you believe it? I told them he wasn't their lap dog and it was about time they started treating him with a bit of respect."

Fuck me. Get Maia fired up and she had a look that'd stop you in your tracks. "Good for you."

He tried to say something else, but Vik's voice was rising, blocking out any attempt at conversation. "What you people do would be quite impossible within the Asian community. To let our old people end up homeless? On the streets? Unthinkable. It is a matter of *izzat* that we look after our families."

"That's all very well to say," Simon countered, "but most of these poor bastards don't have families. So who's supposed to look after them?"

"Everyone has family. If you are a fourth cousin twice removed, you are family. If you come from the same village, you are family. That's *biraderi*. Brotherhood."

God, Vik could be a pompous prick at times. Before he could say anything, Maia leaned forward.

"Tell me, Vik, are you a Sikh, like Baz?"

Vik arched his eyebrows. "Baz isn't Sikh. His father was Sikh, but he was brought up by his mother, and she was English. He doesn't speak Punjabi, and he certainly isn't Sikh."

"Thanks," Baz said. His mouth had a bitter taste in it that had nothing to do with the beer he was drinking. "So, tonight I'm not even half *desi*?"

"I didn't say you weren't *desi*. I said you weren't Sikh. As in, you don't practice the religion."

"So? Neither do you. Or is that pint you're holding a figment of my imagination?"

Maia sat forward, her slim fingers sliding over the condensation on her glass. "Don't Sikhs grow their hair like Baz? And wear turbans?"

"Vik's a *mona* Sikh," said Baz. "Cuts his hair, shaves his beard. His parents don't approve, which is why he's so sodding prickly about it."

Vik shrugged. "Still brought up in it, though, wasn't I?"

"Yeah. You make it pretty fucking clear what you think sorts the sheep from the goats."

Chapter 17

Tom banged his glass down on the table.

"What you having, Maia?"

"Nothing for me," I said. "Only so much fun you can have with an orange juice and bitter lemon."

Tom raised an eyebrow. "Yeah, why are you drinking that muck, anyway?"

I shrugged. "Not feeling great, that's all. In fact, I think I'll make a move in a minute."

Baz reached for his coat. Vik had gone back to arguing with Simon but some of the tension lingered on Baz's face.

"I'll walk you home," he said.

"You don't need to."

"Trust me. I've been cleaning graffiti off the windows of the gallery all day. I'm aching in places that weren't even there this morning, and all I want now is a hot bath and some sleep."

He opened the door and cold air rushed in to meet the fug of the bar, making my eyes water. In spite of what I'd said, I was grateful for the company. I hadn't shaken off the fear that I'd come back one day to find Gary and his mates loitering by our gate.

"Graffiti?" I asked, when we no longer needed to shout to make ourselves heard. "I'm guessing you don't mean Kilroy Was Here?"

"Nothing so innocuous."

"Racist stuff?"

"Yeah."

"Gary and Co …"

His head jerked round. "You've seen something?"

Maybe I should tell him what happened in Broadgate. The group that cornered me was certainly capable of spraying racist graffiti. Were they capable of more than that? If they were, then it would be only fair to put Baz on his guard.

But he was the one who'd inadvertently introduced me to Gary. If I told him, he might think I blamed him for what happened. Worse, he might blame himself.

"I saw him up in Broadgate with a bunch of other skinheads, that's all. Seems like the sort of stunt they'd pull."

"Expect you're right."

I examined Baz's face in the light of the street lamps, thinking about the casual cruelty of Vik's remarks.

"Do you mind my asking—why was your father not there when you were growing up?"

A car came towards us, the glare of its headlights catching him and turning his face to a white mask.

"He died in an explosion at a foundry, couple of months before I was born."

"What about your mum? Why were you fostered?"

He stopped with his hand on the latch and scowled. "You ask a lot of questions."

Heat flared in my face. "I know. Sorry. Bad habit—"

He pushed the gate open and walked ahead of me. At the opening to the yard he spun on his heel, blocking the alleyway. His harsh tones echoed off the walls. "What was it Oscar Wilde said? 'To lose one parent may be regarded as a misfortune; to lose both looks like carelessness?' Well, I must have been fucking careless, because my mother died when I was thirteen."

He banged open the door to the house on the right, where the office and the guys' bedrooms were, and slammed it again behind him, leaving me alone in the yard. I heard footsteps thudding up the uncarpeted stairs. In his room, a light went on.

Well, I'd screwed that up, hadn't I?

I let myself into the other house and lit the fire in the sitting room. I crouched in front of it, warming my hands, my mind drifting from Baz's problems to mine.

I didn't want a baby. Possibly not ever and certainly not now. The logical thing to do, if I did turn out to be pregnant, would be simply to have an abortion. Yet I could feel the tug of that invisible cord, linking me to Ossie.

Six months ago, when Tom and I toasted our results, I had my future all mapped out. I was going to get a job with one of the big pharmaceuticals. Maybe one day make a world-changing breakthroughs, like discovering the viral equivalent of penicillin.

God, how naïve was I? Six months on and not even an interview. A few weeks back, I'd have settled for any halfway decent job that got me off the dole. Now I'd settle for the chance to go back and tell myself not to fuck things up.

Two weeks. That was how long I had to wait before I could find out if I really was pregnant. Two weeks? I didn't know how I was going to last two days.

However uncomfortable I'd made things with my probing, Baz and I were both rostered at the Skipper that next night, which didn't leave much room for avoidance. He was at the serving counter with me when Jerzy came in for supper, yellow teeth shining in his blackened face.

"You fix for me. You Lech Walesa. You negotiate with government. Very good."

He pinned a Solidarity badge to my jumper and left a sooty smudge where his hand touched.

"Now, no hunger strike. Big bowl of soup you give me, please."

"You've made a hit there," Baz said, as Jerzy walked off.

I fingered the badge, my skin warming. "I think I've just been given a medal."

"You did a good thing."

"It was nothing much. I just listened." I took a step closer. "Baz, about last night. I'm sorry."

A silence awkward enough to embarrass a cat was broken by his short laugh.

"I dare say I should stop being so touchy."

"You have every right to be touchy."

He smiled, but the smile didn't climb as far as his eyes.

"You still have both your parents?"

My parents had embarrassed me in all sorts of ways over the years. But never before just by being alive. "Still together, even. How about that?"

"Practically an endangered species," he agreed.

"God knows, they're the most ill-matched couple you can imagine," I prattled on. "They're academics, but Dad's all quiet and bookish and hardly ever sticks his nose out of his study. And Mom's always off somewhere, studying some new tribe in the middle of Africa. All loud and argumentative and tactless."

This time the smile crept into his eyes. "You said you'd spent time in Africa."

I took a j-cloth and started wiping rings of tea and spilt soup from the counter. I remembered how I used to feel, as the school holidays approached and the process of packing for the next trip began. "I think she had this idea of herself as a doting mother who couldn't leave her only child behind. But once we got out there, she'd forget all about me."

"Must have been fun, though?"

"Honestly? Most of the time, what I really wanted was to be left at home with my books. There were times when I hated Mom for dragging me off with her."

Baz started stacking soup bowls in the sink. I thought he'd dropped the conversation and I went back to cleaning up the mess left on the counter.

"I suppose everyone ends up hating their parents sooner or later," he said.

"Definition of being a teenager, isn't it?"

He turned the tap on the hot water geyser and squirted washing up liquid over the stacked soup bowls.

"At least you get the chance to tell yours when you've stopped hating them," he said.

Chapter 18

If he wanted to confront little brother Gary over the graffiti, he was going to have to wait. This early in the morning, he was nowhere to be seen. He and his mates had marked their territory, though. Round the base of Godiva lay discarded beer cans; torn, pink sheets of the Saturday sports pages; a couple of plastic bags that might have been used for sniffing glue. Baz stared at the bags, remembering the time he found Gary throwing up in the gutter, his face almost blue before the ambulance got there …

Though why he should care, fuck knows. Gary certainly didn't. If anything the whole episode had only served to fuel his resentment. Baz passed under the arch at the base of St Michael's tower, turned his face towards the sky and breathed deeply.

The roof of the old cathedral was gone, bombed to oblivion in 1940. The walls were razed to a point above the first row of arched windows and the stone pillars in the nave stood like tree stumps, two, maybe three feet high. Baz walked between them, staring towards the East Window, his eyes seeking out the fragments of ruby glass that glowed like embers in the low-slanting rays of the winter sun.

When he was below the window, he lowered his eyes and let himself look at the cross on the stone altar. A cross made of two burnt timbers lashed together.

He had upwards of five hundred photographs of the burnt

cross, taken from every possible angle, in every possible light. Long shots framing it in the skeletal East Window. Close-ups revealing minute detail. When he closed his eyes he could see the asymmetry of the crossbeam. The slight kink in the base, as if it had turned to face the light. The exact twists of the knot lashing the two timbers together.

Something was dragging the past into the present, folding up the last fifteen years as if they had never happened. He felt it in the growing menace of the skinheads, in Abena's crusading zeal, in Maia's persistent questions.

He had been so angry with his mother just before she died. Angry with a consuming rage that burnt him from the inside. "Definition of being a teenager," Maia said. And in the ordinary course of events it would have burnt itself out, along with acne and mood swings. But he'd never had the chance to forgive her. Or himself.

Another piece of litter fluttered across the nave. He stooped to pick it up, smoothing it out between his fingers.

It was one of their flyers for *Desi Art*. It had a swastika daubed across it and it was singed around the edges.

After that, Baz found swastikas and NFs daubed on their flyers all over town. He took to carrying a fresh supply in his kitbag, tearing down and replacing the spoilt ones wherever he found them, like a surgeon cutting out diseased flesh to stop the spread of rot. But, whoever was doing this, they were quick. Within hours, the new flyers would be vandalised too.

One morning, soon after they moved in the welded metal sculptures that Vik's friend was exhibiting, they found the gallery windows smashed and a brick lying in the middle of the floor. Vik's sign had been overpainted with *Their ant no Blak in the Yunyun Jack*.

"Is this what British education has come to?" Vikram

complained. "We're abused by some *sala* who can't even spell?" But even his bravado was wearing thin. His voice shook a little as he told Baz, "Listen, *yaar*, I have an uncle who is a glazier. I'll call him. He will be here in ten minutes."

Vik went to find a working payphone. Baz unlocked the door. The brick was on the floor amidst the broken glass, wrapped in one of the *Desi Art* flyers. Lying next to it, as if they had been thrown together, was a red plastic lighter. His vision went black. He'd had his hand on the light switch, but he pulled it away and felt along the floor, down the door, sniffing for petrol, paraffin, anything that might ignite. He found nothing.

He turned the lighter over in his fingers, feeling the smooth plastic. Holding it away from him, he spun the wheel. It clicked, but didn't ignite.

Hundreds of lighters like this must be thrown away every day. This one might have nothing to do with the broken window. It could be just a passer-by, grabbing the chance to chuck away an empty.

But he'd seen the one in Gary's hand. He'd heard the threats. *I could burn them out, like them niggers down in London.*

He forced himself to calm his breathing. There was a time when everything around him seemed to conceal a threat of fire. But the world was not going to burst into flames—he'd had to learn that. A brick was a brick, not a firebomb. He slid the lighter into his pocket. When Vik returned, he said nothing.

"What you need is someone keeping an eye on the place," Simon said.

Baz shook his head. "Don't think I haven't thought about sleeping down there."

"You can't!" Maia gave him startled look. "It's got to be too risky."

Before he could probe what she meant, Libby tutted. "Maia, it really isn't going to help if you blow things out of proportion." She turned to Baz with her best Middle England face. "If someone is vandalising the gallery, you simply have to go to the police."

"What planet does she live on?" Simon asked the room at large.

Iain leaned his elbows on the table. "You know the skinheads are saying they're going to demonstrate at your opening?" he said.

"All the more reason to go to the police," Libby insisted.

Simon snorted. "The Front have to get permission if they want to march, don't they? Police will know all about it. Bastards'll get protection an' all."

They stared at one another, wary and on edge, each with their own take on his situation, thinking they had answers. Well, they couldn't do much worse than he had.

"So, if not the police, then what?" he asked.

Simon scraped his chair back. "That's what I was trying to tell you, see? Some mates of mine, they're in this group. CovARA— the Coventry Anti-Racist Alliance. Organising defence squads, they are. Protecting people against the racists."

"Vigilantes?" Libby squeaked. Her face turned very red.

"Politicos," Baz answered.

"Well, yes," said Simon. "But—"

"Look, I appreciate the offer, Simon. But the last thing we need is a turf war between the skinheads and the Workers' Revolutionary Whatever."

Simon scowled. "You gotta make a stand against these bastards, Baz."

Making a stand. Everything he did was making a stand. His being alive was making a fucking stand. What he didn't want right now was to stir up a storm that would bring down the whole sodding pack of cards. "We're putting on an exhibition," he said. "That should be enough."

"That's the trouble with you bloody liberals, butty. Think you can win a war with concerts and bastard exhibitions."

Baz shook his head. "I am not trying to fight a war. Mostly, I'm trying to kickstart a career." He rubbed a hand over his face, feeling an ache deep in his scars. "If we go for the sort of head-on confrontation you'd like—with bricks and bottles and people getting hurt—we'll end up with the Council banning the exhibition. Which, from my point of view, defeats the fucking object."

Simon twitched like a dog that had been leashed too long, but he gave a sharp nod. "Okay. On my life. No trouble. Just let us keep an eye on the place. See they get no chance to break any more windows."

Baz dragged in a long breath. His chest hurt. "All right. But that's it. I don't need any other bastard fucking this up for me, okay?"

The night before the opening, Baz went to the gallery to photograph the exhibits in situ. Libby had typed up and roneoed a catalogue, a single terse sheet to be given out to viewers and potential buyers. His photographs would be their visual record, the thing that would survive beyond the weeks of the exhibition.

He could still smell the fresh emulsion they had put on the walls. He stuck his copy of The Selecter's new album into the cassette player. The sound filled the old butcher's shop, reverberating off its tiled surfaces. He dug out a tripod and some of his old studio lights and lit each piece in turn, working methodically, dredging back to his student days to remember studio techniques he had not used for years. Mohan's two scrap metal sculptures stood man-height on the floor—one of Lord Ram breaking Shiva's bow, the other of Hanuman the monkey god. He needed a wide angle lens to capture their scale and power. The dentist's ceramic hands, arranged in the different *mudra* of meditation—they had to be shot in close up to show their intricate decoration. He wasn't used to working with colour. That was another dimension he had to factor in. The work was unfamiliar and by the time he reached Vikram's paintings, he was sweating under the studio lights.

Vikram's paintings were not easy to capture. Take a picture of the whole, and you missed the extraordinary detail with which Vikram invested each tiny figure. Or take a series of close-ups and miss how the picture as a whole zinged with life, how each one spoke to its subject.

Baz pressed the heel of his hand against the bridge of his nose, staving off a headache. He moved the camera towards the paintings. Away. Tried different lenses. His eyes ached.

The tape ran into silence. Just his own photographs left. He had the negatives of these, of course, so he just needed to capture them as a group on their easels. Baz was manoeuvring one of the polished aluminium frames when he heard a shuffle outside. He swung round towards the window, but he'd made the gallery into a lit stage. Beyond the lights, he could see nothing.

He rested the photograph back on its easel, scolding himself for being so jumpy. It would be Simon, or one of the CovARA mob, checking up. Nothing to worry about. He opened the door, ready to call out a greeting. Mist rose off the frost-covered paving, filling the passage and making it impossible to see more than a dozen yards. He peered up and down the empty pedestrian street, straining to hear. Nothing.

A fancy, then. Or a cat. Pre-opening jitters getting the better of him. He pulled the door to. In the heartbeat before the door met the frame, he fancied he saw, across the empty pavement of Bull Yard, the tiny flame of a cigarette lighter.

Chapter 19

That night, a freezing fog came down, reducing the world to a series of pearlescent globes around each street lamp. The men came into the Skipper with their hair and beards rimed with frost, like so many shabby Father Christmases. I wandered among the tables, picking up plates and bowls ready for washing, returning Jerzy's thumbs up, smiling vaguely at Frank, my head in another place altogether.

Two weeks. It had been two weeks. My breasts had been tight and sore for days now, and my nipples felt as if they couldn't bear anything to touch them. When I had my bath, I'd study the areolae, trying to decide if they were larger, if the bumps on them were standing out more.

I had it all planned. I'd been back to Boots to buy the test kit. I'd take my pee sample here, first thing in the morning, set up the test back at Paradise Road, then leave it while we went to the exhibition. When I got back … well, I'd know, wouldn't I?

I had it all planned, right up to the point when I looked at the result. Mostly, when I tried to see beyond that, my mind faded to black.

"Hello, pet."

The voice behind me came from a softly spoken man with a lilting accent. He was one of three who came in together. Ex-steel workers from Consett, travelling south looking for work. Two of them had shed their third wheel and now sat hunched together in the far corner, poring over a newspaper, while the third man, the one who had spoken to me, sat on his own sipping a cup of tea and looking around him as if he were committing the scene to memory.

I conjured a half smile out of the numbness in my head.

"Not sitting with your friends?"

He grimaced. "We're travelling together for convenience, like. I'll not tag along for much longer. We don't exactly see eye to eye." He held out his hand. "I'm Derek, by the way."

My fingers were sticky with spilt soup from the bowl I'd just picked up. I wiped them on my jeans.

"Maia."

"Pleased to meet you." He folded my hand in a paw that seemed too big for his bony wrist. "You're a sight for sore eyes in this place, Maia, man, let me tell you."

Okay, he was new, but I wasn't about to encourage that sort of thing. "Been on the road long?" I asked, to change the subject.

He glanced sideways at his travelling companions. "It seems like it, pet, aye." He reached into his pocket and dug out a packet of Players. "You mind if I smoke?"

I looked round at the fug that collected every evening beneath the low ceiling. "I don't think anyone will notice another one, do you?"

He lit a cigarette, cupping it as if he were outside in the wind. He noticed me looking at his lighter and he held it up. It was gold.

"Our lass gave us this on our wedding day. Only decent thing I've been able to hang on to."

"You need to be careful with that in here." I watched him slip it back into the pocket of his donkey jacket, which had a curious stain on the back, just below the leather part. It radiated out like a spider's web, as if something had struck him on the back and shattered, leaving a blast pattern. "Have you booked in for the night?" I asked him.

"I believe I have the penthouse suite."

His eyes—pale blue as a swimming pool—sparkled and it was hard not to laugh with him.

"What about your mates?"

He frowned at that, and his eyes dimmed. "I don't think they'd call themselves my mates," he said, leaning towards me. "Between ourselves, I think they resent us."

"Why would they resent you?" I asked, drawn in despite myself.

"Half nowt, pet, that's the way of it." He glanced over his shoulder at his two fellow travellers, his eyes narrowed. "Those two, they lost their jobs last year, when the steelworks closed, like. Me, I lost my job six month earlier, and I fetched it on meself." He leaned forward, blowing out a long plume of smoke. "See, I'm an alcoholic."

Not many men, here or anywhere else, would come straight out and say that. It took me aback and made me look at him more closely. His face had a rumpled look, as if it had been left to dry without being properly shaken out.

"You're brave to admit it," I told him.

"Aye, well. I'm not drinking now, mind. I've been down the AA and that. Haven't had a drink for five month now."

"Can't be easy when you're on the road."

"It's not, pet, and that's the truth."

"Well, I think you've done well. No reason to resent you. They should give you credit for it."

"I appreciate that. But here I am, going on, when it's plain to see you're rushed off your feet. Is there anything I can do to help?"

It seemed we had another gentleman here, like Frank. I smiled.

"No, you're all right. It's getting quieter now. We'll manage."

"Howay, then. I'll speak to you later."

Chapter 20

The exhibition opened officially at midday. Soon after eleven, the exhibitors started to arrive with their families. Vikram's mother pinched Baz's cheeks till they were sore and scolded him for not coming to dinner. Vikram's father, Gurinder-ji, stood ramrod-straight beside her. He pumped Baz's hand up and down and told him he must be, "proud, so proud."

"You, he thinks should be proud," Vik hissed in his ear. "Me, I'm supposed to get a proper job."

"Hey, he's proud of you, too."

"You think?"

Each newcomer brought different smells, filling up the empty spaces and chasing away last night's shadows. Libby, the perfect hostess, with her mushroom vol-au-vents ... Tom's homebrew ... spiced chai ... Gurinder-ji's attar of patchouli ...

Baz began herding people into groups for photographs.

First Mohan Chand, dwarfed by his own metal sculptures, sporting a grin wide enough to light up the whole room. Unlike Vikram, he wore a small black turban, though in every other respect he looked a born-and-bred Coventry kid. His parents stood either side of him, radiating pride.

Next Paras Shah, the dentist, a diminutive Jaina with short-cropped hair and glasses too big for his face, who greeted everyone courteously, and brushed aside any compliments on his own work. Baz photographed him with his wife and Noordin

Kheraj, next to his exquisitely decorated ceramic hands.

Rebeccah in a dove-grey suit with a rose-coloured scarf tied at the throat: he photographed her standing in the horseshoe formed by his own easels. When he embraced her afterwards, he felt how frail she was.

Noordin tucked her arm through his.

"My dear Rebeccah. You were not put off by these rumours of a demonstration?"

"Pah," said Gurinder-ji. "What can a few *badmaash* do, here in the middle of Coventry?"

Gurinder-ji began to hold forth in Punjabi to an audience of polyglot South Asians. Excluded, Baz drifted away, scanning the groups standing and chatting around the room. No Simon. Off with his CovARA mob, no doubt. If the National Front were going to march, no way that lot'd let it pass. Just for fuck's sake don't let them turn it into a full scale riot.

No Maia, either. Didn't realise how much he'd counted on her coming till she failed to appear. God knows why. Like the stone in your shoe. Or the grit in the oyster …

He paced by the window, wanting to get it over with now. Wanting to face whatever they had coming. When the door opened, he swung round. But it was just a bored-looking reporter from the *Coventry Evening Telegraph* who slouched around the room, writing down the names of the exhibitors. You only had to look at him to see he'd rather be covering the footie.

A few minutes after twelve, he heard the drums. *Rat-ta-ta-tat. Rat-ta-ta-tat.* A sound that had once made his mother grow pale and pull him indoors. *Rat-ta-ta-tat. Rat-ta-ta-tat.* A sound hardwired into his brain. *Rat-ta-ta-tat. Rat-ta-ta-tat.* His hands curled into fists. The chanting started, in time with the beat.

National Front! National Front!

The reporter perked up. He peered out of the window like a dog scenting a rabbit. Away to the right, a convoy of Union Flags sailed into Bull Yard. Not a big demonstration. Maybe thirty, all told. Nevertheless it seemed the police would only allow a few into the narrow passage between Bull Yard and Shelton Square. The demonstrators shifted around and a small flag party moved forward. They marched in step, seven of them. Two pairs carrying long banners, one flag bearer, one drummer and, in the middle, a man with a large placard. They lined up outside the gallery, facing inwards. Baz felt the sweat stand out on his face.

The drumbeat was slower now, *rat...ta...ta...tat*, a gallows march. Everyone in the gallery had gathered at the windows, silent, staring, shocked. They read the words on the banners. 'Defend Rights for Whites.' 'Protect Coventry's Shops.' In the middle, held up by a thin-faced man in horn-rimmed spectacles, a placard that read:

```
         We need a
         BUTCHER
           not
         A PAKI
         exhibition
          TODAY
```

"You realise what that bastard thing will look like from a distance?" Iain said.

"Yes. And so do they."

Baz touched the cold glass and, as he did so, the man in the middle locked eyes with him. He had wispy hair, half hidden under a porkpie hat. A long thin nose. Gloved hands that held the placard up high.

You're not the sort to throw a brick through a window, Baz thought. You wouldn't get your hands dirty. And I don't reckon you're bright enough to invent those nasty, clever words. You're a sergeant. You take your orders and make sure there's some grunt to carry them out. Question is, who threw the brick? And which twisted bastard is giving the orders?

Feeling sick and cold, he shifted his focus and saw, beyond the flag party, passers-by turning to stare. One or two gave a half-hearted cheer. A few more booed. Most hurried past, their faces averted. No idea, any of them, what it felt like to stand behind a sheet of glass, confronting people who'd like to wipe you from the face of the earth.

A small figure with spiky blonde hair appeared from Bull Yard. He watched, mesmerised, as Maia made her way behind the flag party. Passing the drummer—a man who looked big enough to pick her up and snap her in two—she stumbled and Baz felt his heart lurch with her.

Chapter 21

The others had gone on ahead. I made some excuse, said I'd be right behind them. Now it was just me and the cellophane-wrapped box containing the pregnancy test.

In the box was a phial of purified water, a test tube with a sheep's red blood cells, a medicine dropper and a special stand for the test tube, with a mirror on the bottom for viewing the results.

I must have done hundreds of simple assays like this in the course of my degree. This was just another one. Whatever the consequences, what I needed to do now was concentrate on process. Working mechanically, I added the water to the test tube, introduced three drops of urine and mixed it. The whole thing must be left where it wouldn't be disturbed, even by a slamming door or loud music. I climbed onto the counter in the disused kitchen of the second house and slid it onto a high shelf. When I was done, I sat on the counter, my whole body shaking.

It seemed crazy, after that, to go and gawp at some works of art and hobnob with a load of people I'd never met. But I knew I couldn't stand my own company for the two hours it would take for the test to complete. So I changed into something half-decent and walked the mile or so back to the gallery.

By the time I passed the long flight of steps up to the ABC cinema, I could hear the shouting. Simon was right. This was too good an opportunity for the skinheads to miss.

My legs carried me onwards long after my mind began to drag me away. By now I could see them. Maybe twenty or thirty, young guys in donkey jackets. Hair brush cut. Fists in the air. Pressing forward towards the thin line of policemen who held open the passage through to the market.

Somewhere in that rabble were Gary and his beefed-up mate; I'd stake my life on it. To reach the gallery, I'd have to walk past them. They'd see me. Recognise me. Okay, there were police restraining them, but I'd been on enough demos to know how quickly that could change. If they were to break through ... I thought of Beefy's breath on my face, Gary's lighter burning my skin.

Jesus, Maia. Get a grip. Did I really think anyone was going to pay attention to me in this bedlam? I forced myself to walk on, past the screaming ranks of skinheads, into the covered channel that lay like a thick neck between Bull Yard and Shelton Square.

A small group of the demonstrators stood in front of the gallery, the police lined up behind them, facing outwards. I could make out faces of those inside the gallery. Baz. Iain. Robyn. Like prisoners in a glass cage.

And that was when I spotted Beefy.

He was at the far end of the group, the straps of the heavy drum digging into the flesh on his shoulders, his thick fingers curled round two drumsticks. He stood to attention, staring forward, his hands beating out a slow menacing tattoo. As I passed, his head swivelled round and a slow grin spread over his face. He took the drumstick, held low near his crotch, and jerked it upwards in a single, crude, unmistakeable gesture.

My plummeting heart collided with my stomach coming up. My legs seemed to move too slowly and I stumbled, but I recovered and carried on. Right outside the door, a man holding a placard called out to me. His voice was quiet, a bit nasal, with a layer of Received Pronunciation thinly veneered over a Midlands accent.

"So you think it's all right, do you, the Pakis taking our shops? Using them to spread their degenerate filth?"

His eyes were the colour of over-ripe gooseberries, and his mouth had formed itself into a sneer. A light came on in my head and I understood. Properly understood. If I was carrying Ossie's baby, I'd no longer be on the sidelines. As far as cretins like this were concerned, I'd have betrayed my race. I'd be filth. Like Ossie, like my child, I'd have something to lose. And everything to fight for.

I looked him in the eye.

"This shop's closing had nothing to do with *Desi Art*. And the degenerate filth I see is right here in front of me."

Chapter 22

Baz saw the face of the man carrying the placard darken as Maia spoke. She swivelled away, shoving open the door. As it swung shut behind her, she seemed to draw a deep breath as if sucking in clean air.

Her arrival sliced through the gathering tension. The group by the window broke away and began to move around the gallery in twos and threes, ignoring the rabble outside. Baz watched Rebeccah and Dr Kheraj take Maia to look at his photographs. The reporter hesitated, his notebook halfway into his pocket. As he headed for the door, they heard the pounding of feet running towards them from Shelton Square.

Those inside the gallery pressed towards the window. Seconds later, Baz caught sight of Simon at the head of a ragged phalanx of militants, anarchists, leftists and hangers-on. Out of breath and shambolic, they scrambled to an untidy halt and unfurled a red and white banner that read "They Shall Not Pass."

For a breathless moment, before the skinheads corralled in Bull Yard spotted them, it seemed neither police nor fascists knew how to respond. Then both sides rushed the passage. The police lines broke and reformed as they struggled to throw a cordon between them, blocking the passageway and trapping a handful of shoppers inside.

Baz felt dizzy. Shit-scared and half furious with Simon for jeopardising the exhibition. Glad someone was standing up to the bastards. Guilty that he wasn't out there with them …

Behind him, Vik seized Mohan's arm.

"Come on, *yaar*. Let's show these fascists a bit of *desi* muscle—"

"Vikram, no!" his father thundered. "I will not have you brawling in the street like a common hooligan."

Mohan moved away from the door. Vikram stood his ground, his colour rising, shoulders juddering with anger. Outside, the rest of the National Front marchers were trying to charge their way through the passage into Shelton Square. A small group of them had made it as far as the second police line and were lifting their arms in Nazi salutes and shouting, "*Sieg heil. Sieg heil.*" Simon's group, enraged, counter-charged.

"You are going to let these *goras* fight our battles for us, *papa-ji*?"

"This is not the way, Vikram."

"And what is the way? To hang our heads and say 'yes, sahib' and 'no, sahib' while they peddle this shit?"

"Vikram!"

The reporter pushed past father and son and grabbed Baz. "Hey, you. Photographer. Chrissakes, get your camera out there and take some pictures."

"Look, I'm not a journalist. Don't you have to …?"

"Listen, pal, how in the name of all that is holy do you expect me to get a photographer from the paper down here before this is over? Now start shooting and let me worry about protocol."

He shouldered through the door. A policeman tried to drive them back inside, but the reporter flashed his press pass and pulled Baz after him. Before the copper could decide whether to argue, a flying missile snatched his attention away.

Baz and the reporter were caught in an airlock between the two lines of police, trapped along with a couple of frightened shoppers and those skinheads who had broken ranks. On one side, a furious pack of skinheads. On the other side, Simon and his counter-demonstrators. Behind them the flag party, standing rock still, their drummer silent now.

Baz lifted the camera to his eye.

As soon as he looked through the lens, he was back in control. This was better than standing helpless behind the glass. This way, he got to tell the story. He adjusted the camera to frame the man with the placard. The man tried to lock eyes with him again. But Baz pressed the shutter release. Locked him into that split second.

In the split-second of blindness while the reflex mirror flipped up and the shutter curtains travelled across the lens, the yelling of the rival factions filled his ears, and he felt the pounding of his heart. Then the viewfinder cleared and he was a single eye again.

He swung his camera and saw a punk girl, thighs red raw between the tops of her stringy stockings and the bottom of her tartan skirt, haul her boyfriend through the ranks of demonstrators by the bondage straps on his trousers and scream, "Fascists!" at the opposition.

In the next frame, the drummer sulked, held back from joining in the fray, frustration playing out on his face.

The newsagent next door to the gallery harangued a policeman. "If this keeps up, I'll have to shut my shop. And who's going to pay for the loss of business, I'd like to know?"

Muffled through the funnel of his concentration, Baz heard the sirens as panda cars pulled up in Bull Yard. He framed Simon, fist raised, then swung round, pointing the camera into Bull Yard.

In a gap that opened in the ranks of sieg-heiling youths, he saw the familiar tattooed head of Gary. Before he could photograph him, a lump of wood struck him on the leg and he fell to his knees. Pain shot up his thigh.

By the time he had scrambled to his feet again, jeans torn, police reinforcements had pressed forward from Bull Yard into Shelton Square, and Gary was nowhere to be seen. Baz tried to sidestep into the gallery.

"Oi, sonny, move," yelled a copper.

"Hey, this is my exhibition."

The copper raised his truncheon and the journalist darted forward, press card at the ready.

"Jason Creech, *Evening Telegraph*. He's with me."

"So get him out of my way, before I arrest him for obstruction."

Creech dragged Baz away in the direction of Shelton Square. Protestors on both sides were grabbing discarded pallets from the market and breaking them up to use as missiles and weapons. Baz saw Simon yelling at policeman. The copper swung his truncheon and Simon dropped to his knees. Several more of the CovARA crowd were being hauled off towards a waiting Black Maria. As far as Baz could see, the police were allowing the fascists to disperse unchallenged.

"I thought we'd gone tits up for a while there. Give it here." Jason Creech held out his hand for the film. Baz wasn't quick enough and he clicked his tongue. "Don't worry. You'll get it back. And you'll get paid if one of them is published. What a blinding story!"

Too dazed to argue, Baz started rewinding the film. Now it was over, he felt sick. The exhibition hadn't even opened before the fascists wrecked things. Not one person outside their own tight circle had seen his photographs or Vikram's paintings.

"You've got a story and I've got a flop on my hands," he told the journalist. "I can't see any bastard coming now after that balls-up."

Creech took the canister of film and held it up between his fingers like a trophy.

"Don't cry over your milk before it's spilt, I say. You give me one halfway decent photograph and I'll have you on the front page tomorrow. They'll be flocking to see you."

He stalked off. Baz stumbled down the few steps to the mini-amphitheatre in Shelton Square and up again the other side, too tired for anything but the shortest line between two points. He'd had no coat on when the journalist dragged him out and the cold began to bite.

The passage leading to Bull Yard was strewn with debris. He saw the broken stave of a placard, a fingerless glove, a cap. Bits of rubble, gathered up to be used as missiles, lay as they fell, discarded when the police arrived in numbers.

He nudged a broken-up pallet with his toe. Gary had been right in among the marchers. The kid was being sucked in and played like a penny whistle. No telling what he might do with all that misdirected anger if some bastard was twisting it for their own purposes …

He leant on the door to the gallery and it opened. Less than an hour had passed since they first heard the drums. Noordin had slipped away but Rebeccah was still there, her face pinched with anxiety. Gurinder-ji was pacing up and down, Mohan caught between exhilaration and rage, Vik nakedly resentful.

Baz looked for Maia. She took a step forward, and the blood drained from her face. She wavered for a moment between standing and falling, before her legs buckled and she crumpled onto the tiled floor, limbs splayed like a puppet with its strings cut.

Chapter 23

When I opened my eyes, Baz's face was close to mine. I could see, in minute detail, the long sweep of his lashes, the smoky grey kohl-brushed look of his eyelids, the black teardrop on his cheekbone. I could smell developing fluid, and sandalwood.

He was kneeling beside me. I tried to raise my head and as I did so, I caught sight of a tear in the leg of his jeans. A glimpse of toffee-coloured flesh through the gash in the denim, the feathering of black hairs. I wanted to slide my hand through the gap, run my fingertips over the sensitive skin on his inner thigh. The thought made the colour rush back into my face and I struggled to sit up.

"God, how stupid." My head was spinning in slow ellipses, as if I'd just come off the waltzers. I stopped speaking, both hands still on the floor, my eyes closed, and tried to push aside the image of Baz's thigh. "I'm sorry," I said, when I could open my eyes again.

He put his arm under mine to help me sit up and I leaned into him, feeling the strength of his support. His fingers were long, the nails short and neatly shaped. More café au lait than pink.

"I'd better see you back, when you're ready to go. I don't want you collapsing again in the middle of Broadgate."

Vikram cleared his throat. "Baz, I appreciate the sentiment, *yaar*. But it's not your concern. Not today. You need to be here."

Baz looked as if he might argue the toss but Libby forestalled him.

"I'll go," she said.

"No!" Libby's offer brought me to my senses. The last thing I needed today was anyone fussing round me. "I'll be fine. It was a bit stuffy in here, that's all. The walk home will do me good. No, Libby. You're very kind. But I'd just as soon be by myself."

By the time I walked back to Paradise Road, the two hours allotted for the test were well and truly up. I climbed onto the kitchen counter, scared in case I blacked out again. It felt as if my whole life had collapsed into this single moment, as if I might be trapped here forever.

I moved the stand to let the light fall on the mirror. My fingers were stiff and clumsy. A positive result would be a brownish-pink ring that formed in the bottom of the test tube and showed up in the mirror angled below it. A negative result—no ring. But I knew even before I looked. The ring was there.

I was carrying Ossie's baby.

Tom must have come through the yard while I was still in the other house. He sat on one of the armchairs in the sitting room easing the laces on his boots, his stubby ponytail brushing his collar.

"Got back all right then, did you?" he said.

"Sure." I moved the test kit from one hand to another, trying to hide what I was carrying.

"Don't know if you ought to be clambering around on kitchen counters," he said. "Could be risky, so soon after flaking out." He dropped his gaze to the test kit and raised it again to my face.

"The assay," I said, as if we were two students meeting in the lab. "It was positive …"

My head went swimmy again. Tom shot up out of his chair, grabbed my elbow and guided me onto the sofa. He took the test kit out of my hands and sat down with me until the room stopped reeling round.

"God, Tom, I'm pregnant." It felt strange, putting into words. As if, even more than the brown ring at the bottom of the test tube, it made it real.

"I did wonder if you might be up the stick."

"Fuck. Is it that obvious? Does everyone know?"

"I doubt it." He gave me a half grin. "I've got three older sisters who've presented me with four nieces and nephews between them. And every one of them has gone mazy and started running to the loo every five minutes as soon as they fell pregnant."

He leaned an arm along the back of the sofa. I could smell beer on his breath, but he wasn't drunk.

"So whose is it?" he said. "Or shouldn't I ask?"

I stared at a patch of worn carpet, trying to get a fix on Ossie's face.

"Want me to beat him up for you?"

I started to smile, and found tears welling up in my eyes.

"You'd have a job. He's in South Africa …"

"Hey! I'll go to South Africa to beat him up if it's as bad as all that."

"The police are probably doing it for you."

Tears were streaking my cheeks. My nose was running and I was getting the hiccoughs. I buried my face in the handkerchief he held out for me.

"I take it this conception didn't take place at long distance? Unless he's got some amazing—"

"Shut up!"

"Sorry."

"It was his last night in England," I said. "I just … We ended up … And I messed up taking my pill and …"

Tom brushed my damp hair away from my face.

"This is Ossie we're talking about, right?"

I nodded dumbly.

"So not just good mates?"

"We were. Except that one time."

I could see the scroll of his ear beneath the straw-coloured line of hair. The blue-grey of his hand-knitted jumper.

"You know the worst part? The worst part is, I couldn't give a rat's arse what colour Ossie is, or what colour the baby is. But after what I saw today, how could I ever—"

"Expose a child to that?"

I nodded.

Yet how could I walk away from it, now that I'd seen what those cretins were capable of?

Chapter 24

Baz fought his way up from sleep through a dream of smoke and flames and a door that was searing hot and would not budge. When he emerged, sweating, into consciousness, his clock radio was broadcasting the tail end of the news. He prodded a few buttons before working out that the ringing sound came from the telephone downstairs in the office.

He stumbled down, eyes half shut, and snatched the handset. He heard pips, and Vikram's voice crackled in his ear.

"Baz? That you? Get your arse down here, man."

The residue of his dream turned his sweat to ice. "Fuck. They've torched the gallery—"

A choking sound came from the phone and after a treacle-slow moment, he recognised strangled laughter. "What are you? Marvin the Paranoid Android? They're queuing up outside."

"Outside where?"

"The gallery, *yaar*. They've got copies of the *Evening Telegraph* and they're queuing to get in."

Baz had collected yesterday's copy of the *Telegraph* as soon as it hit the stands. Creech was as good as his word: they'd made the front page. A couple of column inches and a headline: *NF*

Disrupt Opening. Inside, though, was a full page article reporting the rise of the Far Right in Coventry. Printed next to it was one of the photographs he'd taken during the demo. The scumbag with the placard stared back at him out of the page, just as Baz had framed him. The placard was at an angle to the camera and the writing wasn't clear. But the underlying message was there for anyone to read.

BUTCHER A PAKI TODAY.

And now people were queuing outside the gallery.

They planned to open for a couple of hours, and they were still there at three o'clock. All afternoon they came—the curious, the idle, the bored. Even a few genuine art lovers. He waited for the first signs of trouble—for a glimpse of a thin-faced man, for a brick through the window. Nothing.

Two of Paras Shah's beautiful *mudra* sculptures sold in the first couple of hours. And the Head of Training at Climax, where Mohan was doing his YOP, signed a cheque on the spot for his welded sculpture of Rama, "as a bit of motivation for our future trainees." When Baz stuck the first red dot on a piece, he was light-headed with relief. By the time they closed the door behind the last of the visitors, he felt as if he'd spent the day smoking the best sensimilla. He leaned against the wall, seeing the same look of stupefied bliss on Vik's face.

"We'd better tidy up, *yaar*. Get ready for tomorrow."

"Can't expect it to carry on like that."

"No."

"It won't be the same. A weekday. People at work."

"No. Of course not."

They stared at each other over the top of the cash box.

"Ohmygod, we sold something."

"Amazing."

"Several somethings."

"Fucking amazing."

They both started to laugh. Baz grabbed Vik by the shoulders and they bounced around the room, pogoing like punks, whirling like dervishes, until, howling with laughter, his sides aching, his breath rasping, Baz dragged them to a halt, inches from toppling one of the welded steel sculptures.

"None of mine sold," said Vikram. He was leaning forward, his hands on his knees, a sheen of sweat on his face.

"Nor mine."

"Still, not bad, *haan*?"

"Not too fucking bad."

When he could breathe again, Baz dug out a mop and a broom. Vikram switched the radio to Mercia Sound while they cleared up. At six o'clock, the news came on. And Baz realised what it was that must have wormed its way into his dreams in the early morning. A newsreader's voice. Burning ceiling tiles and locked fire exits, panicking people and forty-eight dead …

… the Queen and the Prime Minister will visit Ireland to offer their condolences to the families of the 48 victims of last night's fire in the Stardust Club in Dublin …

Baz went rigid. Vikram carried on mopping muddy footprints from the tiled floor.

… the victims, mainly teenagers, were attending a St Valentine's Day disco …

"Did you hear that?"

Baz slammed the broom on the floor.

"Forty-eight white kids die in Ireland, and suddenly the Queen and the sodding Prime Minister are falling over themselves to offer condolences? But thirteen black kids, thirteen black *British* kids, die in a fire at a party in London and nothing is said. Nothing is done. "

Vikram stared at him, an odd look on his face. "Baz, you do know they're saying now that the fire in New Cross wasn't an attack? That a couple of black kids got in a fight?"

"What has that got to do with anything?" Anger seared through him, like lightning through pitch pine. "This fire in Ireland, no one is saying it's the paramilitaries, are they?"

"Well, no, but—"

"Don't you see? It makes no difference. They don't need firebombs, or burning crosses, or even cretins with placards. They can just ignore us. They can treat us like we're less than nothing. Less than the animals in laboratories they make such a deal out of protecting. Less than fucking skateboarding ducks on fucking *Nationwide*. We know where we stand."

Abena said, "Thirteen dead: nothing said."

"We're going to march," she told him. "Second of March. We'll have all Black London on the move. They're not going to be able to look away this time. They're going to have to face us."

She said, "You're coming. You have to tell this story."

He half smiled, picturing her blazing into the phone, her anger illuminating the dingy stairwell leading to her bedsit. God, but she'd been dazzling when he first saw her. Like a lighthouse, sending a cone of light out into the darkness to protect the vulnerable. Somewhere along the line, though, he'd missed the essential fact about lighthouses. You attended to their light, or you steered well clear.

"I'll still be in the middle of the exhibition."

"They can manage without you for a day, can't they?"

"I expect so. As long as the National Front keeps off our backs."

Abena laughed. "You come down here if you want to see beefheads. That'd give you something to worry about."

He felt a flash of anger as he thought of the flag party lined up outside the gallery, the mob of yelling skinheads breaking through from Bull Yard.

"Damn it, Abena, we're not just some sideshow—"

"You will be, the day we march. Ain't no one gonna shout louder than us that day."

Hell, it'd be worth going just to see her blaze one more time—burning as if her light could change the course of history.

"Okay, I'll do my best, but—"

"Don't you rat out on me this time, bwai."

"Listen, Abena—"

"Catch you later."

He heard the pips and the phone went dead. Abena had had the last word. Again.

Chapter 25

Tom pushed back the doors of the charity cupboard and released a smell of mothballs into the room. I sat cross-legged on one of two beds and watched him dig through the piles of donated clothes.

"Tell me to belt up if you want," he said, "but have you thought about what you're going to do yet?"

Iain had left a half-solved Rubik's cube lying on the bed. I picked it up and gave it a few random twists. "Everything just keeps turning over and over in my head. Every time I think I'm close to a solution, it scrambles up again."

Tom backed out of the cupboard holding a large, collarless shirt.

"Are you gonna tell Ossie?"

In a corner of my brain, something flinched, as if Tom had poked it with a stick. "I can't. Not until he lets me know where he is."

He tossed me the shirt and dived back into the cupboard, pulling trousers from a black plastic bag.

"When's that gonna be?"

"Oh, God. This year, next year, sometime, never."

I swallowed hard, trying to ignore the stinging in my eyes. Tom backed out of the cupboard carrying a pair of grey flannel trousers.

"What do you think? Will these do?"

"Who did you say they're for?"

"Walter. He's going to the delousing clinic on Monday."

"Uggh! I don't want to know!"

Tom grinned. "Feeling itchy, are we?" He mimed scratching himself until I threw the Rubik's cube at him.

"What about your mother?" he asked, hauling out a basket of assorted underwear.

"Studying kinship systems in the Kalahari. Please God, let her stay there."

"Bless and keep our parents well away from us?"

"Something like that." I began to fold the heavy cotton shirt, pinching it, out of ingrained habit, to make the sharp folds required for packing. Mom, so careless in many ways, was a fanatic about that. She took it for granted I should be able to pack everything I needed for two months into a case I could carry unaided, and still have everything emerge the other end pristine and uncreased. "It's not like she'd be bothered about Ossie being black. It's the sheer bloody stupidity of my being caught that'd drive her crazy. That, and the fact that I'd have betrayed the sisterhood."

"You what?"

"You know. 'I didn't burn my bra in the sixties so you could sit at home changing nappies and scrubbing sinks.' That sort of crap."

I picked up the trousers and attempted to line up the seams. Was that going to be it? Twenty two years of hope and education abandoned at the bottom of a nappy bucket? Sod it, I might not have a career, but I still had choices, didn't I?

Tom dropped onto the bed beside me.

"Hey. C'mon, kiddo." He put his arm around me and I buried my face in the hollow of his shoulder. "Does this mean you're thinking of having the baby?"

"Hell, Tom, how can I have a baby? I can barely look after myself." I wiped my eyes on my sleeve. "Bloody sight easier to have an abortion, wouldn't you say? Mom, Dad, Ossie—none of them'd be any the wiser. I could just carry on like nothing ever happened."

Except I'd know that, for a few days, or a few weeks, I'd carried Ossie's child. His link to the future. Maybe the only future he'd ever have.

I pulled myself upright. I had to stop thinking like that. Be practical.

"I've made an appointment with the Pregnancy Advisory Service. I can see what they say, at least."

"You want me to come with you?"

I blinked at him, nonplussed. "You'd do that? Why?"

He shrugged and gave me a wonky grin. "Just felt like I ought to offer."

"Prat." I poked his expanding beer gut. "You come to the PAS and they'll think you're the one that's pregnant." I expected him to make some crack in return, but his eyes looked steadily into mine. I hugged him. "It's sweet of you. But I think this is something I've got to do on my own."

Chapter 26

The convection heater below the table scorched Baz's shins and left the rest of him shivering. Outside, the sleet was turning to snow, settling on the concrete walkways and being churned to slush by the boots of shoppers hurrying to get home. At three o'clock, it was already dusk.

Baz flexed his fingers to warm them, rearranged the roneoed catalogue sheets again, got up, paced round the exhibits, went to the door, peered up and down the darkening street. It was the second weekend of the exhibition and no one was queuing to get in. On the plus side, no one was demonstrating, the windows were all in one piece and no one had graffitied them for days.

He had just about made up his mind to shut up shop, when he heard something knock against the pavement outside. A figure appeared in the doorway—a Rastafarian carrying a long staff, grey in his beard and his locks. Against all probability on this wintry day, he was dressed in a robe of red, yellow and green. He was struggling to open the door against the snow piling up on the step, and Baz sprang to help him.

The Rasta raised his staff. The handle was a ring held in a carved hand and the stave was painted the same red, yellow and green as his robe. Under his robe, he wore trousers tied at the bottom and cheap sandals over thick grey socks that gave off a smell of wet wool. "Bhajan Singh! Greetings. I am Jah Green of Handsworth."

Before Baz could gather his wits, the Rasta swept into the gallery, wet leather squeaking on the tiles, staff tapping out the rhythm of his walk.

"Most people step around all day, not sighting the things that are right in front of them, is that not so, brother? But you—you have an eye for the juxtaposition of the unexpected."

He pointed the staff at Baz's photograph of a Hindu wedding party emerging from a converted chapel. The wedding guests were resplendent in saris and turbans, the newlyweds garlanded and hennaed. But dominating the foreground were a couple of punks snogging, their lacquered hair like the crests of cockatoos.

"This picture. Is it for sale?"

Fuck me. Was this his first sale? Where was Vik when he needed him—to keep his feet on the ground and stop him giving the picture away from the sheer joy of finding someone who liked his work enough to be willing to pay for it?

"You've picked the only decent one of the bunch," he said, the effort to sound cool making his voice strain.

Jah Green wagged a finger at him. It stuck out at an awkward angle from a hand that was cramped with arthritis.

"Perfectionism may be a virtue in an artist, brother, but in a salesman, it is a weakness." He turned back to the picture. "And how much would it cost to acquire the only decent one?"

Baz negotiated a price that was less than Vik would have demanded, but more than he'd ever expected to make. The Rasta reached under his robe and brought out a thick roll of tattered bank notes.

"As you see, I do not place much trust in the institutions of Babylon." He handed over the cash and returned the billfold to its place under his robe. "Now, let me tell you my business here."

"Wasn't that—?"

"A likkle show of good faith, is all. For an artist I admire." He lowered himself into one of the chairs by the table and beckoned

Baz to join him. "I am interested in this here exhibition because of a festival I organise this summer in Handsworth."

Baz's eyes widened. Shit, this could be better than a first sale: even a small exhibition outside of Coventry could introduce *Desi Art* to a whole new audience.

"You want us to exhibit our work?"

"I want more than that, my friend." The Rasta sat back on the rickety chair, clasping his staff. "We have a saying in the Islands. 'We likkle but we tallawah.' Or as you might say, 'Even though we small, we can do great things.' But I have some sense in here." He rapped his bony forehead. "On my own I can organise a Rasta Festival, or a Jamaican Festival, or maybe even a Caribbean Festival. But I want to do more. I want to put on a festival that brings together all the communities, and for that, I need help."

"What sort of help?"

"Before all, contacts in other communities—"

Baz did some quick calculations. *Desi Art* sprang from a web of connections: Vik's friendship with Mohan and with him, his own links with Noordin Kheraj, which brought in Paras Shah and also found them a place to hold the exhibition. And they all had links onwards, into other communities. Taken together with Jah Green's own contacts, how far could they not reach?

He turned over one of the catalogue sheets, scribbled something on the back and passed it to Jah Green.

"We're having a party when the exhibition closes. Why don't you come? You can talk to the exhibitors yourself."

Jah Green took the paper and tucked it under his robe with the billfold.

"I must speak plain with you, Bhajan Singh. Not everyone in my community approves of what I wish to do. There are those who say that we must stay amongst our own kind. That the way to keep safe in these troubled times is to draw a line around our communities and exclude, not just Babylon, but all who are not of Africa." Jah Green's yellowed eyes studied Baz's face. "I think that in every community there are some like this? Who seek salvation in division, not in unity?"

In his mind he heard echoes of old arguments with Vik's brothers. Mandeep and Daljit were older than Vik when they were thrown out of their home in Uganda. They'd carried their resentment with them.

"You're right," he said. "None of us are immune."

"So you and I, we would be courting trouble."

Baz laughed. "Trouble seems to find me whether I court it or not."

Jah Green rapped his misshapen knuckles together. "Then perhaps we have sown the seeds of a great partnership."

As Baz left the gallery, big flakes drifted through the saffron-coloured arc of the streetlights, settling on pavements, on windowsills, on telegraph wires. A washing line strung across a yard became a chalk line smudged across the blackness. Walls were upholstered with cushions of snow.

If he went straight to the studio, he had maybe an hour to spend going over negatives before he was needed at the Skipper. He cut away over Anarchy Bridge, the narrow footway named for the surreal graffiti that covered its high metal sides. Too dark to read it tonight, and the concrete footway was slick with snow.

Ahead of him, against the darkness of the trees on the far side, Baz could make out the silhouette of another pedestrian. Whoever it was kept stopping and looking back over their shoulder. Baz slowed down. But instead of hurrying on, the figure stooped, picked something up from the ground, and stopped still.

Well, he could dig in, retreat or keep going. And he could see no reason why he should be the one to back down. Ten more strides and he was close enough to make out a donkey jacket and a bobble hat pulled down low. Skinny white face. Hands fumbling with something in the dark. A click sounded and a globe of light appeared around a small flame, throwing shadows upwards, illuminating nostrils and eyebrows and leaving most of the face in darkness.

Gary. That was all he sodding needed.

"You following me, Paki?"

"Well, you're in front of me, little brother, and I'm behind you, so technically, yes. I'm following you. But if you're asking if I'm intentionally in pursuit, then, no. I'm not."

"You just keep away, you hear?"

Gary swept the lighter in front of him. The globe of light swung round, illuminating fragments of graffiti and sending the shadows dancing like puppets. Baz took a step closer.

"Been getting through lighters a bit fast, haven't you?"

"Too right. You fucking owe me—"

"Oh, I think we're more than quits for one broken lighter, seeing what use you made of the last one."

The lighter stopped in mid-swing and Baz had a glimpse of Gary's pinched face.

"Stupid bint's been shooting her mouth off, has she?"

What? Who had the little prick been harassing this time? Rebeccah? She'd have told him, surely?

"Whatever the mardy cow's been saying, I never touched her. A friendly chat, that's all. Put her straight about a few things. If she's been telling you anything else, she's a lying cunt—"

"That's enough!"

Baz strode forward and Gary backed against the metal parapet, brandishing his lighter in front of him like a flaming torch.

"I don't know what other shit you're in, little brother. But, understand, you stay away from my friends."

"I don't let any cunt tell me what to do."

"No? You gonna tell me that stunt at the gallery was all your own idea? Because I got the impression someone put you up to it."

"What you on about?"

Gary looked puzzled. Baz folded his arms.

"A brick thrown through a window? Lighter just like that one lying next to it? Ring any bells?"

Gary shrugged. "Nothing to do with me." His grin flashed white. "Like to have seen your face, though, if you thought someone was trying to torch you." He thrust the lighter towards Baz and the heat from the flame grazed his cheek. "Bit of smoke, bit of flame. Still make you shit in your pants, does it?"

Baz made a grab for his wrist but the kid dodged away. He swung his arm, aiming at Baz's face, but he must have been off balance. His feet went from under him on the slippery surface and the missile flew wide. Something hard and heavy whistled past Baz's ear and ricocheted off the parapet in a cloud of snow. The flame from the lighter died.

As the light went, Baz lunged and grabbed Gary by the lapels of his donkey jacket. The kid hung suspended, arse over the concrete, until Baz jerked him to his feet.

"You give your puppet masters a message from me, little puppet. Tell them we're here to stay—so deal with it!"

Chapter 27

The waiting room was as anonymous as any doctor's surgery. Chairs with wipe-clean covers. Tattered magazines that nobody looked at. Walls papered with health notices that you read and wished you hadn't. A few seats away, a pasty teenager clung to her boyfriend as if he were the only thing anchoring her to the earth. God, why did I tell Tom I had to do this on my own?

I closed my eyes, and a memory ambushed me. On the landing outside our bedrooms. Ossie's hand, palm to palm with mine. The recollection was so vivid I felt as if I'd missed a step and was falling.

"Maia Hassett? Will you come with me?"

A tall woman in a neat trouser suit. I'd half expected this place to be populated with dungaree-wearing Robyn clones, but she was even wearing a little makeup. So much for stereotypes.

I followed her down a corridor and squeezed into a room filled to capacity with a table and two chairs. A pregnancy test stood next to a tiny sink, along with the remains of my urine sample. The walls were a matching shade of weak piss.

"Don't worry, Maia," the woman said. "No one is here to judge you or pressure you into anything."

I knew what I was here to do. Everything else—the counselling, the doctor's exam, the procedure—they were just hurdles to get over before I could get my life back on track.

She asked the obvious questions—date of last period, previous history, current circumstances, did I have a partner?

"He's gone away … That is, the father's gone away."

I tried to concentrate on what she was saying, but my mind tailed Ossie through the South African veldt. He'd been out there five weeks. He must have crossed the border by now. I pictured him standing on a soap box in some township, spreading his gospel of non-cooperation. Sparking a blaze that would set the country alight. Or so he hoped.

The security police would be watching him. He wasn't planning on keeping a low profile. He could be in a police cell already …

"Maia?"

The counsellor passed me a tissue and I realised I was crying.

I blew my nose. "It seems wrong, not to tell him, that's all. But I've no way to reach him."

The counsellor went on talking. About what it would mean to have a baby now, and what it might mean to be bringing up a child in five or ten years time. I told her my parents wouldn't be happy about my having a baby, but they wouldn't disown me, either. I told her I had a job, sort of, and a home that went with it, but I couldn't keep working there with a baby.

"Lone mothers with children get priority when it comes to housing. But you must be realistic. Being a single parent is never easy. And it's even harder on benefits."

I wasn't planning on being a single parent. I was going to have an abortion. Couldn't we just get on with things, before I …?

The counsellor pushed her chair back and stood up to peer into the little mirror under the test tube.

"Well, Maia, I think we can agree: you are definitely pregnant." She frowned as she took her seat again. "Ordinarily this is where we would say that, if you want to proceed, you need to see one of our doctors."

My skin pricked, as if I'd brushed against nettles.

"Ordinarily?"

"One of our doctors has been snowed in. He lives out of town and his village is cut off." She glanced at her watch. "There'd be quite a wait if you wanted to see a doctor today. In any case, we would need two doctors' signatures before we could proceed any further." She gave me an encouraging smile. "Fortunately, if your dates are correct—"

"They are."

"Then time is on your side, up to a point."

"How long do I have?"

She started talking again, about legal limits and complications and different procedures that were used at different stages of pregnancy. I tried to concentrate, but it was as if I'd wandered into the wrong lecture, in a subject I knew nothing about. The words drifted past, uncomprehended.

I thought about Genny and me, back when we'd just found out she was pregnant. A bill was going through parliament that would have drastically reduced women's access to abortion. The two of us went down to London and marched in the big pro-choice rally outside Westminster. Genny's choice to have an abortion seemed so obvious, so clear. Why was I complicating things?

The counsellor leaned forward, her forearms resting on the desk.

"Whatever you decide, don't leave it too long. Even if you want to keep the baby, you'll need to start antenatal care—"

"I won't leave it," I told her.

"Good. Then by all means, make another appointment on your way out, if that's what you want to do."

"Sure."

But the receptionist was talking to the pasty teenager as I came out, and I walked straight past them. I stood at the end of the path leading to the clinic, looking out at a blanket of snow with a single set of tyre tracks slewed across it. The glare was so bright I had to shield my eyes.

I had been pregnant for thirty-six days, and known about it for ten. I knew, because of a library book hidden under my mattress, that the life inside me was an embryo about four millimetres long, floating in the amniotic sac. It had a heartbeat and was forming what would be its spinal cord. It had the beginnings of eyes, a nose and a mouth. In a week, it would have doubled in size.

The counsellor was right. I had to get this over with, before things became even harder.

Chapter 28

The ruined space of the old cathedral was deep-pile carpeted, white and untracked. The unglazed tracery of the windows wore a softened keyline of white powder. Close up, through the camera lens, the snow created patterns of light and shadow, contrasts of texture, white on black. Though white, as Baz knew from the developing room, was never truly white; black was never truly black. It was all a matter of perception—the choice of developing fluid, the length of time in the developer.

He'd never made it to the Skipper last night. He'd lost himself in poring over negatives. Time slipped by, and before he knew it, it was too late to bother with the Skipper. He'd found himself a couple of blankets, curled up on the couch and slept in the cold studio, too exhausted even to dream.

This morning he woke to a world made over by the snow. Simplified. Monochromatic. He took his camera out at dawn, tramping the snow-covered streets until long habit drew him back to this place. Today, even the pitch-and-soot-coloured timbers of the burnt cross were dressed in two-tone garb, the upright flecked white along its windward side, the skewed crosspiece mantled with snow.

He had the camera to his eye when he sensed someone walking up the nave behind him. He took the shot and turned, lowering the camera. Maia stood a few feet away, her thin coat pulled tight around her and the bottoms of her jeans wet with snow. His first thought was that, at long last, here was a chance to capture her on film. Guilt about last night lagged a few paces behind.

"Maia, shit, I'm sorry. I got caught up in things …"

She seemed to pull herself back from a long way away. The cold had made two spots of pink bloom on her cheeks and reddened the tip of her nose.

"That's okay. We had some help. One of the transients gave us a hand, as it happens."

She lowered her eyes, as if half expecting to be told off. Her lashes seemed to graze her cheek, making his finger itch on the shutter release.

"Who was it?"

"Derek. Do you know him? A Geordie. Steelworker, or he was. Only been in a couple of times. But he's okay. A bit of a lifesaver, actually."

"Sounds like I owe him one."

Her face bore traces of an emotion he couldn't identify, like the ghost imprint from a double exposure. She ran her mittened hands along a plinth, gathering snow and shaping it into a ball. When she tossed it into the air, it landed on one of the foreshortened pillars, sending a shower of fine white powder into the air. He lifted the camera to his eye, twisting the lens. Her bottom lip had a trace of blood on it where it had split in the cold.

Just before he pressed the shutter release, she saw him and held her hand up.

"Don't."

"C'mon. That'd make a great picture."

She shook her head and he lowered the camera. But as she let her arm fall, he took the shot from waist level. She caught the sound and spun round, and suddenly he recalled her standing nose to nose with Gary outside the Patel's shop. The sprite and the demon.

I don't know what the stupid bint's been telling you, Gary said.

He was the one who'd brought the two of them together. Only too likely Gary would find a way to take unpleasant advantage. Especially if he thought it would hurt Baz.

"Maia … you know that kid we met, that day I took you to the market?"

"Your foster brother?"

"Yeah, you ever seen him again?"

She shivered. Behind her, the towering West Window of the new Cathedral reflected the ruins of the old, so that for a dizzying moment the two of them seemed to be floating in the air with the angels and saints engraved in the glass.

"Once," she said. "The day Knoxie got ill and I had to go home on my own. I … ran into a bunch of them in Broadgate."

So he'd sent her out there on her own and the little prick …

"Maia, what happened?"

"Nothing. Doesn't matter. Gary recognised me, that's all. Called me a Paki lover."

His grip tightened on her arm and he had to force himself to relax his hand. "He did something with that lighter of his, didn't he?"

Her eyes widened and he caught a flash of their blue-green, like another fragment of stained glass. "How the—?"

"Never mind. Tell me."

She held his gaze, as if deciding how far she could trust him.

"It was foggy, do you remember? You couldn't see your hand on the end of your arm." She glanced back towards Broadgate and shivered again. "Gary held his lighter up by my face, like he was trying to see me better. I thought he was going to burn me, but I guess he just wanted to freak me out."

Anger locked his jaw tight. He kicked off down the steps, his feet sinking into soft drifts, cursing loudly. Maia grabbed his sleeve.

"This is why I didn't tell you. It's not your problem, okay?

You've got enough to deal with." Her arms dropped to her sides. "Besides, nothing happened. Not really."

"Not this time, maybe." He put his hands on her shoulders. Her skinny frame felt frail, as if he might break her if he didn't take care. "He comes near you again, you tell me. Okay?"

Gary had a talent for disappearing. Baz spent a couple of days looking for him, then turned his attention back to the Skipper. If he couldn't do anything about Gary, he should at least check out this bloke who was making himself handy in the kitchen.

Paterson was the name he'd given on the register, which might or might not be his own. People didn't always book under their own names, not if they were paying for themselves.

As a rule, they never let the men into the kitchen. The bolt on the door was there for good reason. Yet, overnight, this guy had turned himself into a sort of trusty. He served tea, collected cups, mopped the floor, generally made himself useful. He had a touch of charm and an endless flow of chat like a barrow boy on the market. Most of the men responded, but not all. Pongo didn't take to him; Baz could see it in the clipped way he spoke to him and in the way every inch of his bearing screamed 'army corporal'. Still, cocky bastards like Derek Paterson had been giving army corporals gyp since they invented soldiering. Didn't mean there was anything to worry about.

"You were a steelworker, I hear," he said, taking a cup of tea over and sitting down next to the Geordie. "My father worked at the steel foundry at Bilston."

"That right?" Derek said, not lifting his eyes from the paper in front of him.

Maybe the guy didn't like authority. Baz, it seemed, was the one person round here who couldn't get him to talk.

Sunday night, and Paterson was there again, an ancient tea-stained cloth around his waist. Baz watched as he moved among the tables, collecting cups. He reached one where a newcomer was sitting and stooped to ask if he'd finished his tea. As the stranger turned his head to speak to Paterson, Baz registered something familiar in his profile. A pointy, long-nosed face. Wispy hair combed over. A pair of horn-rimmed glasses …

The man from the demonstration.

In the time it took Baz to recognise him, the man had weaselled Paterson into conversation. Paterson shot a glance back over his shoulder towards Baz. Shaken out of his inertia, Baz strode forward and stopped in front of the intruder.

"You. Get. Out—"

The man turned his head, but not before Baz saw a 'what did I tell you?' look pass from him to Paterson.

"Are you speaking to me?"

"Get out. Now," Baz repeated. "You're not welcome here."

"Still a free country, last I heard. Why should I take orders from a Paki like you?"

"Because this Paki will call the police if you don't get out of here."

It was an empty threat. The police wouldn't do a thing so long as no violence was offered, and he'd be willing to bet that weasel knew it too.

"You afraid of what'll happen if they hear the truth?" the man asked.

"What 'truth'?"

Baz knew he had made a mistake as soon as he said it. The man half stood, straddling the bench. The Skipper, scenting trouble, fell quiet. The man's voice projected into the hush.

"Ever stop to think why you never get Pakis in a place like this?"

Baz made a lunge for his collar, but the man twisted away with the practised movement of a seasoned demo-goer.

"He doesn't want you to hear because it's people like him that are making sure the Pakis get all the best housing—"

"He doesn't want you to hear because it's racist crap," Baz said.

"—while decent British people like you are left on the street—"

Baz had the Weasel in an arm lock now and was manhandling him towards the door. To his gratified surprise, Jerzy and Pongo were there before him, opening the door and blocking the man's return.

"Fascist," he heard, in a guttural growl from Jerzy.

Pongo looked Baz up and down as the door shut.

"All right, gaffer?"

Baz nodded and rested a hand on Pongo's shoulder. When he turned back to Paterson, the Geordie was bent over a table, wiping it down as if nothing had happened. But a moment earlier, he'd swear, he'd been staring at the group by the door.

"Sorry about that," Baz said. "We've had some trouble with his sort before."

"Sure … gaffer," Paterson said. "No harm done, eh?"

Chapter 29

Derek dumped a stack of cups on the counter and leaned against it, wiping his hands.

"What was all that palaver?" he said.

"Just someone out to cause trouble, I think."

I'd recognised the man from the demo seconds before Baz started yelling. What had that creep been doing here? Was it just chance, his turning up like that? Or something else? The photograph, the article, the exhibition—they'd all drawn attention to Baz. Was someone trying to let him know they weren't happy? That they knew where to find him if he thought of raising his voice again?

And if so, how had they found him?

A mixture of fear and guilt made me shiver. I'd led Gary to Paradise Road, after all. Had he and his mates been watching us since then? Reporting back to higher authority, like some nasty version of the Boy Scouts?

But our unwelcome guest seemed intent on spouting the same noxious crap that's always been used to turn people against the Outsider. *They're* getting what *you're* entitled to. Claim it back before they take everything! He must have been surprised when Jerzy and Pongo helped to throw him out. I wasn't, though. People here knew Baz. It'd take more than a few snide remarks to turn them against him.

"I thought you lot took anyone in," Derek said.

I shot him a glance, sensitive to anything that might suggest criticism of Baz. But he merely looked curious.

"I don't think he was after somewhere to stay."

I let him in to the kitchen and he started drying the stack of plates on the draining board. Transients rarely spent more than a night or two at the Skipper, but Derek had been here for over a week now. His travelling companions had upped and left without a word, so he said, and he had no taste for taking to the road on his own.

"You still thinking of making a go of it in Coventry?" I asked.

He leaned back on the counter, drying his hands on the tea towel.

"Maia, hinny, it's not easy. I'd like to. It's a canny enough place."

"But you're not going to spend the rest of your life living in a night shelter?"

"Well, no. That wouldn't be my choice." He picked up another cup from the draining board and began to dry it. "But that's where the trouble starts, like. To find somewhere to live, you have to pay for it. To pay for it you need a job. And to get a job you need to be able to tell them that you have somewhere to live."

"There are people who can help with all that."

Derek gave the tea towel a flourish. "Trying to keep us round here, are you, pet?" He winked and I flushed. "Only funning. What have you got for me?"

"I know a couple of charities that'd help out with the deposit and maybe the first month's rent. I can write down the details for you, if you're interested."

Derek hesitated, arms loose at his sides. "I don't know, pet. I don't like being beholden to anyone."

"You wouldn't have to be. You could pay the money back once you got a job. It'd be a way to give you a leg up, that's all."

He studied my face, his blue eyes very clear. "You're a strange lass. Why should you care what happens to us?"

"Well, it's not because I've succumbed to your good looks and charm."

I allowed myself to smile as Derek mimed heartbreak. Truth was, researching this kind of stuff had been a convenient distraction. Something to take my mind off the decision I was still dodging. "What do you think? You interested?"

He looked down at the grubby floor. "Phone calls cost money."

"Not much. They're just local calls." I dug in my pocket. "Here. You can use this."

He let me drop the small handful of change into his palm, his face changing colour.

"Thanks, Maia man. I don't know what to say."

"Just do something with it, okay?"

"I will. You have my word."

Chapter 30

Tonight, the office, with its heavy door and its bolts on the inside, felt more like a tomb than a place of safety. If he stayed, he was going to lash out, say something he'd regret. Baz ignored Libby's reproachful look, told Maia he was going and escaped into the night.

He climbed past the canal basin, up the Foleshill Road, through areas he'd photographed for *Desi Art*. A corner shop like the Patels' was still open. Inside, a young lad sat on a stool, doing homework by the light of a single naked bulb. A little further on, a sweetshop had its lights ablaze, its windows displaying pyramids of *barfi* and *laddu* and *jalebi*. Street lights illuminated the exotic scripts on signs he couldn't read. A halal butcher's. A sari shop.

Steam wafted from the door of a food shop. The smell of spice tempted him to sit in the smoky darkness, to eat without cutlery and mop up rich masala with chapatti or naan. As he turned towards the door, it swung open and a group of turbaned men came out, nattering in Punjabi. They swept past Baz as if he didn't exist and, as the door swung closed, he walked on.

He turned into Eagle Street. A woman in a *shalwar kameez* and a heavy coat, her *dupatta* over her head, hurried by, a heavy bag of shopping in her hand. As she passed Baz, she clutched the bag and looked away.

He crossed Stoney Stanton Road, walking along rundown

terraces, past the boarded windows and sealed letterboxes of houses that might or might not be deserted. Here and there, a blast of music from a Hindi film erupted onto the street.

So many things that his father should have taught him. Not only the big things—the language, the culture. Every time he opened his mouth near Vik, Baz was aware of the thousand tiny things he should have learnt from birth.

Too Paki to be white. Too *gora* to be *desi*.

At midnight, he came out near the top of Far Gosford Street, a few minutes' walk from Paradise Road. The night was bitter cold and a fine, penetrating rain had begun to fall.

The only person still up was Simon. He was drinking Tom's homebrew (several pints already, by the look of him) and letting the anarcho-punk sounds of Crass bleed out of the headphones. Baz kicked his ankle.

Simon lifted an earpiece. "What's the matter? You look like the cat got your tail feathers and spat them out again."

"Got any dope?"

Simon grunted and sat up, feeling for his tin in the pocket of his jacket.

"Columbian Gold. Tidy shit. Enough for a spliff if you fancy sharing."

"That'll do."

Baz watched Simon roll the spliff. When he'd finished, Baz took a long drag and let the hypnotic effect spread through his body. Simon, flat on his back, narrowed his eyes at him through the smoke.

"So what happened tonight to make you need this?"

Baz shrugged. "Fucking National Front at the Skipper."

Simon jerked his head up. "You had a rumble and you didn't invite me?"

"Not a rumble. Just some racist cretin peddling his poison."

Baz took another drag and felt himself grow light, as if he was hovering, half an inch above the ground. His mouth was dry and he felt a buzzing sensation behind his eyes.

"What about you?" he asked Simon. "Why are you lying here getting shit-arsed?"

"Fucking St David's Day and no one to celebrate it with but a bunch of bloody English and a Scotsman with the flu."

"Ah."

Simon took another drag and coughed, a hacking cough that went on for several minutes.

"You know the bastard thing of it?" he said, when he had his breath back. "Here, I'm always Simon the Taff. The Welsh bloody windbag. Give us a bloody song, Simon. But go back to Swansea, and what d'you know, it's hey, there's that *sais* from the prep school. Let's get him, boys."

Baz blinked. "Prep school? You?"

"Didn't know that, did you? Headmaster of the local prep school, my dad. Boys in green blazers with gold piping. Little green and gold caps. Elocution lessons from the age of five. How do you think I learnt to fight?"

Baz laughed. "I always thought your dad was a miner."

"De-elocuted myself, didn't I? Bloody Welsh John Peel, me." Simon pointed the spliff at Baz. "Tell anyone, butty, and I'll fucking kill you."

"Not a word."

Seven people living in this house together and were any of them what they appeared to be? Black was never truly black. White never truly white.

Baz held up his arm in front of his face and examined the meandering pattern of blue veins in his wrist. The drug was kicking in now. He could feel it, opening vistas in his head.

"Tell me, is this blood any different to anyone else's?"

"If you prick us, do we not bleed?" Simon declaimed. "If you tickle us, do we not laugh? If you poison us, do we not die?"

National Front, spreading their poison …

"Poison in the blood. Snakes stick their fangs in and—"

Simon struggled into a sitting position. "Know how you deal with a snake?"

"No."

"First you kill 'em—"

"How?"

"Doesn't matter. Then you suck the poison out."

"Out of the snake?"

"Of the place where it—whatsit—bit you. Then you apply a tourney-thing to stop it spreading."

Baz blinked. "What were you? A fucking boy scout?"

"Air cadet." Simon staggered to his feet and attempted a salute. "Daddy's little soldier."

A second later, they were both rolling around on the hearth, laughing uncontrollably, until Baz's eyes grew heavy and he cradled his head on his arm.

When he woke a few hours later, Simon was gone and the gas fire turned down low. He was ravenous. He got up, tripping over the blanket that someone had thrown over his legs. Rolled oats in the cupboard. Plenty of milk in the fridge. He made himself a pot of porridge, and ate it topped off with black treacle.

Chapter 31

That night, I listened to the whispers that eddied through the stagnant air of the Skipper.
Didn't know the gaffer was a Paki.
I was banged up in Winson Green with a black geezer once. As nice a bloke as you could hope to meet. But them Pakis up the Foleshill Road …
Sikhs, aren't them the ones that wear towels on their heads?
Breeding like rats. Stinking out their houses with their filthy food.
Taking over all the shops. Go and buy an ounce of baccy these days and the place smells like a tart's bedroom.
Vermin.
Didn't know the gaffer was one of them.
Transients and casuals, they had the biggest mouths. The hard-core residents kept a morose silence I couldn't fathom. Only Pongo, bless him, spoke up one time, telling two of the muck-stirrers to shut their faces before he did it for them.
"Maia, don't."
"Don't what?"
Libby took the pile of bowls from me and shook her head.
"Open your mouth. Give them a lecture on the evils of racism."
"So, what? You think they should get away with it?"
Libby put the bowls in the sink and plunged her arms into

the soapy water. "There's two of us and more than thirty of them. How long do you think we'd last if we antagonise them?"

"That's just cowardice."

"It's common sense!"

I let her persuade me to keep my trap shut. But later, lying in the dark, listening to the coughs and creaks and groans of the Skipper at night, I remembered Ossie's concept of *Ubuntu*. A person becoming a human being through the way they treated other people.

In the end, Martin Luther King said, we will remember not the words of our enemies, but the silence of our friends.

By the time I got back to Paradise Road in the morning, I was in that state of exhaustion where idleness is impossible. I stormed through the kitchen, washing up the pile of mugs and bowls that had been left by the sink and scrubbing down the surfaces. Then I decided to strip the beds.

Someone, probably Libby, had put lavender bags in the laundry cupboard, and as I took the sheets out, the clean, fresh scent enveloped me. Like most of our things here, the sheets came from charitable donations. People who had never seen the inside of the Skipper dormitory imagined we would be in constant need of fresh bed clothes. Piles of old sheets would appear in our charity box. Twill-woven linen, threadbare and out of fashion. Slippery to the touch. Robyn complained about how cold they were when you first got into bed, and about the fuss of not having fitted sheets. But I liked the ritual of smoothing them out. Tucking them in tight. Making sharp edged hospital corners.

I made up the three beds, put clean covers on the duvets, plumped up the pillows, and then carried the bundle of dirty bedding down to where the big laundry bag was waiting to be taken to the launderette.

Robyn was cutting up potatoes. As I came down, Baz opened the door from the yard. His long hair was straggling out of its silver band and his chin bore a day's growth of beard.

"Well, look what the cat dragged in," said Robyn. "Have a good time last night, did you?" She threw me a look. "Maia, you don't know how lucky you were. At least you got a good night's sleep down at the Skipper. Laughing like hyenas, he and Simon were. Stoned out of their brains at one in the morning."

So Baz had left Libby and me and come back here to get stoned, had he? I felt an echoing spasm of annoyance. One look at his face, though, and I could see he'd been punished enough.

"Come on, Robyn, give the guy a break. We had the bloody National Front at the Skipper last night!"

But Robyn wasn't listening. She pointed the kitchen knife at his chest.

"Abena called. Slipped your mind, did she? Or was smoking dope with Simon just a whole lot more fun?"

"I know. I fucked up. I'll make it up to her."

"How? Something like this isn't going to come along again next week, you know. You can't just not show up and expect—"

I didn't know what Baz was supposed to have done, or not done. But I could see that, given any more pressure he would shatter into a million pieces.

"Robyn, for once in your life, will you shut up!" I said. She gaped at me, open-mouthed and I gave a conciliatory smile. "Now is not the time, okay? Just give him some space."

She looked as if she'd like to argue the point, but with one last flourish of the knife, she stalked off upstairs.

I made a pot of tea and brought some through for Baz. A vein in his temple throbbed and his skin seemed drawn too tight over his skull.

"Hey. Don't beat yourself up. I can't be that bad, can it?"

He rubbed a hand across his face. "Abena, my girlfriend. She's helping to organise this huge protest march in London today. I promised her I'd be there. She must have phoned to find out where I was. No doubt Robyn's told her what I chose to do instead."

"It's hardly surprising, is it, with that cretin turning up last night?"

"Yeah, that's a handy excuse. But the truth is, I hadn't thought about the march in days."

"Do you think that guy came to the Skipper looking for you?"

He swirled the tea round in his mug and stared at it, as if looking for the answer in its spinning surface. "Bastard could play a good game of poker if he had a mind to. But there was a flicker, when he first caught my eye. He wasn't expecting me. I'd swear it."

I felt a half-guilty surge of relief. If this wasn't personal, if they weren't after Baz, then I didn't have to deal with the thought of someone spying on us as we came and went. I didn't have to think that it might be my fault I'd let Gary find out where we lived.

"Guess they know where to find me now, though, eh?" he said. He straightened up, scraping back his chair. "I need to get out of here, before my head explodes." He held out his hand. "Can I show you my studio?"

As he pulled the studio door shut, a cat emerged from under a tripod-and-tarpaulin tent and stretched each paw in turn. Baz picked her up but she wriggled away and shot out the cat flap. His eyes tracked her up the garden, as she stalked a bird. The bike ride had brought some colour back into his cheeks but his movements were still jerky with tension, as though his joints were wound too tight.

"You okay?" I asked. "I've seen you weather all sorts of stuff, but this …"

He pressed the heel of his hands into his eye sockets.

"I guess I thought the Skipper was the one place I'd never have to deal with that shit. That I could just get on with the job." He gave a bitter laugh. "I should have learnt by now—lying never does any good."

"Just because you didn't go out of your way to tell people your background, that's not lying."

"Isn't it?"

He went to one of the cabinets at the back of the studio, took out a small, papier mâché box and set it on a low table between us. On its smooth, lacquered lid, princes and tigers stalked each other through a miniature jungle. His hand hovered, as if he were making up his mind whether to open it.

"For thirteen years, my mother never told me who my father was. I never saw a picture. Never heard his name. All I knew was that he'd served in the RAF during the war, and that he died when a blast furnace blew up at the steel works." His hand hovered over the box, as if he were making up his mind whether to open it. "She lied, Maia. And it did no good. It never does any good. They always find you out."

"What do you mean, 'they find you out?' Baz, who found you out?"

"The National Front. The British Movement. Whatever the hell they were calling themselves that week." He hunched forward, long legs folded up. "I reckon someone traced us back to Bilston. Talked to the neighbours. Looked up the names of the men who were killed in the foundry explosion. She didn't keep her secret as well as she thought she did." He ran his fingers through his hair, loosening strands of it again. "We were always having graffiti scrawled on our door. Dog shit pushed through the letterbox."

"Oh, God."

"She'd tell me it was a mistake, that they'd mixed us up with the Gills next door. God knows, they got enough of it as well. But I don't buy it, not after …"

He fell silent again. I tried to imagine what it must have been like, growing up like that. Even more than Ossie's stories, it made me feel like a spoilt princess. Because it had happened here, in England. Because it could happen again.

Baz straightened up, as if shrugging off something that pressed down on him. "So you understand, if they're going to come after me again, I'd sooner meet them out in the open. No use skulking in shadows thinking they can't see you. They can."

I studied the pulsing vein in his temple, the lines etched around his eyes. It was a brave stand. But I understood only too well why his mother wanted to hide her small child away.

"How did you find out? About your dad, I mean."

He slid the box around the table with the tip of his finger, like a piece on a draughts board, forward, left, forward.

"I found some stuff she'd kept hidden. Photographs. Papers. My own birth certificate." His eyes opened, his pupils dilated like wide, dark pools. "I looked at it, and I didn't recognise my own name."

The pain and anger of that teenage boy was clear in his eyes.

"She must have wanted to keep you safe."

"She took a chunk of my life and locked it away in a suitcase. Kept it hidden from me as if I had no right to know who I was."

He was still staring at the painted box on the table.

"Was that your father's?" I reached towards it, but his hand scooped it up, shifting it out of reach.

"Mrs Gill, the lady next door? I used to call her Auntie Harjit … She brought me this after my mother died. I reckon my mum must have told her. She and uncle-ji were always trying to teach me stuff. Bits and pieces of Punjabi. Things about Sikhism. The best way to make *roti*. Funny that. She could tell our neighbour, but she couldn't tell me."

"Maybe she wanted Mrs Gill to teach you the things she couldn't?"

He laughed, and the sound was so bitter it made my mouth purse. "And here I am. Still too Paki to be white, too *gora* to be *desi*."

"Are you going to let anyone tell you that's a problem?"

Easy for me to say. But from somewhere deep inside me, a memory replayed itself. The market in Dakar. A group of men sitting drinking tea and playing chequers. They smiled at Pinda and me, and I smiled back. Then an African man passed, holding two light-skinned children by the hand. The men pointed at him with the soles of their feet, which I knew was very rude, and shouted '*Toubab la!*' When I asked Pinda what it meant, she said *toubab* was what her people called white folk. She said the man had married a white woman and people didn't like it because they believed the white woman would take the man away from his roots and the children would grow up in the wrong ways.

If I had Ossie's child, who would teach it all the stuff I didn't know? About all the things that made Ossie who he was? About being an African and a Xhosa? About *Ubuntu*?

And who would teach it to grow up in the spaces between two cultures?

Chapter 32

Baz stared at the little papier mâché box. Auntie-ji had said it was from Amritsar, where the Golden Temple stood. His father was from Amritsar.

After a time, he allowed himself to ease off the lid. A circle of plain steel gleamed against the silky fabric of the lining. His hand poised for minute before closing over the bangle. He slipped it over his wrist, feeling the metal cold against his skin, like a handcuff.

The first thing of his father's he ever saw. The last to survive.

For as long as he could remember, it had lain on top of his mother's wardrobe: a battered leather suitcase he was forbidden to touch. The one place in the house where dust was allowed to settle.

At thirteen, he was tall enough to reach it.

The clasps were pressed down and at first he thought they must be locked, but they were just stiff from disuse. First one, then the other gave way with a soft clunk. He lifted the lid.

A paisley shawl lay on the top, packed in layers of tissue and smelling of lavender and mothballs. Underneath, a length of sari silk—red and embroidered with gold thread, like the ones

Auntie Harjit next door kept in her dowry chest. "Red is the colour brides, Baz, *beta*. Not this white the *gorey* insist on."

But what would his mum be doing with a wedding sari?

He lifted the corner of the silk. Underneath lay a package wrapped in a linen handkerchief that sat heavy in his palm. He unfolded it and found a plain bangle made of heavy white metal and a pair of wooden combs. Below that was a strip of blue linen, at least five yards of it, and a pair of what looked like white cotton shorts.

He felt again in the suitcase. Something was buried in the folds of the shawl. A curved shape, smooth to the touch. He drew it out, gasped and nearly dropped it.

A small, curved blade in a polished wooden sheath, hanging from a wide ribbon embroidered with symbols he recognised but couldn't read. He'd seen one like it in Auntie Harjit's house. Knew it was carried by all adult Sikhs.

The *kirpan*.

Auntie Harjit had explained it all to him once, but he hadn't paid attention. Only the little sword had caught his imagination. If this was a *kirpan*, though, then the other things—the bangle, the combs, the shorts, the linen that could be folded into a turban—they were the other symbols of Sikhism. The other four of the five Ks. And they were in his mother's bedroom, which was bonkers.

The final thing in the suitcase was a battered cardboard shoebox, its lid tied with a scrap of ribbon. He unknotted it, his mouth so dry he thought his tongue would seal itself to the roof of his mouth.

Inside was a yellowed piece of paper, a pedlar's certificate, issued by the Wolverhampton police. Beneath that, an old black and white photograph of a man standing next to his mother. A man tall and proud in his RAF uniform, a medal pinned to his chest. A man like Uncle-ji from next door.

He lifted the photograph, holding it by the edges. Underneath was a birth certificate, made out with his own date of birth, and his mother's name, but in the name of a stranger. Male. Bhajan Singh Lister.

He didn't understand. He wanted to cry, like some stupid little kid. When soft footsteps padded across the carpet, he hid his face in the counterpane.

His mother didn't shout. She sat beside him and stroked the short dark hair at the nape of his neck. That was worse than if she'd shouted. He jerked away and thrust the photograph into her lap.

"Who is that?"

She took it and held it by the edges. "It's your dad. Sanjit Singh. On our wedding day."

"My father was a Sikh? Like Uncle-ji? Is Uncle-ji my real uncle, then?"

"No, Mr Gill never met your dad, Baz. But your dad was a Sikh."

"And is he dead? Or did you lie about that too?"

His mother's face got all screwed up, but he couldn't tell if she was angry or sad. Then she kind of ironed her features out again. Put on the same calm face she'd always worn. Only now it looked like a mask.

"No. He is dead. He died before you were born, in a blast furnace explosion, just as I told you."

Her headscarf was still tied over her hair, beaded with rain. She fingered the red silk sari, letting the delicate material slip between her fingers. "He gave me this as a wedding present. I never did wear it."

"You were ashamed of him? Is that why you lied?"

"Baz, duck, you have to understand, I was on my own with a new baby. And people said such things. I thought it was better if we moved where no one knew about Sanjit."

"Including me."

"You never met your dad. I didn't want you to have to pretend. To lie."

"You didn't mind lying yourself though, did you? To me?"

"Baz, I—"

He waved the birth certificate in her face. "You didn't even tell me my own name!"

"I was going to tell you, when you were old enough."

"I'm thirteen! How long were you planning to wait?"

He could still taste the anger he'd felt that day. Feel the way it had ripped his world apart, setting him on one side, her on the other.

And then she'd died, before either of them could repair the damage.

He stared at the steel bangle circling his wrist. By rights it should have been cremated with his father. Another sin of omission on his mother's part. Auntie Harjit had only given it to him because it was too late to do the right thing. It was never really his.

He pulled it off his wrist, placed it back in the box, and locked it once again in the cabinet.

When he got back to Paradise Road, Abena's march was on the television news. Baz watched as the line of flatbed trucks crawled across the black and white screen, the marchers following behind. Tall, narrow banners flapped in the breeze. 'Thirteen Dead: Nothing Said.' 'Blood ah Gonna Run if Justice Nah Come.' The names of thirteen children.

A handful of times that evening, he tried ringing the communal phone at Abena's place, but either nobody answered or a succession of bored voices informed him she was out. It was morning before he heard from her.

"Abena—"

"You didn't come," she said.

"No." He let a silence fall, while he thought what he could

possibly say. "They tell you about the National Front coming to the Skipper?"

"Sure. They told me. You didn't tell me. But they did." Her voice was like the crackle of dry tinder.

"So how'd it go?"

She snorted. "You see the papers? Twenty thousand marched with us. Twenty thousand black people. Twenty three arrested afterwards because they say we make trouble."

"Abena—"

"I'll tell you who makes trouble. The newspapers make trouble. 'The day the blacks ran riot.' Raas claat!"

She exhaled in a long hiss.

"We march through Wapping, and we expect the beefheads. But we cross the river into Fleet Street, and you know what? People hang out of the newspaper offices and shout abuse at us there too."

"Fuck." He felt sick. For her. For all of them.

"Don't know why I'm surprised," she said. "A free press we may have, but no one gonna tell me it unbiased."

"It's not all of them."

"No?"

Abena fell silent. He reckoned he had one chance to redeem himself and this was it.

"Look, Abena, I'm sorry—"

"Save it, Bhajan. I don't want to hear it."

She didn't sound angry any more. She sounded weary.

"Seems to me there's always something. Always a reason you can't come, a reason not to be here when I need you."

"I'm not making this stuff up," he said.

"No?" Anger flickered in her voice again. "Maybe not. But the fact is, you're never going to be there to support me. And I'm tired of waiting around for you to take an interest."

"I am interested. Abena, I'll always support you. You know that—"

"Don't make promises you can't keep, Bhajan."

"I mean it."

"You know the saying, 'what come bad in the mornin', can't come good in the evenin'?" Her blistering disappointment stung all the more because he knew it was at least half true. "You're not going to change, Baz. And I can't do this any more. It's finished. We're finished."

"Look, Abena, I—"

"I'm going to hang up now. I'm not at my yard so don't try and call back."

"Then where—?"

"That's not your business now."

"Well, can you at least—?"

"Goodbye, Baz."

He heard a click and the phone went dead. He listened to the hum for a moment before lowering himself into the chair, still clasping the handset.

She wasn't at her place. So where was she? Had she found another man already? One of her co-workers at the community centre, maybe? A knee-jerk jealousy overtook him as he ran through the potential candidates. That fit-looking one with his own sound system—he would be her type. Her voice had changed since she moved down there, picking up the Jamaican street patois they all used. Now he fancied he'd caught echoes of the sound guy's inflexions. He pictured them together, dipping and grinding to sound of Dennis Brown's silky voice.

He slammed his fist on the desk and pain shot up his arm.

"Baz? You okay?"

Maia stood in the doorway, backlit by the dim light of a winter's afternoon, looking more like a sprite than ever. He flexed his hand, easing the soreness.

"Abena and I—we just split up."

"I'm so sorry. Do you want me to go?"

"No, please! Stay."

She came in, her movements contained but graceful.

"Is this all because of the yesterday? Because of the march?"

"It's been brewing for a long time, I guess."

Just saying the words out loud put his jealousy into perspective. If he was honest, any passion he'd felt for Abena had long since faded to admiration. And admiration could be a chilly emotion to take to bed.

Maia on the other hand … In the past few weeks, she'd wormed her way under his skin. Extracted confidences from him he hadn't shared in a long, long time. How had that happened? Recently, she must have come into his mind more times in a few hours than Abena had for days on end. And now he had no reason—

"Come to the wrap party with me on Saturday."

The words were out before the rational part of his brain could stop them. Her eyes widened and he realised how it must sound. "Just as a friend. Please, I could use a friend right now."

He watched different emotions chase their way across her features.

"I can't. I'm working Saturday."

"No point being the gaffer if I can't fix that." Before she could say anything, he went to the foot of the stairs and hollered up. "Tom, you doing anything Saturday night?"

Tom's voice drifted down, edged with suspicion. "Nothing special, no. Why?"

"You don't want to come to the wrap party, do you?"

Baz heard a snort of disgust.

"I'd rather have my toenails pulled off one by one with a pair of pliers."

"Then I guess you won't mind swapping with Maia so she can come?"

Tom hesitated long enough to make him sweat.

"If it's what Maia wants."

Baz looked back at Maia. She was curled up in the big chair, looking guarded, as if waiting to see his next move. If he pressed her too hard, he would lose any chance he had. He sat down again on the office chair and held out his hands, palms upward.

"Is it what you want?" he asked.

Chapter 33

Tom levered himself up on the desk, planted his feet on the chair and started folding a piece of scrap paper into an aeroplane.

"Made another appointment at the PAS yet?"

I tensed and glanced towards the yard. Baz had gone to start on dinner and the two of us were alone in the office. The others had either gone out or were in their rooms. Still ...

"Keep your voice down, will you? Somebody might hear you."

"Well, did you?"

"None of your business!"

Tom gave me the sort of look a teacher would give a wayward child. "Don't you think getting that sorted might be more important than arranging a date with Baz?"

For a moment, I had a queasy vision of myself as the subject of one of my mother's research papers. 'Study of kinship ties and social relationships of a pregnant female':

Subject impregnates herself by absent male. Shows no sign of taking responsibility for child. Attaches herself to new tribe and engages in mating rituals with tribe's alpha male.

Screw that. Screw my mother. And screw Tom, too.

"I didn't arrange anything. Baz asked me, in case you didn't notice."

"Didn't exactly blow him out, though, did you?" His face

softened and he gave me a conciliatory smile. "Look, Maia, you want to go out with Baz, that's fine—"

"I wasn't aware that I needed your permission."

"You don't but—"

"And I'm not going out with him. I'm just going to his party. As a friend."

His eyebrows shot up. "Have you noticed the way he looks at you recently?"

"Don't be stupid. He and Abena have only just split up."

"You telling me blokes don't make eyes at girls when they're still going out with other girls? Or is Baz just a biological oddity?"

I had a sudden image of those dark eyes with their smoky grey lids, and a feeling of static electricity brushed over me.

"No, you're wrong."

He shrugged. "Fine. Good. I'm wrong. But there's still a clock ticking here, kiddo. And you need to get things sorted."

I hesitated. A well of thoughts and feelings I hardly dared admit even to myself bubbled to the surface.

"Tom, what if I've decided to keep the baby?"

I wanted him to look pleased. I wanted him to give me a big hug, to tell me 'that's great.' But instead he stopped in the act of making the final fold to his plane and glowered.

"Why?"

"What do you mean, why?"

"Why do you want to keep the baby? You making some sort of political gesture? Pissing off the National Front? Trying to hold on to some sort of connection with Ossie? What?" He finished the aeroplane and launched it. I felt the rush of air as it glided past my cheek. "Only one good reason to keep this baby, Maia, and that's because you want a child. Anything else and you're both going to end up fucked."

The first thing I saw as we approached the gallery was Baz's big photograph of the punks at the Hindu wedding. It had been shifted into one of the two bays, and Vik had pasted the latest cutting from the *Evening Telegraph* in the window. 'Asian Art a Great Success,' it announced; 'Coventry defies the racists by flocking to exhibition.'

"Do you suppose that counts as sticking two fingers up?" Baz asked.

Vik grinned. "Too right, *yaar*. We've earned it."

Around us, red light bathed the walls of the gallery. A sound system that looked capable of knocking out some serious welly took up a big part of the floor. Food piled on two tables filled the room with the smell of spices, and Mohan was busy opening bottles of Spanish champagne. Tom might be right: maybe this was another way to avoid facing reality. But it felt good, for just one night, to let go and enjoy myself.

A few minutes before kick-off, Vik pulled Baz's Ska compilation tape out of the player. Mohan flung open the back door and a group of young men piled in. They wore long white shirts, wide trousers and saffron-coloured turbans, and they carried a bizarre mixture of instruments. There was an electric guitar, a bass, keyboards. But also a big drum, carried slope-wise on a strap, and a weird thing that looked more like a single-stringed barometer than anything you could play music on. Baz shot photographs as they arranged themselves.

"They're called *Sona*," Mohan said. "Bhangra Gold. You gotta hear it."

When they started to play, the sound was like nothing I'd ever heard. The stringed instrument opened by twanging out a melody and was answered by the seductive beat of the drum. The singer threw back his head and produced an ululating sound that formed a contrapuntal beat. The other instruments joined in one by one, weaving between the two rhythms.

"That's the *dhol*," Mohan shouted in my ear, pointing to the drum. It was decorated with saffron-coloured tassels and the drummer was playing with one bent stick and one straight. "And that stringed one there is the *tumbi*. Traditional Punjabi instruments, you know? Music to get the harvest in. But listen to what they've done with it."

People were arriving in large numbers now. The men were mostly in Western dress but the women wore a rainbow of styles—saris, *shalwar kameez*, fashionable pegtop trousers and long-sleeved shirts. I couldn't be sure in the press of people, but it looked as if I might be the only Westerner there.

Feet tapped and bodies began to sway. A circle of dancers formed, energetic and sinuous –hands clapping, wrists twisting and shoulders shaking. Baz's flashgun kept going off, catching moments of the dance and freezing it. I was thrown back to memories of village festivals in Africa. My mother busy with her Kodak Retina. Me standing in the shadows, envying the dancers, feeling alone and utterly outside.

Then Mohan grabbed my hands. I was sucked into the whirl of bodies. Out of the corner of my eye, I saw Baz taking photographs of a jaw-droppingly beautiful girl with long, intricately plaited hair. Her back was straight like a professional dancer's and she danced as if he were the only person in the room.

"Harvest, you see?" Mohan shouted in my ear. "You scythe, then you thresh and then you sift."

I tried to copy him, but hopeless. I scythed when I should be threshing, sifted when I should be scything. Nobody seemed to mind, though and after a while the adrenalin kicked in and neither did I.

After a couple of dances, I couldn't keep it up. I told Mohan I had to get a drink and made my way across the room. The girl with the plaited hair joined me and smiled. Close up, she was even more beautiful. No wonder Baz was interested.

"Nice dancing," she said, over the din.

"I hadn't a clue what I was doing."

"It showed." She grinned and clinked her glass against mine. "Bhangra was a man's dance, you know, back in the Punjab. Not that anyone thinks like that any more." She held out her hand. "I'm Narinder, by the way. Vikram's cousin."

"Maia."

She poured a long glass of orange squash. At least here I didn't have to worry that I looked conspicuous if I stuck to soft drinks. The band started another song.

"They're amazing. How long have they been playing together?"

"About a year, I think. I don't know them all that well. They're sort of friends of friends."

She cocked her head on one side, listening. "They're changing the lyrics, singing about Baz and Vikram."

People were laughing. I could hear a chorus repeated over the hypnotic beat.

"What are they saying?"

She shook her head, a smile playing on her lips. "It's rude."

Baz broke free of a crowd of admirers and arrived to pour himself a drink. In the heat and the crush of people, patches of sweat had appeared on his sleek black roll neck. Narinder gave him an appreciative look, and I tried to see if it was reciprocated. But before I could judge, he was whisked off once more. Narinder watched him go, a small frown on her face. Then she leaned over to speak in my ear.

"Vikram told me Baz has split with his girlfriend. Does that mean he's going out with you now?"

"What? Oh, God, no. We're just friends." And friends don't get jealous, I reminded myself, grateful for the wash of red light.

Narinder tracked Baz with her eyes before wandering off in pursuit. But if she wanted to corner his attention, she had no luck. People kept coming up to him, patting him on the back, shaking his hand, refilling his glass. I heard snatches of bellowed conversation as I moved about the room.

"You must meet my cousin. He is an artist too …"

"Baz, congratulations! You've really put us on the map …"

"My uncle is in publishing. He might be able to get your

photographs into a magazine…"

"You must come and see Surjit … Jaswinder … Imran … They want to say hi."

It didn't stop.

Sometime after ten, the band took a break. Baz put his Ska compilation tape back on and the noise level dropped to the point where you could talk without having to shout. As ever, come evening, my morning sickness had disappeared and I was ravenous. I stood for a while, nibbling at samosas and pakora, aware of voices nearby, a man's and a woman's. They were speaking in Punjabi, and it sounded as if they were arguing. When the woman broke into English, I looked round automatically.

"You wonder why I don't want to go out with a Punjabi boy? When you're all like little princes with *laddu* in your mouths, wanting everything done for you? At least he's different."

It was Narinder. And the one arguing with her was Vik. Vik caught me looking and scowled. He grabbed his cousin's arm and drew her away.

At eleven o'clock, the band came back on and Baz materialised at my side. He had shed his camera with its bulky flashgun and reflector.

"Are we going to have that dance?" he asked, as if I were the one who'd been too busy to spend time with him.

Something about those dark eyes of his seemed to bypass the rational parts of my brain and go straight for a more primitive centre. I let him take my hand and lead me towards the dance floor. Halfway there, I tripped.

"Why don't you get rid of those heels?" Baz shouted in my ear. "You'll find it easier if you can feel the floor."

I looked down and saw that his feet were bare, his toes well spread. Sexy feet. I'd noticed that before.

"What if someone treads on my toes?"

"Trust me, I'll look after you."

I stashed my shoes under one of his easels and we joined the dancers. He was right. The steps were easier when you were connected to the ground. I felt the euphoria rise again, and it wasn't just the music. His body, moving close to mine, was playing fast and loose with my hormones.

We were still dancing when Vikram climbed up and took the microphone from the singer. A blast of feedback screeched from the speakers and the crowd groaned. "*Sat sri akaal! Namaste ji! Asalaam alaikum!*" he shouted, and the audience yelled back. He spoke for a time in Punjabi, raising laughter and applause at intervals, then he turned to Baz and switched into English.

"But the person who we have to thank for organising *Desi Art*, is Bhajan here, who has done a pretty fair job, despite never having learnt God's own language. He found us this location, managed the publicity, kept his head when the Nazis were running riot outside. And thanks to him, I am happy to say, we sold every single one of the pieces we had on display!"

A huge cheer went up. People turned and began applauding Baz. Vik waited for the noise to die down.

"Baz may have organised this exhibition, but it takes a true *desi* to organise a *mela*. *Arré, chak de phatte*! Raise the floorboards!"

In the light of the argument I'd overheard, Vik's words took on a double-edge. But if Baz felt it, he showed no sign. He was grinning, head thrown back, soaking up the mood of celebration.

The dance floor was now so full, every move threatened to mow down another dancer. Baz grabbed a couple of drinks and led me back to the semi-circle of easels where we'd hidden my shoes. I sipped the squash, looking round at his now familiar photographs. My God. Every one of them sold. Two weeks ago, when we were facing down the National Front, that would have seemed about as likely as Gary swapping sides and putting on a turban.

Baz's fingers brushed against bare skin where the back of my dress was cut low and I shivered.

"Have you enjoyed yourself?" he asked.

"More than I ever expected."

He was standing close enough to talk without shouting and I could feel the heat of his thigh against mine.

"I'm glad you came, Maia. I know I left you on your own too much but, believe me, it's made a difference, knowing you were here."

"You've had no shortage of admirers tonight."

"That is not why you're here." He cupped my face, fingertips skimming my jaw, his thumbs touching the hollow of my throat. "If you and Vik have anything in common, it's that you're neither of you ever guilty of flattering my ego."

He stooped his head and I caught a whiff of sandalwood on his hair. His lips when he kissed me were warm and dry, the inner surfaces barely moist as they parted, soft and delicate, and tugged at my lower lip. A charge of electricity ran over my body and out along my limbs. For as long as we kissed, I was still the young woman I might have been a few months ago. Free and without responsibilities, enjoying the touch of a man who was making her feel like the centre of the universe. Then Mohan broke in on us.

"Someone here wants to talk to you, man."

Baz's hands lingered on my waist. "Don't go anywhere," he said. And he slipped away after Mohan.

And just like that, all my fears and responsibilities snapped back into place. I pushed through the crowd. Outside in the yard, it was pitch dark. Above the high walls, I could see a sprinkling of stars. A thin frost had formed on the cobbles and on the door to the outside loo. I squatted above the seat, holding the full skirt of my dress out of the way.

Even supposing Baz meant what he said, that it wasn't just the champagne, the euphoria, the effect of being on the rebound—I had a baby on the way. Tom was right. The counsellor was right. Every bugger with their head screwed on was right. I had to sort that out before I even thought about anything else.

Chapter 34

Baz saw Jah Green standing in the doorway, spliff in hand. The scent of ganja clung to him, mingling with the spice and sweat and booze of the party. The Rasta's threadbare African robes were stained red in the light, his staff gleaming like mahogany. A serious looking young man in wire-rimmed glasses and a short-cropped Afro hovered at his side.

Too bad he'd locked his camera away when he went to find Maia. He'd have loved to photograph them. But even as he thought it, he was aware of the room parting around them, of hostile stares amidst the curiosity. He pushed his way through the crush of bodies.

"*Irie*, brother. I am not too late?" Jah Green hailed him. "I had a likkle business to attend to first."

"Not a problem. I'm glad you're here."

Jah Green waved the spliff in the direction of his companion. "It was important for me that Emmett, here, see your work. After all, it is going to share wall space with some of his."

"Truth is, he needs someone to drive him," the younger man said, smiling sideways at the Rasta. "But he likes to dress it up a bit."

"You're a photographer too?"

The young man held out his hand. "Emmett Bailey. I've been taking photographs of my community in Handsworth."

Jah Green ushered them towards the window. "You have my

picture in pride of place, I see?" He struck his staff on the floor and beamed as if the picture were one of his own children. "I have an eye, you know. Emmett can tell you. I am never wrong."

Studying the photograph through his wire-framed specs, Emmett began to ask questions. What sort of camera did Baz use? What kind of film did he favour? What exposure had he used for this photograph? Did he wait a long time for the right shot, or did he just happen upon it? What about in the developing? Did he have difficulty getting the right amount of detail in the darker background? How many attempts had he made before finding the one that satisfied him?

Baz answered, peppering the conversation with questions of his own, feeling the exhilaration of engaging with another photographer. After a time, he realised Vikram was hovering nearby and waved him over.

"Vik! You've got to meet Jah Green. And this is Emmett Bailey, another photographer."

"Ah, Vikram Kalsi. The painter. I hear 'nough good things about this here exhibition," Jah Green said.

"Thank you. We're very pleased with how it's gone." Vik's voice sounded flat.

"I don't know what Bhajan tell you. I myself am putting together an exhibition, as part of a likkle multi-racial festival. This summer, in Handsworth."

"Well, good luck with that."

Vikram started to leave and Jah Green raised his voice a notch. "My hope is that all of you who were in *Desi Art* will take part."

Vik rocked back on his heel, treating Baz to a blistering stare.

"Perhaps you haven't heard?" Vik said. "All our exhibits have sold."

"My festival is not until August. Maybe you'll have time to produce some more work before then?"

"My canvases take a great deal of time."

Jah Green shrugged.

"A pity. But perhaps your colleagues will find they have a likkle more time on their hands?"

"Perhaps."

As Vik started to walk away, Emmett blocked his path. "It would be a shame for a group of artists who have overcome so much to be held back by prejudice," he said.

"Yes, it would. Pleasure to meet you, Mr Bailey." Vikram held Emmett's eye for a moment, then sidestepped round him and slipped away into the crowd.

"God, I'm sorry—" Shame filled Baz's mouth. Jah Green held up his crooked hand.

"Do not vex yourself, my friend. I tell you, I have 'nough troubles the same in my yard."

"I'll talk to him. This isn't like him." As soon as he said it, he was aware of how much this sounded like the sort of excuses that the *goras* make for one another … *He didn't mean it anything by it. You're taking it the wrong way.*

He caught up with Vik close to where the band was playing and grabbed his arm. Vik wheeled on him.

"Are you out of your mind, *yaar*?"

"No. But I think maybe you are. Have you forgotten what you told me when we thought this was all going to go belly up? That if *Desi Art* didn't work out, you'd be stuck working for your *pyo* for the rest of your life? Wasn't this what we were hoping would happen?"

"What you were hoping for, maybe."

"It's not good enough for you? Why? Because he's black?"

Vik stared at Baz, his lip curling to show a flash of canine.

"You think I'm a racist?"

"Fucking looks like it from here."

"So tell me, *yaar*, exactly how is he going to advance your career?"

"What do you think? A multi-racial Arts festival. A chance to take this to a much bigger audience—"

"And who do you think are going to turn up at this Rastafarian dope fest of his? The big London Art critics? Or the drug squad?"

"God's sake, Vikram, he's smoking dope, not selling it!"

The noise level dropped as the band finished one number and his voice carried more than he had intended. Narinder appeared at his side.

"Who's smoking dope? That Rasta? God, I wish he'd give me some."

"Narinder!"

Vik looked as if this might send him over the edge. Narinder gave him a playful push.

"Cool it, *bhai*. I'm not going to do anything else to shock you tonight."

She looked up at Baz and smiled, as if she were conspiring with him against Vik. But at that moment, over the heads of the crowd, Baz spotted Maia, making her way to the door. He pushed Vik aside and threaded his way through the press of people. He could see the V of her dress where it was cut low at the back, showing off a triangle of pale skin. The tapering curve of her calves, the ankles set off by the high heels she had now slipped back on. All evening, he'd been pulled this way and that by a rip tide of conflicting demands. He'd wanted to tell her she made him feel as if he was opening up after being clamped shut for such a long time. But even when he'd kissed her, they'd been interrupted.

She was fumbling for her anorak now, amongst the pile of coats near the door. As she bent forward, he saw the hollow made by her collarbone, imagined the taste of it on his tongue.

"Do you have to go?" he asked. "If you can hang on another hour or so, I can take you home myself."

Somewhere in the direction of Bull Yard, a car hooted.

"That's my taxi. I'm sorted. I'll see you in the morning, okay?"

She pushed her way out the door. He watched her cross

into the square, her thin figure buffeted by the wind funnelling between the buildings, until she was lost beyond the wall of the Three Tuns.

Chapter 35

As soon as I woke up, I knew I'd done something stupid. It wasn't Baz's fault. He wasn't in possession of the facts. But I was. I knew I was pregnant. I knew I shouldn't get involved with anyone till that was sorted. But I'd let those damned eyes get the better of me.

I didn't trust myself to see him again. Not till I'd got everything straightened out in my head. I had to get out, avoid any early morning encounters over cereal and coffee. So I went for a walk, zigzagging through the backstreets, past closed-down businesses and boarded-up houses, staying away from the familiar route up to town. Letting the morning air clear the fug out of my head. I spotted a blanket and an empty bottle of cider in an underpass and wondered who had kipped here. On the landscaped green beyond the underpass, trees were coming into bud. Purple-headed crocuses were pushing their way through the thawed earth of the corporation flower beds.

Two months since Ossie left.

Sometimes, when I tried to picture his face, I saw instead the grainy newspaper images we'd carried on our banners. Steve Biko and Desmond Tutu. Nelson Mandela. When I forced myself to focus on Ossie, what I saw were the scars on the backs of his legs where he was beaten by the police during the Soweto uprising, the callus on the inside of his first finger, the crease in his neck. Not his face.

And last night I'd kissed Baz.

You could say, so what? I'd always had boyfriends. Ossie always had girlfriends. That wasn't what our friendship was about. Ever.

Except now I was carrying his baby. Whichever way you looked at it, that had to count for something. If only I could figure out what.

I was through the green and out the other side when I recognised where I was—at the top of Warwick Row, a few hundred yards from Bull Yard and the entrance to the gallery. Baz was due there to clear up after the party, and I wasn't ready to face him. I dodged past, head down, hands in pockets. As I reached the bottom of Hertford Street, a diesel engine started up. As I glanced over my shoulder, the red nose of a fire tender nudged out of the passage. Before my brain had processed what I saw, my feet raced back towards the gallery.

A police car was angled across the passage. I slid past, remembering how I'd manoeuvred round the phalanx of skinheads on their opening day. Dreading what I would find on the other side.

A jagged hole was smashed through the window where Vik had stuck the newspaper article. On the other side lay a pile of charred wood, some shards of glass, and the buckled metal frame of Baz's photograph. Oily soot fanned out across the ceiling.

Further back, beyond the bay, the room looked pretty much like any room the morning after a party. The band's sound system was gone, leaving a gap at the heart of the room. Empty bottles, paper plates, napkins and spilt food littered the floor. On the table nearest the window, soot grimed the white paper cloth. Yet the rest of the exhibits—the ones that had been pushed out the way to make room for the dance floor—appeared undamaged.

Baz and Vik stood inside the doorway, talking to two

policemen. Vik looked taut as an elastic band, bouncing on the balls of his feet, ready to make a fight of it. But Baz looked as if he were holding himself upright by sheer effort of will.

The door rasped against broken glass as I pushed it open. The older of the two policemen, distracted from eyeballing Vik, peered at me over the top of his half-frame specs. The younger gave a cheery smile. Vik scowled. Baz continued to stare at a point in space a few feet behind the policeman.

"This young lady one of the exhibitors, sir?"

Vik looked as if he might start telling the policeman precisely what 'desi' meant.

"I'm a friend of Mr Lister's," I said, to forestall him.

"Bit of a party going on here last night, I gather. Were you here, Miss …?"

"Hassett. Yes I was."

"And what time did you leave?"

"I got a taxi about half past twelve."

"And at that point, nothing had been damaged? Things hadn't started getting rowdy?"

Vikram gave a bounce of irritation. "This wasn't some drunken prank that got out of hand—"

The policeman continued to look at me, as if Vik hadn't spoken.

"No," I said. "Everything was fine."

"And you, gentlemen, if you could tell me what time you left here last night?"

Vik flipped a glance at Baz, who was still not speaking. "About half past two, or thereabouts," he said. "I left with Baz."

"And you were the last to leave?" the policeman asked. "No stragglers left behind to finish off the drink? Anything like that?"

"We left. We locked up. The place was empty," Vikram said.

The policeman scribbled a note, moistened his finger and flipped over a page.

"And it was your photograph that was burnt, is that right, Mr Lister?"

"Yes. That's right." Baz seemed to drag himself out of his catatonic state and focus on his interrogator.

"Any reason why someone should have targeted that particular picture?"

I felt a collective intake of breath. I guess all three of us were thinking of reasons why that photograph might have offended the sort of people who throw bricks through windows. But Baz just shook his head.

"And, all these pieces had been bought and paid for, is that right? Including the one that has been destroyed?"

"Yes, I told you," said Vik. "Every work sold."

"And the photograph that was destroyed can be reproduced, I presume. So it's just the damage to the building. But you'll be insured for that, naturally?" He pushed his glasses back up his nose and crooked his neck, examining the smoke damage on the ceiling. "You know, you're lucky those ceiling tiles didn't catch fire or the whole lot could have gone up."

Baz glanced upwards too, and a shudder passed over his frame. The policeman snapped his notebook shut.

"More than likely it was a random act of vandalism. Happens a lot these days with empty shops and that."

Vik snorted.

The policeman stopped in the act of sliding his notebook back into his pocket. "You don't agree, sir?"

Vik rolled his eyes and I saw the policeman press his lips into a thin line. I could tell he wanted to file this away with all the other incidents too minor to be bothered with. Vik was getting in the way.

"You do realise we were the target of a far right demonstration at our opening?" he said.

"And a bit of a counter demonstration from the far left, as I heard it."

"And before that, the outside of the shop was sprayed with racist graffiti. And the windows were broken."

"All of which you reported to the police, naturally?"

"Well, no, but—"

The policeman tutted. "That's a pity, that is, sir. It makes it much harder for us to do our job if people don't give us the full picture."

"This may be vandalism, but it wasn't random," Vikram snapped. "This was a racist attack."

"I don't see the evidence of that myself. And there's no need to shout if you don't mind, sir."

Vik thrust out an arm towards the policeman, checking him. "You can't just brush this aside. There's been a clear and sustained threat—"

The policeman stared at the hand on his shoulder until Vik dropped it.

"I don't know how you do things where you come from, sonny," he said, "but here in England you'll find we proceed on the basis of evidence, not allegation. And if you continue to take that tone with me, I shall have to ask you to come along to the station for questioning."

"About what?" Vik demanded.

"Let's start with assaulting a police officer, shall we?"

Something about the situation must have penetrated the wall Baz had erected around himself. He seemed to gather himself together and draw his voice up from the depths of his diaphragm.

"Vik, I am sure the police will do everything they can. Sergeant Conway, thank you for your time. You've been most helpful."

Vik shifted his weight onto his back foot. The policeman gave a curt nod.

"Yes, well. Thank you for your co-operation, Mr Lister. Mr Kalsi. Miss. And if you get any further information for us," he added, with a sharp look at Vik, "you be sure and let us know."

Their heavy police boots crunched over the floor. The older one paused in the doorway. "I'd get this broken glass cleared up if I were you, before someone gets hurt."

As soon as they were out of sight, the tight hold Baz had over himself seemed to snap. He staggered back against one of the tables, his breath coming in harsh gasps, as if he'd inhaled smoke. Vik paced up and down, fists clenching and unclenching.

"What do they think? That we set light to the place ourselves, for the insurance? At least the fire brigade could see what was under their noses. Brick through the window, petrol sprayed all over your photograph. What do they want? A signed confession written on the brick?"

He came to a halt in front of me, glaring as if I was part of the whole diabolical conspiracy. I glared back.

"This is getting us nowhere. When do you have to hand back the keys?"

"Tomorrow morning."

"Then we need to get this mess cleared up; we need to get someone to patch up that window, and we need to get the exhibition dismantled."

Vik looked like he wanted to challenge that 'we'. But then the fight seemed to fizzle out of him.

"I'll call my uncle. He'll repair the window."

"Good," I said. "Then let's get on with it."

When Vik had gone to find a payphone, I put my arms round Baz. I could feel him shaking, even through the heavy fabric of his greatcoat.

"Baz, what is it?"

His face turned towards mine, his eyes blank.

"She died."

The room felt suddenly ice cold.

"Baz, no one was here. I heard Vikram tell the police. You two were the last to leave. No one was hurt."

A tear formed in the corner of his eye and settled for a moment on his teardrop mole, before sliding down his cheek.

"She was trapped upstairs. She died, Maia. She died."

Chapter 36

As soon as he could be sure that his mother wouldn't poke her head round the door again, he pulled his father's things out from under his bed. The photograph lay on the top, one edge ragged. He'd torn it in two, the day after she let him keep it, ripping her out of the picture and burning her image in the waste paper basket with a match stolen from the kitchen.

He stared at the black and white figure of his father, alone on the steps. Sometimes, now, between the turban and beard, he caught a likeness to his own face. Was he supposed to grow his hair, wear it in a topknot on his head, like Inderpal? Get Uncle-ji to take him to *gurdwara*? How should he be, now that he was someone else?

As usual, the answers didn't come. He put the photograph back in the box and stowed it deep under the bed. He lay down, his face to the wall, and pictured his father in the next room, getting ready for bed. Saying the bedtime prayer, like uncle-ji. It would be so much easier if his father was here to tell him what to do.

He hadn't been asleep long when a noise outside woke him. He heard a scuffling and two sharp bangs and levered himself up to peer round the curtain. The night was moonless and dark, but he thought he saw two figures on the path. Cherryknockers, banging on the door and running away. Some nights they'd keep it up for hours.

He wanted to fling up the sash and yell out, 'Yes, I'm Sikh and I'm proud of it!" But a kernel of fear held him back. He remembered the gang of boys he passed on the way home from school last week. Up an entry, kicking at something on the ground. A turban and a bundle of clothes that lay there without moving. He'd hurried past, glad that his hair was still short and his skin just looked a bit tanned. Trying not to think that he was denying his father, just like *she* had.

He dozed off and the next thing he knew, she was shaking him awake. He jerked away but she shook him again, insistent.

"Baz, wake up. They've set the door on fire."

He sat bolt upright, all feeling draining out of him, and allowed her to hand him his dressing gown. The smell was like the time he and Inderpal had left the roti on the stove. He groped with his feet for his slippers, but she tugged at his arm.

"Baz, duck. We've got to get out."

The oilskin drugget felt cold and slippery underfoot as they ran down the stairs. Smoke stung his eyes, half blinding him, and he stubbed his toe on the plant stand in the hall. All they need do was get out the back door. They kept the key in the lock, so you could just turn it and let yourself out. But as they reached it, his mother stumbled. Her outstretched hand struck the key and it spun away, skidding across the floor.

"Oh, Lord. Find it, Baz."

They were both coughing now, the smoke choking them. She wetted two tea towels and gave him one to tie over his mouth and nose. Together they crawled over the floor on their hands and knees. Thick black smoke rolled across the ceiling, a shimmering layer of hot air bellying underneath.

"You keep trying, Baz. I'm going to go upstairs and try and shout for help. Mrs Gill will hear me. She always says her sisters only have to sneeze in the Punjab and she's awake."

She was gone, and he was alone. He stood and tugged at the door. The handle was hot, like a pan handle on the stove. The air scalded his lungs. He looked back. The flames had reached the foot of the stairs. Over the roar of the fire, he could hear his mother shouting as she struggled with the sash.

And then … and then … and then …

Why couldn't he remember what happened next? Why couldn't he remember why he'd got out and his mother hadn't?

The firemen had found him lying in the garden, the wool of his dressing gown burnt away, the back of his pyjamas melted into his skin. They told him that when he came to. But he didn't remember any of it. He barely remembered the almoner who came to the children's ward to tell him his mother was dead. The woman had sat by his bed all afternoon, waiting for him to cry.

His first clear memory after the fire was Auntie Harjit coming to see him, on the day they discharged him from hospital.

"It's the only thing they found, *beta*. The fire took everything else. But this was saved for you. *Waheguru*. Take care of it, Bhajan. It is yours now."

She left the little box on the bedside table, the bangle inside wrapped in a scrap of silk.

Maia's arms were round him and his face was buried in the oiled wool of her fisherman's jersey. He couldn't tell how much of his scrambled memories he'd mumbled out loud.

Her hand caressed his cheek. He covered it with his own and kissed her palm.

"It's okay. I'm okay. It was just seeing it like that. Brought it all back …"

He felt as if he had been strung up on a meat hook and used as a punch bag. But he was on his feet again now. Muscles aching but his body functioning.

He remembered the prayer his mother—no great churchgoer—would occasionally repeat. *Yea, though I walk through the valley of the shadow of death, I will fear no evil …*

No wonder his mother, with dangers threatening on every side, had found comfort in it. *Thou preparest a table before me in the presence of mine enemies …*

He'd spent so long being afraid of the fires rekindling. Now they had, he felt purged. Whatever else they did to him, he'd survived this. That must mean something.

Chapter 37

I had put my arms round Baz when the frightened little boy hovered just beneath the surface of the adult. Then the boy slipped away and the adult Baz was back. But it was too late. The walls I'd tried to construct around myself were as thin as dust. Just for an instant, when his lips touched my palm, I was naked. And he had seen.

Thankfully, after that, Baz switched his attention to clearing up. He charged around, tipping paper plates, plastic cups and leftover food into bin bags, while I found a dustpan and broom and tried to reassemble my defences.

I worked my way towards the window, sweeping up shards of broken glass. At the seat of the fire, the floor had bubbled in the intense heat. Some remnant of the chemicals given off in the fire caught at my throat and I imagined the destructive force of the heat bearing down on that small boy as he huddled in that kitchen …

His mother hadn't died in an accident. She'd been murdered because she married a man with coffee-coloured skin and eyes that were brushed with kohl. Because he'd worshipped in a *gurdwara* instead of a church. Because they'd had a child called Bhajan.

Beefy's face swung into focus in my mind's eye. Gary holding the lighter up to my face. The man at the demo. … *Degenerate filth … She's a Paki lover, that one … Like a bit of curry with your dick …*

Hunkering down to pick up one of the larger pieces of glass, I sliced my finger on its edge. Baz was at my side almost before I cried out. He took my hand in his.

"Doesn't look too bad. You'll live." He took out the first aid kit and bandaged my finger, as though I were one of the men at the Skipper after a Friday night rumble. "There." He finished it off with a piece of sticking plaster. "You better let me clear up this glass. Don't want you fainting on me again."

His eyes met mine and, just for a second, I had the sensation of swinging over a vertigo-inducing drop. I knew, if I let myself, I could fall for this man in a big, big way. But with everything else going on, I'd have to be insane.

The lump of concrete that had crashed through the window had come to rest by one of the table legs. I picked it up and carried it outside. Whoever threw it, whoever sloshed petrol through that gap, did they run off once they set the fire? Or did they stay to watch their little drama play itself out?

Only too easy to fit one face to that picture. Gap-toothed, shaven headed, tattooed. Looking for a new high. Getting off on the power of destruction.

"Baz, have you thought …?" I hesitated, not sure if I was letting emotion rule over logic. "Do you think it could it have been Gary who did this?"

Baz paused in his sweeping and looked back towards the window as if, like me, he was picturing the scene last night. "I dunno. He's a nasty piece of work with an entitlement complex but—"

Before he could complete the thought, Vik reappeared in the doorway, his body springy with tension, his voice cutting across Baz's. "Man, I tell you, Narinder is going to have my balls in a vice. My uncle says if she's not safe, even out with me, then he'll keep her under lock and key until she's married …" He seemed to twig that he'd interrupted something. "*Achcha*, which nasty piece of work are we talking about today?"

"Gary."

"That squirt Rebeccah used to foster? Why?"

Baz glanced at me and shrugged.

"He did make threats against those people in the shop," I said.

Baz gave an exasperated sigh. "Little prick's obsessed with that bloody shop!"

"And he's got a thing about playing with lighters," I said.

Vik looked from me to Baz. "Something you're not telling me, *yaar*?"

Baz ran a hand over his face. "Gary's got himself mixed up with the skinheads who were at the demonstration."

Vik's shoulders rose until they were almost square with his ears. "Mixed up how, exactly?"

"I'm not sure." Baz walked over to the window and stared through the jagged hole at the grey, damp scene outside. The vein in his temple was throbbing again.

"I never told you but, when the window was smashed that first time, I found a lighter on the floor next to the brick. And the night before the opening, when I was photographing everything, I was sure someone was out here, watching me. Someone with a lighter."

"Jesus!"

"You never said anything, *haan*?"

"It was a cheap plastic lighter. Must be hundreds like it thrown away every day. And there was no petrol, nothing anyone could have used to start a fire."

"What about the night before the opening?" Vik said. "The person watching you?"

"When I thought about it, it could have been anyone. Someone walking past and lighting a fag. Even now, all this adds up to is a load of coincidences and a dose of paranoia."

"Don't you know it ain't paranoia if they really are out to get you, *yaar*?"

Baz went on staring out the window, his body unnaturally still.

"So what are you going to do?" I asked.

"What can we do? The police aren't going to believe a word of it. They made that clear."

Vik made a tense angular movement, like a feint at the beginning of a fight. "I don't know about you, man, but I'm not going to wait around for those *haramzadey* to throw a firebomb into a house full of people instead of an empty shop!" Baz shook his head and Vik thumped his shoulder. "Come on, *yaar*. You of all people should understand that."

With so many people in Coventry spoiling for a fight, it wouldn't take much to ignite the tinder. A breath of wind would have it burning out of control. And Vik was like a struck flint, showering sparks.

"You want to be careful," I told him. "Don't set off something you can't control."

"And what do you suggest?" Vik said. "That we turn the other cheek, like good Christians?" He plucked at the front of his shirt. "In case you don't know, we Sikhs carry swords round our necks, not crosses."

"Then you should have learnt to pick your fights by now."

He threw me a look that could have curdled milk. God, if Baz wasn't there I'd have crowned him with one of this own paintings.

"What exactly are you doing here, Maia?" he said. "Ticking boxes in the Observer's Book of Multiculturalism? Been on a couple of Anti-Nazi League rallies, met a few black and Asian students at university—now let's do the ethnic art trail?"

"Vik, for fuck's sake!" Baz said.

But Vik was in full flood. "You know *nothing*. At least with the ones that throw bricks I know where we stand. But you people—"

Baz grabbed a handful of Vik's shirt front and yanked him up, so that his toes grazed the floor. "Enough! You go around antagonising our friends as well as our enemies, we'll have nobody left."

Vik went limp, as if the bile had leached out of him. "*Achcha*," he said, as Baz released his hold. "Let's hear what she has to say."

He didn't apologise, but I guess his vocabulary didn't run to apologies. I held his gaze, slowed my breathing, making him wait.

"Actually, I think you should do exactly what you have been doing."

"Oh, well, thanks, that's a big help."

"You said it yourself, last night, remember?" I said. "Putting that newspaper cutting in the window was like sticking up two fingers to the fascists. And they retaliated. But think about it—they must have been shitting themselves, thinking they'd done you a favour."

"So … what, then?" Baz searched my eyes, as if the right answer must be just on the tip of my tongue.

"So you carry on. Do more exhibitions. Get yourself out there. Get yourself noticed. In the papers. On the radio. Anything. You'll do more damage to them that way than you ever will taking the battle onto the streets."

Baz smacked his fist into the palm of his other hand. "What did I tell you? That festival in the summer …"

Vik's mouth worked as if literally chewing it over.

"The *gori* has a point, *yaar*," he said.

Baz laughed, a full-throated laugh as if he really believed, in that moment, that everything was going to be all right.

"Maia, I think you've just made history. You've got Vikram to see sense."

Chapter 38

Narinder's father arrived to fix the window, still scolding.

"Only nice Punjabi boys, you tell me. Nothing can happen to her, you say. Now I find she misses by a hair's breadth being burnt alive? And this is what you call keeping her safe?"

Baz adjusted his grip on the handles of the porter's trolley supporting one of Mohan's metal sculptures and eased it backwards through the door, leaving Vik to take a telling. Mohan followed him out, his face lined with tension. The van he'd borrowed stood a few feet away, its tailgate down, the back cleared to make space.

By the time they had Hanuman, the monkey god, strapped into the van alongside Rama and his broken bow, they were both sweating. Baz sat down at the rear, flexing the feeling back into his fingers. Mohan squatted beside him.

"Tough break, your picture getting torched. Guess I'm lucky those scrotes didn't melt my babies down for scrap."

Baz screwed his eyes shut. For the past few hours he'd pushed it aside. But it was all still there, just below the surface.

"Makes you feel kind of dirty, doesn't it?" Mohan said.

"That was said with feeling. You having trouble?"

Mohan shrugged. "My little brother's had some hassle from the skinheads up at the Precinct. And there's a friend of mine …"

Mohan's normally cheerful face darkened and he turned away, reaching into his haversack.

"What?"

"Doesn't matter." Mohan pulled out a stainless steel water bottle, took a swig and passed it to Baz. "Some bastards are always going to think like that. What you gotta remember is—it's not your problem; it's theirs. You just gotta get on with life."

At last, they had the shop back in as good a state as they could manage. Tomorrow Baz would hand back the key and make what apologies he could to the landlord. The insurance would take care of the rest. And *Desi Art* would be over.

He paused, staring at the floor. Around the core of the fire, the tiles were lamp black, fading to leopard spots of ochre and umber. Where the fuel had splashed, running along the channels between the tiles, blackened branches grew outwards, linked by drifts of smoke like smudged charcoal.

The feelings that had buoyed him up and carried him through the first few hours of cleaning and packing had seeped away. His muscles ached as much from tension as from exhaustion.

Whether they chose Maia's way or Vik's, they'd be taking the fight to the enemy. And with the cold, hard certainty of a photograph shot in bright light, he saw what that would bring. More attacks, more demonstrations, an escalation of violence. People getting hurt—killed, even …

But what was the alternative? To hide in the shadows, like his mother did? Anger curled inside him. Not that. Never again. If he couldn't stop what was happening, he could at least stand against it. That was what his father's *kirpan* represented, after all: the principle that you act to prevent violence being done.

Whatever it cost.

Maia's shoulder brushed his and a little of his tension earthed itself through her touch.

"Know something? You've been amazing today. Everything you've done. Everything you've put up with." He raised her fingers to his lips. "Vik's a little sod when he's in a temper. Doesn't care who he hurts."

His free hand pressed into the small of her back. He could feel her heart beating against his chest.

"You left last night before I could tell you something," he said.

"I did?"

"You did." His eyes searched her face. The whole day had been a whirlwind of emotions and reactions through which he'd spun like a top, till he'd come to rest here, with this woman. When had he ever laid himself open to another human being like this? They'd barely begun to know each other, yet whenever she was near, he could feel the tantalising promise of real intimacy. Something so dizzying, so terrifying that he felt compelled to make light of it. He swung her round as if they were dancing.

"Don't ask me why, Maia Hassett, but from the first day I met you, you got under my skin. Like a tick. Like an itch I can't scratch—"

She thumped his chest.

"Bhajan, that has to be the most unromantic proposition I've ever heard! Rotten trick, making me laugh like that."

"I have this mad idea that we're meant to be together. And I don't see any way to test it out except to give it a go."

Her face tilted upwards and he kissed her, feeling her body relax into his and his own body respond.

They parted in the yard at Paradise Road and he let her go with no more than a press of his fingers on hers. Standing in the drizzle, he watched her slip away through the bright lights of the kitchen and into the sitting room. What they had between them was like an unfixed image. He had to be patient, allow time for things to develop. But his body ached in protest.

She wasn't there at breakfast and to take his mind off her absence, he forced himself to tackle the phone call to the gallery owner. He had been dreading it, but Noordin was right. The landlord understood this kind of trouble.

"No one was hurt. That, you thank God for and never mind the rest. Buildings can be repaired: human beings are a different matter."

Baz had just replaced the phone in its cradle, feeling as if a little bit of his faith in human nature had been restored, when Simon stuck his head round the door.

"There's a guy outside says he wants to talk to you. Jason somebody? I think he's a journalist. Want me to get rid of him for you?"

"No, that's fine," he said. "I'll deal with him."

Jason Creech leant against the wall, hands in the pockets of his tan leather bomber jacket, jaw working at a piece of gum. When he saw Baz, he pulled himself upright and held out a hand.

"I heard someone tried to burn down your gallery yesterday."

"Word travels fast."

"Hey, gotta keep your finger on the pulse in this business." The reporter followed Baz through the green gate and into the office. "Any idea why they chose yesterday morning to attack? I mean, you'd had no trouble since the opening, had you?"

"We think that could be down to you lot. That article you wrote saying how well we did? Could have put someone's back up."

"You got a problem with the *Telegraph* covering the story?"

Baz shrugged. "Law of unintended consequences, that's all."

Creech sat on the plastic office chair and crossed one ankle over his knee. "What's your gut feeling? Is this just general racism? Or is there an element of personal vendetta?"

"Why would you think it's anything personal?"

"Well, see now. I understand one of these skinheads who have been causing all the trouble is your foster brother."

"How the hell did you—?"

"Is it true?"

"Get lost!"

"Tell me, what sort of relationship do you have with your foster brother?"

"That's none of your business."

The journalist clicked his pen against his teeth. The noise made Baz clench his fists on the arms of the chair.

"Come on, Bhajan, cut me some slack here."

"So ask me something different."

"Fair enough." He folded his arms across his chest. "It is true, isn't it, that this is not the first time you've been attacked?"

Baz relaxed. Here at least, he was on safer ground. "Well, as you know, the windows of the gallery were broken once before when we were setting up. And we had racist graffiti sprayed over the frontage several times—"

"Matter of fact, I was talking about when you were a kid, Bhajan."

"What?"

It felt like a punch in the face. He stared at the journalist, who stared coolly back. Who had he been talking to? Who'd fed him this stuff?

"Your home was firebombed when you were a teenager, yes?"

"That has nothing to do with—"

The words were out before he could stop them. Creech's eyes widened. "So it's true?"

Shit.

"But your mother was killed in that attack?"

Baz scraped back his chair. "Go fuck yourself."

"Come off it. That's got to be a matter of public record. A few hours' research in the archives and I'd have the whole story."

"So do the bloody research. You'll get nothing from me."

Chapter 39

By morning, I knew I had to tell Baz I was pregnant.

It wasn't the start anyone would want for a relationship. In fact it could end any chance of a relationship before it even began. But I knew that if I swung one more time over that dizzying precipice he opened beneath my feet, I was going to fall for him so hard. And if that happened, I had to know he was willing to catch me.

It was my turn to cook supper that night. I thought if I could cook something special, it might make it easier to have that impossible conversation. And I remembered something Pinda used to cook when we were in Senegal. A spicy bean stew with sweet potatoes and peanuts that always tasted to me of comfort.

The key to making the stew work was the sweet potatoes, but threading my way round the concentric circles of stalls in the Market, I almost despaired of finding them. Then, way out in the furthest rim, I caught the sound of Reggae from a West Indian stall.

"What's your pleasure, darlin'?" asked a man in dreadlocks.

His stall seemed to sell everything from chillies and limes to bootleg dub tapes. When I made my purchases, he handed them over with a broad smile.

"Soul food, darlin'. Best thing in the world."

"I'm counting on it."

All the way home, I rehearsed what to say. I could hear Tom's voice in my head. *Dressing it up ain't going to help, kiddo. Just spit it out. If he can't take it, he ain't worth it.* But I'd never in my life spent so much time rearranging so few words.

By the time I got to the green gate, I had goosebumps up and down my arms. I wasn't planning to tell Baz until tonight, but my head was so crammed with one thought, I was half convinced I had a sign over my head saying 'bun in the oven.'

I was pushing my bike up the alley when this young guy strode towards me. His face looked familiar, though I was too distracted to place him. As he passed, he gave me a penetrating stare, as if the sign was real and he was reading it. I flushed crimson.

Baz was in the yard. I'd have preferred to avoid him, if I could, until I was ready for my big confession. Fumbling for something to say, I felt my face go an even deeper red. Baz's eyes shifted from the guy's departing back to my face. If anything, his scowl deepened and as I came up, he stuck his foot under my front wheel and brought me up short, making the handlebars bang against my belly.

"So what was your price for selling me out to the Press, then?"

"What?"

He looked at me with the eyes of a stranger, cold and accusing. "Don't pretend you don't know. That reporter from the *Telegraph* was remarkably well informed about my childhood." Faces were appearing at the windows now, drawn by the sound of his raised voice. "That is where you've been, I imagine. The *Telegraph* offices?"

After everything he said last night, this is what he thought of me? I packed my feelings into a tight hard knot in my stomach, and tilted the bike. Dark green spinach leaves poked out from the basket, and below them, the reddish skin of sweet potato.

"I've been out getting food. Ask Simon. He saw me go. I haven't had time for any side excursions to the *Telegraph* or anywhere else."

The anger leached from his face and he slumped against the wall. Beside him, a rusted bicycle stood on its saddle, the front wheel removed from its forks, the rear wheel spinning.

"That reporter knew everything we'd talked about yesterday, Maia."

"And you think that I'd—?"

"I saw the way Creech looked at you and I …" He raised his head and the curious faces at the windows drew back into the shadows. "Maia, only two other people knew that stuff. And Rebeccah's kept her counsel for fifteen years."

"Let me guess," I said. "The other one's Vikram?"

"Vik … Fuck." The colour came and went in his face as he digested this. "I should have known it was too easy, the way he just agreed to everything." He aimed a kick at the bicycle. "Keep us in the frigging papers—well, he's done that, hasn't he?"

He prowled across the yard, dragging a dark cloud with him. "Vik's my best mate and I can't believe I'm saying this. But sometimes he and Gary are like two prints from the same image. They're both so God damn angry, you never know what they're going to do next."

"Whatever else Vik might be, he's no Gary. I can't see him throwing a brick through a window. Or starting a fire."

Baz gave a gallows laugh. "No. He'd just egg the other side on until they threw the brick, and then hit them over the head with a two-by-four."

At last he came to a halt in front of me and seemed to remember I was there.

"Maia, I am so sorry. I had no business jumping to conclusions like that. If it makes any difference, I don't make a habit of kissing a girl one day and hurling accusations at her the next."

"So, just me then?"

I gave him a smile that only papered over the cracks. His anger had flared and fizzled and was gone as quickly as it came. Part of me could even see his point. He and Vik had been friends for years and he'd only known me a few weeks. Of course it was easier to think that I'd been the one to shop him. But that didn't make it hurt any the less.

He reached for me, but I held up my hand, warding him off.

"We can't do this, Baz."

He glanced back at the house.

"You mean because those nosy parkers are gawping at us through the windows. Sod 'em. Let them look—"

"No. I mean, we … I can't do this."

He blinked, unsure of his ground for once. "Hey, I know I acted like a complete arse. If I were you, I'd probably kick me in the bollocks—"

If I were me, I thought, the old me, the before-I-got-pregnant me, I'd kick you in the bollocks, have a row with you, punish you for not trusting me, and then go out with you anyway. Because I like you. So much.

But the baby changed everything.

Anyone I went out with, I had to be able to trust absolutely. Not just with me, but with my child. And he'd shown me we weren't ready for that.

"I'm sorry."

The night Creech's article came out, Baz went straight to the office at the Skipper. Usually the spare pair of hands did kitchen duties, but neither Libby nor I felt like arguing. He'd closed himself away for the last day and a half. Speaking to no one. Avoiding the expressions of sympathy. But most of all, avoiding me.

I felt raw. And lonely. After all, Baz was the one person in this whole mess who had half a chance of understanding what I was going through. But it would have hurt a lot more if I'd allowed things to go on, allowed my heart to get caught up with his, and then he let me down.

God, though, I hated knowing he was just the other side of

the office door.

After a while, Knoxie came in with a group of travelling unemployed. He and another semi-regular called Joey had evidently spent the afternoon helping to relieve the group of their redundancy money in liquid form. One of them, a kid of about nineteen, had to be supported between two others.

Charlie Singer was strumming away on his guitar and I half expected the simmering feud between him and Knoxie to boil over again. But the group had their heads together, muttering, and after a while I forgot about them.

Derek turned up almost two hours after we opened, looking edgy and pale, his thin bony hands fidgeting over the counter. A copy of the *Evening Telegraph* stuck out from the pocket of his donkey jacket.

"Hello, pet. Sorry I'm late. Do you need a hand in there?"

"Do you want something to eat?"

"Nah. I'm not hungry. I could murder a cup of tea, though."

He let himself through into the kitchen and poured a cup, drinking it greedily. Then he was back, jaunty as ever. I put him to serving the soup while I buttered more bread, licking margarine off my fingers when no one was looking.

"Listen, pet. I've a favour to ask you."

"Sure. Ask away."

"I've found someone who'll help me with a deposit for a flat. So I've been looking in the paper, seeing what's available, like." He thrust his hands into his pockets, looking sheepish. "But I'm no good at this sort of thing. When I were married, it were always our lass that'd spot if there was damp in the walls or cockroaches in the kitchen. We'd have ended up living in some right dives if it had been up to us, I can tell you."

"You want me to come and look with you?"

"Maia, pet, would you?"

I saw the relief on his face and smiled. "I'd be glad to. Though I don't know how much help I'll be. You should see some of the places I lived when I was a student."

"Well, two heads and that." He smiled his face-transforming smile. "I can't thank you enough for this, Maia, man. This could really turn things around for me. And before I forget, I've got something for you." He scrabbled into his pocket and produced a tiny handful of coins. "Fifty five pence, wasn't it? The money you lent me for the phone?"

"You don't have to—"

"I wouldn't want anyone to say Derek Paterson doesn't pay his debts." He ducked his head, his smile growing shy. "Besides, it makes me easier in my mind asking you this favour, like."

I started to thank him, but was distracted by growing signs of a disturbance among the group with Knoxie. Baz came out of the office, and I saw Knoxie look up and nudge the man next to him. The two of them tracked Baz across the room and Knoxie's neighbour shouted to Charlie.

"Oi, Music Man, you know 'Disco Inferno'?"

"You want a request, son, you can chuck us a tanner like any other bugger."

Knoxie grinned. "C'mon, pal, we'll hum a few bars and you can join in."

It was one of those moments between lightning and the thunder. When you know what is going to happen but it is too late to do anything about it.

Chapter 40

COVENTRY ARTIST SURVIVES
SECOND RACIST ATTACK

… The Desi Art exhibition, which attracted protests from Far Right groups when it opened, ended in disaster on Saturday night when extremists smashed a window at their gallery and made a bonfire out of one of Bhajan Sing Lister's photographs. This is the second time that Lister has fallen victim to racist thugs. Thirteen years ago, an arson attack on the family home in Leamington Spa left his mother dead. Lister, then a teenager, was lucky to escape with his life …

Baz froze by one of the tables in the Skipper, staring again at Creech's article spread out in front of him. Bhajan *Sing* Lister. Sing without the 'h'. Half the Asian population of Coventry used 'Singh' as a surname—you'd think a fucking reporter could get it right.

He'd have laid odds no bugger here would get past the football and the horse racing and actually read the bloody thing. Seemed he was wrong. Still, tomorrow it'd be wrapping a poke of chips. No one would remember.

Over in the corner, Charlie Singer was working on the riff for a new song. He kept snagging on the same place over and over, and the table next to him was getting twitchy. Baz heard shouts and catcalls.

Knoxie was laughing himself into a fit of coughing. Next to him, a hard-faced git called Joey, recently released from Winson Green, was leering, gums showing above his teeth. The rest were strangers. He stared at them, trying to work out if the insult was deliberate. The man on Knoxie's right caught Baz's eye and began to beat out a rhythm on the table. One after the other, men round the table joined in the chant.

One, two, three, we all agree. Pakis burn better than petrol.

The words hit him like a force ten gale. He wanted to overturn the table and kick the benches out from under every one of them. He wanted to grab the smirking ringleader by the throat and strangle him. He wanted to stuff a copy of the *Evening Telegraph* down Knoxie's throat. He—

The grin vanished from Knoxie's face and he grabbed his neighbour by the collar.

"What the fuck do you think you are playing at, pal?"

The man's arms flailed. "It was a joke. Just a joke."

"Tell that to the gaffer," Knoxie said. "It's his mother that's deid."

Around them men were standing up. Hands travelled towards belts. The man on the far side of Knoxie leaned forward. "What's the matter, cock? Had a sense of humour bypass?"

Without letting go of the first man, Knoxie wheeled, dragging his captive with him. "And who's you to tell me what to laugh at, you dickless cunt?"

"Dickless? You checked that with your mother, cock?"

"Say anything more about my mother, cunt, and I'll shove your teeth so far down your throat you'll have to stick your toothbrush up your arse to clean them."

Baz was tempted to let the whole bloody lot of them rip each other to pieces. All around the room, men were shifting position, marking one another as if they were opposing football teams. If he lost control, this place would be like Millwall after losing a game to West Ham. And he had others to think about. Libby. Maia …

The thought of Maia galvanised him. He wasn't going to let her get caught up in a riot. As Knoxie wound his head back and prepared to use it as a club, he stepped between them.

"Enough!"

"What's your problem, pal?" Knoxie stopped in mid-swing, looking baffled. "I'm just trying to explain to this shit-for-brains here that your ma wasnae a Paki."

"Great. Thanks, Knoxie. But you still can't plaster his brains all over my bloody walls."

One of the other incomers strained forward, jeering at Knoxie. "Yeah, get back in your fucking cage, y'cunt."

Knoxie jerked convulsively. Pongo and Jerzy were hanging off an arm each, holding him back. Round the other side of the table, Paterson threw a restraining arm around the man who'd made the jibe. For a moment, the only sound was the noise of a dozen men breathing heavily. Then Walter, who had been rocking himself back and forth, began muttering, "O God, the Father of heaven: have mercy upon us miserable sinners …"

"Right, all of you. Sit down and shut up!" Baz said. The men shuffled and grumbled, but one after the other, they sat. Baz leaned forward, his fists on the table. "Any of you pull a stunt like that in my gaff again and you're barred. Is that clear?" A grudging nod travelled round the table. Baz risked a glance over his shoulder. "Pongo, take Knoxie somewhere to cool off, will you? And Derek, fetch some tea over here. Help us all calm down."

Baz sat at the incomers' table. A kid who'd come in rat-arsed had dropped off to sleep and was snoring with his mouth open. The others glanced round uneasily. Another copy of the

Telegraph lay in the middle of the table, open at Creech's article. When Derek brought the tea over, Baz swept it out of the way.

He schooled himself to talk to them, to find out where they were from (Nottinghamshire) and why they were on the road (British Sugar closing their factories and putting them out of work, leading to some bitter jokes about where the sugar in their tea would now come from). It was a drearily familiar story.

When, after half an hour, he got up to return to the office, one of them grabbed his arm.

"No offense, cock, okay? We meant no harm. Just a bit of a joke, y'see?"

He freed his arm gently but said nothing.

"You're okay. You know that, cock? You're okay."

He'd left a pile of post on the corner of the desk, to be dealt with later. Most of them were letters from the DHSS, for those men who used this place as an accommodation address. The pile had slipped and a new envelope lay on top. Plain brown, like all the others, but hand delivered. Addressed to 'Bhajan Sing Lister'. Same ignorant spelling as in the article.

When he slit open the envelope, a single folded sheet fell out. Inside, the message was spelt out in newsprint, cut and glued onto the coarse notepaper:

NEXT TIME YOU WON'T BE SO LUCKY

A familiar, sick feeling crept over him. *They know where you live. They know who you are. They can find you anytime they want.*

He crumpled the paper and hurled it at the bin. A moment later, he thought better of it and fished it out.

The letter had not been with the others when he picked them up. At some point this evening, someone had come into the office and left it on the desk. Not one of the incomers—they'd been in his sights the whole time he'd been out of the office. Which meant it had to be one of the Skipper regulars. Did they know what was in the envelope or were they just the carrier pigeon? And was the whole business with the Nottingham crew staged? Or had it just been a handy distraction?

Fuck. What a mess.

"Baz?"

As Maia pushed open the door of the office, he stuffed the letter into his pocket.

"God, that was horrible. How you managed to sit and drink tea with them afterwards Are you okay?"

"Yes … No. Shit, I don't know." He wanted to reach out and hold her, bury his face in her hair. But she had made it painfully clear that that wasn't what she wanted. "Having Knoxie on your side tends to be a bit of a mixed blessing."

He could feel the crumpled paper, rough under his fingers. It would be a relief to tell someone about it. But if someone in the Skipper had brought it in, he'd didn't want her—or any of the volunteers—looking into the faces of the men they'd come to trust and trying to work out which one had done it. That was his burden.

Instead, he said, trying to make light of it, "You ever had anything made public that you really, really wanted kept private?" and wondered why her face changed colour as if it had caught the setting sun.

Chapter 41

Somehow we made it through the night. The warring factions fell asleep, and so did Libby and I. And in the morning the Notts contingent seemed keen just to eat their porridge and get out. By the time I'd finished washing up the breakfast things, Derek was waiting for me.

"Are you up for this, then, pet?"

"Sure, why not? It's a good day for it."

It was, too. A good day not to be going back to Paradise Road. A good day to have other problems to occupy my mind. I set out with him in high hopes, imagining finding the perfect little bachelor pad from which Derek could launch his new life. It wouldn't be much, of course, but decent and clean.

By late morning, my optimism was strained. We'd looked at half a dozen 'rooms to let' in unpromising streets in some of the poorest parts of the city. So far, we'd found plaster peeling off the walls, cockroaches under the sink, signs of bedbugs on the mattress. And those were some of the better rooms.

This latest place seemed different. The hall was clean and recently decorated. And the only smell was a faint aroma of curry.

The man who'd answered the door was a middle-aged Pakistani with a greying moustache and greying cardigan. His hands were cracked, callused and stained with nicotine, and skin round his eyes was deeply lined. The cardigan was darned at the elbow with wool that didn't quite match.

"I was living here many years," he said as he led us, single file, up the narrow stairs. "Now my wife, my family are in close neighbourhood and we are making bedsitting flats."

Derek fidgeted on the small landing while the man unlocked a door.

The room had a sofa bed, a couple of gas rings and a small sink, a gateleg table with a yellowing Formica top and one chair. A cheap patterned carpet covered the floor, jarring with wallpaper that featured circles of orange, cinnamon and pink. It was soulless, second hand and depressing. On the other hand, it was clean and dry and it showed no obvious signs of infestation.

"It's a good room, Derek," I told him.

He glanced sideways at the landlord, Mr Arain, who was standing as far away as the tiny space allowed, hands clasped behind his back.

"You don't think it smells a bit funny?" he asked, in an all-too-audible whisper.

The landlord began to struggle with the sash. "You may at any time open the window and let the air come in," he told us.

Derek turned away. Still in a loud undertone, he said, "It's one thing I can't get used to down here. All these Pakis everywhere. Like your gaffer with the ponytail."

Oh, not you too, Derek. Not after last night.

"You can't say Paki, Derek. It's like calling someone ..." I couldn't bring myself to say 'nigger'. "It's like calling someone a spade."

"What's wrong with calling a spade a spade?" Derek looked blank and I couldn't work out if he was joking. "Don't get me wrong, like. I've nothing against them. It feels a bit weird, like, having a darkie for a landlord, that's all."

"Derek!"

"Sorry."

"Look, it's the best we've seen."

"You're not wrong." He looked around at the hallucination-inducing wallpaper. "You think he'd let me give it a lick of paint?"

"Ask him."

He raised his voice, as if talking to someone hard of hearing. Mr Arain's face showed he had been through this before. Many times.

"Look, mate. I like the room okay. But I don't like the wallpaper. What would you say if I wanted to paint these walls?"

He pantomimed painting. A furrow appeared between the landlord's brows.

"I have already been having much much expense."

"Oh, nah, nah. I'd do it all myself, like."

"You would be paying all the money?"

"Aye. Fair enough."

The landlord glanced at me, the furrow remaining. "And you will not be bedsitting with female persons?"

"What? Oh, nah. Maia here is just helping me look for a gaff, like."

"I work at the Night Shelter in Fob Watch Lane," I explained.

"Shelter?" I could see he understood everything that implied. "You will not be drinking alcohol and making nuisances?"

"Nah, nah. All in the past, that, mate."

"Then I am thinking this is acceptable to me." Mr Arain said.

Chapter 42

On the highest point of the bridge over the canal, Baz paused. The tall building that housed Kalsi Clothing had once been a weavers' topshop; now the Kalsis produced cheap clothes for the catalogue industry. Baz had first come here with Vikram, one Christmas holiday after they met at Art College. He remembered meeting Gurinder-ji in the tiny glassed-in booth that served as an office, trying to sound respectful while raising his voice over the constant whir and clatter of the sewing machines.

He'd taken photographs on that first visit, too—the tall building with its mullioned windows reflecting in the sluggish waters of the canal. Vik clowning around on the tow path, holding an orange *Nishan Sahib*, the triangular Sikh flag. Being scolded by his oldest brother.

"You can't see the razor wire," Vik commented later, looking at the prints,

"What razor wire?"

"*Desi* special, *yaar*. They twist it out of family honour and blood ties and work ethic. With special pointy bits that finish with 'you will break your mother's heart.'"

Baz's initial blast of fury over the newspaper article had dissipated, blown away in the disappointment of Maia's rejection and the shock of events at the Skipper. All the same, Vik had to understand that he'd crossed a line. There was other stuff unresolved between them too. Stuff that would fester if they didn't have it out.

Vik's brothers, turbaned and bearded like their father, occupied the office today. As Baz pushed back the sliding door, they looked up from a set of figures they were studying and Mandeep gave him a bright, white smile.

"*Kiddan*, Baz? How's it going?"

"Morning, Mandeep. Vik around anywhere?"

"Down in the stores area. But do us a favour, *haan*? Don't distract him for too long."

Daljit grunted. "Hard enough to get that lazy *khota* to do any work these days."

Baz climbed back down the steep stairs, past the washhouse smell from the steam irons on the middle floor, down to the low-ceilinged store room on the ground floor.

"You see what they have me doing?" Vik said, when he saw Baz. "My brothers are upstairs discussing how they're going to fulfil the latest contract when they haven't got enough machines and two good workers are off sick. Meanwhile, I'm down here humping bales of cloth."

"Quit moaning and I'll give you a hand," Baz said. "That should keep Mandeep off your back."

"It'd take more than that to keep that *sala* off my back." Vik grabbed a bale and carried it over to the hoist. "I keep telling them, *haan*, I'm an artist. I could design fabrics, branch out, take the business in a whole new direction. But no, it's Vikram move this. Vikram shift that."

Baz regarded the back of his head with a mixture of affection and exasperation. To Vik, Baz's almost complete lack of family ties was a source of bafflement and occasional envy. For him, family was something that permeated every aspect of life. "The *desi* telegraph's got branches everywhere, *yaar*. You can't take a dump without someone reporting on how it smells."

"You do realise you caused a shitload of trouble, getting that stuff about me spread all over the papers," he told him.

"Yeah?" Vik grinned. "Trouble was the name of the game, wasn't it?"

Baz held back a rush of anger. "God's sake, Vik, we nearly had a fucking riot at the Skipper."

"You telling me your tame winos read the article?"

"We had a bunch of unemployed lads from Nottingham singing 'Disco Inferno' and a Scotsman the size of a house trying to ram someone's teeth down his throat because they said my mother was a Paki." The corners of Vik's eyes creased up and his mouth twitched, as he fought laughter. "All right! All right! It does sound ridiculous when you put it like that. But sod it, Vik, I have a right to decide who I tell about my past and when."

"*Arré*, I'm sorry. But, hey, look at the publicity we got. The *gori* was right, *yaar*."

Baz's gut gave a sharp twist. "God's sake, Vik, she has a name."

"All right. Maia was right. We have to keep this in the public eye. That way, we drive the agenda."

"It doesn't feel like driving the agenda. It feels more like being a ball in somebody else's game of ping pong. We need a plan, not just going off at half-cock every five minutes. And we've got to find other ways to exhibit our stuff, or what's the point?"

"We will, man. I have a good feeling."

Vik shouldered another bale and ambled towards the hoist. Shit, better just get this over with. "Listen, I talked to Jah Green again this morning. The Rasta who came to the wrap party?"

Vikram's body tensed. Dumping the bail, he snatched up a clipboard and held in front of him like a shield.

"I thought I'd made it clear I don't want anything to do with him."

"Hey, you want to pass up an opportunity, that's your lookout. But you could at least give me some of your contact names, let me see who else might be interested?"

"You're not listening," Vik said. "You want to get mixed up with that charlatan, that's up to you. But you're not dragging my friends and family in with you."

Daljit was right. Vik was as stubborn as a donkey. A stupid *khota* braying at the orchestra because he couldn't play the fiddle.

"Jesus, Vik, what *is* your problem?"

Vik flung the clipboard down and it clanged against the hoist.

"My problem? My problem, *phenchod*, is you don't seem to have the first idea what you're getting yourself into. You think you've found yourself some great guru who's bringing people together—?"

"At least he's trying. He's even calling his Festival *Healing of Nations*—"

Vik slammed a fist into a bale. "*Healing of Nations*? How stupid do you think I am?"

"I don't know? How stupid are you?"

Vik leaned across the stack of bales like a teacher across a desk. "Healing of Nations means cannabis. Marijuana. Pot. Ganja. Whatever you want to call it."

"Okay. I admit. He uses. It's a Rastafarian thing—"

"Is that supposed to make me feel better?"

"It did last time we shared a joint."

The response was off the tip of his tongue before he could stop it. Vikram glanced nervously over his shoulder.

"That is different," he hissed. "And keep your voice down, will you? If Mandeep heard you."

But Baz was too angry to be quiet.

"You know where the Rastas learnt about ganja?" he asked. "From the Hindu *sadhus*, that's where."

Vik spat, and a gobbet of spittle landed between Baz's feet.

"You want to know about the Rastas? I'll tell you about them, shall I? Your fucking *sadhus* have been terrorising my cousin's family in Handsworth. They don't dare let the children out of the house now. They've had their windows broken, their kiddies' bikes stolen—"

"And you're going to tar them all with the same brush? A black man in dreadlocks can't be anything but a drug-dealer and a thief and a hooligan?"

"*Phenchod*! My family lost everything they built up, over three generations in Africa to the—"

"To the what? To the *kaale bandar*? Is that what you were going to say?"

"Shut your face."

"… black monkeys …?"

"I have never said that—"

"No? But Mandeep has, hasn't he?"

Vikram flushed deep mahogany. "I'm not the guardian of my brother's tongue!"

"No? And what about the rest of you? Just because you don't say it, doesn't mean you're not thinking it."

Silence fell like a dead weight. Vik's face contorted, its colour coming and going.

"You don't understand. You will never understand. You're nothing but a *gora*—"

Baz felt a pain in his chest as if Vik was crushing his lungs. *Too Paki to be white. Too* gora *to be* desi. That was supposed to be their joke. The two of them spitting in the eye of a world that tried to pigeonhole him and failed. But was that how Vik had seen him all along? 'Not one of us'? Had the joke been on him from the start?

He dug the crumpled paper out of his pocket and threw it at Vikram.

"Yeah. Such a *gora* they want to kill me for it. As you reminded them. Perhaps you'll be satisfied when they finally succeed."

He couldn't face going back to Paradise Road. He went to his darkroom, intending to start work on a new print of Jah Green's 'Punk Wedding' photograph. But instead he lost himself in developing the film he had taken in the snow-covered ruins of the old cathedral, just for the one stolen image it contained of Maia.

The picture wasn't bad. But it had been shot at waist-level, its framing left to chance, its timing governed by her moment of distraction. Her face was turned away, the shadow cast by the great arch half obscuring it. What he'd hoped for was a picture that showed her face in one of those moments of unguarded openness, when he came close to touching the real Maia. Or one that showed her as the sprite that haunted his dreams. This was neither. But it was all he was likely to get, now she'd made it clear she meant to keep a distance between them. Hell, it was probably cheating to print the image at all. But he was far too bruised to think about such niceties. He'd take his comforts where he could find them.

Coming out of the darkroom a couple of hours later, Baz found Rebeccah leaning on a spade, her face bleached of colour like an overexposed print.

"Hey—what have you been doing to yourself?"

Rebeccah brushed back a lock of hair, leaving a streak of earth across her face. "I took a fancy to having a rockery," she said, "here at the bottom of the slope. I've been trying to lift some turf. It's a bigger job than I realised, though. I think it's going to take me some time."

A thin film of sweat beaded her face, and her lips had a violet tinge.

"I should call a doctor—"

"No, Bhajan. I'll be fine. I just tried to do too much at once, that's all."

He knew her well enough to know there was no point arguing. He steered her to the bench at the base of the wall and made sure she was settled comfortably.

"Tell me what you want done."

"Absolutely not. You have quite enough on your plate. The rockery will simply have to take a little longer, that's all."

"Trust me, a bit of hard labour is just what I need right now."

He knew that she was seeing the dark shadows under his eyes, the lines from lack of sleep. After a moment, she relented, and allowed herself to relax into the warm sunshine. Baz lost himself in the rhythm of digging, letting the ache in his shoulders blunt the ache in his mind.

He and Vik had worked in this garden once, planting a pair of plum trees for Rebeccah. The trees were well grown now. White blossom was beginning to show along their branches, and by mid-summer they would be heavy with tiny, purple-skinned fruit. Rebeccah always remembered to pick a basket of plums for Vik to take to his mother, who would turn them into a sweet, pungent chutney.

He plunged the spade into the heavy, clay soil and felt it jar against solid rock. Two rocks in fact, wedged together. He worked his way round until he'd loosened them, then squatted down and gripped one. Yanking hard, he pulled it free, but his hand slammed into the rough edge of the second. His knuckles flowered red. Swearing under his breath, he dug for a clean handkerchief and wrapped it round his hand.

"You need to be careful with that," a voice behind him said. "I trust your tetanus inoculation is up to date?"

Noordin Kheraj stood on the gravel path. He carried an irregular trapezoid of stone that sparkled in the spring sunlight. Its underlying colour was silver grey, but running through it were patterns in bas relief, shaded pinky brown—some shaped like the cut surface of a lemon, others like the ribs of a fan. It was a stunning object, and Baz found himself staring at it, trying to work out how he would capture those contrasts of texture on film.

Rebeccah rose to her feet. "Noordin, what a lovely surprise."

"A piece of coral limestone. For your rockery," the doctor told her. "It emerged from the ground one year after the monsoon rains washed away the soil in my garden. Such a foolish thing to bring all the way from Zanzibar, but I could not bear to leave it behind."

"Noordin, this is much too beautiful to put in my rockery."

"I insist. It came from a garden and it should return to a garden. Imagine how it will look, surrounded by sedum and saxifrage. Much better than in my dusty old study."

"Then perhaps I may keep it in trust for you."

They wandered off, the Latin names of plants tripping off their tongues as they discussed plans for the rockery. Was he reading too much into this? They had both been alone a long time. And they fitted together like a pair of gloves …

"I have to go," he told them. He slipped an arm through Rebeccah's. "Noordin, will you make sure this woman takes care of herself? She gets these notions in her head and forgets she's not as young as she was—"

"I'm not quite in my grave yet, Bhajan," Rebeccah said.

Baz shook his head. "She was almost blue when I found her," he told the doctor. "Gave me a fright. You must tell her to get herself checked out."

"Bhajan, stop fussing. I'm perfectly fine, am I not?"

A look passed between the two old people, and he realised with a sharp pain that Noordin could easily know more than he did about Rebeccah's health.

He planted a kiss on the top of her head and shook the doctor's hand. "Just promise me you'll let me know before you start moving rocks again."

Chapter 43

After a week or two in the bedsit, Derek's clothes were dirty, he had bags under his eyes and I noticed a hole the size of a five-pence piece in the sole of his shoe. When I asked how the room was, he blew out his cheeks.

"That wallpaper's bollocks, man. I daren't strip it, or that Arain bloke would be after us. So I've had to paint over it. But that pattern's the very devil. Every time I think I've got it covered, the paint dries and these brown and yellow circles start showing through. Like eyes, they are, man. I should think the room's about half an inch smaller all round now, with the amount of paint I've put on."

He laughed, but his eyes looked hollow. When Knoxie came in, his breath reeking of whiskey, he flinched away.

"It is pretty rank," I said.

"To tell you the truth, I kind of like it. And that's the problem."

"Derek, you're not tempted, are you?"

"I've told you, pet. That's all behind us."

He finished his drink and began clattering out mugs, making a show of being busy.

"It's hard, like, when you've been a working man all your life. When you're on the dole, you don't see anyone from one day's end to another. Except maybe the bloke you buy your fags from and that."

"Well, you know we're always glad to see you here."

I thought about the way his 'mates' had given him the cold shoulder, the first night they were here. Just how long he had been to all intents and purposes alone? It wasn't good to be so isolated.

"You still going to the AA?" I asked, hoping I sounded more sympathetic than officious.

He carried on spreading marge on a sliced white loaf, taking exaggerated care to meet the corners.

"It's not easy, being on the road and that. There's not always a meeting where you happen to be." He let the words hang and when he spoke again, his voice was subdued. "If you must know, pet, I haven't been since I left Consett."

"But you can start again, can't you, now you've got your new place? If nothing else, it might be a way to make contact with other people."

"Aye, pet, maybe." He flipped the last slice of bread onto the pile and gave the counter a half-hearted wipe. "Truth is, I thought I might have found a job by now, what with having a settled address and that. But I've been all over looking, and there's nothing doing." He flipped me a sideways look, his eyes half hooded. "I wondered, with my gaff being a Paki place. Maybe they think—"

I stopped dead, the plate of bread in my hands, and turned to face him. "Listen to me, Derek. I'm sure that has nothing to do with it."

"Nah, nah," he responded, a little too slowly. "I'm sure you're right, Maia, man."

"It's the same for everyone these days. Something will come up. You just have to be patient. "

Once the queue at the counter died down, I took a bowl of soup and went to sit at one of the benches. As I ate, my mind turned over the conversation with Derek. Had that scumbag from National Front latched onto him, after the night he turned up here, gone on feeding him his poison? No. Surely what Derek was saying was common currency, *Daily Mail* stuff? No need to go inventing paranoid fantasies.

"Feck, lass, don't they feed you at all? You're shook as the day I first saw you."

The Don Quixote of Fob Watch Lane.

"Hello, Frank. Haven't seen you in ages."

"It's the spring, lovely girl. Come the long days and I get itchy feet, like there's some traveller in me. But I never goes far. More like a homing pigeon, my mam used to say. I flies off, but I always comes home to roost."

He looked thinner, I thought. Or maybe he just had fewer layers of threadbare clothes padding him out. He seemed chipper enough, though.

His eyes narrowed and I saw he was frowning over my shoulder at Derek. "I see that one's got his feet under the table."

It wasn't like Frank to be uncharitable. Could it be he jealous of Derek's new standing?

"He's just helping out, Frank."

"Mebbe." His face cleared and he gave me one of his gappy smiles. "Will you tell your man from me, I'm sorry for his troubles."

"Tell ... Baz, do you mean?"

He worked his stumpy tongue round his mouth as if he was winkling something out from between his teeth. "I may not have been around, but I hears things. The gaffer should know, we're not all in that way of thinking."

I smiled at him tenderly. Little man with a huge heart. "He does know that, Frank, I'm sure."

"Mebbe so, lovely girl. But a man can need reminding from time to time."

Chapter 44

Abena, Maia, Vik: one by one, he'd alienated all of them. Even Rebeccah was keeping secrets from him now. *Desi Art* was finished, the Skipper threatening to turn hostile. If not for Jah Green assuming he could turn up miracles for this damn festival, he'd fuck off and leave them all to it.

At least, thanks to Noordin, he had Paras Shah's phone number. And Paras was happy to talk to him about exhibiting at the *Healing of Nations*. "On one condition. You must allow me to take a cast of your hand."

So, on a day when clouds as black as crows chased each other across a Prussian blue sky, Baz made his way to the dentist's surgery.

"You will remember that for each of my models, I choose a *mudra*," Paras said, once Baz was settled in the workshop behind the examination room. "A position of the hands that I believe says something about them. For you, I think it should be the *dhyani*, the *mudra* of meditation."

The *mudra* of impotent rage would be nearer the mark, Baz thought, though he couldn't expect a peaceable Jaina like Paras to understand that. He let Paras show him how to rest his right hand on top of his left, palms upward, with his thumbs touching. He practised until he could put his hands into position with his eyes closed. "You won't be able to see what you're hands are doing," Paras explained, "so you must be able to find the *mudra* as if blindfold."

While Paras filled the galvanised container with water and stirred in the powder to make the alginate ("very similar to what I use for dental moulds, though this takes a little longer to set"), Baz wet his arms, took off the excess water with a paper towel and sank them into what looked and felt like warm pink yoghurt.

"Move your fingers a little," Paras said. "That will remove any air bubbles. And settle into the *mudra*. Have you found it?"

"I think so."

"Then you must now keep as still as possible."

Almost at once, he could feel the increased resistance against his skin as the alginate set. He had a moment of panic and had to fight the urge to pull his arms free. It was succeeded by a feeling of release, as if he was relinquishing his worries along with his freedom of movement.

"You are comfortable?"

To his surprise, Baz realised that he was.

"In that case, tell me more about your friend's festival." Paras perched on a stool alongside him and folded his hands on the counter.

"Before you commit to anything, I should tell you, Vikram won't have anything to do with it. He thinks the whole thing may be a cover for some kind of Rastafarian dope-fest."

He hadn't meant to say that. Better not to go looking for trouble. But something about the Jaina demanded honesty. Paras blinked at him through his thick glasses. "Do you also think this is a possibility?"

Baz's jaw tensed. "No. I think Jah Green is straight up. But Vikram and I had a bloody great argument about it. He's furious about the whole thing."

"*Arré*! I am grateful to you for telling me this."

"Does that mean that you've changed your mind?"

Paras pushed his glasses back up his nose. "No, indeed. But I think perhaps I should meet this Jah Green for myself sometime."

"Of course."

"Now, Bhajan, I think that the alginate has set. You may begin to wriggle your fingers and draw your arms out."

The gel-like substance clinging to his arms resisted for a second before the surface tension broke with a faint pop and his arms rose out of the mixture. After so long holding them in one position, they seemed to float by themselves. Baz was surprised to see how little residue clung to his skin.

While Baz washed his arms, Paras poured plaster into the alginate, rocking the basin back and forth to ensure that the whole space was filled. When he was done, he led Baz through into another room, where three more sculptures waited in various stages of development. One was a plaster, straight from the casting process, and Baz was fascinated to see the detail that was reproduced—fingerprints, pores, fine hairs, all clearly visible.

"From this positive cast, you see." Paras explained, "I must make a negative mould, also of plaster. And into that I put the slip, which is a sort of liquid clay. And the slip dries to make a sculpture that can be glazed and fired."

"It must take hours."

"Days. Weeks perhaps, if the piece is very complex."

The second sculpture was a ceramic blank, in a partial stage of decoration, its colours muted. The third was glazed and fired. The complex patterns covered the hand and wrist with the delicacy of a lace glove—cobalt blue against the pure white of the underlying glaze.

"Tell me," Paras asked, "do you recognise this hand?"

Baz looked more closely. It was a left hand, the little finger and the ring finger touching the thumb, the index and middle fingers upright. Even through the decoration, you could see that the hand from which it had been modelled was lined and callused. The ring finger bore the imprint of a ring, the setting of its simple round stone picked out with Paras' delicate brush strokes.

"In the *prana mudra,* the *mudra* of life," Paras said. "It seemed appropriate for a healer."

"It's Noordin's hand, isn't it?"

"Very good. Very good indeed." Paras beamed at him, his glasses slithering down his nose. "Noordin has been most kind to me, ever since I came to this country. He is a man who has had everything taken from him, yet there is no shred of bitterness in his heart."

"He always puts other people first," Baz agreed.

Paras brought his hands together, as if making *Namaste.* "You tell me that you and Vikram quarrelled over Jah Green. Forgive me for interfering, but have you made peace with him again?"

Baz flinched as if Paras had prodded an exposed nerve. "It's not as easy as that," he said.

"Forgiveness is seldom easy, my friend. Yet without it, we are like someone nursing a bad tooth until the pain becomes too great to bear."

A hundred yards from the surgery, Baz crested a bridge and looked down into the canal. On the parapet, a faded circle of white paint marked the spot where fire wardens had drawn water to douse the fires of the Blitz. A rusted supermarket trolley poked out of the water, arse end up.

From here, the canal crawled a mile through weeds and silt before it emptied into the basin at Draper's Fields. A winding half a mile along, it slouched past Kalsi Clothing. And Vik …

To hell with Paras Shah and his parables of forgiveness. The only problem with not speaking to Vik was that, without him, he had no way to track down Mohan Chand. All because Vikram was too stubborn to give him a sodding phone number.

An empty cigarette packet blew against his leg and Baz stooped to pick it up. After a moment, he fumbled in his pocket for a pencil, tore the packet open and wrote 'Miss you, Vikram, you miserable bastard.' He dropped it in the water and turned aside, not waiting to see whether it snagged on the trolley or whether, against the odds, the canal carried it on its way.

Chapter 45

Walking through the Lower Precinct, I was pulled up short by the window display of City Pram. Pushchairs, prams, double buggies: the whole paraphernalia of child rearing. Could I really be pushing one of those in a few months' time?

"You don't have to go through with this," Tom had said, last time we'd talked. "You're only, what? Ten, eleven weeks pregnant?"

But already I was feeling as if it were too late to change my mind. According to the book hidden under my mattress the baby was two inches long. Foetal nerve cells were multiplying fast. Synapses were forming. It had reflexes. Soon I was going to feel the baby move. That was a whole different matter to ridding oneself of a clump of undifferentiated cells.

"Maia, having a kid on your own is a big deal even without all the other shit you're having to wade through. No one's going to think the worse of you if you decide to have an abortion."

No one, I thought. No one except myself. No one else to speak for Ossie.

Standing outside the shop now, I watched a couple move towards the window and scrutinise a big Silver Cross with maroon upholstery. The man had his arm round the woman. The woman's belly swelled the outline of her coat. My reflection floated in the window, a ghostly interloper. Hardly mother material. Jeans worn through at one knee. Oversized jumper snatched from the charity bag. Spiky hair, starting to grow out.

In my head, Ossie's reflection joined mine, his hands resting on my shoulders.

"Where I come from, *nosisi*," I heard him say, "if a man goes away to work, or he gets sick, all the neighbours will see to it that his children are looked after. We say a child is a child of the whole village."

Trouble is, Ossie, I don't have a village. There's just me. And I don't know if I can do this on my own.

I shut my eyes against the sharp sting of tears. When I opened them again, Ossie was gone. In his place stood a thickset guy with a shaven head and a skinny kid who had tattoos growing over his skin like ivy. Behind them, two or three others in Levis and bovver boots had shed their donkey jackets to display knock-off Ben Shermans and red braces.

"Hey, it's the Paki-lover."

"Whadja doing here, Paki-lover?"

"Got a bun in the oven, have you?"

It was just aimless spite. They couldn't know. But a numbing cold settled in the small of my back and my face flamed. Gary stared as if I'd grown two heads.

"Fuck me, she is too. Look at her. The Paki-lover's up the duff."

Beefy clenched his fist and leaned towards me. I could see the pustules on his acne erupting from his bull neck.

"Got a Paki in there, have you, slag?"

Anger obliterated every other feeling. I stared right at him, forcing myself to meet his eyes. He drew back his fist, aiming for my belly. I caught a flash of metal that might or might not have been from his skull and crossbones ring and felt a moment of bowel-loosening fear. Then a pair of policemen appeared, walking towards us like angels in blue serge. Gary shoved Beefy in the small of the back and the four of them wheeled away, their thumbs in their belts. Just before they merged with the crowd,

Beefy looked back.

"Just remember. That kid comes out black and we'll come after you. You and your half-caste brat."

Chapter 46

When had he last managed more than four hours sleep? Baz couldn't remember. Sleep wouldn't come these days, at least not at night. He'd dropped off on the top deck of a bus and woken to find himself creeping through traffic.

Blinking sleep from his eyes, he saw a knot of skinheads run into the road from the Precinct. One was Gary, the blue tinge on his skin unmistakeable even from up here. The others he didn't know. He watched them cross the road, to where more shaven heads lolled against Godiva's plinth.

As Baz watched, a man sidled up to Gary. Not a skinhead, this one, but a thin-faced weasel of a man in a brown suit and a trilby. As the bus crawled round the square, he took some leaflets out of his pocket and started handing them out to the prone and semi-prone figures around the statue.

Even before the bus stopped, Baz was down the stairs and off. He plunged into the traffic, forcing a taxi to swerve and blare its horn. Another bus crossed in front of him and by the time it had passed, the Weasel had gone to ground.

Gary stood in the lee of the statue, a bundle of leaflets in his hand. Baz gave a shout and the kid wheeled round, dropped the leaflets and took to his heels, running over the green, across Pepper Lane and into the narrow confines of Hay Lane. Baz snatched up a leaflet and gave chase, feeling the cobbles under his feet, hearing the metal segs on Gary's boots clatter like horses' hooves. He reached the High Street in time to see his quarry dive into the twisting alleyway beyond, and ran on, no longer sure what he would do if he caught up with him. When the alley emptied into Salt Lane, there was no sign of Gary.

Baz stopped, breathing heavily, and listened for the sound of Gary's boots, but all he could hear was the rumble of traffic.

The leaflet he had crumpled in his hand was crudely printed, black on off-white paper, with a couple of Union Jacks across the top. Underneath, in large letters, was the headline:

```
               CALL TO ARMS.
   Young Patriots, you are soldiers in a war.
      The colours of your uniforms are the
              colours of your skin.
    If you have the courage to fight for your
               race and your nation,
                    JOIN NOW!
```

Underneath it said, `Recruitment Drive`, with a date, a time and a venue.

His stomach heaved. He had to lean over a wall and drag air into his lungs to stop himself from puking. When he had command of himself again, he looked again at the flyer.

If nothing else, here was hard evidence.

Baz pressed the buzzer on the duty desk and asked for Sergeant Conway.

"You asked us to come and tell you if we had any new information," he said, when the Sergeant appeared. "These were being given out on Broadgate this morning."

He handed over the leaflet. The sergeant took it and read it methodically, peering through his half-frame specs. When he had finished, he pushed it back across the table.

"Extremely distasteful, I agree, sir. But I fail to see how it connects with your vandalism case."

Baz took a deep breath. No point losing his temper like Vik and getting himself thrown out.

"The man handing out the leaflets was the same man who led the demonstration against the opening of our exhibition. The one whose picture appeared in the paper. He's also been to the night shelter where I work, stirring up trouble among the men."

"What sort of trouble?"

"Telling them it's all the fault of the Asian community that they have no homes. That sort of thing."

"Go on."

Conway's face gave nothing away. Baz cleared his throat and carried on.

"Well, like I say, he was talking to the skinheads round Lady Godiva. One in particular, a kid called Gary Treddle. I used to know him." He could hear himself talking faster and faster, sounding less and less convincing. "He's always liked messing about with fire. I've heard him threaten other Asian businesses …"

"Mr Lister, all I am hearing is that none of these people look favourably on our Asian community. That's hardly news. None of this connects to you or your gallery—"

"I had an anonymous letter," Baz said.

The sergeant took off his glasses.

"Indeed. And when was this?"

"After the newspaper article. The one about my mother being killed in a fire. It said 'next time you won't be so lucky.'"

The policeman held out his hand. "May I see it?"

Baz felt his colour deepen. "I threw it away."

Conway sat back with a grunt. "Mr Lister, I don't see how you can expect us to help you if you insist of disposing of evidence! You tell me that the windows of your gallery have been defaced, but you clean it up before you bother to tell us about it. And now we have this anonymous letter that disappears before you can show it to me." He stood up, pushing back his chair. "Please, don't waste my time any further unless you have something concrete to show me."

"What about this?" Baz said. He brandished the leaflet in Conway's face and the policeman lowered himself into his chair once more. "Isn't this something concrete?"

"Mr Lister, however you or I might feel about statements like that, the plain fact is, there is very little I can do about people who use a photocopier to distribute a few leaflets."

"What about the Race Relations Act? Surely this ... filth ... constitutes racial harassment?"

"I expect so, yes."

"They're advertising when and where they're going to be recruiting. You could go and arrest them, can't you?"

The sergeant rubbed the bridge of his nose. "Mr Lister, believe me, I do not have the manpower to spare to attend political meetings, however strong the temptation might be to do so."

Baz stared at him. The sergeant's face remained unmoved. Was this a simple statement about overstretched resources, or a coded warning that he was on enemy territory?

"Well, thank you for your time, sergeant."

"No problem. Oh, and Mr Lister, next time, perhaps you might think of coming to us first, before you destroy the evidence."

As he stood on the steps outside the police station, fat drops of rain began to fall. He was tired, so tired. And he had nowhere left to go.

Chapter 47

I didn't dare follow Gary and Beefy back up the Precinct and risk walking into them on their own turf. Instead, I turned right and trudged round the long curve of Corporation Street, following the all-but-vanished line of the old city walls. Spring sunshine lit up inky black clouds and shone spotlights on the lime trees shaking out their new spring leaves. The road seemed endless.

As I reached the place where the five storeys of the de Vere Hotel spanned the road, the wind gusted. A cloud blotted out the sun and rain fell, fast and fierce. I had to make a decision fast. Turning inwards towards the Cathedral would give me more cover, but it meant going that much closer to Broadgate. The skinheads belonged in the concrete jungle to the west, though. I'd never seen them in the ancient lanes behind their favourite roost. I flipped an imaginary coin, and turned up the flight of steps leading to Hill Top.

I was half way up the cobbled rise when the rain turned to hail. The effect was as if someone had cranked up the gradient. My feet scrabbled for purchase on a surface made slick with frozen ball bearings. By the time I'd struggled to the top, the hailstones were the size of marbles. People were huddled together under the canopy that joined the old cathedral to the new. Holding my arms over my head to protect my face, I ran for cover and all-but collided with the familiar folds of a grey army greatcoat.

"Maia! You all right?"

Hail thundered against the copper roof and fell like glass beads down the open sides. Baz gripped my hands. Back at Paradise Road, the past couple of weeks, we'd made sure we were never alone together for long, kept conversation strictly utilitarian. But here, taken unawares, I could feel the current flowing between us.

"Shall we go inside?" Baz yelled over the noise. "You're frozen."

We pushed our way through the glass door in the base of the West Window. As it swung shut behind us, the fusillade of hailstones was reduced to a muffled drum roll and the sound of the organ swelled to fill its place. The quiet made us shy again and both of us looked away, anxious to avoid each other's eyes.

"You been in here before?" Baz asked.

"Once, for my graduation ceremony."

As I said it, the shadow of Ossie slipped between Baz and me. I remembered how we'd sat in groups by course and degree, arranged in alphabetical order. Us Bachelors of Science in our blue hoods on the left hand side. Ossie away on the right among the red hoods. Master of Arts. No one there for him among the guests ranged at the back or peering in from the steps of the old cathedral. He joined my parents and me for lunch afterwards and let my mother lecture him on African affairs.

Baz and I made our way up the nave, Ossie's shadow keeping pace. The main walls were vertical louvres of plain grey stone, angled towards the towering figure of Christ behind the altar. Like some conjuror's trick, the whole edifice to rest on pairs of pillars that vanished at the base in impossible stiletto points.

I don't know how to do right by both of you, I thought. Ossie, you're my best friend but you're the other side of the world. And you never asked for this. You gave away everything before you left. A clean start, nothing to tie you down. Least of all a child.

And Baz, God, do you remember how I said you carry other people's problems on your shoulders? I know why. Because half the time you make it so easy for us. As if we can just go on piling stuff on you and you'll just go on taking it. But this baby is nothing to do with you.

Baz touched my shoulder and a shock ran down my arm. I turned towards him and he pointed back the way we had come. We were standing in the chancel. The slats in the louvred walls were angled towards us now, their recessed windows filled with vertical slits of colour, vibrant as a diffraction pattern.

We crossed behind the main altar. Neither of us said anything, but I felt my mood lift. As we came back to the West Window, the notes of the organ died away. The sun broke through the last of the storm clouds, illuminating the curved wall on our left. Jewel-like colours radiated around a central lozenge of pale gold, as though the organ were playing chords of light.

In front of me, I could see the breadth of Baz's shoulders, the grey wings of his coat. In the past couple of weeks, he'd taken to twisting his long ponytail into a knot at the back of his head. Not so easy now to mistake him for a southern European.

He crossed the stone floor and stopped by a limestone boulder that had been hewn into a font. When he touched its roughened surface, I realised I had stopped breathing.

"We all think that we can wipe the slate clean, don't we? That we won't make the same wretched mistakes that our parents did. But in all probability, we're just going to find a whole new way of screwing things up."

My throat constricted. I reached out, not quite daring to touch him.

"Does that mean you'd never have children?"

He took such a long time answering I wanted to will the words back into my mouth.

"I dunno. No, I think one day ... maybe."

I ran my tongue over my teeth to try and bring some moisture to my mouth.

"If you could wish for one thing for your children, what would it be?" I asked.

This time he turned to face me, his face assured.

"To be able to walk in their own skins. To be proud of who they are."

As if someone had overheard, I felt a touch on my shoulder, and a whisper in my ear like a blessing. *Remember,* nosisi: *a child is the child of the whole village.*

Chapter 48

The sun was shining out of a blue sky again, as if no such things as hailstorms had ever existed. A plan was starting to form in his mind, born out of the first embers of optimism. Could he use his camera to record the skinheads' activities? Get their faces on film so that when trouble came, he had a ready-made rogues' gallery to help identify the perpetrators? It wasn't much, but it would make him feel less like a punch bag.

But right now, he wanted to spin out this time with Maia, make the most of every second before the next storm clouds gathered. He wanted to put off the moment when she told him, sorry, this had been very pleasant, but it changed nothing. Tucking her arm through his, he said, "Listen, do you have any pressing desire to have Iain's root vegetable hotpot again tonight?"

"Not really, but I suppose I ought—"

"How do you fancy fish and chips?"

Her eyes widened and her mouth formed into an O. Just for a moment she looked like a child who's been offered a trip to the sweetshop.

"Oh, my God. I haven't had anything as decadent as fish and chips in months."

He grinned. "C'mon. We'll get supper at Fishy Moore's, then I'll deliver you to the Skipper."

They walked in companionable silence down Priory Street

past the Polytechnic. As they passed the Students' Union, Maia stopped.

"Did I hear you say you were looking for Mohan?"

"Yeah ...?"

She pointed to a bulletin board announcing forthcoming events.

"That's his mates' band, isn't it?"

In the middle of the board, a poster on orange paper announced:

```
          CHAK DE PHATTE!
          ASIAN SOC DISCO
          Live Music from
                SONA
          8pm till midnight
          Thursday 9th April
```

"Bugger me." He gave her arm a squeeze. "Seems like you're my good luck charm."

Plenty of time to get back there, he thought. He could even get changed first. If Mohan wasn't there (and there was a good bet he would be) the band would at least be able to put him in touch. Better still, they might be interested in playing the Festival themselves.

Maia gave him a dry, sideways look. "So while I'm spending a night at the Skipper," she said, "you're swanning off to a Bhangra gig?"

"Not to put too fine a point on it, yes."

He gave her a lop-sided grin of apology and she prodded a finger to his chest. "Just make sure you find out where they're playing next. Bloody brilliant, they were. I'd love to hear them again."

"Is that a date, then?"

"Maybe." But her face was inscrutable again.

They bought their fish and chips and crossed the road, past the weathered remains of Priory Gate and into Lady Herbert's Garden. Baz spread his coat on a bench still damp from the hail, and they sat together, their shoulders touching. Maia pulled off a hunk of haddock with batter and ate it.

"God, I'm telling you, there's only so much vegetable hotpot and lentil bake a girl can take." She stuffed a chip in her mouth and rolled her eyes heavenward. "What is it about eating chips with your fingers that makes them taste so good?"

"Has to be 'cos you can lick them afterwards." He demonstrated, drawing out the action, and watched her pupils dilate. He could kiss her now, he thought, and she wouldn't stop him. Or he could just go on enjoying the moment, savouring it, not doing anything to spoil it. He leaned back against the bench, his eyes narrowed, studying the slope of her cheekbone, the delicate pallor of her skin.

A soggy weight landed on his shoulder. A limp chip lay in a green mess like pigeon shit. And the smell …

"Curry sauce. I fucking hate curry sauce."

Two more chips landed, one on Baz's leg, another on Maia's arm. Baz got to his feet, his legs unfolding till he was at his full height. Two young kids, nine or ten at most, were the grass, their own pokes of chips still steaming. One backed off, but the other stood his ground.

"Bleeding Paki," he yelled. "Why don't you fuck off home?"

Baz could have mashed their faces in it, rubbed it in till they smelt curry for a week. He made to grab their collars and they legged it out the gate and back down Hales Street.

Shit, they were kids. Just kids. He took out a handkerchief and started dabbing at the sauce, smearing it round. After a minute, Maia took the handkerchief from him and began to blot the mess more effectively. When her eyes met his, a bubble of desperate laughter begin in his gut and rose up out of him. A moment later, she was laughing too. They leaned against each other shaking helplessly, tears in the corners of their eyes.

"God, though, Baz. Ten year olds," Maia said, as sobriety returned. "Where do they learn it from? They don't spring from the womb, fully-fledged bigots."

Where? They drank it with their mother's milk, heard it as they were dandled on their father's knee, copied it from older brothers and sisters.

"How long before they turn into little Garys?" she asked. "How long before they're chasing Pakis through the Precinct and marching around with banners saying 'Protect Rights for Whites'?"

"God knows. Three, four years at the most?"

A cold shudder ran through him. He'd been lucky, he knew that. Most of the time when he was out and about, his 'get-out clause' protected him. Other people lived with this sort of thing day in, day out. And now, wearing his hair in a knot, sitting here with fair-haired, pale-skinned Maia, he was a target too. And so was she.

She laid her hand on his and he felt some of the knots inside him unravel. "Frank had a message for you. I almost forgot. He said, 'tell the gaffer, we're not all in that way of thinking.'"

"He's a good man, is Frank. If we just had a few more like him and a few less like those little sods." He rubbed his hand over his face. "How do we stop it, Maia? How in the hell do we stop it?"

Chapter 49

"You look cheerful," Tom said when I got to the Skipper that night.

Was I? I had a momentary flash of the terror and fury I'd felt confronting the skinheads outside City Pram. God, was that only a few hours ago? Almost without my noticing it, Baz had lifted me out of a quagmire. Or maybe I'd caught some of the altered mood in the Skipper.

A different sort of punter had come through the doors shortly after opening.

"I see yellow's on the broom again," Charlie Singer said, when he saw them. "They're tinkers, wench. Travellers."

They weren't the most restful bunch. Some of the transients muttered that they hadn't expected to share with a bunch of bloody thieving pikeys. A chippy from Northampton nearly started a war when he accused a tinker of stealing his tools (found shortly after, safe under his mate's coat). And at one point, one of the tinkers reached into his pocket for a blade, threatening to chiv a cousin over some ancient vendetta, and had to be restrained by members of his own family.

But they were quick, bright and sparkling—like silver trout in a pool of flatfish. They had burnished skin and heather in their voices. And their high spirits were catching. Charlie Singer played 'John Barleycorn' and 'Donnybrook Fair', and one of the tinkers sang and another got out a penny whistle. Tonight, no one complained about the music.

I found my foot tapping along as we dished out what seemed like twice the usual number of cups of tea. Singing was thirsty work.

"Pity Derek's not here," I said, when Tom joined me in the kitchen. "He'd enjoy this."

"Where is he, anyway? I thought he'd become a permanent fixture."

"Don't know. It has to be a good sign, though, doesn't it? If he's too busy to come down here? Maybe he's got himself a job."

The whole room was roaring along to a chorus of 'The Rambling Rover', when Tom came out of the office, looking puzzled, and said someone was on the phone, asking for me.

"At least I think it's for you," he said. "I can hardly make out what he's saying."

I shut the door behind me to shut out the clapping and stamping, and picked up the phone. "Hello? Maia Hassett here."

An indistinct voice fizzed out of the phone. "Why you are bringing this madman to my house?"

For a moment, I clung to the notion that this was a bizarre wrong number. Then the voice continued, "You are the young woman from Shelter, please? You are bringing me this Mr Paterson?"

I swallowed hard, my short-lived bubble of euphoria shattering. "Mr Arain. Is there a problem?"

"There is very much a problem. There is a problem of drinking. You say he is not drinking but he is all the time drinking drinking. And now he will ruin me with smashing and bashing in bedsitting flat."

"Mr Arain, please, slow down a minute. I don't understand—"

"I want him out of my house. Now. If I see him, I am calling police. Are you understanding me, please?"

"Yes, but—"

The sound of the phone banging down exploded in my ear. I put the handset down and stared at the cluttered notice board. It couldn't be true. Not after everything Derek had promised. Yet what reason could Mr Arain have to make up a story like that?

Tom stuck his head round the door. "Everything okay?"

"I'm … not sure. Derek's had an argument with his landlord. And it sounds like he's drinking again."

Our eyes turned to the vacant spot behind the counter. Not such an optimistic sign after all.

Tom put his hand on my shoulder. "It's probably all a fuss about nothing, kiddo. You know how these things get blown out of all proportion."

"Yeah. Sure."

"Nothing we can do about it tonight, anyway."

"No."

But a knot of anxiety lodged itself in the pit of my stomach.

I must have dozed off after locking up, because I woke to a volley of banging on the outside door. Tom was already awake, his legs dangling from the top bunk as he let himself down. I scrambled up and together we tumbled into the main room.

Tom put his eye to the spy hole and turned around, looking startled.

"It's Derek."

"What? Then let him in."

I reached for the bolts, but Tom forestalled me.

"You know the rules Maia. No one's allowed in after lock up."

"Don't be ridiculous. It's Derek."

I made another feint for the door and Tom blocked me again.

"He's got a bottle in his hand, Maia. If you ask me, I'd say he's been drinking pretty hard."

Another tattoo of knocking rattled the door, raising groans from the dormitory.

"What do you usually do if this happens?" I whispered.

"If they won't go away, we have to call the police."

"Tom, no! Not for Derek."

"Then you see if you can talk to him."

He stepped aside and I laid my hands on the cold, blank surface of the door and peered through the spy hole.

"Derek?"

"Maia, man, is that you?"

"Derek, we can't let you in. It's after lock up."

"I know, man, but I've got nowhere else to go." Through the spy hole, I saw him look away, shamefaced. "I've messed up, Maia. I've messed up. But I'll put it right, if you'll just let us in."

"Don't, Maia," said Tom.

"You can come back in the morning—"

"No!" Derek smacked his two hands against the door. Seen through the spyhole, his face seemed to seethe forward. "Maia, man, you don't understand. That Paki bastard's set the police on me. If I stay out here they're going to find me for sure."

"Derek, what have you done?"

His glance twitched away, scanning the alley. "Let us in and I'll tell you."

I glanced over my shoulder at Tom, who signalled a desperate 'no'.

"It's all a stupid misunderstanding, pet. Honest."

I took a step back and pulled Tom away with me. "It's not like he's just another resident," I said. "He's practically one of us."

"That's not exactly true—"

"Maia, man, give us a chance to explain," the voice on other side pleaded.

Tom and I stared at each other, out of our depth and frightened.

"For God's sake, Tom," I hissed. "He's rolled up his sleeves and helped us often enough, hasn't he? Even once he had his own place."

"But he's drunk. You don't know what he'll—"

"I'm letting him in."

"Maia, don't be bloody stupid."

I tugged at the bolts. Hearing the sound, Derek pressed forward.

"I promise you won't regret this, pet."

"I'm calling Baz," Tom said.

"Fine. If you're going to grass me up, shut up and get on with it."

The last bolt shot back. As Tom made for the office, I pulled open the door and stood squarely in front of it.

"You need to give me the bottle first," I said, dragging as much authority into my voice as I could manage.

Derek dodged past me, still clutching his bottle, moving on the balls of his feet like a boxer.

"Don't you worry yourself, pet. I'm not like them in there. I'm not going to start a fight or be sick all over the floor."

But when I tried to reach for the bottle, he jerked his hand away and hugged it to him, his lips pulled back into something like a snarl.

Chapter 50

A little after eight, Baz made his way back to the Lanch Students' Union. He'd been back to Paradise Road and dug out the grey tonic suit and narrow black tie that made him look like a stray member of The Specials. At the door of the bar where the gig was being held, he submitted to having a red star stamped on the back of his hand. Inside, he could see a disco set up to one side and, at the back of the room, oversized speakers crowding a small stage. A familiar figure in a neat black turban squatted at the back, fiddling with some leads.

Baz made his way across the dance floor, through scattered couples bopping listlessly to Kim Wilde, and tapped Mohan on the shoulder. The young man glanced round.

"Hey, man. What are you doing here?"

"Saw the poster. Thought I'd come and check you out. Not very busy is it? I think those guys on the door may be trying to bounce people in."

Mohan grinned. "Don't you worry. Once Sona come on, they'll be fighting them off."

"I believe you." He smiled, remembering Maia dancing barefoot at the gallery. "Listen, now I've caught you, there's something I wanted to talk about. Can we arrange to meet up sometime?"

Mohan glanced at his watch. "Soon as I've finished soldering this jack, I'm going to grab myself something to eat. I've got about twenty minutes. You can join me if you like."

"Sure."

While Mohan finished his wiring, Baz looked round the room. The couples on the dance floor were Asian mostly; some, but not all, girls dancing together while boys looked on. But unlike the party-goers at the gallery, they were dressed uniformly in jeans and t-shirts, indistinguishable from the students propping up the bar outside. Baz loosened his tie and shoved it in his pocket.

"There," Mohan said; "Mic was cutting out when we did our sound check but that should sort it. Time for a pie and a pint."

Baz bought them both a pint, while Mohan got himself pie and chips. They took a seat near the snooker tables, where the clack of balls blended with the atonal beeps of the games machines.

"How's your course going?" Baz asked.

"Driving me nuts, man," Mohan replied, between mouthfuls. "It was okay while we were doing welding and that. But now it's Social and Life Skills." He pulled a disgusted face. "This morning, right, they had us videoing ourselves doing interviews." He leaned back, surveying the students milling round, drinking pints or cueing balls or playing video games. "Sometimes I wonder if I'd have been better off staying on at school, going to Poly or University like this lot. But then the volunteers at your place, they've all got degrees, haven't they? And they can't get jobs either. So what's the point?"

Baz shrugged. "People are always going to need welders, aren't they?"

"You'd think so, wouldn't you?" He took a long swig of his pint and dug into his pie again. "So what did you want to talk to me about? Not my YOP, I'll bet."

Baz explained again about Jah Green's invitation.

Mohan stopped, a forkful of chips halfway to his mouth. "I'd love to, man," he said. "Seriously. But it's going to depend whether I can get access to equipment. Climax were cool about my doing stuff in their machine shops. But I'm not there any more. And my course is finishing soon, so I won't be able to use the college workshops either. After that, it's back to whether I get a job or not."

"Like you said, it's the same for everyone."

"If I don't get a job, my dad will say it serves me right for not listening to him," Mohan said. "He never wanted me to be an engineer. He doesn't think there's any future in it. That's what he was, you know? He was a machine tool fitter at Triumph, till they shut down the plant. Now he can't get work anywhere. He's sweeping up, nights, here at the Poly. A *churha*, just like his father."

"What does he want you to do?" Baz asked.

"My auntie and uncle, right, they have this sweet shop up the Foleshill Road." Mohan pushed his plate away. "That's where my dad thinks I should go. But it drives me crazy. You have to stand there all day, smiling and smiling, with the *goras* either despising you or treating you like a stop on some Asian tourist trail. And then there's the high caste types, who won't touch your food 'cos your family used to be sweepers." A grin sparked across his face. "I guess I could always go and work for the Kalsis. Humping bales with Vik, what do you think?"

Baz felt his mouth go dry. "You don't get any high caste shit from the Kalsis, then?"

"Nah." He speared a forkful of chips and moved it round his plate, mopping up the last of the gravy. "My parents never used to talk about caste when we were growing up. But I always knew Gurinder-ji was good to my mum and my aunties. Some of the other women could be a bit funny, but if Gurinder-ji heard anything, he'd soon put a stop to it. Didn't make him too popular, sometimes."

Mohan's words broke over Baz like a wave of cold water. He didn't say anything to Mohan—how could he?—but, inside his head, voices squabbled back and forth.

That's the man you accused of being a bigot.

I never said anything about caste …

You said enough.
Okay, maybe I jumped to conclusions …
Made sweeping generalisations. Thought in stereotypes. Tarred everyone with the same brush.
All right! Enough!
Mohan had got to his feet and was looking at him oddly.
"You okay, man?"
"Yeah, sure. I was just … thinking about something else."

Sona were every bit as good as Baz remembered from the night of the party. True to Mohan's prediction, by the time their set finished at eleven, the dance floor was packed and the bouncers had their hands full.

The effect of a couple of hours' energetic dancing was to purge some of the poison that had been clogging his system. On the way back to Paradise Road, his limbs aching, he told himself he would go see Vik in the morning, try and sort things out between them. Just as soon as he'd had some sleep and cleared his head.

He reached the quiet of the empty house and let himself into the darkened office. As he fumbled for the light switch, the phone began the ring. He reached to silence it before it woke the rest of the house and heard Tom's voice, laced with an edge of panic.

"Baz. Thank God. I'm sorry to ask you, mate, but can you get yourself down here? We've got a right bugger's muddle on our hands."

Chapter 51

Something in Derek's eyes reminded me of a dog we once had. Soft as anything most of the time, but go near him when he had a bone and he'd growl and snap.

"I thought you'd stopped drinking," I said.

"You don't begrudge a gadgie a drink, do you? After the day I've had?"

He prowled across the floor, bottle clutched close to his chest. I sat on one of the benches, hoping that, by being still myself, I might calm him.

"What's been going on, Derek? Mr Arain called here."

He made a hawking sound in his throat and took a swig from the bottle. "Stupid Paki. There's no talking to them, mind. I told him it was all a misunderstanding, but he wouldn't have it."

"Derek—!" I bit down my retort. Until I had that bottle off him, I needed him on side. "What happened?"

He swung away, pacing between the rows of tables, his stained donkey jacket hanging loose from his shoulders. Tom came out of the office and telegraphed that he'd called Baz. I was glad. Even if Baz was angry, even if he fired me, I couldn't handle this on my own. I'd been stupid ever to imagine I could.

Derek was marching up and down, his gestures wilder than ever. He swept past, his arms held out wide, as if trying to catch me in the net of his fantasies.

"You know, it might not be such a bad thing after all. That

was no sort of place, that, all cramped into one room and a Paki for a landlord. This could be my big chance. Find somewhere decent, show 'em what I can make of it. Then they'll have to give us a job."

"Derek, you're not even going to get your deposit back, let alone your rent in advance."

He stopped for a minute, swaying. He cocked a finger in my direction. "I should skelp it out of him, stupid Paki. Knock his bloody teeth out and take it back in gold."

"What?"

The words hit me like a slap in the face. I stared at him in disgust and he caught my look and subsided a little. "Nah, nah. Fair dos. I did do some damage, I suppose." Then he brightened again. "Not to worry. We'll go back to that charity."

"Derek, for crying out loud, no one's going to—"

But he wasn't listening.

"They'll see I can't be blamed for what happened. Maybe even give us a bit more, set us up somewhere more suitable, like."

I felt as if I'd opened the door to let the cat in and found myself trapped with a tiger. When Baz appeared in the still-open doorway, I could have wept with relief. He moved forward, dropping his coat over a bench and taking in the scene as he came. His long shadow, cast by the light in the alleyway, drew a line across the floor. Derek finished one leg of his prowl and recoiled as he came face to face with a man considerably larger than he was. He smiled a humourless smile.

"Evening … Gaffer."

He left a split second pause before the 'gaffer', gave it a fractional overemphasis. But Baz showed no sign of having heard.

"You need to hand over that bottle," he said. "Or I'll have to ask you to leave."

"I don't know as I want to do that."

Derek did a quick about turn and sidestepped into the next aisle. Baz circled after him, as if he had all the time in the world to sort this out.

"It's my understanding that you shouldn't be in here at all, seeing as you got here after lock up."

Derek's face turned a deeper shade of puce. "Do you think I give a monkey's for your poxy rules?"

"Perhaps not. But either you hand over that bottle, or you leave quietly, or I'm calling the police. Now."

"All I want is a quiet drink."

"I think you've had more than enough to drink—"

"And you can keep your neb out of my business!"

I was a few feet away, in the same aisle as Derek, Baz the other side of the table in the next aisle. Derek's eyes swung from Baz to me and back again. He still had the neck of the bottle clasped in his hand. I saw him swing his arm back and crack the base against the side of the bench. The time that followed seemed to be sliced into hundredths of a second, each one freeze-framed before my eyes. I waited for his hand to come back up, a jagged-edged weapon pointed straight at us. But it didn't happen. The bottle didn't shear at the neck like it did on the telly. It shattered into a thousand diamond-edged slivers, most of them now clenched in Derek's fist. Derek's head swung round and his mouth dropped open, as the first scarlet gobbets of blood dripped from his fingers. He tried to open his hand but the glass had dug into his flesh.

"Someone get his hand over his head," Baz yelled. "Tom, get Dr Kheraj."

My feet had grown suckers and were holding me tight to the floor. Tom appeared in the door of the office, caught sight of the blood and turned green. Baz made to vault over the tables. But I was still the closest—and perhaps the one Derek was most likely to tolerate near him.

He'd dropped to his knees and was staring at his lacerated flesh. I took hold of his arm and it moved without resistance, like the arm of a teddy bear that had lost its stuffing. I felt a stickiness spreading over my fingers. Baz appeared at my side with a First Aid kit.

"I hope to God I know what I'm doing," he muttered. He took a crepe bandage and tied a rough tourniquet round his arm. By now, Derek's head was down and his back heaved.

"Bucket!" Baz roared, and Tom appeared with a bucket in time to catch the worst of it.

The glass had missed the delicate webbing of veins on the wrist. With the hand elevated and the tourniquet in place, the tide of blood was stemming. Yet the shards of glass remained, like the bizarre mutations of a horror film, some experiment gone wrong. I wanted to look away, but my eyes held on, focusing, zooming in, till I could see the pink edges of the wound, fluted like the lips of an oyster. Then a line of creamy white. And below that, a layer of burgundy red, like a steak cut by a butcher's knife.

I felt my own stomach contract and almost let go the arm. Derek had no strength to hold it up on his own. I felt the weight as it dropped and held on, and the moment of nausea passed.

It could have been minutes or hours that I sat, holding up Derek's arm and trying to empty my mind. But eventually I heard Dr Kheraj's voice and turned to see him—crumpled linen suit pulled on over a pair of paisley pyjamas.

"Let's see what we can do for the young man, shall we?"

He put his bag down on the table next to Derek and bent over. Derek was slumped over the bench, all the fight taken out of him. But he looked up as the Doctor approached and his face changed. He jerked back and clutched his hand to his chest.

"Get away from me."

Dr Kheraj drew a long breath through his nose.

"Mr … Paterson, is it—? I would like to see if I can get the glass out before—"

"Don't you touch me! Fucking Paki."

The doctor turned away, his face drawn and tight. "I'm sorry, Bhajan. If he will not let me treat him, I must get him to the hospital. I have no choice."

"Should I call an ambulance?"

"From here, at night?" The two men exchanged looks. "If he could be persuaded to go in my car, it would be quicker to take him myself."

I could feel how the whole room had retracted from the man on the floor, as if he had an infectious disease. And this was my mess. I had to do something to clean it up.

"Come on, Derek," I said. "We need to get you to hospital."

I coaxed him to his feet, shielding his mutilated hand. Dr Kheraj stayed behind me, out of sight, as I walked Derek out into the alley.

"I'm going to have to stay here," Baz murmured as we passed. "I don't want to leave Tom to manage on his own."

I nodded, not trusting myself to speak. I slid beside Derek into the back of the doctor's battered Austin Maxi, keeping up a meaningless flow of soothing noise to distract him. I hoped he wasn't going to see Dr Kheraj in the driver's seat and try to throw himself out of the car. He started to shiver and I took a plaid blanket I found folded on the back seat and wrapped it around him.

"I think it may be best if I do not come in," the doctor murmured as we pulled into the hospital car park. "I will wait for you here—"

"You don't have to …"

"I will wait for you here," he finished. "When you need me, come and find me. *Khuda hafiz*, Miss Hassett."

Derek came with me, docile as a bellwether. He hadn't much strength left. A few feet from the doors of Casualty, he turned the colour of a hospital bed sheet and began to shake. I looked round for help and an orderly with a wheelchair appeared, like an angel of deliverance, and relieved me just before he crashed to the floor.

When Derek had been taken away for treatment, I made my way out to the car park. I wasn't leaving without Derek, and Dr Kheraj, apparently, wasn't leaving without me. We got ourselves cups of scummy tea from the machine and joined the army of ghosts in the waiting area. My head was aching and the tea made me feel sick.

"I'm sorry. I've made such a mess of things."

"How so, Miss Hassett?"

"I was the one who let him in tonight. After hours, because I felt sorry for him."

"Ah."

"And not just that. I helped him find his digs. I got him a room in a house with this Pakistani guy. And I knew he wasn't comfortable with …"

I stopped, knowing how bad what I was about to say would sound.

"With an Asian landlord?" the doctor finished.

I nodded, feeling wretched. But Dr Kheraj's pock-marked face showed nothing but compassion.

"I don't think Derek's an out-and-out racist. I truly don't. He's just … ignorant. But he's a recovering alcoholic. He's vulnerable. I should have seen it was more pressure than he could handle. It wasn't fair on him or the family he was lodging with. Goodness knows what he's gone and done, apart from being foul to you—"

Dr Kheraj held up his hand to stop me. "You think it's possible he may have harmed this family?"

"I don't know. I can't imagine he'd … But I had this phone call, earlier on, from the landlord, Mr Arain. He was pretty upset—"

"Arain? Is this Abdul Saleem Arain? From King William Street?"

"Yes! At least, I don't know his full name, but he lives in King William Street. Do you know him?"

"A little." Dr Kheraj steepled his fingers. "He was one of the first of his community to come here. Since then he has sponsored many others from his *biraderi*. Until recently, many of them were living in the house on King William Street. But now, I believe, most have brought their families from Pakistan to join them."

"He did tell us his wife hadn't been here long."

Dr Kheraj looked thoughtful.

"Abdul Saleem has had a good deal of trouble over the years, because of his prominent role in the community."

"What sort of trouble?" I asked.

"The usual sort, Miss Hassett. Words of hate sprayed onto doors. Bricks thrown through windows. Dog's excrement put through doors. A few ignorant men beating him up on a Saturday night."

"My God."

My mind caught the scent of leather from the big chair in my dad's study, and I heard his voice reading aloud from *A Christmas Carol*. Each year, we'd read a chapter a night, finishing on Christmas Eve with Scrooge's deliverance. Of all the things the ghosts revealed, what disturbed me most was the Ghost of Christmas Present drawing back his robes to show the two emaciated children, Ignorance and Want, from whom all the wrongs of the world flowed.

"It's happened to you too?" I asked the doctor.

"I live in what might be called a 'nice' neighbourhood. For the most part, my neighbours do not bother me. I have never had to live in darkness because my windows are boarded up …"

"But you've suffered harassment?"

"Few of us are immune."

I laid my hand on my stomach, imagining my child, living in fear in a boarded-up house. Like Baz. Like the Arain family, possibly. Like how many others in Coventry? All over Britain?

"How can you live with it?" I asked.

"With the dog shit?"

"With knowing someone hates you so much."

"My dear Miss Hassett, I am an Ismaili. A hundred and fifty years ago, my people left India and settled in Africa to escape religious persecution. Fifteen years ago, the Africans rose up and threw the foreigners out of their country so that they could rule for themselves and we Ismailis came to Britain. One day we may be forced to leave Britain also. But not yet, I think."

Chapter 52

Baz crossed King William Street with Noordin, their shadows stretching and contracting as they moved out of the circle of one street light and into another. The doctor pointed to Abdul Saleem's taxi, parked in the road outside the house.

Even before they reached the Arains', Baz knew that something was wrong. A bulge filled the doorway, a shadowy excrescence that made his skin creep. The doctor saw it too, and quickened his pace. In the yellow light of the streetlamp, it was the colour of earwax. Grinning hideously, curved teeth jutting from its jaws, a few hairs still protruding from its snout, its fluted ears parodying the arches of a mogul palace.

A pig's head, fixed to the door like a monstrous knocker.

The doctor made an angry noise and strode forward. Grabbing the creature under the jowls, he heaved. Then he staggered back, retching. The dead head vomited a blackish stream, drenching his pale suit. The sweetish smell of a butcher's shop filled the night air.

Blood. Blood pouring from the dead pig's mouth

"*Bismallah*! What is occurring out here?"

A sash creaked open and a man began to scold. His eyes widened as he saw Dr Kheraj covered in blood and he muttered something that sounded like a prayer.

"It's okay," Baz called up. "It's not his blood. No one is hurt."

"What is happening?" the man demanded. "Who are you?"

Dr Kheraj collected himself with a visible effort and moved into the light.

"*Asalaam alaikum,*" he called up. The man at the window hesitated, then the greeting was returned and the doctor began to speak rapidly in Urdu.

Baz dropped his jacket on the garden wall and slipped back into the shadows. The pig's head still grinned at him from the door, blood dripping from its jowls. He studied it. Forewarned, he could see how the trick had been managed. A blood-filled sac had been placed in the mouth so that anyone trying to lift the head was bound to push upward on the jaws, piercing the sac with the tusk-like teeth and causing the mouth to spurt blood.

He took a hold behind the jowls, where there were no moving parts, but his hands couldn't grip. Flesh yielded under his fingers and gave off a smell of putrefaction. He lifted, trying to prevent it tipping forward, but the weight was unbalanced. In the end, the only way to take the weight was to hug it to him. Its ears brushed his cheek and he could feel the dregs of the blood seeping into his shirt. The stench was under his nostrils and he struggled not to gag. Sergeant Conway's voice in his head cautioned him not to destroy any more evidence. Screw that. He couldn't leave it here. He remembered some bins, thirty yards away near an entry.

Behind him, he heard the chain rattle on a door. The door opened and the flood of incomprehensible words grew a little louder. He staggered to the bins and ditched the head in the nearest one. It would give someone a hell of a fright come the morning, but he couldn't help that. As he dropped it he saw maggots writhing in the neck cavity and turned away to vomit.

He half expected, on his return, that the door would be closed again, but it stood open. A man in a *kurta* and *dhoti* beckoned to him.

"Come. Come. You must wash yourself. Terrible thing. Terrible. That this should be happening to you in my house …"

Dr Kheraj had been spirited away to the bathroom upstairs. In the scullery, Baz glimpsed a thin, dark-skinned woman bent over a sink, sluicing out the doctor's pale suit.

"Come. Give me your shirt. My wife will wash it for you."

"That's really not—"

"Please, please."

He crooked his hand impatiently. Baz peeled off his shirt and followed his host upstairs, feeling humbled. In the bathroom, Noordin was kneeling over the bath in his underwear, his face deathly pale. The water in the bath had turned pale rust, as if it had leached the colour from his skin. The doctor scrubbed at his nails with a big, old-fashioned nailbrush.

"Do you realise that, because they have let us in like this, because they are washing the blood of a pig from our clothes, they will have to purify themselves, this house?"

Baz stared at him, his eyes glazing over.

"Should we have refused to come in?"

Noordin shook his head, deep lines of anger scored on his face. "They feel they owe it to us, because it was done at their house, because they were the intended victims."

Baz watched the blood eddying away from his own hands into the water, swirls and curlicues of red. The doctor pursed his lips.

"Do you think that that young man at the Skipper—?"

"I wish I knew, Noordin. I hope not."

Unlikely that Paterson would have the knowledge or the understanding to set up a stunt like this. But only too likely that someone else, more knowledgeable, more malign, could use him as their patsy. He thought of the leaflets he had seen in Broadgate. *Young patriots, you are soldiers in a war …*

When Baz and Noordin had both washed, they sluiced the bath, careful to wash away every trace of the pig's blood—conscious that nothing they did could clean away the taint of *haram*. Outside, Abdul Saleem presented them both with clean, pressed *kurtas*, and Dr Kheraj with a *dhoti*.

The three of them sat on the floor around a low table, in a room overcrowded with mismatched furniture. Abdul Saleem's wife brought tea, her eyes lowered and her hair modestly covered. A clock on the wall ticked loudly. It was gone three in the morning. The taxi driver had more than likely been up since six in the morning and he'd need to be up again in a few hours, to start his next shift. God, what a life.

"Abdul Saleem, do you know how this could have happened, or when?" Dr Kheraj asked, speaking in English for Baz's benefit.

"We already know you had some trouble earlier in the evening," Baz said.

The taxi driver nodded his head from side to side. "Yes, yes. I am sorry to say this is true. I have rooms, in another house. A man who is renting one of them, he brings alcohol in my house when he is promising me this will not happen. I am telling him, you bring alcohol, you are not living in my house. Out. Go. He is most angry. He is breaking chairs and so on, and then he is going."

"There was a lot of damage?"

"In truth, more mess than damage. When I am first seeing it, everything is upside-down like cyclone blowing. But then I pick up, and maybe one chair broken, some cups. A table …" He makes a chopping motion with his hand on the edge of the table.

"Chipped?" Baz suggested.

"Yes, chipped. But otherwise is not so bad, *Alhamdulillah*."

"*Alhamdulillah*," Dr Kheraj echoed.

Baz sipped his tea. It was the same sweet, milky mint tea he remembered Auntie Harjit endlessly brewing on her gas hob.

He had never acquired a taste for it, but it would be ungracious not to drink it.

"What time did this happen?"

"Between nine, ten o'clock, not many taxis are wanted. I am coming home to see my wife, my children. Then I am hearing noises from bedsitting house, and inside I am finding as I told you."

"Did you call the police?" Noordin asked.

He made a hawking sound. "The police are coming, coming; writing, writing, and doing always not one thing to help. I tell Paterson I am calling police, but no, I do not call them."

Of course you don't, Baz thought. Here's me, going round destroying evidence because I don't believe the police will do anything even if I shove it under their noses. Why should you have any more faith in them than I do?

"And later on," Noordin persisted. "Did he come back?"

"I am finishing my shift twelve o'clock, come home. Still everything is very well. I go to bed. Sleep. Hear nothing till you fellows shouting, shouting and blood everywhere."

Noordin's face had hardened. "If Paterson has done this," he told Abdul Saleem, "we can take the police to him."

Abdul Saleem sat up, moustache twitching.

"You know where he is? How are you knowing this?"

"Wait." Baz held up his hand. "Midnight? You're sure nothing was there at midnight?"

Chapter 53

I couldn't sleep after Baz left with Dr Kheraj. I lay on my back staring at the boards under Tom's bunk, hearing him snore, remembering the grim look on the doctor's face. Hard as I found it to imagine that Derek would harm the Arains—after what I'd seen tonight, how could I doubt it was a real possibility?

Just before six, I heard Baz come back in and got up to join him. He must have been back to Paradise Road, because he'd changed out of the suit he was wearing the night before, but he couldn't have managed any more sleep than I had. He looked as if he had been put through the wringer every which way and then hung out to dry.

"How's Mr Arain? Is he okay?"

"He's not been hurt. Not physically."

"Thank God—"

"But some bastard nailed a rotting pig's head to their door."

He let that sink in—what it would mean to a pious Muslim like Mr Arain. The depth of the insult.

"You don't think Derek—?"

He shook his head. "Mr Arain told us he saw nothing when he came home from his shift at midnight. And Tom said Paterson was here banging on the door just after half eleven. Whoever put it up there, Paterson's in the clear."

Relief gave way to anger. Derek had squandered every chance

he'd been given. Lied to me. Abused my trust.

"Baz, I'm so sorry. If I hadn't let him in here last night …"

Baz didn't answer. He was writing something in the register. When he had finished, he pushed the book towards me. "Maia, I know you two have been close but …"

After Derek's name, were the letters 'DNA'. Do Not Admit.

"You're going to bar him?"

"He threatened us, Maia." Baz said. "If the punters think someone can get away with pulling a weapon on us, we're none of us safe."

It was almost time to close up before Derek slunk out of the dormitory, cradling his bandaged hand against his shoulder. He shuffled to a table in the corner with a cup of tea and Baz sat down opposite. I followed, feeling like the Prisoner's Friend in a Court Martial.

"How are you this morning?"

Derek glared at Baz and said nothing.

"I understand you've lost your digs."

Derek wiped his hand across his mouth.

"Landlord told us not to come back," he mumbled.

Baz took a deep breath. "How much do you remember about what happened last night?"

"Enough."

"Do you remember how you hurt your hand?"

Derek stared at the bandages. It looked as if his hand had bled more in the night.

"I broke a bottle," he said.

"Broke it to use it as a weapon?"

Derek said nothing.

"You threatened my staff. You have to understand, no one threatens my staff."

Derek said nothing. He didn't move. I knew what was coming

next and, angry as I was, I could have wept for him.

"I am sorry to say this," Baz told him, "but I am going to have to ask you not to come back here tonight. For the safety of my staff, I cannot allow anyone who uses a weapon in here to stay. Derek Paterson, you're barred for six months."

Derek stared from Baz to me, looking bemused.

"Do you understand me?" Baz insisted. "If you come back again tonight, you won't be admitted."

Derek's face splintered, his bland, non-expression shattering into a look of shock and anguish. He stared over Baz's shoulder at me.

"Are you going to let him do this to us?"

"You crossed a line, Derek," I said. "We've got no choice."

"After everything I've done here?" His voice rose. The men around him turned looking for the source of the commotion. "I'm not some sodding wino, you know. I've not just come in here, drunk my tea, slept in my bed and gone, like the rest of these tossers. I've sung for my supper. Even after I had my own place, I came back here and helped out. And now you're going to turn us out just when I need you? Well, fuck you."

He pushed back his chair and pulled his coat round him, shouldering it over his injured arm.

"I reckon that gadgie you threw out was right," he said. "You Paki bastards look after your own and leave the rest of us to go to hell. Well, I've news for you, mate. This is our country and we're going to take it back."

As he started to push his way out, I realised I hadn't given him the instructions from the hospital.

"Derek, you're going to need to see a doctor. Your dressings will need changing and you may need—"

His swimming-pool-blue eyes froze over.

"I thought you were different," he said. "I thought you cared."

"I do care. But that doesn't mean I'll—"

"You're just like all the others." He looked over my shoulder towards Baz. "Take that Paki's side against me, would you? Well, I don't need you, and I don't need your Paki doctors pawing me about. Now GET OUT OF MY ROAD."

I jumped back, angry and sick at heart. The men shrank away, opening a path between him and the door. The last I saw was the look of pain on Derek's face as he jarred his arm barging the door.

Chapter 54

Baz had scrubbed himself raw in the shower, in the early hours of the morning and again just now, but the stench of the pig still clung in his nostrils.

When he asked Maia to walk with him, she got to her feet readily enough. But as they emerged into the darkening spring evening, she looked as if she were bracing herself against a storm. She kept her head down and he could see the little nubbly bone at the nape of her neck, the fine, fair down tapering towards it below her short-cropped hair.

At the end of the road, she turned, her face half ashamed, half defiant.

"Listen, if you want me to go—"

He gawped, a feeling almost of panic rising inside him.

"Why would I want you to go?"

"Because the whole bloody thing was my fault. Not just letting Derek in last night. I trusted him from the start—"

The constriction in his chest eased.

"You were doing your job. We're supposed to help people if we think they can be helped. If it comes to that, I messed up too. I had my doubts, but I did nothing and let you all turn Paterson into a trusty. But, if we're going to fuck up, frankly I'd rather it was because we trusted someone too much than because we wouldn't give them the benefit of the doubt."

She looked at him, her eyes narrowed, as if trying to make

her mind up about something. "So what did you want to talk to me about?"

"Not yet. Just come a bit further."

They were walking now parallel with the sandstone wall bordering the old London Road Cemetery. He stopped where the wall butted a low, shrub-planted bank.

"This should do it."

She laughed and, to his delight, the tension seemed to ease out of her.

"You're going to break into a grave yard?"

"Not scared are you?" he teased.

"Just give me a leg up and we'll see who's scared."

Once they were both over the wall, he took her hand and led her up the bank and into the maze of paths that wound among the weathered monuments—the angels with broken wings, the canting crosses, the cherubs with their faces worn blank. Most of the trees had buds just softening the skeletal outline of their shadows, but here and there dense clusters of spreading darkness showed where yew trees presided over the dead.

In an open area above a small slope, where the graves were marked with simple headstones, the smell of new-mown grass lingered in the air, together with a hint of camomile. Somewhere in the west, a sickle moon hung low over the horizon, half hidden among the trees. The sky above them was darkening, stars beginning to appear. He laid his coat on the grass.

"Baz, what on earth are we doing here?"

He lowered himself to the ground and held his hand out to her. "Not on earth," he said. "In the sky."

Maybe it was lack of sleep, but tonight it seemed as if he could feel the headlong, spinning rush of the earth through space. He could hear the soft exhalation of her breath, and the little rustling sounds as she turned her head or stirred her arms. Just above their heads, a star pricked into life.

"You make a wish?" he asked. "You know. *Star light, star bright, first star I've seen tonight ...*"

"I'm a scientist. Aren't I supposed to say they're just big balls of burning gas in the sky?"

He chuckled. "Fibber. I bet you did wish."

The dazzling canopy overhead was deepening every second, as more and more stars flickered into visible range.

"Which star did you wish on?" she asked.

He pointed to a bright light above the eastern horizon, steady and unwinking. "That one."

She laughed. "I hate to spoil it, but isn't that a planet?"

"Not a big ball of gas in the sky then?"

"No."

"Damn," he said. "And it was such a good wish too."

Overhead, the Plough took on its familiar shape.

"Do you know what Hindus call the Plough?" he asked her. He felt the shake of her head against his arm. "They call it the Seven Rishis, the seven wise men. The Pleiades are their wives. And the North Star is Mount Mehru, the centre of the universe."

"How do you know?"

"My neighbour when I was growing up, he was an amateur astronomer. He had this beautiful old telescope he'd brought all the way from India. If we children were good, sometimes he would set it up on a winter's evening and let us look through it. And he taught us all the old Hindu names for the constellations."

Her profile was silhouetted against the deepening blue of the night sky—the rounded hillock of a brow, the sharper peak of a nose, the valley of her mouth, sheltered by lips. Her chin as delicately shaped as a pebble smoothed in a river. He reached out and brushed her lips with his finger. The gathering dusk was like his darkroom, magnifying his sense of touch and smell.

"Tell me what you wished for," he murmured.

"Wishes don't come true if you tell."

He felt her shiver and turned to wrap the greatcoat around her. At the same time, she half sat up and they were caught in accidental embrace. Breast to breast. Hip to hip. Thigh to thigh. Her hand on his hair. His hand on her shoulder. He could feel all the curves that her clothes concealed. The soft protuberances of her breasts. The curvature of her belly. He inclined his head to kiss her and she brought her fingers up to touch his lips, forestalling him.

Chapter 55

I could see the darting movements of bats overhead—tiny things, no bigger than sparrows. I thought of the fruit bats the size of mangos that would drop from baobab trees outside our compound in Senegal at sunset, before opening their wings and soaring over the city, filling the air with rustling and turning the sky black.

Pinda said that evil spirits lived in the baobab trees and we shouldn't walk under them after dark. She also said the spirit in the kapok tree inside the compound would protect us. My mother said it was all nonsense, but I shouldn't ever say so to Pinda.

Back in England, kids at school said that ghosts lived in Highgate Cemetery, and dared each other to run past the gates. Cemeteries never scared me, though. I was too used to people maintaining friendly relations with ancestor spirits. Pinda, for one, kept a full jar of water by the kitchen window, just in case one stopped by for a drink. More nonsense, though Mom wrote it all down in her notebook.

"Tell me what you wished for," he said.

My almost-wish formed like vapour in my mind. If we could stay here in the deepening twilight, feeling the evening breeze in our faces, hearing the rustlings of small night creatures, smelling the grass, and watching the stars appear one by one in the canopy of the sky. Safe from the ghouls outside the cemetery walls …

But this wasn't just about Baz and me. Another life was sharing space with mine. Its cells dividing and multiplying, becoming more complex day by day, hour by hour. Laying snares for me, catching me in a web of emotions I'd never expected.

When he slipped his arms around me, he smelt of sandalwood and wet wool, of photographic chemicals and good clean sweat. I wanted to stay there and breathe it in. I wanted to let him kiss me. But I didn't. I put my fingers to his lips.

"Baz—"

A half-laughing smile played over his lips and he gave a little groan of frustration. He drew my ring finger into his mouth and sucked it.

"Baz, I'm pregnant—"

His body stiffened. I felt him roll away and sit up. The silence was so dense it seemed to stuff up my mouth. I stared at his back, trying to remember everything I'd planned to say, but before I could get any words out, he moved away through the gravestones, diminishing until he vanished into the shadows. After a time, I started to shiver.

I picked up his coat and wrapped it round me, smelling the familiar mixture of sandalwood and Dektol. A hollow shell of an embrace, everything gone except the scent and a tiny residue of body heat.

"Know what?" I yelled after him. "Screw you!"

I tore my eyes away from the spot where he'd disappeared and started to walk. Baz might spout all that crap about giving people the benefit of the doubt, but when it came to me, he seemed to jump at every opportunity to think the worst. Well, I was pregnant, not leprous. If he couldn't handle that, he could fuck off.

I kept turning the wrong way on the twisting paths, circling round and passing the same weathered monuments, ghost white in the dark. Baz's coat trailed on the ground, sweeping a train of rubbish behind me, like that guy from the Skipper the first night I was there. About a million years ago, when Ossie had just left.

When I knew nothing. When I understood nothing.

A barn owl passed overhead and a few moments later I heard it screech. I stumbled upon the wall and followed it to the point where the raised bank provided easy access. I clambered up and sat for a moment with my feet dangling. A wisp of mist wrapped itself around a lamp post and I thought again of the ghouls that lay beyond the cemetery—the marauding skinheads, the kids throwing chips, the arsonists and the graffiti-spraying bigots.

Before Ossie left, I could never remember feeling unsafe on my own at night. But then, before Ossie left, I could never have imagined creatures living so close by who would destroy a child for no other reason than the colour of his skin.

God, I missed him. I missed the comforting solidity of his physical presence. Missed his soft-spoken assurance that the world could still be redeemed. That there was hope, even for a spoilt princess like me.

I looked back at the sky, but the street lights had swallowed all but the brightest stars and the rising mist shrouded those that remained.

Truth was, we were never meant to bring children into the world on our own. And Ossie wasn't coming back.

Chapter 56

He hadn't meant to go far. Just to put a little distance between them—get his head clear before he opened his mouth, so he didn't sound like a complete arse. But once he began to walk, he kept going, down the slope, into the trees. Only when the walls of the ruined chapel loomed over him like the white bones of a Greek temple, did he wake up to what he'd done.

He turned back, hurrying now, but when he reached the place where he'd left her, she'd gone. He began to run, shouting out her name, but no one answered. Then he saw her, sitting on the wall, close by where they'd climbed over. He called again, but just at that moment she slipped off the wall and dropped into the street below.

God, he must be the last person on earth she'd want anywhere near her right now. But he couldn't just leave her to walk home on her own. Not with all the crap that had been going on. He followed, keeping her just in sight, until he was sure that she was safely back in Paradise Road. And then he made his way to the studio.

He woke in the dark. He was sprawled on the couch in the studio, his limbs stiff. His head ached and his mouth felt as if someone had been using a vacuum cleaner in it.

Fuck. He'd only sat down and closed his eyes, just for a minute to try and think. But he must have fallen asleep and now it was nearly morning.

He forced himself off the couch, muscles protesting, and turned the hotplate on underneath the kettle. Thoughts of Maia flooded his head.

She was pregnant.

With some other bastard's child.

Did it that matter? She wasn't with the father any more, was she?

Deep down inside, though, he knew that made no difference. She might not worry on her own account if she had chips thrown at her or had Gary abusing her in the streets. But she'd never let that happen to her child. She'd want to keep as much distance between herself and him as she could. That wasn't racism; that was maternal instinct.

Mrs Peel rubbed herself against his legs, and he scooped her up and held her, protesting, while he buried his face in her long calico fur and cursed. Everything else came back to him in a diorama of twisted images—the anonymous letter, his quarrel with Vik, the Weasel distributing leaflets, the pig's head on Abdul Saleem's door and the smell of the blood on his clothes, Paterson's shredded hand and the look on his face when Baz told him he was barred.

Eventually, the cat wriggled free and mewed for food. The act of opening a tin and filling her bowl forced some order into his mind. He reminded himself he'd planned to go and see Vik this morning. To patch up whatever could be patched up, before he had no friends left at all.

He made tea, and out of habit, turned on the radio to hear the news. A bland BBC voice read the day's headlines.

Riots broke out in Brixton last night after crowds mistook the intentions of police trying to assist a coloured youth who had been injured …

He turned up the volume and listened as the newsreader told of cops being stoned and police vehicles damaged.

Abena would be in the thick of it. Trying to calm things down, maybe. Or more likely arguing with the police. Telling them exactly why charging in like the Heavy Brigade was the wrong way of doing things. If she didn't end up hit by a flying brick, she'd be arrested for sure.

As he listened, his mind shifted gear. From spinning uselessly, it began to grip onto a new thought. He'd never been able to go near the fire-ravaged house in New Cross, but this was different. He could take his camera. Try and find a grain of truth amongst the chaos. After months spent boxing shadows all over Coventry, it offered a solid purpose.

Maia had left his coat draped over a chair in the office. He picked it up, smelling the grass, a hint of her perfume. The scent flung him back to the cemetery, to Maia lying next to him. He forced away the sense of loss and went upstairs to his room. Working fast, he grabbed a selection of clothes and stuffed them into a bag. His camera went in too, along with a large supply of film.

He could be at the station in half an hour if he hurried, but he had to say something to Maia before he went. He'd behaved like a total wanker last night, and to bugger off to London without apologising would only compound the offence. Leaving his bag in the office, he crossed the yard and went into the other house. The door to Maia's bedroom was ajar. At least, with Robyn on duty at the Skipper, she would be alone and they could talk in private. He tapped softly, then pushed it wider.

The room was empty, the two beds unoccupied and both apparently unslept in. Compared with the sprawling mess on Robyn's side of the room, Maia's space was startlingly neat and contained. No scattering of books and magazines across the floor. No clutter of toiletries on the shelf behind the bed. The only sign of habitation was his own t-shirt, the one she had borrowed the first night she arrived, neatly folded and laid on top of her pillow.

He felt of a flicker of panic, but repressed it. She had been back here last night; he knew that. He'd followed her and seen her go through the door. And she always was an early riser. When she wanted to be on her own (never an easy task at Paradise Road) she'd take herself off for long walks before breakfast. She'd be striding along somewhere now, eyes focused on the middle distance—cursing him roundly and mentally grinding him under her heel.

He could wait for her to come back, but there was no knowing how long she'd be. Better to leave a note and take his punishment when he got back.

He found a pen and a piece of paper and sat down on the edge of her bed to write. After a few false starts, he managed to assemble half a dozen inadequate sentences.

> *Dear Maia,*
>
> *Congratulations. That was what I should have said last night, isn't it? I'm sorry. You took me by surprise, and I behaved like a complete arsehole.*
>
> *I have to go away for a couple of days, but I want you to know, I understand. You've got other priorities right now and that's only to be expected.*
>
> *I'll see you when I get back. Take care of yourself (and of the baby).*
>
> *Baz.*

Not great. But it would have to do. He folded the note and put it on the shelf behind the bed, then snatched it back. No point leaving it where anyone might read it. He tucked the note between the folds of his own t-shirt, kissed two fingers, and touched them to the fabric where it would lie against the hollow of her throat.

In the back streets behind the Community Centre, Abena's bronze Austin Princess listed on its suspension. Baz patted the roof, remembering the battery that was forever in need of charging, the gears that screeched whenever you tried to put it in reverse.

Reggae bled from the open doors of the Community Centre, the sound curiously hollow. A huddle of community workers stood in the middle of the empty hall. They were arguing—he could tell that even from the doorway. Voices rose against the music, fingers pointed, hands sliced the air.

In the middle of it all stood Abena. She had a scarf tied over her short-cropped hair, arms akimbo, legs set wide apart. She looked exactly as she had the last time he'd seen her, that, as if it were only hours ago he'd walked out of her bed-sit.

As he came into earshot, a studious young black man in wire-rimmed spectacles said, "This is about access to public spaces: black street culture versus the police thinking they have to rule the street."

"Raas claat, Wesley. You're not in college now, man," someone said and there was a short, tense burst of laughter. Half a dozen voices crisscrossed each other, weary, on edge.

"There's man and man out there convinced it was Babylon stabbed that dread yesterday."

"After the way things been, folk ready to believe anything."

"Face it, man, whatever we do to calm things, it's just delaying the inevitable."

"So what *can* we do?"

They faded to a halt, as if acknowledging they were going

round in circles.

"Hello, Abena," Baz said, in the silence that followed.

Abena swivelled round and her eyes widened. She dragged him aside.

"What you doing here?"

"I wanted to see if you were all right."

She looked him up and down, like a poor specimen at a cattle market. "Bit late for that, don't you think?"

"Just because we broke up doesn't mean I have to stop caring."

Abena gave her head a toss. "Bwai, I'm still waiting for you to start caring."

"That's not—" He stifled the automatic protest, rolled with the blow. "Look, I didn't come here to quarrel with you."

"So why did you come?"

Before he could answer, a man appeared behind her. He had dreadlocks and was wearing Rasta colours over a pair of pale slacks. The dub poet, the one with his own sound system.

"Who's the coolie?" he said.

Abena gave Baz an angry glance and shrugged the guy off.

"This is Baz. We used to work together in Coventry."

The dread looked Baz over with eyes that held no welcome. "You may not have noticed," he said, "but this ain't such a good time to be paying a social call."

Baz let his jacket fall open, revealing the camera he had half concealed.

"You want people to know what's going on around here? Then let me take the pictures."

The Rasta looked from him to his camera and shrugged.

"Can't hurt, cha," he said. He glanced at Abena.

"Last time I hear, it's still a free country," she said. "Theoretically." She gave Baz a look sharp enough to cut through any amount of crap. "Just stay out of my way, raas claat."

On the surface, it was a normal Saturday. People were out and about in the spring sunshine. Market stalls were doing brisk trade. Shoals of black youths moved through the streets. But every few yards along the Railton Road, police vans from the Special Patrol Group stood, their doors shut and their windows blacked out. Police officers patrolled in pairs, never more than a few yards from the next patrol.

Shortly before five o'clock, Baz followed a group of dreads into Atlantic Road. The crowd was thickening, like the air before a thunderstorm. He jostled his way forward, to where two men who were clearly plain-clothes cops had stopped a cab driver.

"Yo!" someone said in his ear. "You got a camera and thing. Get up on that roof and make sure you see what really happen."

Before he could answer, he was hoisted up, with a handful of others, onto the roof of the All Star Takeaway. From here, the crowd was a sea of heads, their bodies foreshortened. They eddied round an island formed by the cab and the policemen, turbulent but still in check. Then a black youth, standing between the bollards and the kerb, started to argue with the cops. Within moments, one of the police vans from the Railton Road broke ranks and cut through the crowd. The doors opened, the youth was bundled into the back and the van moved off.

A brick sailed over the heads of the crowd and clanged into the back of the police van. Its doors flew open, and at the same time, a police officer staggered out of the crowd, gasping and winded. Shit. From another vantage point, it could look as though the brick had struck the copper. Far too much scope here for both sides to add two and two and make a whole lot more than four.

The van jerked away under a hail of missiles and the crowd surged after it. Baz scrambled down from the roof. Police officers were pouring in from every direction. The cars along the road had come to a dead halt, unable to move. As Baz pushed his way through the crowd, one of the drivers met his gaze. He looked stunned.

Further along the pavement, a senior police officer in uniform was being mobbed by people shouting complaints. Baz saw one of the workers from the community centre approach him. The policeman kept looking at the crowd and shaking his head. Someone shouted in Baz's ear that the Beastmen were armed with metal bars. Someone else screamed back that he'd seen them wearing National Front badges.

True or not, they were ready to believe it. A hail of bricks and stones flew towards the police. Baz ran with the crowd into Coldharbour Lane. His finger on the shutter release, the motor drive whirring, he caught the moment when they turned their fury on the police vans and managed to roll one over. Its doors burst open and several police dogs scrabbled out, yelping, their handlers stumbling behind. Then his film ran out. As he pressed himself into a doorway to change it, the police charged, driving the crowd back along Coldharbour Lane. Traffic began to crawl forward, car drivers shaking their heads as if waking from a nightmare.

Baz jostled his way back into Atlantic Road and found Abena with the young politics student.

"If I were you, I would get your car out of here while you can," Wesley told her.

Abena kissed her teeth. "Come on," she said to Baz. "You may as well make yourself useful."

The Princess was in a short side street leading away from Atlantic Road. As they reached it, part of the group that had been chased away by the police charge doubled back into the side street from the far end. They were shouting, swinging whatever they had in their hands, banging on cars, dustbins, anything that got in their way, the sound like a steel band gone feral.

Baz scrambled into the seat beside Abena. Fifty yards in front of them, at the junction with Atlantic Road, the police were throwing a cordon across the street. The only way out was to turn the car round and go through the crowd. Abena started the engine and began to ease forward, trying not to draw attention. She executed the first part of a three-point turn, then pushed down the clutch to go into reverse. And, as they always did, the gears crashed.

They both turned and looked back up the road towards the crowd, but the youths had spotted the cordon and turned away, running south down Rattray Road. Shouts of *Babylon haffe dead*! faded after them.

Baz stopped holding his breath. Abena turned the car along the same way the youths had run, going slowly so as not to overtake them. The uproar grew louder until, at the bottom of the road, noise cascaded towards them like the clash of rival sound systems.

At least a hundred youths had gathered at the junction and more were joining them all the time. Baz could see the underside of a car that had been turned over, and a hail of missiles. The police were using dustbin lids as makeshift shields.

"We're not going to get out this way," Abena murmured. She glanced over her shoulder, and once again eased the car into reverse. Baz wiped his palms on his jeans.

When the gears crashed, a few heads nearest to them turned. Then, like the start of a chain reaction, more and more turned until a sea of eyes stared back at them. As Abena began to inch backwards, the crowd surged round them, hands drumming on the bonnet, on the roof, bodies pressing close, playful and deadly as a wave breaking round a rock. Abena, outwardly composed, slid the car back into neutral.

A fist grabbed the door handle. Baz felt the car begin to rock underneath them. Gently at first, then more and more violently. He clutched the grab handle above the passenger door and stared at the faces pressed against the window. How far gone were they? What would they be prepared to do? They'd survive being rolled (probably) but what if they decided to torch the car?

Fear swelled his throat as his lungs fought for air.

The face of a youth appeared at the windscreen, grinning and whooping. He had a wide mouth with beautiful, even teeth, and a mop of baby-dreads. Baz could see the vault of his nostrils, pressed wide against the glass. He made an obscene gesture towards Abena, and then hesitated.

"*Cha*, I know you," he mouthed, over the roar of the crowd.

He wriggled away and disappeared, to reappear by Abena's window, banging at it for her to roll it down. The crowd on her side eased off to let him through and a sudden heave on Baz's side almost had them over. The youth banged on the roof and there was a lull.

Abena eased the window down a hairline crack. Baz forced himself to keep schtum, aware that at best he was on sufferance, at worst a liability. Abena was the one with the street cred to get them out of this. All he could do was hold his tongue.

"I know you," the kid said. "You that sistren from the community centre."

"And you're Joker," she answered. "You with the Cool Runnings sound system."

"Cha! You remember."

"Who's the white guy?" someone yelled.

"That's no whitey. That's a coolie-man," another voice answered.

Someone jostled Joker and he snapped his fingers. They were covered in rings.

"Wh'appen?" he asked Abena. "Where you taking this car?"

"Just taking it out of the way for now," she told him. "I'm gonna to need it on Monday to go by the Cash and Carry, get supplies for the Centre."

That was a smart move. Abena held Joker's gaze, staring him down until, with a sharp nod of his head, he made up his mind.

"Let this one go, sight?"

The crowd let out a collective groan but more people had recognised Abena. They eased back to give the car breathing space. Abena shifted into first gear. Hands were still beating a tattoo on the roof, though less urgently now—more a salute than a threat. As Abena sped up, the crowd fell back until at last they were driving alone down the middle of the road, with the crowd receding in the rear-view mirror. A stray stone struck the back windscreen with a crack. Abena jumped and jerked the steering wheel, then corrected herself and drove on.

They took an erratic path at first, avoiding bins thrown into the road, broken glass, bricks and stones and other missiles. They'd be lucky if a couple of tyres didn't need replacing. Yet in a few hundred yards, the disturbances were left behind.

Baz's shudders began as the tension was released, little ripples at first and then shakes that juddered through his arms and legs. He couldn't look at Abena, but stared out the window as they skirted Brockwell Park. Here a suburban Saturday proceeded undisturbed, the riots just a nightmare fantasy.

Abena pulled into a tree-lined side street round the south side of the park, near Tulse Hill. When she turned off the engine, her hands stayed locked to the steering wheel. He put an arm around her and she leaned into him. He could feel her Afro against his cheek, soft as a baby's blanket. It was hard to know who was comforting whom. But almost before he could remember how sweet it could be to hold her, Abena pulled away and climbed out of the car.

"Raas claat."

She walked round the car, inspecting the damage. A few dents and scratches had been added to its existing tally, one wiper was hanging loose and the stone had taken a chip out of the rear windscreen.

"Got any money?" she asked. "We better see how far the bus gonna take us."

Chapter 57

The Piccadilly line Tube juddered and rattled between stations. I perched on the end of a blue upholstered bench, opposite a man in a cap who held his newspaper close to his face, poring over the sports pages. The front page headline read:

BLACK THUGS RAMPAGE THROUGH BRIXTON

The carriage was emptying and filling up again at each station, the character of its occupants shifting as we went past Knightsbridge and South Kensington and headed out towards Hammersmith. Black faces supplanted the white. More copies of the same newspaper appeared dotted round the carriage. More pairs of eyes stared bleakly at the headlines.

Baz had been predicting this sort of trouble for months. I remembered that first night at Paradise Road, Baz telling us how he'd nearly been arrested in Brixton. How I'd thought it was a stupid boast, a vain grabbing for attention.

I mustn't think about Baz. I'd wasted most of the previous night on that, huddled under the quilt that I'd once shared with Ossie. After a time, when I'd given up on sleep, I started packing the stuff I didn't need into the trunk under my bed. The things I wanted in the next few days—a change of clothes, underwear, toothbrush—I stuffed into a backpack. The last thing I did was slide Ossie's book into the outer pocket of the backpack.

I reached for it now, to reassure myself it was still there, my fingers lingering on the tattered paper cover. As I did so, I noticed a black man on the other side of the aisle, sitting bent over a bag of tools. Something about the shape of his head reminded me of Ossie—or maybe I was just projecting. When he saw me looking, I gave him a smile and turned away.

I knew that Baz hadn't come back during the night, because you could always hear the creak of the gate from my room. I left his t-shirt folded on my pillow. I'd have said goodbye to Tom, but I could hear him and Iain both snoring, so in the end I just shoved a note under his door. Three quarters of an hour later, I was on the train to London, snaking out of Coventry on the same route Ossie had taken.

By the escalator going down onto the Tube at Euston Station, a poster advertised the Pregnancy Advisory Service. 'Pregnant?' it asked. 'Happy about it? If not, phone (01) …' A payphone stood at the bottom of the escalator, next to the booking office window. I dug around for some change. Straight after I made the call, I caught a train to Hounslow.

The Tube jolted over a set of points, almost bouncing me off the bench. The frame of my backpack jabbed into my stomach and I gasped. My neighbour closed the sports pages with an elaborate rustling, turned to the front page and scanned it. Then he lowered the paper to his lap and glared at the black man with the tools.

"As far as I'm concerned," he said, "Enoch was right. If it was up to me, I'd send every man jack of them back where they came from."

A couple of hours later, I lay on Genny's bed in the terraced house in Hounslow and stared up at the ceiling. A circular indentation above the bed showed where a big light fitting had once hung. Now the ceiling rose had been removed and a single bulb dangled there, shrouded in a paper balloon.

Genny sat cross-legged on the bed next to me, glass of Frascati in her hand. The remains of a picnic she'd put together lay strewn around us.

"I thought I could do it," I told her. "I really thought I could go ahead and have this baby. Hang on to a bit of something good, for Ossie."

"You can, if that's what you want," Genny said. "You just need to get away from that awful place."

"It's not the place. Coventry's no different to anywhere else. People like us just don't see it most of the time."

"So what are you going to do? Do you know?"

My fingers plucked at the candlewick bedspread, making a bald patch in the ridges. I saw again the poster by the escalator. A girl about my age looking scared. I had to swallow a couple of times before I could speak.

"I made an appointment with the PAS. For Monday."

Genny stopped twirling her glass between her fingers. "Sweetie, are you sure?"

"Oh, crap, I don't know. What choice do I have?" I touched my glass to hers. "Don't look so tragic. You of all people should know it's not the end of the world."

She frowned. "It was different for me. I got drunk and knocked up at the end of a party."

"*I* got drunk and knocked up at the end of the party."

She shook her head and her neat bob of hair swung round her. "With Ossie, though. It's not the same."

"That's the problem."

She fell silent. I felt a rush of resentment, tinged with guilt. How the hell did she know what it was like?

And how the hell did I know I wasn't making excuses?

"Do you think I don't hate myself for saying it?" I said. "But the truth is, if I'd got pregnant by, I dunno, Tom—"

"Tom? Yeugh!" She pulled an exaggerated face and I chucked a pillow at her.

"Shut up. Tom's all right."

"Tom's an idiot."

"Whatever. If he was the father, I'd just be trying to make up my mind. Do I want this baby? Don't I want this baby? Simple." I saw the look on her face and amended. "Okay, not simple. But straightforward, anyway. But with this, everything gets bound up in who and what Ossie is."

She reached for my hand and squeezed it. "Not really. When it comes right down to it, it's about you being a mother."

"That's what Tom said."

"Mmm." Her nose wrinkled. "Maybe not such an idiot after all."

No one understood. It was as if the past three months had driven a chasm between me and the people I used to know. A chasm I thought that Baz might have been the one to bridge.

Don't think about Baz.

"How can I not worry about Ossie being black?" I said. "When I think about having his child, I feel as if I'm deliberately bringing it into a world where it will never be safe. Quite apart from the fact that I'm a white woman and I can't teach it anything about being black. But when I think about having an abortion, I'm terrified I'm getting rid of it just because it's not white."

My breath came in a juddering sob and my eyes misted over.

"Oh, sweetie!" Genny wrapped her arms around me until I'd stopped shaking. Then she poured the last of the Frascati into my glass.

"I shouldn't."

"Oh, yes, you should." She held the glass out to me. "C'mon, you need it."

Obediently, I took a swig and it slid down my throat, numbing me. This was almost the first alcohol I'd drunk since I found out I was pregnant, and just having a second glass was making my head swim. Or maybe that was lack of sleep. Two nights now I'd lain awake almost the whole night, my mind stretching and flexing and giving me no rest.

"Listen to me," Genny said, taking my hand in hers again. "First of all, I know how much you and Ossie adored each other. Everyone said you were like brother and sister. No way are you a racist—"

"Yeah, but—"

"And secondly, I know a bit about what it's like living under threat of danger. And, believe me, if that ever put people off having children, the population of Northern Ireland would have collapsed years ago."

"I know. I know. But tell me honestly, would you have had a half-Protestant, half-Catholic kid and stayed living in Belfast?"

I read the answer in her eyes.

Chapter 58

Their bus stopped fifty yards away from the junction where they'd encountered Joker. The driver looked from his passengers to the mob filling the road and back again, sweat beading on his face. In the time they had been away, the youths had beaten back the police. More cars had been turned over and plumes of black smoke billowed.

"You haffe get off now," the driver said. "I cyan go no further."

Abena grabbed Baz by the sleeve and they hurried onto the pavement. The driver stayed in his seat, staring straight ahead and clinging to the steering wheel like a captain determined to go down with this ship. A posse detached themselves from the pack at the junction. His camera at waist level, Baz captured them as they boarded the bus. Two of them levered themselves up on the hubcap, climbed in behind the driver and roughly evicted him. He stumbled round the front of the bus and stood on the pavement, rubbing his hand through his greying hair. His uniform trousers bagged at the knees and the jacket rode up at the back.

More youths drifted away from the junction and surrounded the big double-decker. They heaved at its side, trying to topple it, but it stood firm. One youth in an outsize leather cap broke from the others and jumped in the cab. The engine coughed a few times and growled into life.

"Lord, I hope they no blame me for this," the driver said.

It was like watching a stunt sequence in a film. The bus rolled forward, veering from side to side. In front of it, a vanguard of jubilant youths advanced on the police line. Baz ran after them, his mind detached, his camera capturing a line of police, truncheons waving. The youths scattered but the bus pressed on. One policeman, not much older than the kids on the other side, snatched a brick from a tumbled garden wall and flung it, with a sort of desperate savagery, at the oncoming bus. There was a loud crack and the bus swerved. The bus-jacker leapt off, rolling into the curb. The bus carried on, canting at an impossible angle until, with a graunch of folding metal, it careened into a wall and came to a halt, leaning drunkenly.

A few yards further on, gangs of youths, black and white, were tearing down corrugated iron fences round a building site, grabbing bricks, iron bars, pieces of wood, anything that could be used as a missile. Baz caught an image of them mad with glee, *in control* for the first time in their lives. Fifty yards away, as if in another world, a young black man escorted an elderly white woman to shelter.

Baz followed Abena towards the police line at the top of Atlantic Road. As they drew near, he could see riot shields held above the heads of the police. Smoke stung his eyes and the air stank of burning petrol. The urge to panic pricked, just beneath his skin.

A black youth squatted by an overturned car, a milk bottle in his hand. Baz saw him drain petrol from the tank into the bottle and pass it to an accomplice in a Rasta hat. More bottles flew over the heads of the crowd towards the police, cloth wicks already burning. As they arced over, petrol spilt out, some of it running down the insides of the shields. One policeman hurled his shield away as the padding on the inside began to burn. Another knocked him to the ground and rolled him over to put out the flames on his clothes.

One of the Community Centre workers grabbed Abena.

"Come. We're going to try and negotiate with the police, get them to withdraw before things get worse."

Abena and her colleague slipped away down the side streets. A little way away, a group of policemen sat on the curb, exhausted and frightened. They were smoking and one of them had blood trickling from a gash on his head. In the time it took to photograph them, he lost Abena.

He made his way north towards Electric Avenue. The police had been sucked out of the area round the market, drawn to the battle zone a few streets away. Stall holders and shop keepers were gone too, shutting up and hurrying to safety. In their place came looters. A skinhead in the window of an off-licence was handing six-packs of booze out to the waiting crowd. Jewellery was scattered across the pavement like an Aladdin's cave in the midst of hell. A headless tailor's dummy burned in Burton's window.

Baz tracked south, following the noise of the ongoing battle. He kept coming up against dead ends and wrong turnings. In one narrow road, a boy of about ten staggered along, arms laden with stolen goods. A middle aged woman threw open her front door.

"Elroy? That you, Elroy? Your mama know what you're up to? If you don't burn in hell, your backside surely going to fry if she find out."

The sky was dark now, but lit with yellow flame. A fire engine was making its way up the road under heavy police escort. A hail of missiles came towards them. Bricks. Bars. More petrol bombs. A pub on the corner was ablaze. Thick black smoke rolled across the sky.

A piece of railing struck his shoulder. Pain spread down his arm. Sweat poured down his face and his lungs struggled to take in air. With a huge effort, he rubbed a sleeve across his face to wipe the sweat from his eyes, and forced himself to look.

If your pictures aren't good enough, you aren't close enough. That was what Robert Capa had said of Omaha Beach on D-Day.

That's what one of his lecturers had drummed into him at Art College.

He moved one leg and then the other and … it was okay. So long as he had his eye to the viewfinder, it was okay. His mind and eye became part of the mechanism, controlling where it looked, what it recorded.

In desperation, the firemen were turning their hoses on the rioters. Baz felt a fine spray of water, shockingly cold. Closer to the engine, a young man was knocked off his feet.

Half crouching in the gap between a house and its low surrounding wall, he changed his film. His hands shook so much he couldn't fit the sprockets into the holes at the side of the film and when he tried to stand up his legs almost gave way underneath him.

The mob was being beaten back now. Baz took photographs at random, hardly bothering to frame the shots. The street he was in was dark, its power lost when another burning building collapsed. Most of the rioters had slipped away through the alleyways, back into the maze-like estates beyond. Behind the blank façade of the night, the sound of reggae spilt into the air. Brixton was celebrating.

Baz sunk against a wall. His shoulder still ached where the missile had struck him and he'd twisted his ankle slipping in the oil from an overturned car. Smoke and petrol fumes clogged his lungs.

On the other side of the road, one of the terraced houses had been turned into a make-shift clearing station for casualties. As he watched, the door opened and a figure came out, shoulders slumped, scarf tied over her head. He watched her cross the road and come towards him, and as she passed, he reached out his hand.

"Hi," he said hoarsely. "You okay?"

Abena's face was smeared with soot, and her hands had burns across the palms. She and her colleagues had had their shot at negotiating, she told him. But the police and the crowd were worlds apart, and nothing came of it. For most of the evening, she'd been helping with the casualties.

"You need the hospital?" Baz asked.

"I'm not spending what's left of the night sitting in casualty."

She took him to an attic bedsit that was a carbon copy of the last, in a squat not far from where he'd seen the car that morning. They both showered—bringing a hammering protest from the room across the landing, where the occupants had just got to sleep—and Abena held her hands under cold water. When she crawled into the narrow bed, Baz settled in her old wicker armchair, the red and gold kente cloth draped over him.

"Want to come in with your Milk and Honey?" Abena asked, lifting the covers. "For old times' sake?"

For a split second, he was tempted. His body ached with wounds visible and invisible. But …

"I thought you and that Rasta were an item?"

She gave him a long stare.

"Your loss, bwai," she said at last, turning away.

After a minute, her face still to the wall, she said, "You with that *maga* white girl Robyn told me about?"

"She's not just some skinny white girl."

"I'm just saying, bwai, be careful of the choices you make. Times like these, they matter."

In his mind's eye, he glimpsed Maia's face in the moonlit cemetery, the moment before she told him she was pregnant.

"You have no idea," he murmured.

The room fell quiet. He fell asleep, thinking of Maia and her baby, as the first of the city sparrows began their dawn chorus in the trees outside.

Chapter 59

For a while, when I first started school and was still on half days, my father would bring me to his office in the afternoons. I'd sit in a chair in the corner, drawing or looking at books, while he marked student papers and looked at bigger books with more words and fewer pictures. I suppose I should have been bored, but never was. Spending time with my mom was like being caught in a strobe light—alternately ignored or subjected to intense scrutiny. My father was diffuse, like background lighting. He'd smile from time to time, pass me a sweet, ask some companionable question or other. But mostly we were just content to be together.

On Monday morning, after I'd gone once more through my counselling at the PAS, and said yes when previously I'd said maybe, I was shown into an office that was a clone of my dad's. Its mullioned windows looked onto the tops of the plane trees in the centre of the square. The wooden desk was battered and scuffed, and its ancient swivel-and-tilt chair creaked when the doctor sat on it. But instead of leather and mint imperials, the room smelt of antiseptic. And the man behind the desk had a clear stare to match the strip light running like a scar across the high, plaster-moulded ceiling.

"You understand that I need to establish whether there are legal grounds for me to recommend abortion?" he said.

His goatee beard was prematurely silver, and his ear, the one

I could see, was the shape of an ammonite.

"The law as it stands requires me to establish that there is a risk to the mother's health if the pregnancy were to proceed."

I felt as if my brain had pins and needles. Was I at risk? Surely I was perfectly healthy? Perfectly capable of bearing a child? Then …

"However," he went on, "the law allows me to take your actual and foreseeable environment—your social and economic circumstances—into consideration."

"Okay …"

"Most doctors accept that a woman's mental health may be damaged if she is forced to undergo pregnancy in circumstances which she finds intolerable." He folded his hands in front of him and smiled. "So. Tell me about your circumstances."

It was like taking a viva for an exam I hadn't prepared. What if I said the wrong thing? What if he decided my mental health was in no danger?

"Just take your time," he said.

"Well, I've been volunteering for a charity in Coventry and living in a house that belongs to them. But if I have the baby, I can't go on working for them. And then I'll have no income and nowhere to live …"

"What about the father?"

An image of Ossie blurred and morphed into one of Baz and back again in the space of a heartbeat. I blinked hard.

"The father's out of the picture. Out of the country, in fact. I don't even know how to contact him."

"So there is no one to support you?"

"I suppose my parents would help—"

"But you are over twenty-one. Not a dependent?"

"No."

"And you're a graduate? With good career prospects? Or as good as anyone's can be said to be these days?"

"I guess."

He made a few notes, then he pushed his chair back and

stuck his legs out in front of him.

"It's not for me to tell you what to do. Ultimately, the choice has to be yours. But if you were my daughter, I believe I would say: have the abortion and then get on with the rest of your life."

My mind, which had been sliding over the surface of his words as if they were Teflon coated, found some traction and clung on.

"Yes."

"Yes? You mean, yes, that's your decision? You want to go ahead with the abortion?"

The air seemed to have left the room. I couldn't breathe, and my vision contracted to two pinholes of light in a grey mist. I concentrated and the doctor's face swam back into view.

"Yes. I want to go ahead."

"Then we'd better see about examining you."

I tried to put my head in another place, while his gloved hands poked and prodded inside me. But all roads led back to this room. Me with my legs drawn up and my knees apart, like a frog pinned out for vivisection. Naked from the waist down because I hadn't the sense to wear a skirt.

God, Ossie, I need you here. But if you were here, I wouldn't be, would I? Not like this.

My knees began to shake uncontrollably, jigging up and down as if they had a mind of their own. The doctor put out his hands to steady them.

"You can relax. I'm all done for now."

I sat up too quickly and my head spun. I waited until the walls had anchored themselves to the floor, then gathered up my clothes.

"You've been a while making up your mind to come to us," the doctor said, when I was once more seated in the chair by his desk. "That limits our options a little bit. You'll need to come in for a D and C, and as soon as possible, I'd say."

It sounded scary, putting it in words like that. "Will I need to stay in overnight?"

"That shouldn't be necessary. But you will need to bring certain things with you, and prepare for having a general anaesthetic. That means not eating or drinking before you come in. And having someone to look after you for a day or so afterwards. The nurse will give you all the details before you go."

He filled out a form, signed it with the usual illegible doctor's scrawl and passed it to me.

"You'll need the signature of a second doctor, but that can be arranged before you leave today. And good luck. I'm sure you've made the right decision."

Chapter 60

Broadsheets and tabloids alike screamed of 'an orgy of arson, looting and destruction', perpetrated by 'black thugs' and egged on by 'outside agitators bent on the complete collapse of civil order.' For three nights, Baz read, a community had been 'terrorised by vicious hooligans high on drugs.' The police, 'society's guardians,' had behaved with 'exemplary steadfastness and courage in the face of sustained attack.'

"They think it was drugs that drove those kids crazy?" Abena railed. "They think they need 'outside agitators' to tell them to get mad? And looting? If they imagine only black people helped themselves, then they're living in some fool's paradise."

The police kept the Tube station closed all day on Sunday. It made for an easy excuse to stay on and help Abena pick up the pieces. In the afternoon, they stood among the jeering crowds as the Home Secretary toured the areas of devastation, looking like a lumbering bear surrounded by angry dogs.

On Sunday night, the authorities flooded Brixton with over a thousand police and sealed off the area as far as the Kennington Oval. Overhead, the police's new 'Nightsun' helicopter hovered, its searchlight cutting a swathe through the darkened streets. On television, the Home Secretary announced that he had, "seen enough to convince me that there has been a serious breakdown of law and order."

The broadsheets on Monday morning were no better. There could be 'no excuse,' they said, for such a direct challenge to the rule of law in a community already suffering from 'endemic petty crime.' Other poor people didn't riot, did they? Poverty was therefore not a factor. Police harassment was not a factor. It was greed, lawlessness and drugs, pure and simple.

"For fuck's sake! Do they actually believe this crap? Are they so blind they can't see why kids have been driven to riot?"

Abena shook her head. "I have to work," she told Baz. "From what I hear, the courts are setting exemplary fines, making it difficult to post bail. Those kids will need help."

He could feel her eyes on him as he gathered and sorted his photographic equipment, tucking the precious rolls of exposed film deep in his inside pockets.

"Baz ... those pictures in the papers? You know they say the police are using them to identify trouble makers?"

He turned and met the cool beam of her stare.

"Just ... be careful of the choices you make," she repeated.

He kissed her cheek. It felt as if something that had been ripped apart was now finished, its loose ends tucked away. He and Abena were in two parts, but made good.

"I'll see you around," he said.

Baz closed his eyes as the train wound its way past Milton Keynes' concrete cows. For all the madness of the past few days, the Brixton disturbances had never deteriorated into a race war. The white kids on the streets on Saturday night had been hurling missiles alongside the black kids, not at them. There was hope in that, wasn't there?

And what about him and Maia? Was the father of her baby still in the picture? If not, did the fact that she was pregnant really mean they couldn't be together? He knew it must seem that way, seen through the lens of the past few weeks. Look at the way she'd had chips thrown at her, just because she'd sat next to him on a bench in a public place. And that was before you took that little bastard Gary into account.

But it needn't be like that. In other times and other places, maybe … He'd always said he'd pack it in here one day and go travelling. Collecting photographs for his portfolio. Would Maia come with him? He allowed himself to toy with an image of her in the passenger seat of a little car like Rebeccah's, their belongings bungee-roped to the roof.

He was getting ahead of himself. Way ahead of himself. All the same, by the time the train pulled up at Coventry Station, he had almost convinced himself they stood a chance. If only he could wind back the clock to that moment on Friday evening when Maia told him she was pregnant, start over without being such an arsehole …

Maia wasn't in the sitting room. And no one else seemed altogether pleased to see him.

"Maia's gone," Tom said. "She left Saturday morning."

"Gone where?" He stared at them, willing the words to mean something inconsequential. Something less final.

Libby touched his hand. "Baz, she packed her things and left. Stuck a note under Tom's door."

"So where is she?" he demanded. "When's she coming back?"

"I don't think she is coming back," Iain said.

"Don't be stupid!"

He pushed past Robyn and ran up the stairs two at a time. Everything in the bedroom was exactly as he left it. He sat on the bed and felt between the folds of the t-shirt. His note was still there. Untouched. Unread.

With a groan, his head sank to the pillow and he buried his face in the shirt. He could smell her hair, her skin.

Downstairs again, he slammed his hands on the table.

"What did you say to her?"

A circle of accusing eyes stared back.

"What did *you* say to her, more like?" Simon said. "The two of you go off together Friday evening. She comes back on her own and goes up to her room without speaking to anyone. Then Saturday morning, she's gone."

"What was in the note she left you?"

Tom shrugged. "Just that she was sorry to let us down, but she had stuff to deal with. That she'd send for her trunk when she knew where she was going to be—"

"I want to see it."

Tom shook his head.

Baz leaned forward, his fists clenched on the table. "I said, I want to see it!"

"And I say it's none of your bloody business."

He looked round at them. Tom, Iain, Robyn. Libby on the sofa. Simon hidden behind a copy of *Searchlight*.

A sound was building up inside him, an unstoppable roar of shame and frustration and loss. Libby flinched as it burst from his lungs and he slammed past her into the yard. He wrenched the gate so hard he was in danger of dragging it off his hinges, and kicked it shut again. A man delivering flyers took one look at his face and gave their door a wide berth.

Baz turned the other way, towards London Road. It was the middle of the day and the cemetery was open. He entered through the main gates, threading his way along the paths till he found the place where he'd brought Maia three days before. Here, on the bank above the lines of simple white crosses, it was possible to imagine that no one had walked since he and Maia lay there, breast to breast, hip to hip, thigh to thigh.

She hadn't planned to go. Not before he walked off and left her. If she'd changed her mind, it could only be because he put her in an impossible situation. She'd tried to tell him, over and over, that it couldn't work. And when he'd pushed her to tell him why, the answer had sent him off in a storming sulk. He'd driven her away as surely as if he'd told her to fuck off. But where had she gone? And was she safe?

A light rain began to fall. He dropped to his knees on the grass, turned his face upwards and let the rain wash away the salt.

Chapter 61

My instructions from the PAS were: not to eat less than five hours before my appointment; after that, not to drink less than two hours before my appointment, and then only water; not to smoke, not to chew gum; to bring a nightdress or a long baggy t-shirt; to bring sanitary towels …

"Thanks," I said, as Genny handed me a worn blue shirt. Seemed I was destined to go round borrowing other people's t-shirts.

"Never mind the fecking shirt. I should be going there with you."

"I'll be fine."

"Trust me, you'll not want to be alone."

"I'll be alone whether you come or not. They don't allow anyone in if you're having a general anaesthetic."

"Then what about when you're waiting?"

"Genny, please!"

I turned away but she put her arms around me, not letting me go.

"Maia, what is it?" She gave me a little shake. "C'mon. I know you. What are you not saying?"

I screwed my eyes tight and gulped down the pain in my throat.

"I can't bear the thought of having a witness."

"Oh, Maia." She pulled me to her and hugged me tight.

"You're not doing anything wrong. You know that, don't you?"

"My head knows that. It's just …"

"Your heart says otherwise?"

I nodded mutely.

"Maia, listen to me. You don't want me to come with you, then fine. But they told you, you can't just walk out on your own after a general anaesthetic. You'll need some looking after, at least for a day or two."

"So I'll call you when it's over."

"Promise me you will?"

"Promise."

I tried to look brave as I waved Genny goodbye, but by the time I got to Bedford Square, I was a jellyfish, all rubber limbs and a stomach that wanted to turn itself inside out.

In the garden at the heart of the square, the giant London plane trees were coming into leaf, their trunks mottled olive, grey and light brown. By a small pavilion with a green roof, a woman sat reading a book. If I could have just a few minutes of that tranquillity, it would give me courage. I circled the railings, peering through the shrubs like a little child shut out of a sweetshop. It took two laps before I spotted the old-fashioned sign, half obscured by shrubs. *Bedford Square. Private. Access to Key Holders Only.*

Nothing for it, then, but to head for the clinic. As I climbed the steps, a grinning stone face leered down from the Palladian arch above the door. I stuck two fingers up at it before I pressed the bell.

A small, round West Indian nurse showed me into a cubicle with a hospital bed and lemon-coloured bedding. The greying hair at her temples reminded me of Pinda. Pinda running my bath when my mother was once again staying late at the university. Pinda saying goodnight and tiptoeing away to sit on the veranda, singing to herself while we waited for the sound of the ancient, asthmatic Seat that would bring Mom home. She patted my hand.

"You just take a little time getting undressed and making yourself comfortable, dear," the nurse said. "Then I'll come back and we'll put a pessary in, to make you nice and relaxed, down there, you know?"

She slipped away, silent on her white soft-soled shoes. I let my backpack slip to the floor. Oh God, what if she could tell the baby wasn't white? Would she think that was why I was getting rid of it?

My fingers fumbled with the zip on my skirt. For the last few days, my jeans had become impossible to do up. At thirteen weeks' gestation, the baby was three inches long and could blink, swallow and suck its thumb.

If I was going to do this, it had be now, before it was too late.

The skirt dropped to the floor and I started on my shirt. I could see myself in the mirror over the sink, skinny and angular still, my belly just convex, my boobs swollen and mapped with blue veins. The gown was hanging on the back of the door. I took a step towards it and a wave of emotion scoured through me. Tears fought their way through cracks and chinks until the force of the flood waters took my legs out from under me and I folded up on the bed and wept.

I wept for Ossie and Baz and the whole bloody mess of an equation I'd tried to solve and failed. I wept for Baz's mother and for poor Mr Arain. For all the 'niggers' and 'Pakis' and '*toubabs*' and 'half-castes' who'd faced their tormentors day after day without letting go of their dignity.

I cried for the innocence I'd lost and the burdens I never wanted to shoulder. For thwarted plans and disappointed hopes. I cried until I had no tears left, and even then sobs convulsed me like dry heaving.

When the storm passed, I washed the snot and tears from my face and dried it on a paper towel. I felt lighter, as though the tears had washed away a hundredweight of chains.

I had found the strength I'd been missing.

Chapter 62

When Baz reached the garment factory, a lorry was backed up against the loading bay. The driver leaned against the cab, smoking a fag, leaving Vik to unload the large consignment of cloth. As Baz approached, Vik straightened and stood with his arms folded.

"I wondered when you'd show your face round here, *gora*."

Baz's jaw tensed, but he jerked his head towards the back of the lorry. "Want a hand with that?"

Without replying, Vik hoisted a bale and carried it over to an empty corner of the storage sheds. Taking that as assent, Baz shouldered another bale.

"If you're going to do it, do it properly," Vik snapped. "The label needs to face outwards." Choking down a retort, Baz turned the bale round.

They toiled without speaking until the lorry was empty and the consignment of cloth stored. As the lorry drove away, Vik broke his silence.

"Want some tea, *haan*?"

They climbed the steps of the old weaving sheds, past the steamy air of the pressing floor and into the chatter of the sewing room. Women in brightly coloured *shalwar kameez* stooped over the machines or stood at cutting tables. Baz scanned the room, trying to spot Mohan's mother. He had an uneasy feeling that, if Vik had told his family what he'd said, Mandeep and Daljit would be all set to throw him in the canal. But he saw no sign of the two brothers. And Gurinder stood up and shook his hand in a soldier's grip.

"Bhajan, you have not been to see us in a long time."

Baz felt himself breathe easier, but the fact that he'd wronged Gurinder-ji still scalded his conscience.

"It's good to see you, sir," he said.

"You must come to dinner with us soon. Some of my wife's *sarson ka saag, haan*? What do you say?"

"I'd like that, sir."

Vik poured some *masala chai* from a big enamel pot.

"Be careful with that long hair out by the machines," Gurinder called after them as they left the office. "Thank God, at last you have learnt to tie it up."

As soon as they were out of earshot, Vik grinned.

"You remember the first time you came to dinner at our house?"

Baz remembered. "You'd just cut your hair, and your father gave me the third degree about why I'd grown mine long and who my father was and why I didn't wear a turban or a beard."

Vik posed with one hand in the small of his back, mimicking Gurinder-ji. "'*Arré*, what is the world coming to? My son cuts his hair and you wear it loose like a wild man.'"

Baz laughed. "Your mother kept saying, 'Not over dinner, *ji*. And your father would reply, 'I'm only asking, *ji*. The young man does not mind, *haan*?'"

"And then *ma-ji* would give you another portion to show she didn't think that was any way to treat a guest."

"Uuggh! I ate so much that night I thought I was going to burst."

They sat at the top of the shaft where the bales came up, legs dangling over the edge, and drank their tea.

"How are you, Vik?"

"Okay. Sick of this place."

"Nothing new there, then."

"Piss off."

Another silence rolled past.

"Hey, how's Abena?" Vik asked. "I thought about her last weekend."

"I was there," Baz said.

"You were there? During the riots?"

In his mind he caught a whiff of petrol. *Right in the thick of it. And it was like being in the middle of a war zone.* He cleared his throat.

"Saturday night, yeah. Took about a dozen rolls of film. I've started developing them. Got to be at least a few worth printing."

"This a new career as a photojournalist?"

"Dunno about that." He rubbed his eyes. "I'm getting an idea for something I could do here, though. Take some more pictures of the opposition, try and show people the fucked up stuff that's been going on."

"Lens is mightier than that sword?"

"Something like that." He glanced at his friend's taut face, at his jigging foot. "What about you? You done any painting?"

Vik jerked his head towards the office. "Don't give me the chance, do they?"

They both fell silent. Baz shifted uneasily on the edge of the lift shaft.

"Look, Vik," he said. "The things I said last time …"

"Forget it."

"No, listen. Mohan told me what your parents did for his family. Shit, anyway, I was way out of line, and I'm sorry."

Vik took a crumpled piece of paper out of his jacket pocket and smoothed it on his leg. Baz saw the cheap white paper, the crudely cut newspaper lettering.

"They send you this, *haan*?"

Baz wiped his hand across his mouth. "It was after the article came out about my mother's death." His voice caught in his throat and he had to swallow before he could speak again. "The envelope. It had the same spelling mistake. You know, 'Sing' without the 'h'?"

"Ignorant *saley*." Vik stared into the shaft, the colour coming and going in his face. "You know I never meant for anything like this to happen, *yaar*?"

"I know."

They held each other's gaze for a minute. Baz could see the thin film of his own bravado mirrored in Vik's eyes.

"You're right about taking pictures of them," Vik said. "They're scared of you, *yaar*."

"Bollocks."

"Why do you think it's you they go after? They're shitting themselves. That camera of yours shows things they don't want people to see.

Before Baz could answer, he heard the stuttery sound of a VW Beetle pulling into the yard.

"*Phenchod!*" Vik scrambled to his feet. "Mandeep. Gotta get back to work." He turned to Baz, his fingers slicking back his hair. "Look, I haven't changed my mind about that Rasta's exhibition. I won't take part. But I'll give you some names of people who might. Just … be straight with them, *haan*? Tell them why I'm not doing it."

"I did. When I spoke to Paras—"

"I know. That's why I trust you."

They ran down the steep steps. At the edge of the loading bay Vik slapped Baz's shoulder.

"Listen, *yaar*, you be careful out there among these *gora*."

Chapter 63

I phoned Genny from a payphone at the clinic, and told her I'd decided to go home. Then I walked to Goodge Street and caught the Northern Line to Hampstead.

The hall of the tall, redbrick townhouse smelt of floor polish and muddy boots. By the look of the clobber piled up there, my mom was back from the Kalahari. She and Dad were in the drawing room, a tray of tea and scones laid out between them—afternoon tea being one English custom Mom had adopted with a passion.

"Maia. Sweetie!" she said.

My dad smiled at me from his place on the sofa. He was sucking on one end of his metal-framed glasses, a habit he'd picked up since Mom made him throw away his pipe. I sat next to him and he put his arm round me and kissed the top of my head.

"So," Mom said, pouring tea into a china cup, "to what do we owe this pleasure? I thought you were hell-bent on showing us we're not needed any more?"

I rubbed a hand over my belly, my mouth dry.

"Actually, Mom, there's something you need to know."

It took my mom about twenty-four hours to get past the 'how could you be so stupid?' phase and try to take over my life.

Once she'd got over the idea she was going to be a grandmother (I'm far too young!) she came round to the idea of being midwife, birth partner, and (for all I knew) wet nurse as well. The Golden Mean was not a concept Mom ever embraced.

"Giving birth is a perfectly natural experience," she said, over breakfast. "Western women make far too big a deal of it, if you ask me. Just think of all those tribeswomen going out into the forest on their own."

Just think of the neo-natal deaths, I wanted to say, but didn't.

Whenever I could, I crawled away to my small, white-sheeted bed at the top of the house, making the excuse I was 'still very tired'. I'd close my eyes for a while and try to come to terms with the path I had chosen.

Until that moment in the clinic the baby had been an abstraction, an experiment I had to decide whether to continue or to terminate. But somewhere in that storm of weeping, I'd found a fierce attachment to this extraordinary being with the odds so stacked against it.

I'd ditched any romantic notions of a gallant protector keeping me and the baby safe. Whatever was coming, the two of us would face it.

Preferably without the two-edged sword of my mother's 'help'.

Submitting to a rare dose of maternal cosseting was pleasant enough for a couple of days. Grandma Brook's traditional American recipes came out, and we ate pancakes with maple syrup, and bran muffins, and homemade Boston Baked Beans. Mom went to the library and came back with armfuls of books about nutrition during pregnancy, and we had broccoli with dinner every night.

"Of course, there's no point trying to do anything before

Easter. But as soon as the holidays are over, we must make you a pre-natal appointment. You'll go to Dr Gillespie, naturally."

I shuddered. Dr Gillespie had looked after me since I was a baby. He'd chucked me under the chin and given me lollies when I had to have an injection. The thought of him poking around like the doctor at the clinic was plain weird.

"And we must get you into the NCT. Goodness, I hope it's not too late. You practically have to book their classes before you conceive."

God, how many times had I been through this, growing up? How many projects had she taken over, how many problems had she tried to solve for me, only to get bored before she'd seen it through and leave me high and dry? My school days were littered with the corpses of my mother's abandoned enthusiasms.

"Mom, this is my baby. I can take care of it myself."

"And you've done such a good job of that so far, haven't you?" Her pen scratched across the page of her notebook, planning Easter (or was it my pregnancy?) like a military campaign. "Have you had a single pre-natal appointment yet?"

And of course, that was why she always took over. Because she never believed I could manage as well as she could. And because she could make me believe she was right. I scuffed the toe of my shoe along the floor, reduced to the role of truculent schoolgirl.

"I only made up my mind to keep the baby a couple of days ago!"

She laid her pen down and put her hands on my shoulders, tilting her face up towards mine.

"Sweetie, you're still very young. This is a big step and you're going to need all the help you can get."

"Yes, well. Not necessarily from you."

The colour rose in my mom's face. "Maia, just because I don't want to see you tied down with a baby—"

I knew it. Before long, in her mind, the child would be hers. She'd be planning to take it off to a mud hut somewhere, telling everyone how she'd sacrificed everything to bring up her grandchild.

I wasn't sure if Mom even listened when I tried to tell her about Ossie, about who and where he was. As for Dad, he and I had always communicated without saying much. It was the only way to get a word in edgeways. But that evening, he took me into his study and scrutinised my face in the light from his antique desk lamp.

"You always did know how to make life difficult for yourself, even as a toddler." He shook his head. "You know what a hard road it is you've chosen?"

"I haven't thought about much else for the past three months."

"And, head and heart, it's what you want to do?"

"Head and heart, yes."

"Then I suppose you'd better have my blessing."

Mom had a big family gathering planned for Easter Sunday. The evening before, she stood over a pile of ingredients in the semi-basement kitchen, preparing a marinade for the vast shoulder of lamb she had ordered. I was peeling cloves of garlic, my fingers absorbing the pungent smell.

"Granny Hassett will have to be told, of course," she said. "After dinner will be the best time. We don't want to spoil the meal."

"And what do you think is going to spoil it? The fact that I'm pregnant or that fact that the father is black?"

Mom laid down her bunch of rosemary and stared at me, wide eyed.

"Maia, what a thing to say!"

"You need to face it, Mom. My baby's father is a black South African."

"Well, thank heavens it will be growing up in England and not in South Africa." She raised her Elizabeth David hachoir and brought it down energetically on the chopping board. A smell of garlic and rosemary filled the kitchen.

"Mom, contrary to what you seem to think, growing up in England is not a cast-iron guarantee against racism."

She gave a sort of trilling laugh that made me want to slap her.

"Sweetie, you don't have to listen to people like that. You're better than they are. Anyone seeing you and your beautiful baby will see how silly they are."

"For God's sake, Mom. You can't just turn a deaf ear to these people and hope they'll shut up." I put my hand over my belly. "This child is going to have problems you and I can't even imagine. How can you give it any sort of help or support if you won't even acknowledge that?"

She came round my side of the kitchen island and rubbed my arms, the way she used to when she was building me up for something I didn't want to do (like spending another summer holiday in a remote mud hut).

"Sweetie, I'm colour blind. You know that. I don't even notice what colour people are."

"Do you think it's going to help if you stick your head up your own arse?"

"Maia!"

I shook myself free.

"It's fine to sound off about far away countries, isn't it? God forbid you should acknowledge the problems people have on your own doorstep."

I ran from the kitchen and up the three flights to my bedroom. By the time I got to the top, I was winded. Scary how much of my oxygen supply this baby was using. But if I stayed with my mother, I was going to suffocate. Always assuming I didn't kill her first.

Someone needs to carry on here, nosisi, Ossie had said. Well, it might not have been the path he had in mind, but I'd chosen my road. And leafy, liberal Hampstead was a wrong turning.

When I came back down carrying my backpack, my father was standing on the landing, sucking his glasses. The sun, low over the horizon, glinted off his bald head.

"You all right, poppet?" he asked.

"I'm sorry, Dad. I can't stay. She's going to turn me back into her little girl, and I can't handle that."

"Where will you go?"

"I'll let you know when I figure it out." I kissed his cheek. "Don't worry. I won't do anything stupid."

"Indeed. I should think you've used your quota of stupidity for one year, don't you? You're like your mother—no, don't look at me like that. She always thinks any obstacle can be overcome if she throws herself at it with enough energy, and nine times out of ten, she's right. I'm the one who stays at home worrying about the consequences."

"Dad!"

He gave me that clock-stopping look he used when he asked something of absolute importance. "Just promise you won't be too stubborn to pick up the phone and ask for help if you need it? I want that grandchild of mine taken care of."

"I promise."

"Get on with you, then, before I remember where I put the key to the coal cellar."

My mom was at the top of the basement steps as I reached the hall, still wearing the PVC apron with 'Cinzano' written across it.

"You know, you should try staying here to work one summer," I said. "There's more to England than Hampstead. You might surprise yourself."

She gave a half smile. A suspicion of redness showed around her eyes. "Well, maybe it is a little less … dull than when your father first brought me here. But, Maia, sometimes we need somewhere safe and dull to come back to. Between the adventures."

"I know." She opened her mouth to speak again but I cut her off. "But this isn't just an adventure. It's going to be my life. And I have to come to terms with that, in my own way." I hesitated, then gave her a peck on the cheek. "Bye, Mom. I'll see you before too long."

I jumped on the first southbound Tube to Euston and took the escalator, up past the PAS poster ('Pregnant? Happy About It?') and onto the main concourse. I thought of Baz's mother, running away with her newborn child to the place where no one knew who his father was. She thought she would be safe, and all that happened was that she didn't see them coming. Going back to Coventry had a perverse logic to it. At least there, I knew the face of the enemy. No one in Paradise Road was going to pretend everything was for the best in the best of all possible worlds.

I stopped a guy in a British Rail uniform.

"I can't see a Coventry train on the board."

"You won't. Not till tomorrow. Last one's just left."

"Last one? But it's only—"

"Easter timetable, sweetheart."

I considered making a dash to Genny's in Hounslow before the Tube shut down too. But I was tired. I sat down on one of the red metal benches near the ticket office. The station was emptying, the departure board erasing itself as one train after another left without being replaced. The light outside faded and the forecourt acquired an echo.

I watched an old man in an oversized coat ferret in a rubbish bin, before sitting on the bench next to mine. He gave me a furtive look, dug in his inside pocket and brought out a half-eaten sandwich, which he stuffed in his mouth as if he thought I might snatch it from him. I smiled at him and after a while he smiled back.

Most of the lights on the station had been turned off by now. I began to notice figures moving in the shadows. To begin with, they avoided me, but after a while, they seemed to accept I was roosting there for the night and treated me like one of them.

From time to time, a couple of coppers from the Transport Police would pass through and they'd rise like pigeons and flit away. Once, the old man on the bench next to me stayed asleep when the others fled and was shaken awake.

"Excuse me, *sir*," the policeman said, "these benches are for the travelling public only." The old man shambled off, unprotesting, into the cold. The policeman watched after him until he was lost in the darkness of the courtyard.

"Sorry about that, miss," he said.

"He wasn't doing any harm."

"Rules is rules, miss," he said. "May I see your ticket?"

Night passed and light began to filter through the glass frontage. Just before nine, the station buffet opened. I looked around for my companions, but they'd vanished at first light. I bought myself a nasty cup of tea and a bacon sandwich. The smell of garlic still lingered on my fingers. In a few hours time my family would be sitting down to marinated roast lamb.

But these domesticated phases of Mom's never lasted. In a few days or a few weeks, she would be lost in her latest research project. Forget to come home for days on end. Telephone a 'good night' if you were lucky. Well, fine. I wasn't going to waste any more time waiting for her.

Chapter 64

Baz carried a crate of accumulated rubbish outside. At the foot of the slope, the rockery was almost finished. He'd hauled the big stones into place the week before and Rebeccah had placed Noordin's coral limestone at its apex. Now it only wanted for the threat of late frosts to pass before she planted it up.

Rebeccah had a brazier going and was feeding it with dead wood and dry cuttings. The smell of wood smoke drifted down the garden. Sweetish. Not unpleasant. He forced himself to climb the path, stopping a little way off when the heat from the fire began to warm his skin.

"Any chance I could use that to get rid of some old rubbish?"

As he dropped the first batch of photographs into the fire, the flames leapt up and a new, more chemical smell cut through the wood smoke. He stood his ground, forcing himself to override his primitive, animal brain. Just before the photographs shrivelled and burnt, he thought he saw Maia's face engulfed in flames. A pain twisted his gut and he flinched away, screwing his eyes shut. Rebeccah's hands folded over his.

"Are you sure about this, Bhajan? All these photographs?"

The smoke caught his throat, making his voice harsh. "I need the space."

"Would you like me to deal with them for you?"

He felt a swell of gratitude. But he wasn't a child any more.

"Turn and turn about," she said, forestalling objection. "Can you spare me some time tomorrow morning? To help out at the Meeting House?"

He and Rebeccah had been working in the garden round the back of the Quaker Meeting House for about an hour when the first Friends began to arrive. He could see them through the open French doors of the vestibule. Quietly spoken, saying a few words, they greeted one another and began to drift up the stairs to the silent Meeting room. Then families began to arrive. Some children ran by, laughing. A few people came outside, shook hands and commented on their progress in the garden.

Rebeccah pulled off her gardening gloves.

"There," she said. "I think that's broken the back of it. Thank you, Bhajan. No need to stay if you don't want to. I can finish the planting after Meeting."

He watched her through the big windows as she climbed the stairs, half relieved and half disappointed she hadn't asked him to join her. A profound hush settled over the building. He leaned into the spade again, feeling the not unwelcome ache in his muscles. The smell of newly turned clods of earth and the rich odour of compost filled his nostrils. A robin eyed him from the top of a nearby fence-post.

A latecomer hurried through the door. Baz recognised him: an elderly Attender who always waited to hear the Sunday Service on Radio 4 before coming out. As children, they'd set their watches by him. When he arrived, it was time to get up and go down the stairs to their own Meeting below.

Sure enough, a gaggle of children ran down, shushed by the accompanying grownups. They disappeared into their own room and the hallway fell quiet again. Baz moved to the back door and stepped inside. His trainers were claggy with earth. He took them off and set them next to Rebeccah's wellies. Barefoot, he walked up the stairs.

He slipped in and sat near the door, his feet noiseless on the warm cork tiles. The room was so familiar it made his heart contract. The chairs were arranged in a flattened circle, several rows deep, Rebeccah in the innermost row, her head bowed. Next to her, a man with a tiny baby swung a Moses basket to and fro.

After a while, the quiet enfolded him. A cloud of dust motes danced in the sunshine above a bowl of daffodils. Easter, he thought. Quakers never made a thing of it, but someone always brought daffodils.

A discreet shuffling broke the stillness and a man rose to his feet. Kenneth, one of those who could be relied upon to speak at almost every Meeting—some words of inspiration, the wonder of God's creation, that sort of thing.

Kenneth waited with his hands folded, gathering his words to him. When he spoke, his voice reminded Baz of Walter delivering the day's lesson to his ragged congregation. "Friends, we are here on this beautiful Easter Sunday, the sun streaming through our windows, warmth in the air, the promise of new life in the soil."

He could swear he'd heard words like these on successive Easter Sundays all through his teens. Yet when Kenneth raised his head, something had obliterated his usual twinkling smile.

"Most of you will be unaware that, yesterday, a terrible storm cloud passed over our city."

Chapter 65

Paradise Road had welcomed me back into the fold as only Paradise Road could. Robyn squealed. Tom hugged me tight. Simon said, "Prodigal daughter? Fresh out of fatted calf, we are. Better come back next week," and buried his grin behind a newspaper. Libby and Iain started cooking. But there was a Baz-shaped hole in the middle of the room and everyone was skirting round it.

And now he was back, filling the room as he always did, staring at me as if trying to decide if I was a figment of his imagination.

Iain coughed. "I think these two need a wee time on their own."

One after another, they melted away and still Baz didn't move.

"Look at you. You actually look pregnant." His hands reached for mine and he pulled me to my feet. His white cheesecloth shirt clung to his chest and set off his coffee-coloured skin. And those dark brown eyes looked the way I remembered them just before he started to kiss me.

"You damn well walked away, Baz. You left me in the middle of a cemetery!"

"I know. I left you a note, but you never … God, Maia, I thought I'd never see you again."

"Was the thought of my being pregnant so horrifying?"

"Is that what you thought? Oh, fuck ..." His eyes closed and his hands gripped the back of a chair. "Maia, think about all those times you've been caught up with the racists. Gary trying to burn you with his lighter. Those bloody kids throwing chips. Every time, it's been because of me. Because you've been seen with a 'Paki'. I'm not stupid. I know you're not going to want to inflict that on your kid."

"No, I'm not. But I won't have much bloody choice." I took a step towards him. "Baz, with or without you, this baby's going to be a target for racists."

"What do you mean?"

"The father. He's black."

He rocked back on his heels, as if I'd slapped him. "Are you and he still ...?"

"He's in South Africa. He doesn't even know."

"Right."

He passed a hand over his face. "I've been a dickhead, haven't I?"

"Pretty much."

I could see the teardrop mole at the corner of his eye, the vein throbbing in his temple. My own heart seemed to be tripping over itself and I had the bittersweet taste of irony in my mouth. Fresh air. I needed fresh air.

"Can we go somewhere else? Preferably *not* the cemetery?"

"Anywhere you like."

We sat on a bench in Swanswell Park, next to a pond that was overdue for dredging. I could feel Baz's hand, his little finger touching mine.

"Maia, where did you go when you left here?"

A couple of little girls leant over the murky water, feeding bread to the ducks. Their mother called to them to be careful. After a time, Baz's hand crept away.

"You're right. It's none of my business."

I wrapped my arms round my stomach. It hurt to say the words, but I owed him some honesty.

"I was going to have an abortion."

"Because of what I—?"

"No!" I felt a wisp of anger at his presuming so much, but it evaporated as quickly as it formed. "You'd shown me how hard it would be, having a mixed race kid with an absent father. And I wasn't sure if I was tough enough to cope."

"It is," he said. "And you are."

I looked away across the pond. The little girls had gone and the ducks had returned to dabbling in the weeds.

"So what made you change your mind?"

"I guess I reached a point where all the problems in the world were less important than the fact I wanted this baby to live."

Baz put his hand over mine. I could feel the warmth of the sun on the back of my neck, and the breeze on my face. A line of ducklings paddled in their mother's wake, as if linked by an invisible cord.

"So, the other night, in the cemetery, you weren't telling me to piss off out of your life?" he said.

"Not before you walked out on me, no."

"And now?" His thumb drew circles on my knuckles. "You don't have to deal with this on your own, you know. Not unless you want to."

"Why would you want to get involved? This isn't your child."

"Because it's yours."

He laid his hand on the curve of my belly. I could feel the weight and the warmth of it through my skirt. This was how it was supposed to be. Enjoying the moment. Looking forward to the future.

Just beneath his hand, I felt a flutter, a wriggle, not much more than a bubble of wind.

"Oh, my God …"

Baz sat bolt upright, his hand flying off me as if he'd burnt himself. I trapped it and brought it back to its resting place.

"It moved. I felt the baby move."

My baby was alive. Not in five months' time, but here and now. Through a haze of mingled terror and happiness, I saw a smile form on Baz's lips.

Then, just as before, his face closed down. He pushed off from the bench and staggered to the edge of the pond, staring out over the water.

"You have to get out of here, Maia. You have to take that baby somewhere safe."

"What? What are you talking about?" I grabbed his arm and shook it. "Baz, you have to stop fucking with me like this!"

When he turned round, his face was a mask, his jaw rigid with tension.

"The skinheads killed someone, yesterday afternoon. They chased a Sikh student down the Foleshill Road and through the Precinct. Stabbed him in the Barracks car park, left him bleeding to death."

"Oh, God ..."

"He was about to start college, Maia. He had his whole life ahead of him and they cut him down like he was nothing." His eyes, when they focused on me at last, were so sad I could have drowned in them. "Maia, you have to get back on that train, before something else happens."

"No!" I felt tears welling up and shook them away. "What have you been telling me all this time? Running away does no good."

He opened his mouth to argue, but no words came out.

"If I want my child to grow up safe, I'm going to have to stand my ground and fight, whether it's here with you or somewhere else on my own. So if you meant what you said about my not being alone—"

He took my hands between his and held them up against his heart.

"I meant it."

"Then I'm staying."

Chapter 66

If anyone wanted to get rid of the entire Asian population of Coventry, Baz thought, they'd just handed them an opportunity on a fucking great plate.

The seats in the borrowed school hall had filled as soon as the doors opened, but still people poured in. Almost all Asian, almost all men. A few white faces salted the mix, Simon amongst them. A scattering of women, in Western dress or *shalwar kameez*. Baz spotted Narinder among a group of college friends, her hair coiled into an elaborate ponytail. Behind them, Mohan stood with the guys from Sona, his face strained. People crammed the aisles and blocked the exits.

Baz's interior demons painted flames on the ceiling tiles, heated the stuffy air to ignition point, blew smoke in his face and turned the babble of voices into the fire's roar. In his head, people screamed. Scrambled over the chairs. Trampled one another to get to the exits.

Not. Now.

He drove the demons back to hell and elbowed through the crowd to where Vik was standing.

"You know what this is going to be, don't you?" Vik said. "Some bunch of 'Community Leaders' telling us how important it is to behave ourselves, not make a fuss. As if I hadn't heard enough of that from my *pyo* already."

A small delegation marched onto the stage, self conscious

and out of step. Gurinder-ji was there, and Abdul Saleem. Their leader, a man in a deep blue turban, advanced on the lectern with the air of a Prime Minister approaching the dispatch box.

"Who's that?"

"Jaswant Bal," Vik told him. "They're saying he'll be a councillor at the next election."

"He'll be in parliament, by the look of him."

"Good afternoon. *Sat sri akaal, namaste ji and asalaam alaikum,*" Mr Bal intoned over the babble of voices. "Welcome, all of you. I am pleased to see that so many have turned up to support us. Before we begin, perhaps we could each of us offer a prayer in silence for the victim and his family?"

Heads bowed and the room held its breath. Mr Bal cleared his throat and gathered their attention once more.

"I must report to you first on a most productive meeting this morning with our local constabulary." He spread his hands to show that he spoke for all of them on the stage. "The police, actually, are doing their very best. As you will know from reading the papers, they have arrested five youths for this terrible murder."

No names released as yet, of course. But Baz had a sick feeling that one would turn out to be his erstwhile foster brother. When they announced the arrests, he'd gone out prowling the streets, frantic to know, one way or another. But Gary was nowhere to be found.

"... and we have the assurance of the Chief Constable that any attack on a member of the Asian community will be treated as would any attack on a white individual."

Jaswant Bal paused to draw breath and someone at the back of the audience grabbed his chance.

"We're not going to sit around and ask the police to please stop the nasty people hurting us." Heads craned to see who spoke. He was on his feet, a bareheaded young man in a patterned jumper. "This is our home, and I say we fight to protect it."

An angry rumble of approval came from the younger

members of the audience. Jaswant Bal held up his hands for quiet.

"Please, please. I understand your frustration. But fighting is not the way. Our plan is to make a peaceful demonstration of our opposition—"

"Bit late for that," a voice shouted.

Mr Bal made another attempt to command the room, but the mutiny had taken hold. Baz caught a glimpse of Mohan, shouting.

"We have to show these racists we can stand up to them!"

More yells of agreement. Vik put his hands to his mouth and bellowed, "Let's show them a fight!"

Gurinder-ji strode forward, skewering his son with a glance.

"It will not help any of us if we become violent. Our best response is to protest, yes, to show that we will not submit to violence, certainly, but above all to remain peaceful and law-abiding citizens."

"We've tried it that way and where has it got us?" Patterned Jumper called.

"We're not going to be like you, uncles, and bow our heads when the *goras* call us Pakis."

"This is our home and we're not going anywhere."

"And if we do as the blacks have done and riot in the streets, where will that get us?" Gurinder asked. "You want the police crawling round our community as they are round the blacks? You want our women stopped in the streets like criminals?"

"What makes you think we need protecting, *haan*?" a young woman called from the far side of the hall. One of Narinder's group, her hair cropped short so she stood out from the other women. "You think you men are the only ones who can organise yourselves?"

Jaswant Bal edged Gurinder away from the lectern.

"Please everyone. We have no intention of being passive, or taking this lying down or whatsoever. If you will listen please to our plan ..."

Grudgingly, the room fell quiet.

"Understand, this is not the murder of one young man," Mr Bal told them. "It is an assault on all Asians living in Britain and it is incumbent on us to respond accordingly." His gaze swept the room. "Do you not all have connections? *Biraderi*? *Zat*? Family living in other parts of the country? We must see to it, all of us, that friends and relatives come from all over the country. We must make ordinary British people sit up and take notice. Television, the Press, they must be made to understand what is happening in our towns and our streets."

Mr Bal brought them to a pitch of tension then lowered his voice.

"This march will be peaceful. This march will not be marred by hooliganism and mindless violence. We will show people that this atrocity has been perpetrated on decent, hard-working people, who know how to behave in a civilised society."

"See what I mean?" Vik said, as the meeting began to disperse.

"It's not such a bad plan," Baz said.

"No?" Vik threw him a look of disgust as they were half led, half carried out the door by the press of people. "If they think the beefheads are going to let a bunch of Asians march right through the middle of Coventry and not try to pick a fight, they're even stupider than I thought."

Mohan, some of the Bhangra band, Narinder and her friend, and the young man in the patterned jumper who had kicked off the first protests were all on the drive outside. Mohan whacked his fist into his palm. He still had that intense look, as if someone had lit a fuse in him.

"Fight, hah! We won't start a fight, but you can be sure there'll be one."

"I don't know about anyone else," Vik told them, "but I'm not sitting around for a month before we show those *haramzadey* we won't be kicked around. I say we hold our own march, this weekend. Who's with me?"

Patterned Jumper jerked his head. "I'll be there." He scribbled down a phone number on a piece of paper which he thrust at Vikram. "Call during the day, when my *abu* is at work."

"Cheers, Saeed. *Bara changa.*"

"I'm in," Mohan said, and the rest of the Sona line-up murmured assent.

"What about us?" Narinder said. "You going to be like your father and tell us the women are meant to stay behind and make food for the *langar*?"

Vik frowned. "If I let you come, my uncle will kill me."

"If you *let* us come?" said Narinder's friend. "The little prince thinks it is up to him whether to allow us to come?"

She was about five foot nothing but, in Baz's opinion, she looked more than capable of whipping them all into line. Vik shrugged.

"Fine, fine. And you can have my balls in a jar, too, once uncle-ji has finished cutting them off." He turned to Baz. "What about you, *yaar*?"

He stared round the circle of tense faces. A thin brown line of *desi* kids, trying to stop the fascists without starting a bloodbath. Some chance. But they had to try, didn't they?

"Sure," he said.

"And bring your camera, *haan*? If there's going to be a ruck, we want people to see it."

Chapter 67

"Would you like to hear your baby's heartbeat, Miss Hassett?"

"We can do that?"

I was lying on the examination table in Dr Kheraj's surgery. I could feel its stiff paper cover under my fingertips, hear my own heart pulsing in my ears.

The doctor had weighed me, measured me, poked me, prodded me, tested my urine for sugar and protein, asked questions about Ossie and his medical history that I was in no position to answer, and scolded me gently for leaving my first antenatal appointment so late. Now he moved the cold nose of a transducer over my stomach and a sound came from the speaker that at first I thought was just white noise. But it had a soughing rhythm.

"Is that …?"

"That is the sound of your blood in the placenta."

He moved the sensor, pressing a little, feeling for the right place.

"There."

A sound like horses galloping over turf. *Ta-da da-da. Ta-da da-da. Ta-da da-da.*

"That's it?"

"That is it. Your baby's heart."

Ta-da da-da. Ta-da da-da.

"It's so fast."

"One hundred and forty beats per minute," Dr Kheraj smiled. "Around twice the rate of a healthy adult heart."

"And that's as it should be?"

"Absolutely as it should be. It seems you have managed well without us doctors so far, Miss Hassett. You have a very healthy baby."

I had felt so many contradictory things about this pregnancy. I had felt fear and frustration, the oppressive weight of responsibility and a fierce protectiveness. Lying back on the doctor's couch feeling that cold sensor pressing against my stomach and hearing my baby's heart, I fell utterly in love. And like any fool in love, I couldn't hide it. Even now, standing in the cold, waiting for Vik get start the march started, I had to keep reminding myself why we were here and stifle a tendency to grin from ear to ear like a besotted idiot.

Barely a dozen of us had gathered outside the school that Saturday morning. Vik. Baz. Mohan and the Bhangra musicians from Sona. A young Muslim called Saeed. Narinder and a friend of hers called Sumitra. Simon and me. What we thought we were going to achieve, I wasn't sure. But to do nothing was an admission of defeat: Vik kept repeating that like a mantra, and we each had our own reasons to believe him.

Vik chivvied us into a rough formation and handed out homemade placards. The policeman assigned to keep us in order clapped his gloved hands and said, "Lovely day for it, lads."

Baz took my hand and tucked it into his pocket. In the past couple of days, the temperature had plummeted, sending our rough sleepers scurrying back to the shelter of the Skipper. This morning, a dusting of snow formed in the air, only to melt the instant it struck the pavement.

For the first few hundred yards, Vik tried to stir up enough enthusiasm for a chant. Then we turned onto the Foleshill Road and the group fell quiet. This was same route along which, a week ago, a boy had tried to run for his life. For a time, all I could hear was the slap of shoes in the slush. Then Mohan shouted, "Come What May We're Here to Stay!" and voice by voice, we all joined in.

We were hoarse by the time we crossed the Ring Road and tramped on into a half-deserted Precinct. A handful of curious heads turned as we marched past. A few people looked sympathetic; more turned indifferently away. The more we were ignored, the louder Mohan shouted, until his skinny shoulders shuddered with the effort and his voice cracked.

A small cluster of skinheads stood on the far side of Broadgate, snow on the shoulders of their donkey jackets. I could see them, their fists in the air, shouting abuse. A bus went past, its heavy tyres churning up a spray of salt and slush. As it passed, the skinheads' chant became audible.

There's one less Paki, one less Paki …

The sour taste of nausea filled my mouth. I saw Beefy at the front of the group. He looked me in the eye, his lip curled back in a snarl.

The sound of the chanting stretched out, like a tape played at the wrong speed. My foot seemed to take forever to complete the forward swing of its stride. Unable to look away, my head swivelled back as, with slow deliberation, he raised his hand and ran a finger across his throat.

My eyes snapped forward again. A snowflake landed on my eyelashes and I blinked it away. I could feel the solidity of the road against the sole of my foot. Baz's arm jogging me as he struggled with his camera. The collar of my woollen coat scratching my neck. In my head, I could hear my baby's heartbeat, galloping away over the pounding of my own pulse.

Chapter 68

He could feel Maia's palm brushing his, their fingers twined, tips pressing from time to time as if sending each other messages in secret code. When she slipped and nearly fell on the slick road surface, he clasped tight.

He shouldn't have let her come—though God knows what he could have done to stop her. She looked so fragile. Snow dusted her hair just as it had in the photograph he'd burnt. But the hair fell softer now, framing her face instead of making a spiky crown. And how anyone could have missed the way her shape was changing was beyond him. Her breasts were fuller, her stomach distinctly convex. Even her face had filled out a little, and her pale cheeks had a faint rose blush to them.

What would have happened if it had snowed last weekend? If the boy had slipped and fallen along this route? Would the skinheads have set upon him and killed him right here, or would people have come out of their houses to defend him?

He looked round at the rows of mesh-curtained windows. A door opened and an elderly Sikh stepped out, pullover and scarf over his *kurta*, his feet in a pair of thin leather mules. He stared at the marchers and looked startled when the policeman said a cheery, "Good morning!"

The policeman greeted everyone they passed, with a sort of relentless bonhomie that seemed designed to prove what a good guy he was. But a few hundred yards down the road, a car came out of a turning and failed to see the march till the last moment. It slid on the icy surface, slewed across the road, and stopped halfway over the white line. The policeman banged on the bonnet.

"Stupid bloody wog. Why don't you look where you're going? You shouldn't be allowed to drive in this country if you can't control a car."

And these were the people they were expected to trust to investigate the death of a young Sikh. Maybe they would do their duty as diligently as they would for any other citizen, but was it any wonder some people found that hard to believe?

He could remember some of the crass things the police had said after his mother died.

You people have some sort of Festival of Light thing round about now, don't you? Sure you weren't chucking firecrackers around yourselves? Got a bit out of hand and now you're trying to blame someone else? Is that what happened, sonny?

He'd told one sympathetic officer that he thought he'd recognised one of the faces he'd seen on their front path. But nothing happened to them, and after that he was too scared to tell anyone else. Everyone, it seemed, had their own idea of what had happened and wanted him to confirm their version of events. He heard it in the tone of their voices, in the expectant pauses while they waited for him to speak.

Only Rebeccah listened. And even she didn't hear everything.

"You here to use your camera, *yaar*, or just to make up the numbers?"

Vik's voice snapped him out of his reverie. Ahead of them, in front of Godiva, a loosely organised bunch of skinheads yelled obscenities. Baz raised his camera, zooming in and scanning their faces. And suddenly Gary was there, spitting swearwords into the road.

He centred him in the frame, hearing the motor whine as he took shot after shot. He could see the gap between his teeth, the tattoos livid against this neck. *I'll take these pictures and show them to anyone who'll look, and I swear to God, Gary, if you're involved in any way …*

Something jolted his arm, knocking Gary out of shot. Mohan, shaking with frustration, was attempting to break ranks and take the skinheads on. Simon, the demo veteran, flung out an arm to block his way.

"Don't, boyo. They're not worth it."

Mohan rounded on him. "Don't you tell me what to do."

Simon held up his hands. "Hey, I just—"

"What the fuck do you know about it, *gora*?" Snail trails of tears tracked down Mohan's face. "Have any of your friends had a knife in their guts because they had the wrong sort of face?"

Oh, God, Mohan, you knew him, didn't you? Was he the friend you started to tell me about?

He went to put an arm round Mohan, but Vik was there before him. He gripped Mohan's shoulders and spoke in a rattling burst of Punjabi. Saeed and the guys from *Sona* closed round them, a circle of *desi* solidarity. Baz moved back and felt Maia take his hand and squeeze it.

They had stopped dead now, by the bus stop on the south side of Broadgate. The policeman shot a nervous look over his shoulder. Baz could see him calculating that, if his ragged flock didn't keep moving, the skinheads on the green might get bold enough to cross the road, and he'd be in the middle of a punch up.

"Come on. Move it along," he said, shooing them with his arms. "You can't stand here."

Mohan glanced up, said something in Punjabi, and spat. Whether he spat at the policeman or not, Baz couldn't have said. But the wind was getting up, and a gust took the spittle and carried it with fatal inevitability onto the policeman's cheek.

Shit. Here we go, Baz thought. Mohan and the policeman held each other's gazes. Then the copper took a large white handkerchief from his pocket and wiped the spittle away.

"Move it on," he repeated. "Keep moving forward."

Mohan snatched a placard off the drummer from Sona and strode on. The rest hurried after. Baz let himself breathe again. They continued, subdued, along the fag end of their route, even Mohan's chanting reduced to a half-hearted mumble. At the end of the route, a van was waiting. Vik gathered up the placards.

"That was fucking pathetic. What do people think? That they'll come out and fight the racists so long as the weather is nice? Next week," he told them, as he and Saeed climbed into the van. "Same time. Same place."

It wasn't a request.

Chapter 69

The sleet that had seeped through our clothes on the march turned to snow by evening, falling heavier hour on hour. Around nine o'clock, I heard a knock on the Skipper door, so faint I almost missed it. Frank stood in the doorway, his fisherman's jersey sodden. His face was greenish grey, with two bright spots on his cheeks, and he looked as if he had been hit, once in each eye, by a professional boxer. He took a few steps into the room, muttered, "Not feeling so good, lass," and went down like a toppled chimney.

Pongo helped me to carry him through to the dormitory, while Iain called Dr Kheraj. We sat him on the edge of the bed and peeled the wet jersey off him. His whole body shook and his breath rasped. When we lay him down, I saw how the run-off from his jumper had drenched his canvas trousers and the slush from the road had seeped up the rest. I undid his fly and Pongo lifted his hips. Frank's exposed legs were mottled blue and red. I was sure the Frank I'd met in January hadn't been this thin, or this weak.

"He told me he was feeling poorly," Pongo said. "Plus his leg's been giving him gyp. He's been dosing himself up, drinking more'n usual."

I touched Frank's hot, clammy forehead.

Dr Kheraj listened to Frank's chest, took his temperature, checked his eyes for their reaction to light, and turned to us, lips pursed with concern.

"I hope you have both had your immunity to tuberculosis confirmed?"

"Condition of the job, with that many homeless people at risk," Iain answered. "But we've never had a case here."

"Impossible to be certain until the tests have been done, but I fear this may be your first." He looked down at the little man huddled on the bed. "I doubt if I can get him a hospital bed tonight. Can we move him anywhere more private? If it is TB, he should not here with the other men."

"There are beds in the office where we sleep," Iain said.

"It could be too late. He's been in the dormitory most nights," I said.

"Then we must hope that we are not digging the well after the house catches fire."

With the doctor's help, Iain stretchered Frank into the office on a mattress and laid him on the bottom bunk. I hung back, watching him inject something into Frank's emaciated arm.

"Doctor … is there any risk to the baby if I stay with him?"

"I promise you, Miss Hassett, if your immunity is up to date, the men in the dormitory who have not been inoculated are far more at risk than you or your baby."

"Right. Sorry."

"Not at all. It's right that you should ask." He packed his things back into his leather bag and started to button his coat. "If our friend's breathing gets worse, you must call me at once, you understand? Whatever the time."

I looked back to where Frank lay on the bottom bunk. A bundle of bones under a blanket, all his resilient spirit gone.

"Will he be okay, do you think?"

"He is weakened from living on the streets. And malnourished. But if we can keep him somewhere warm and dry, if he'll accept treatment and stick to it, if he eats …"

"That's a whole lot of ifs, especially for someone who lives on the streets."

Dr Kheraj patted my shoulder. "He has a good soul, this one," he said. "*Insha'Allah*, he will recover."

"We'll look after him," Iain said.

"I'm sure you will." He pulled on his astrakhan hat. "Miss Hassett, Mr McHoan, *Khuda hafiz*."

The night wore on, hour after hour, punctuated by Frank's grating cough. We left the office door open but the stench of sickness still overlay those Skipper smells I hardly noticed any more. I didn't get much more sleep lying on the top bunk than I did when it was my turn to watch over Frank. I kept remembering the little man who greeted me on my first night. The man who always had a smile for us, even on the worst days. Who acted like he was taking care of us, not the other way around.

In the morning, Iain had to lean his whole weight into the front door before it would open. Six inches of snow filled the alleyway, more where it had drifted. But it had finally stopped falling and, where the April sun touched the roofs, meltwater dripped from the eaves.

I made a double ration of porridge and we went on serving for an extra hour. Men came in whose skin was the waxy grey of incipient frostbite, and Iain wrapped their hands in towels to warm them before he allowed them to touch the hot mugs of tea. Just as the last person left, Dr Kheraj came back to say a bed had been found at the hospital for Frank.

The snow brought one more transformation to my life.

The day after the big fall, Iain was woken by a dousing of ice-water. A patch of roof tiles had slipped under the wet snow, leaving a ragged wound through which the melt water had seeped until, saturated, the ceiling above his bed gave way. With his and Tom's room uninhabitable, the sleeping arrangements had to be reworked. Baz volunteered to sleep in the studio, Iain and Tom moved into Libby's room, Libby moved back in with Robyn, and it was unanimously decided that, because I was pregnant, I should take over Baz's double bed.

It doesn't take long for half a dozen people to carry a few belongings from one house to another. But Baz and I were still feeling our way towards each other, trying to avoid any more false steps. Being unceremoniously dumped in his room felt like being slammed into fast forward.

"So, Maia-*jaan*, what happens next?"

His black shirt was open at the neck, and his hair coiled up the way he mostly wore it these days, like an illustration from the *Mahabharata*. I looked at our feet, lined up next to each other on the soft numdah rug. No question how he made me feel—how he'd always made me feel. But ...

"It's kind of weird, don't you think? Like an arranged marriage?"

As soon as I said that, I could have swallowed my tongue. But Baz just chuckled.

"Maybe this will make it easier."

His fingers caressed my throat and his lips touched mine. When he fell back on the bed, I let myself fall with him, till we lay side by side, my head pillowed on his shoulder. I twined my fingers through his long hair. Just one comb held the knot in place, the end twisting round and round the initial loop like a piece of rope. I started to loosen it and it unravelled, cascading over his shoulder and brushing my skin. I shivered.

His hand moved towards my breast and hovered so I could almost feel the static charge in the air. "When we got to this stage before, I seem to remember you stopped me."

"And I seem to remember when I told you why, you walked away. Full stop."

He sucked his teeth.

"I did, didn't I? Well, I'm pretty sure I don't want to stop this time. What about you?"

Chapter 70

Baz blew gently on her eyelids till they closed, kissing first one, then the other. Maia snuggled closer. He could feel her skin, satin soft against his, her little frame, delicate as a bird's. Their fifth night together and he was still surprised to find it wasn't a fantasy run out of control.

"What time does the march set off?" she murmured.

"Uh uh. Not this one."

"What do you mean, not this one?" She propped herself on one elbow. "I hope you're not going to start thinking you can tell me what to do, just because we're—"

"I wouldn't dare," he said. "Look, Maia, Vik and Saleem have pulled out all the stops for this. But the other side will have done the same thing. What worries me is, it's going to be big enough to attract real trouble and not big enough to be properly marshalled."

"I can take care of myself. I've been to enough demos—"

"You weren't pregnant then."

"So what am I supposed to do? Lock myself away in a box for the next four months? We all take risks, Baz. I could be knocked down by a bus tomorrow, for crying out loud."

"That doesn't mean you'd step out in the road without looking, though, does it?"

He could see the pattern of colour in her irises, drawing him in towards the pupils. His hand strayed to where her breasts were making hillocks in his old t-shirt, but she was not to be sidetracked.

"You're going, aren't you?"

"Yes, I'm going. But all that might happen is I get bashed up a bit. Worst case for me, I break a few ribs. Worst case for you …"

She looked away, staring out of the window into the darkened street. He lay down and curled his body against hers, nuzzling the nape of her neck. Her back stayed rigid.

"Baz, what if they're carrying knives?"

In the shade of the trees, one hillock of gravelly ice clung to existence. Elsewhere the sun had chased away all sign of last week's freak storm. Saeed had got hold of a cheap megaphone that periodically let rip with a screech of ear-puncturing feedback. He was using it to rouse upwards of a hundred people who swilled around the makeshift podium.

"Think we'll get away without a fight, this time?" Mohan asked. He looked calmer, as if he'd vented some of his anger.

Vik clapped his arms. "With everything that's happened? You must be joking, *yaar*. Anyway, I don't care. Any beefhead comes after me will get what's coming to him." He checked to see no one was watching, then lifted his denim jacket and showed them a knife about six inches long, clipped to the back of his belt so it lay, concealed, along the waistband. "If they want a fight, they've come to the right place."

"Have you lost your mind?" Baz felt himself go numb. *Fuck*. If Vik could be that stupid, who was to say …? "Apart from anything else, if the police find you with that, they'll do you for carrying a concealed weapon."

"My *pyo* carries a *kirpan*, doesn't he?"

"A *kirpan* is ceremonial—"

"A *kirpan* represents your ability to defend yourself and to uphold Sikh values. Which is what I'm doing."

"You think the police are going to see it that way?"

With an ill-formed notion of getting the knife and throwing it into Swanswell Pool, Baz grabbed at Vik. The two of them teetered at the edge of the water.

"Oi! Knock it off, arseholes," Mohan said. "That cop's watching."

"Shit."

He let go and Vik tugged his jacket straight. The march was at last heading towards the park entrance, the column of marchers narrowing to pass through the arched gateway. He looked across at Vik and shuddered.

"Just for God's sake keep that blade out of sight."

Chapter 71

"What can I do you for?" said the duty manager of the day centre. His soft, plump hand shook mine. The windows were open and the blare of the megaphones carried across the street. Baz was somewhere amongst the crowd, awaiting the order to move off, but all I could see were the trees fringing the park.

"I'm trying to find out what happened to one of our regulars," I told him. "He got into a bit of trouble about a month ago and hasn't been round since. I wondered if he'd been here. Derek Paterson?"

The manager went on laying out mugs along the counter top, his eyes bored. "We don't go much by names here. We don't have a register, not like the night shelters. There's no call for it."

"Well, maybe you'd remember him. He's a steel worker from Consett? You can't get all that many Geordies round here."

He paused, one mug hovering above the counter. "There was one chap. I remember the first time he came in. Sounded like one of the Likely Lads. Would that be him?"

"Ever see him with his hand bandaged up?"

The man tugged at his earlobe. "Now you come to mention it, I reckon I did. Just the once, mind. Can't recall seeing him at all after that."

So another dead end. I'd already tried the Sally Ann. And the Cyrenians.

"Sorry, love, that's all I can tell you."

I made my way back outside. Across the road, the megaphones were directing the marchers to line up. My palms itched. What if I ignored Baz's warnings and just followed along behind? At least that way I'd know he was okay. And if trouble started, I could just get out the way

Halfway down the path, a man was dragging on a match-thin roll-up. I'd seen him once or twice at the Skipper. An ex-boxer with a cauliflower ear and a nose that had given up all pretensions to shape. Mick something or other.

"That one you're looking for," he said, "is it that fella who was doing teas at the Skipper a while back?"

"What?" I was watching the first marchers appear through the stone gateway and for a disorienting moment, I thought meant Baz. "Have you seen him?"

"Not for a few weeks, like your man said." He wagged a finger at me. His hand had a tremor and ash kept tumbling from the end of the roll-up. "You want to mind yourself, if you go looking for the likes of him."

"Why's that, Mick?"

I thought he'd say something about the fate awaiting young women who went chasing after single men. But he looked stern.

"First time I saw that one, he was with two of his muckers. Only they didn't seem so friendly, if you know what I mean."

"Yes, I know." I fidgeted, trying to see past him. The marchers were moving out of the park, but try as I might, I couldn't pick out Baz from the crowd. "They had a down on him because he was a recovering alcoholic."

Mick spat into a holly bush, his saliva nicotine brown. "My arse and Katty Barry," he said. "Meaning no disrespect."

He looked so outraged I almost laughed.

"The day I'm talking about, the two of them, the one you're looking for and one of the others, they were having a right carry-on. More than a scrap, mind." He paused for dramatic effect and I stole another glance across the road. "One of them was accusing your man there of killing a fella."

I felt a jolt, as if a burst of electricity had shot through me.

"C'mon, that's just fighting talk."

The little boxer sat down on the wall and took a few deep breaths, as if the effort of telling the story was taking it out of him.

"Your man on duty here that day, he had the pair of them thrown out, and the third fella went not long after. But not before he'd told us all what happened."

"So what did happen, supposedly?"

Mick frowned. The tremor in his hand got worse and he tucked it under his other arm.

"Seems the one you're after, he went into work off his face with the drink one day. He turned on some conveyor belt that carried the steel plate. Trouble with it was, a fitter was there repairing a roller on the belt. Poor bloody bastard was crushed to death."

"Oh my God—" I shuddered and tried to shake the image from my mind. "Okay, okay, but even if that's true, Derek had been trying to put all that behind him. He'd been sober for months—"

"That's as maybe, darlin'," the boxer said. "But I'll tell you what it was I didn't care for. Fair play, the other fellow was goading him. But your man didn't seem to be sorry for what he'd done. It was like it hadn't touched him at all, if you know what I mean."

I felt my skin turn to gooseflesh.

"No, you've got that wrong."

"I hope so, darlin'," Mick said. "But I'm a fighting man. I've seen men would have killed me in the ring if they could. And I'm telling you straight, the look in your man's eyes that day put the heart crossways in me."

Chapter 72

As the front of the march reached the place where the four arms of the precinct crossed, it slowed to make the turn. The end concertinaed into the middle, until the marchers clustered round the fountain, staring up towards where at least fifty beefheads occupied the higher ground. Baz felt his pulse become a drumbeat inside his own head.

The small police escort fanned out in front of the marchers. Baz could see a nerve throb in the neck of a young policeman. The skinheads began to move down the incline in a slow march. Through the high-powered lens on his camera, Baz could make out swastikas, spiders' webs, NF signs inked on their pale skins. He saw their lips move and realised they were singing something. Softly, to begin with. He couldn't make it out. Then louder until the whole pack was baying.

One dead Paki, one dead Paki,
One dead Paki, one million to go!

He could see colour washing out of faces around him. Bodies pressed closer, one or two noticeably shaking. At the front of the advancing pack, a red-faced skinhead with a neck as thick as his thigh walked with one arm stiffly at his side.

Twenty yards away, they stopped. Vik shouldered his way

through the marchers. He seemed to draw all eyes to him, as if the tension building in the crowd was channelled through his skinny body.

"Murdering bastards," he yelled.

The big, red-faced skinhead pulled his lips back into a grotesque smile. "Murderers? To be murderers, we'd have to kill something human, wouldn't we?"

He looked round for appreciation of his witticism, then opened his coat, and Baz glimpsed the thick wooden shaft he'd concealed underneath it.

"We're exterminators, scum. Gonna squash you Paki filth like bugs."

Baz's heart expanded until he had no room in his chest to breathe. Vik's muscles were knotted tight, his shoulders pulled up level with his ears.

"When are you cretins going to realise? Come what may, we're here to stay. And there's nothing you can do."

"You hear that, lads? He thinks there's nothing we can do."

They started to chant in time to the stamp of his boot, the sound rising to fill up the Precinct.

THUMP. THUMP. THUMP. THUMP.
Out! Out! Out! Out!

A wedge-shaped charge scattered the handful of police and drove deep into the marchers. Baz saw an axe handle swing through the air. Heard a sickening crunch. Caught a glimpse of black turban on the ground. A curled up body. Mohan? Fuck. He looked round for Vik but he was lost already in the scrum of bodies. For fuck's sake, let him keep that blade out of sight.

Contorted pairs of bodies reeled past him, holding fistfuls of each other's clothes. He held the camera above his head, struggling to keep on his feet, and shot blind. He could see fragments of what was going on. A small skinhead clung to the shirt front of a marcher, trying to rip off his Anti-Fascist League badge. A broad-shouldered Sikh lowered his head and rammed his turban into a skinhead midriff. Someone's boot, kicking and kicking and kicking.

A fist slammed into his guts and he doubled over. No way of telling if it was a skinhead or one of their own. Winded, he elbowed his way out, using his height to find the weak points in the roiling mass of bodies. Someone grabbed his coat. He yanked himself free, and almost lost the camera. A woman with a pushchair ran past, mouth open, frozen in an Edvard Munch scream. An elderly man backed towards the fountain, swiping his walking stick back and forth through the air.

Baz ducked into the doorway of Richard Shops, arm aching from holding the camera over his head. Behind him, an ashen-faced assistant hurried to lock up. When he glanced her way, she slammed down the steel shutters. He caught a frame of them as they rolled down. Coventry, shutting up shop.

How long had that lasted? Ten minutes? Fifteen? *Fuck.*

Baz leaned against the wall, hands on his knees. Most of the combatants, *desis* and skinheads alike, had scattered at the first sign of police reinforcements. The remaining die-hards, too caught up in battle rage to notice the sirens, were scooped up and hurled into the backs of vans. Now, half an hour later, the Precinct was eerily quiet.

"The police should never have let that happen," Vik said. "They were supposed to be protecting us."

In ones and twos, the demonstrators drifted back as the last of the blue lights flashed away. Perhaps a third of the original march had gathered under the Wimpy rotunda. Mohan had a bruise on his face and a boot mark across his t-shirt. Saeed's jumper was torn. Vik's knuckles were red and swollen.

"If the fascists had been marching, the police would have

looked after them," Saeed said.

"So, let's take the fight to them," said a voice from the back. "We know where to find the bastards."

Baz tensed, his eyes on Vikram, watching his friend's hands clench and unclench.

"No," Vik said. "Not this time. This time we go to the police."

There was a rumble of disagreement, but no one challenged Vik. As they gathered outside Police Headquarters, a senior policeman came out, looking rattled. He would speak, privately, to 'nominated representatives,' he said. Vik and Saeed were thrust forward.

As Vik pushed past, he pressed something into Baz's hand.

"Here. Look after that for me." As Baz started to protest, he shook his head. "Don't look at me like that, *yaar*. I can't take it into the police station with me, can I?"

"You shouldn't be carrying it in the first place."

Bloody hell. He was standing outside the police station with a sodding knife in his hand. Baz thrust it into one of the deep pockets in his coat, just as a reporter hurried over to speak to the demonstrators. Not Creech, this time. It was some old hack with a greying moustache. Baz hung back, listening, as one story jostled another for attention. The reporter scribbled away.

"And how would you answer those people who say all immigrants should be repatriated?" he asked.

"Fucking racists, we have rights—"

"You can't send us back to Africa. The blacks threw us out—"

"I was born in Coventry, man—"

"My grandparents left India before the war. The village they came from, it's part of Pakistan now—"

Mohan's voice rang out in a sudden lull.

"What about Baz?"

"Who's Baz?" asked the reporter, catching this among the tangle of point and counterpoint.

The crowd shifted and he was left face to face with the reporter.

"So what's your story?" he asked.

Over his head, Baz saw the door of the police station swing open and close again. The crumpled sheet of paper with its crude anonymous message swam before his eyes. Was he asking for trouble? Too late to worry.

"My father was from the Punjab and my mother was from Bilston," he said. "Where are they going to send me? They'd have to cut me in two."

The reporter's pencil flew over the notebook, chicken-scratches of shorthand to be deciphered later. "And your name is?" he asked, without looking up.

"Bhajan Singh."

"Bhajan Singh? You're Bhajan Singh Lister, from that exhibition thingy?" He pursed his lips in a silent whistle. "Well, thank you very much."

He started to walk away and seizing the opportunity, Baz called after him.

"They published one of my photographs a few weeks back. Maybe they could use one this time?"

"Sure, I'll ask them."

But Vik and Saeed were emerging and the reporter was off on a different scent. At the same time, a car pulled up in Little Park Street and Gurinder-ji and Mr Bal hurried out.

Mohan gave a low whistle. "Bet the Press'd like sources half as efficient as the *desi* telegraph."

The two of them cut the reporter off from his quarry and took command of the steps. Mr Bal spoke, ostensibly to the reporter but loud enough for the assembled group to hear. He disparaged the lack of restraint among the young and drew attention to the march planned in a couple of weeks—which would, of course, be well organised, well marshalled; no indiscipline tolerated. He knew how to work an audience, all right. By the time he'd brushed the reporter aside and returned to his car, half the youths were looking sheepish and starting to sidle away.

Left on his own, Gurinder advanced on his son, his face enough to make Baz profoundly glad he was not the object of its anger.

"Have you any idea how badly this reflects on us? This piecemeal, march here, march there. You are like children taunting one another."

Vik glared at him, fists clenched by his sides.

"They've taken one of ours. We'll take one of theirs, if we have to."

Gurinder-ji drew back. "Blood for blood? Is that what you would have? Do you forget what the Guru has taught us? *Do not turn round and strike those who strike you; kiss their feet and return to your own home.*"

"If I kissed those bastards' feet, they'd give me such a kicking you'd be taking me home in a bucket. Is that what *you* want, *papa-ji*?"

Gurinder stared at his son. "I will expect you at home in half an hour," he said, his voice low. "We will talk there. And there is to be no more marching before the 23rd!"

As soon as his father had gone, Vik turned to Baz.

"Give me the knife."

"You've got to be fucking kidding me."

"What do you think I'm going to do? Go kill myself some beefhead?"

"After what you just said to your *pyo*? Yeah, it crossed my mind."

"Nah, man. I'm not that stupid. But if they come after me, I'll defend myself. I promise you that."

Baz fingered the sheathed blade where it lay among the filters and spare film. The touch of it made the bile rise in his throat

"Still stupid enough to ask me for a knife right outside the police station."

Vik threw up his hands. "*Achcha*! Fine, we'll go somewhere else."

He jerked his head for Mohan and Saeed to follow, and the four of them moved away, Vik in the lead, his movements stiff.

Chapter 73

The sound of the marchers faded away, leaving behind a trail of crisp packets and dropped leaflets.

Boxer he might be, but Mick surely had the blood of Irish Shanachies in his veins. I couldn't remember anyone giving me the heebie-jeebies like that since Pinda told me those bedtime stories about evil spirits that lived in the baobab tree.

But my mom had drummed into me the necessity to distinguish fact from the human impulse to mythologise. Life on the streets fed a low-level paranoia. I'd scarcely met a long-term resident of the Skipper who didn't think at least one of his fellows was out to get him. The mildest of men could be accused of being, 'ready to kill me stone dead while I sleep.'

Okay, I'd seen what Derek could do when he was drunk. He'd have blinkers on. He wouldn't see anything but what was straight in front of him.

And he had a temper. Christ, we'd all seen he had a temper.

But in the back of my mind, I could see a different sort of man altogether. The man who'd shown me the lighter his wife gave him on his wedding day and admitted he was a recovering alcoholic.

Whatever the truth of it, though, Derek was going to have to find his own road to hell. I couldn't waste any more time looking for him. I had more pressing things to worry about.

The route of the march wasn't the quickest way home, but I figured I might catch the tail end, see they were okay. Smithford Way was half dead, with shops shut up as if the malaise gripping the city had finally smothered it. Even Tiffany's—the club where The Specials recorded 'Too Much Too Young'—had posters plastered over its glass stairwell giving notice of its farewell concert.

Near the fountain at the crossroads of the precinct, I caught sight of the debris. An overturned bin. A placard snapped in two. A torn jacket. A couple of axe handles.

My knees gave way and I sat on the lip of the fountain, breathing gulps of air. The baby gave one of its tremulous little kicks and I pressed my hand to my side.

Baz is doing a better job of looking after you than I am, little one. If it had been down to me, you'd have been in the middle of that.

Baz…

I felt my skin go cold, as if a wind from last week's storm had blown through the cracks. I stared at the splintered axe handle lying abandoned on the ground. It had a dark stain on the end. Was that blood?

Where was Baz? In the hospital? In a police cell?

In the morgue …?

As soon as my legs would hold me, I ran. If everything was all right, he'd be home by now. And I had to see for myself that he was okay.

But he wasn't at home. Five sodding hours I waited before Baz got back to Paradise Road. Five hours fretting myself to a frenzy.

"And it never crossed your mind once to just phone me?"

"I'm sorry. I went to the studio after we left the police station—"

"You went to the studio? While I was here, imagining you

with your head stove in or a knife through your guts—?"

"Maia, I'm fine."

"Let me see that for myself."

"Trust me—"

"Take your damn clothes off!"

Half laughing, he did as he was told. I knelt beside him on the bed and began a fingertip search. I found two bruises on his ribs that hadn't been there in the morning, and kissed them therapeutically. Then I rolled him over to inspect his back.

Ridges and indentations of scar tissue radiated from a point below his left shoulder, reddened in places but mostly pale. His right side was largely clear, as if he had been turned at an angle, his right shoulder leading, when the fire hit. I'd learnt how some of the thickened skin had lost sensation but, in between, he could be exquisitely sensitive to touch.

I poured some oil onto my hands and ran my fingers down his spine, then splayed them outwards, the pads of my fingers skimming the surface of his skin. He moaned. Gradually I allowed myself a deeper touch. I felt him relax and some of my own tension drained away. Eventually, with something between a groan and a growl, he rolled over, pinning me under him.

Chapter 74

When he woke, Maia was curled on her side, one arm flung out across the pillow. The warm weight of her arse rested in the bowl made by his bent legs and her short hair tickled his nose.

The clock ticked past six o'clock. If he was to stand a chance of getting a photograph in the Monday edition, he had to get back to the studio. He kissed the delicate skin of her inner arm and her scent caught hold of him, drawing him back to lie beside her. He broke free of its soft snare, wrote, 'Gone to the darkroom. DON'T WORRY!' on a piece of paper and left it by the clock.

All the way to the studio, his mind lingered with Maia. Her body was changing day by day now. Her belly swelling under his fingertips. Her breasts growing harder, their nipples darkening. A fine brown line had started at her pubes and was running upwards towards her navel. He liked to follow it back down, kissing or licking, to feel her push her hips up towards him

The darkroom, though, exerted its familiar discipline. Schooling himself to concentrate, he began setting out what he needed. Developing tank, spiral, and cap. Developer, stop bath, fixer. Extractor fan on. Film ready to hand. A last check to ensure he could see in his mind's eye precisely where everything was. Then turn off the light.

Darkness heightened his sense of smell. Even the yellow metal canister of the Kodak film had its own special odour. Feeling with his fingertips, he rolled the film onto the spiral, loaded the spiral into the tank, and then fitted the lid. Now the film was light proof once more and the light could go on. He poured the soup through the lid, smelling the sharp tang of Dektol, then capped it, and started the timing process. Two inversions … wait … two more inversions…

Maia had asked him to go with her to the scan. To see her baby before anyone else—before it was born, even. Imagine if that had been possible thirty years ago. His father might have seen him, at least once, before he died. Hell, he didn't even know whether Sanjit Singh had known his wife was pregnant, or whether he'd died, as Maia's Ossie might, without ever knowing he was going to be a father.

Focus. Keep an eye on that timer. Twenty seconds to go, pour away the soup and refill with water. Now the stop bath—the smell of vinegar filling his nostrils. Then fixer. A familiar tug on his tendon as he inverted the tank again.

His mother had gone through her pregnancy alone.

Maia had opened a chink in his buried adolescent anger and confusion and let through a glimmer of understanding of what that must have been like. Marrying Sanjit Singh had cut his mother off from her old life, and his dying had cut her off from everything. Small wonder moving to Leamington had seemed like a fresh start. Small wonder, perhaps, when her son was born with skin fair enough to pass for white, she'd chosen to bury the truth …

The timer on the counter shrilled to tell him five minutes were up. He washed off the developer then pulled the film from the spiral, drawing it between ring and index fingers to clear the oily residue clinging to the surface. He held it to the light just long enough to check it wasn't spoilt, then pegged it in the drying cupboard and stood back.

Maia was not going to go through this on her own: that was a promise. Whatever else happened, she would not have to make the choices his mother had.

The best part of the work in the darkroom was the moment, hours later, when he took the dry negatives from the cupboard and examined them for the first time. Souping the film was largely a matter of chemistry after all. But if the raw material was sound, then a thousand possibilities existed between negative and print.

He cut the roll of negatives into strips, laid them out in his light box and studied them through a loupe. In spite of the crazy conditions in which he'd shot the film, he had some good frames. Sharp and in focus. The images raw and visceral. What was the old rule for photojournalism? 'F8 and be there.' Meaning (as his old tutor had explained) 'give yourself plenty of exposure latitude and don't miss the bloody shot!' Well, the rule looked to have paid off.

The pictures from the middle of the ruck, those were the ones the paper would go for. A skinhead riding the back of a demonstrator, teeth clamped onto his ear—yeah, that was the stuff to get a newspaper editor excited.

As a failsafe, he went back and checked the rest of the film, just to make sure he hadn't overlooked something better. He had maybe ten pictures of the skinheads just before they broke ranks and charged. There was something eerie about the way every pair of eyes was trained on the same spot—the spot where Vik had stood and hurled defiance. But on this final pass, he saw something he'd missed before. An exception. One figure in that whole crowd who looked straight into the lens.

Gary.

He spotted it in one frame, and then moved the loupe onto the next, and the next. In that whole series of pictures, Gary never took his eyes off Baz.

Chapter 75

Simon snatched my copy of the *Evening Telegraph* and waved it at Baz.

"Half a column? Is that it? I thought they were going to use one of your pictures?"

"So did I. Apparently, a bunch of kids rumbling in the precinct isn't enough to justify the column inches." Baz shrugged. "Maybe by the time this city's torn itself apart, they'll wake up to what's going on."

Robyn peered over Simon's shoulder. "They got your name in there, anyway." She read aloud from the last paragraph of the article. "Bhajan Lister, Coventry artist, speaking to our reporter after the disturbances, defied those on the Far Right who call for compulsory repatriation—"

"Yeah, great, thanks. I know what it says."

He glanced towards where I was checking, for the umpteenth time, I had everything I needed for the scan.

"You don't have to come," I told Baz. "If you'd rather—"

"Are you kidding? Let's get out of here."

The room in the hospital was barely big enough for the bed, one chair and the bulky monitor on its wheeled trolley. The sonographer moved the probe over my swelling abdomen and the pattern of white snow on the screen lurched. Baz, wedged onto a stool between the wall and the bed, turned to look and his long legs jolted the frame, making the picture jump. The sonographer frowned and pressed the probe into my side.

"There. The baby's head."

She clicked a button and something whirred at the back of the machine. I stared at the screen, trying to fight back my disappointment. I might as well have been looking at one of those random-dot thingies that always failed to turn into 3D images for me.

I turned to share a bemused shrug with Baz, and found him staring, transfixed. Then, as though my brain at last decided to play along with the optical trickery, something appeared on the screen. An elongated sphere of denser white dots. A sphere, my eyes insisted, that had features.

"Oh!"

The probe moved and the picture swam again.

"It's hard to see, but that's the spine."

"That sort of arc?" I guessed.

She nodded and shifted the probe again.

"That's an arm, look. And a leg." A nudge inside me and then, "There," she said, "If I do it again, it's moved."

"Oh, my God. Did you see that? It was a kick." I reached for Baz's hand and he squeezed it. "That was my baby."

"No doubt about that, love," said the sonographer. "And a good size for dates too. You're doing very well."

She studied the screen, made a few notes.

"Do you want a picture for yourself, love?"

"Could I?"

"Let's see if we can get him to pose for the camera."

"Him?" Ossie had a *son*?

"Figure of speech, love. Figure of speech."

My heart slowed again to something like a normal rate. The machine gave a final whirr and then the light blinked back on.

On the bus on the way back, Baz seemed to withdraw again.

"You okay?" I asked, when as last I could tear myself away from staring at the pattern of white dots on the little Polaroid I was holding.

We were going past a school and the boys were out on the playing fields in football kit. He traced something on the window with his finger.

"It's just … I'm stepping into another man's shoes, aren't I? Ossie should be the one seeing those pictures of his first child."

I felt a pang of contrition. I'd had so little time to think what this situation was doing to Baz. Hell, he must feel every day as if he were navigating hidden rocks. I tucked my arm through his.

"It's just the way things have turned out. Nobody's fault. If it helps, though, I'm pretty sure Ossie would be glad I had someone looking out for me."

"Even some arsehole he's never met?"

"I reckon he'd trust my judgement about the sort of arseholes I choose to associate with."

I could see the tension ebbing from his shoulders, a smile starting to play about his lips.

"And what's your judgement telling you?"

"That I can't think of anyone I'd rather share this with," I said.

It was the middle of the day and the bus was practically empty. He gave me a lingering kiss that was only interrupted by the *ching* of the stop bell. We both looked up, abashed at being caught behaving like teenagers. And froze.

Leaning on the pole at the bottom of the stairs was a figure in rolled up jeans and high-laced Doc Martens. His khaki t-shirt exposed a neck and arms covered in Celtic knots and something that looked like the twisting tendrils of a stylised tree, growing from his wrist up to his shoulder. On his bare head, that inverted, perverted peace sign showed through a growth of fine, fair stubble.

I braced myself for a torrent of abuse. But he just stood, eyes moving from Baz to my bump and back again.

The bus lurched to a halt and the doors opened. Gary didn't move. I stopped blinking, as though my eye contact were the only thing keeping him from attacking. Even the baby lay still.

"Oi! I've got a timetable to keep," said the driver. "You getting off this bus or not?"

Gary jerked as if he'd been poked with a cattle prod. As his feet touched the pavement, he looked up at our window.

"Slag," he mouthed.

The bus lumbered off. Until we rounded the corner and I could no longer see the bus stop, Gary was there, staring after us.

Chapter 76

What was that little bastard up to? First on the march and now on the bus. Staring, staring, staring. Was it just coincidence he was there? Or had he followed them to the hospital?

It was one thing if he had to put up with the little creep stalking him, but Baz was damned if he was going to let Maia get dragged into his stupid games. He tried looking for him, to warn him off, but though the usual ragtag detachment of skinheads still sprawled most days under Lady Godiva, Gary was nowhere to be found.

So Paras' invitation to view the finished *mudra* statue came as a welcome distraction.

The dentist opened the door, blinking at him through his thick glasses, as bright and full of energy as if his day had just begun.

"Bhajan, how splendid to see you. Come in. Come in. I believe you are going to like what I have to show you. Come on through. Are you tired? May I get you a cup of tea?"

"You're sure you don't mind my coming out so late?"

"Please, I am often here at night. I suffer a little from insomnia, you see, and when I am here, my wife may sleep in peace."

"I've brought my camera. I'm hoping you'll let me take some

photographs."

"Of course, of course."

The sculpture stood in the centre of the white table, its colours all the more vibrant for the simplicity of its setting. The two hands were cupped, the fingers laced together, just as Paras had instructed Baz to hold his hands. One could imagine them frozen in the moment of scooping water from a stream.

"It is one of the most difficult moulds I have constructed," Paras said. "It required many, many parts. At one time I feared I would never be able to assemble it as I wished. But as you can see, it has not worked out too badly."

"It's beautiful."

The white glaze was patterned with a network of blue lines, accentuated with flecks of yellow the colour of sunshine. "Your name, you see? Here, along your right thumb. Bhajan, written in *Gurmukhi*."

Gurmukhi, the written form of Punjabi. And his own name one of the few words he could recognise—its first letter like the mirror image of an elaborate E.

"I don't know what to say. It's astonishing."

Paras beamed. "This will be the centrepiece for my exhibition at the *Healing of Nations*. Do you think your Rasta friend will approve?"

"I think he'll love it."

Midnight was striking from a nearby church as he left the surgery. Passing the chapel-turned-temple where he'd photographed the punks at the wedding, he saw the full moon rising over its roof. As he steadied the camera on a parked car to capture the image, he fancied he saw a figure at the corner of Eagle Street. Hands in his pockets, chin tucked down. Staring.

Gary.

He screwed up his eyes and when he opened them again, the

figure had gone. Fuck me, what was he like? He was seeing the little bugger everywhere. He'd wake up and find him perched on the end of the bed next, like some tattooed incubus. Get a fucking grip.

He put the lens cap back on the camera and headed off, humming, 'Too Much Pressure' to chase away the shadows. A hundred yards down the road, he heard a crash and a *whoomph*, and a blast of compressed air struck the small of his back.

For a second he was rooted to the spot. Then he ran back up the road. As he came level with the temple, Paras ran towards him.

"I heard a noise like a thunder clap in the monsoon. Then I saw fire leaping, leaping."

Flames poured from a window at the side of the temple and a thick pall of smoke rose over the rooftops. A gust of wind brought with it the choking smell of ash.

His camera was still round his neck. Automatically, he raised it to his eye and framed a shot of the fire. More people were coming out onto the street and Paras went to urge them to keep back. A man in a white *kurta-pyjama* pushed his way through the small crowd, wailing loudly.

"Aaiie—the holy *murti*. They are inside."

"Someone's inside?"

In an instant, Baz was a child again, crouched in the kitchen tugging uselessly at the locked door, smoke and hot air bellying over his head. *Someone was trapped.* His body lurched towards the temple, even as his rational mind screamed at him to stay put. He stumbled as far as the gate, then Paras barred his way.

"Bhajan, don't. No one is in there. Sri Uttamram Patel is concerned for the temple's sacred statues."

The man tried to push past. "You don't understand," he pleaded. "It is my duty to save them."

Paras clasped the man's forearms. "It is not your duty to risk your life, my friend. There is nothing more you can do tonight."

In the distance they heard the approaching wail of fire engines.

White faced and sobbing, the man struggled for moment, then went limp.

"How could this have happened? We leave oil lamps burning in the shrines, of course, but I am always so careful."

Baz forced himself to look at the blazing building. The intense heat radiating from it made the air shift and bend. If the fire had started inside and blown the window out, glass would be lying on the ground below. Even in the dark, flames would reflect off the shards. But the glow of the fire revealed nothing but the tarmacked surface of the yard.

The fire engines trained their hoses on the shattered window. Noise crammed Baz's head: the throb of the pumps, the crackle of the flames, the hiss of water turning to steam. The sounds mingled in his mind with memories—waking on the cold ground, the fireman's rough hands lifting him, a glimpse of the house, all but invisible behind a wall of flames …

The scar tissue on his back throbbed. To shut it out, Baz took more pictures of the arcing jets of water, illuminated by the fire. The flames subsided, but smoke and steam continued to pour from the window for a long time.

Eventually the firemen deemed it safe to inspect the building from the inside and Uttamram Patel unlocked the door. As he watched them go in, Baz felt the fear inside him, like a wounded animal whining to be put out of its misery. He had to do this. He had to do this now, or the fear would win.

With a cold sweat collecting on his skin, he followed, reattaching his flash gun. The smell inside was foul and choking. Their feet splashed through water that spread outwards from the window. The firemen's big torches cast cones of light, illuminating eerie sections of the scene. Uttamram moaned as the beam picked out the charred stump of a statue, brass oil lamp lying blackened at its feet.

Baz attempted a couple of photographs, with not much hope they'd show anything worth seeing. But the photographs were not the point. The point was he'd made it into the building. When he'd proved that to himself, he stumbled back outside and was sick in the bushes. A white-haired lady with her coat on over her nightie handed him a cup of tea and he drank it gratefully, the hot liquid scalding his throat.

Only as the fire engines rumbled away did he remember the shadowy figure he'd seen moments before he felt the blast.

Chapter 77

Baz stumbled into our bedroom in the early hours of the morning, dragging with him the harsh reek of smoke. He was trembling violently and his laugh sounded as though it might crack and spill an ocean of tears.

"First they burn the photograph, then they go for the real thing. You might almost think they're trying to tell me something."

He buried his face against my chest and I held him until he pulled away.

"That smell … I went inside. It smelt like … Oh, God, I never wanted to smell that again. And it's all over me."

"We'll get you a bath."

"It's three o'clock in the morning."

"Fuck that."

After an hour, he was still in the bath. When I went to check on him he had dozed off and the water was growing cold. I helped him out and he sat on the bed and let me run the comb through his long hair. Then I wrapped it in a towel and he lay down like a child, his body curled up tight, and fell asleep.

I lay down beside him. Strands of damp hair clung to his forehead. From time to time, his face contorted and his body twitched, as if his mind were still trapped in the burnt-out building. Once or twice, he cried out, but he never woke.

When he rolled over, I spooned my body against his and put

my arm around his chest. His body grew still and after a while he sank into a deeper sleep. A little before dawn, I slept too and when I woke, he was lying propped on one elbow, watching me. I blinked sleep out of my eyes and forced them to focus. He looked pale and, despite his sleep, deep shadows underscored his eyes.

"You okay?" I asked.

"I'm … better."

He kissed me. His erection, pressing against my leg, seemed part of the tension that filled his whole body. When we made love, he came with a sob and buried his face in my shoulder.

We dressed slowly, back to back, as if the raw emotion had made us shy.

"I thought I might visit Frank later," I told him. "Why don't you come?"

"I need to see Rebeccah." He stood up, pulling his hair into a tight band. "Tell the old bugger we miss him."

The old bugger was still on his own in a side ward, though he was officially out of isolation. He looked shrunken in his hospital robe, as if by washing away the layers of grime they'd washed some of Frank away too. But he sat up when he saw me and gave a wide grin.

"It's good to see you, darlin'. I've been missing the crack something fierce."

"Nurses not succumbing to your charms, Frank?"

"Sure, they're sweet things, but they're always too busy to come and pass the time of day." He pointed to the brown paper bag I was carrying. "What's that you've got there?"

I handed over a bag of oranges from the market.

"Feck, could you not have smuggled me in a poke of chips and a bit of baccy? I tell you, all this healthy stuff is doing me no good at all."

He took my hand and squeezed it hard, his grip still remarkably strong. "Eh, but that Dr Ker-ash, he's a good man, now, wouldn't you say? A good quack and a good man. Fair play to him, it makes no difference if you're a lush or a lawdy-daw; he'd look after you the same."

"Oh, Frank, I'd forgotten how much good it does me to talk to you! Too bad not everyone sees things that way."

Frank's cheery face ruffled into a frown.

"The gaffer's okay, is he?"

I thought of Baz last night, reeking of smoke and shivering in my arms.

"He's … fine, Frank, thank you."

He nodded his head to a crumpled pile of *Evening Telegraphs* lying by the side of the bed.

"I saw his name in the paper the other day, after that bit of aggro in the Precinct. And now that bomb going off." He struggled to sit up and I shifted some pillows to help him. "You're too young to remember this, now, but right at the start of the war, the IRA boys planted bombs in cities all over England. Did you know that? There was one right here, in the middle of Coventry. It went off in Broadgate, in the basket of someone's bicycle. Killed five people and injured near a hundred."

He lowered his voice as if, even now, this was something that should not be talked about, and I had to lean forward to catch what he was saying.

"My da had just come over from County Mayo. He'd a job starting in the munitions factories that would let him send some money home for my ma and us childern. Well, the English workers, they went on strike, didn't they? Said they didn't want to work with a pile of murdering Micks. And so my da was laid off, and many other good men besides. And he never worked again until after the war, even though the men that planted the bomb were caught and hanged."

He folded his hands piously on the crisp white sheets of the hospital bed.

"So you see, some of us, we understand, if you take my meaning. We know what it is to be a long way from home and no one wanting you there. You tell that Dr Ker-ash fella he's doing a grand job. Will you do that for me?"

"Of course."

He sat back, as if satisfied he'd accomplished his mission. He was starting to look pale and I knew I should go soon.

"What about you, though?" he said, prodding a gnarled finger towards my bump. "It looks as if you've got a bit of news too, since the last time I saw you."

"Guess there's no hiding it now, huh?"

"Eh, but you'll make a fine mother, lovely girl. Anyone with half an eye can see that."

"Thanks." No one had said that to me before, and I found myself close to welling up.

"Got a fella to look after you, have you?"

I thought of Baz wrapping himself round me at night as if sheer bulk could shield me from the world's ills. Baz worrying over me even while his own world was going up in smoke.

"Yeah, I think I do. A good 'un."

He nodded. "I know you modern girls think you can do without all that. But a child changes things, you know."

"I know, Frank."

He patted my hand again. "Now, I think you'd better make yourself scarce before that Sister lurking out there has you thrown you out. They're powerful fierce when they're crossed, these nurses."

He winked at me and lay down, his eyes half closed.

"And if you come back again before they have me out of here, see if you can't do something about that poke of chips."

Chapter 78

Noordin's rose-coloured stone nestled between the fleshy bronze leaves of a little stonecrop and the pink-tinged rosettes of a houseleek. Rebeccah knelt beside her new-made rockery, planting little mossy clumps of creeping phlox. Baz sat on the grass beside her, passing the plants to her as she called for them.

"I thought I saw him," he said. "Just before the bomb went off, standing in the shadows."

"But you're not sure?"

For the umpteenth time, he ran the images through his mind, trying to pick the truth from the shadows of anger and frustration. "Honestly? I'm not sure anyone was there. It could be my mind playing tricks. The last few weeks, it's been as if, everywhere I turn, he pops up like a bad conscience."

"I said I thought you were becoming the focus of something in his mind."

"Or he's becoming the focus of something in mine."

He watched her dig a hole and work in a little compost. How many hours as a teenager had he spent like this? Somehow, he'd always found it easiest to talk when Rebeccah was bent over some task in the garden, her hands buried in the dark soil.

"I don't know what I should do, Rebeccah. If I have evidence about these fire bombings and I withhold it …"

She took the plant he held out and lowered it into its new

home, patting the soil down around it. "There's something else you should know," she said, and the tone of her voice brought him to full alert. "You met Abdul Saleem Arain, I think?"

"Yes."

She brushed hair from her eyes with the back of her glove. She looked the way she did when she was about to speak in Meeting, gathering her words together and inspecting them before letting them loose.

"Noordin called just before you came. Last night, around the same time as you were at the temple, someone threw a firebomb at Abdul Saleem's house—"

Baz felt his vision go black, as if he'd stood up too quickly. Rebeccah put her hand on his arm.

"It's all right. They're fine. No one was hurt. The children were all asleep in the two front bedrooms. It doesn't bear thinking about what could have happened. But by some miracle, the bomb hit the bricks between the two windows and bounced off into the street."

Baz found he could open his eyes again. The garden swam back into focus.

"What now? Will they be safe?"

"His wife and children are going to stay with family in Bradford for now. And the members of his *biraderi* are helping to board up the windows in case the bombers return. Not much of a defence, but it's something."

He thought of the houses he'd seen along Eagle Street. Boards across their windows. Letter boxes nailed shut. People living in semi-darkness, like rats under the floorboards.

"Why Abdul Saleem? Do they know?"

"Noordin thinks it's because of the march. He's one of the principal organisers."

The cold, black feeling washed over him again. "Vik's father, he's one of the organisers too."

"I know. He's been warned. All the committee members have."

He stood up, his limbs stiff and uncooperative as though he'd been in one position too long. The cherry tree at the back of the garden was shaking its petals over the lawn. In a damp corner by the water butt, purple irises unfurled to reveal deep yellow centres. Clematis crept over the roof of his conservatory-studio.

"What's happening to this city?"

He swung a kick at clay flowerpot, lying on its side by the path. It flipped up in the air and landed with a crack, sending Mrs Peel fleeing, ears flattened, into the rhododendron.

"A season of madness," Rebeccah said.

"You think it will pass?"

"I've lived long enough to know that things generally do. Though it seldom seems that way when one is young."

Chapter 79

Dr Kheraj phoned the day after I visited the hospital. He sounded strained.

"Miss Hassett, I've been intending to call you, but time has run away with me. It seems Mr Duffy has been on the medication long enough now for the tuberculosis not to be actively infectious. The hospital staff would like to discharge him and have him manage his treatment himself."

"Good grief. Do they know his circumstances?"

"In theory, yes. In practice, I fear they have little idea. Miss Hassett, it's vital that Mr Duffy completes the course of his medication. The recommended procedure in these cases is a supervised treatment regime. That is, someone is responsible for administering the drugs to the patient and ensuring that they take them. In normal circumstances, that would be the GP, but I fear if I ask Mr Duffy to come to come to my surgery on a regular basis …"

"Half the time, he won't turn up, or—"

"Exactly. But as I understand it Mr Duffy is a regular patron of the Skipper?"

"Yes, he's in pretty much every night." I thought I could guess what was coming. "You want us to keep the medicine and give it to him when he comes in at night?"

"I know it is a lot to ask, but …"

"No, it's fine. I'm sure it'll be fine." Should I check with Baz before I made a promise like that? No, sod it, if it was a problem, I'd go down every night myself. "But look, Dr Kheraj, I don't know if we can do anything to stop him drinking. Not if he's back on the streets."

"That does not matter. These drugs can be given in combination with alcohol if they must. Though it is better for the patient if …"

"I get the message. But I don't know if Frank will."

There was a soft chuckle on the other end of the phone. "Miss Hassett, I am asking for help, not miracles. Miracles are a matter for Allah, praise be upon him."

"Do you think he might have any to spare for a lapsed Catholic with a bad limp and a bit of a drink problem?" I asked.

"'There is special providence in the fall of a sparrow', is that not so? Your Mr Duffy is a rather bedraggled sparrow, but I do not think he has done much harm in this life except to himself." He paused, and I could see the gentle, tolerant smile that would be shaping his face as he spoke. "Thank you, Miss Hassett. *Khuda Hafiz*."

"Dr Kheraj, what does that mean? *Khuda Hafiz*?"

"It means to leave you in the hands of God."

"Then I leave you in the hands of God, too, Dr Kheraj."

As I put down the phone, something caught my eye. Today's mail was already arranged in a neat pile on the desk, but a single brown envelope lay on the mat. It must have been hand delivered, because there was no address, just my name written in block capitals.

Standing in the sitting room with a cup of tea, a few minutes later, I ran my thumb under the gummed flap and pulled out a single sheet. It felt like cheap art paper, the sort of stuff they give to the infants' class, and it was folded in two. I flattened it out and stared at the contents.

The infants' class could have done a better job. Scraps cut out of newspapers and gummed on unevenly, glue oozing round the edges and leaving the paper shiny. I felt the heat come and go in my face and became aware that, one by one, the others were turning to stare at me.

Baz was on his feet and across the room in two strides, taking the paper from my hands. I heard him suck air into his lungs, and his hand clenched into a fist.

```
         FUCKING SLAG
     STOP MIXING WITH PAKIS
 OR YOU GET WHATS COMING TO YOU.
```

The others crowded round us. The letter was passed from hand to hand. Baz snatched it.

"Where did you find this?" he demanded.

I noticed with curious detachment that my hands were shaking. I took charge of one of them to gesture vaguely. "On the mat, next door."

"Here, in Paradise Road?"

"Yes." I couldn't see why he was harping on about it. And then I did.

"So whoever did this knows I live here …"

A flash of memory: a figure strutting away, coattails stuck out behind him. *So this is where you do-gooders live. Good to know. Might come in handy one day.*

"Gary. He saw us on the bus. He called me a slag—"

Baz shook his head. "He doesn't know about this place. If he was going to pull a stunt like this, he'd use the Skipper. Or the studio."

"But he does know. He followed me home once, months ago. I never told anyone because … Well, because it didn't seem important at the time."

Baz's face changed, as if a curtain were lifting in his mind. I waited for him to say something, but he went on staring at a spot half way between him and the door. Libby cut into the silence.

"Maia, I'm serious. You have to take this to the police."

The letter lay on the table where Baz had dropped it. I picked it up.

"Got your lighter on you, Simon?"

"If you're thinking of taking up smoking, *bach*, I've got some weed just now, guaranteed to make you forget all your troubles."

I held out my hand and he fell silent and dropped the lighter into my palm.

"Only one thing to do with filth like this—".

I flicked the top of the lighter, but Baz's hand shot out and grabbed my wrist.

"Libby's right. We have to take this to the police."

Chapter 80

Once again, it was Sergeant Conway who saw them in the cramped interview room at the back of the police station. His mouth pursed as he read the crude lettering.

"I'm sorry you've been subjected to this unpleasantness, miss." He looked up from examining the letters stuck on the cheap paper and gave Baz a hard stare. "And it's gratifying you chose to come to me this time before destroying the evidence."

Baz felt Maia shoot a question at him, but he blanked it. He unrolled the photo from the demo and pointed to an enlarged image of Gary. "We think he may be the one who sent the letter."

Sergeant Conway inspected the photograph, then took off his glasses and folded them.

"I take it you have your reasons for making such an allegation?"

Yes, I bloody well do, he thought. *I tried to tell you last time, but you wouldn't listen.* He stifled his temper.

"He keeps following us. At least it seems that way. The other day, he was on the same bus as us. He called Maia a slag." He jabbed at the letter. "Same word here. And it came to our house. Of all the lowlife that might have the motive to send a letter like that, he's the only one who knows where we live."

Conway smoothed the photograph flat on the desk and

tapped Gary's head. "He has a name, this young man?"

"Treddle. Gary Treddle. You had him up on glue-sniffing charges a couple of years back."

"Did we now?" He slipped the glasses back on and considered the photograph again. "No harm in seeing if we can't eliminate him from our enquiries, I suppose."

He was about to take his hand away and let the photograph roll up when Maia leaned forward. Her face, which had started to recover some of its colour, had gone white again.

"Let me see that again."

Without taking his eyes off her, he pressed it flat and she took it from him. Her hand shook as she studied it. Then she turned it for Conway to see.

"There's someone else." She pointed to the bull-necked skinhead in the middle, the one who had squared up to Vik. "I don't know his name, but I recognise him. He's threatened me. Twice."

"When you say threatened, miss, what exactly—?"

Her eyes darted towards Baz, her colour flaring. "He was the one who grabbed me in the fog. Remember?" The sergeant cleared his throat and she dragged her gaze away from Baz, hand fluttering to her throat.

"He said, if they came to power, they'd lock up people like me who mixed with other races, and throw away the key—"

Someone had put a clamp round his chest and was squeezing it tight. He stared at Maia as if she were a stranger.

"Why didn't I know about this?"

She threw him a look, almost pleading, and Conway held up his hand.

"Please, sir, let Miss Hassett finish. You say he threatened you a second time?"

She nodded. She had her head down and was staring at the table, as though she were ashamed to admit any of this.

"About a month back, he saw I was pregnant and he said … he said if the baby wasn't white he'd come after both of us."

"So this letter could have come from him?" the sergeant said.

"He doesn't know where we live, though," Baz objected. "The letter came to the house."

"Gary could have told him. They've always been together when I've seen him. Like Gary's his shadow."

Conway tapped the desk with his pen. "Maybe we should have a word with both of these gentlemen," he said. His eyes switched back to the letter. "I suppose any number of people have handled this by now? I thought as much. People never stop to think of the trouble they might be causing—"

"I'm pretty sure I was the only one who handled the envelope," Maia said.

Hope flickered on the policeman's face. "You don't still have it, I suppose?" he asked.

Maia fumbled in her pocket, then laid a creased brown envelope on the desk next to the letter. Conway took it by the edge.

"You understand, we'll have to take your fingerprints, in order to eliminate them?"

He stuck his head out the door and shouted down the corridor, calling for a constable. Baz nudged Maia and frowned a question at her, but she shook her head and looked away. Conway came back in.

"One other thing, sir. I understand from some of the other witnesses that you were the first on the scene when that temple was firebombed the other night?"

"Yes, sure. I guess I was."

"Any particular reason why you haven't come forward as a witness?"

Conway's face was poker-blank—no telling if there was anything behind the question. Baz shrugged.

"I didn't think I'd have anything to add. I was down the road when the bomb went off. By the time I ran back, flames were coming from the window. Plenty of others saw that."

"All the same, I want you to make a witness statement. Perhaps while Miss Hassett is having her fingerprints taken?"

He had finished giving his second statement, and Maia was cleaning ink off her fingers, when a thick-set man in a brown suit stuck his head round the door.

"Oi, Conway, a word if you please."

"Sir." Conway excused himself and went outside, closing the door behind him. The senior officer's voice resounded through the thin plywood.

"What are you doing still pissing about with these time wasters? I thought I told you to get rid of them."

Conway coughed. "Sir, I'm just—"

"We've got a murder enquiry and two counts of arson to investigate, and you're worrying about some tart's hurt feelings? This isn't Dixon of bloody Dock Green, sergeant. Get rid of them."

Maia's face flared red. It took every ounce of Baz's hard won self control not to go out there and rip the bastard's head off. Footsteps died away down the corridor. A slow count of ten later, Conway came in, his face struggling visibly for control.

"Sorry about that, miss. But I think we're done here now, aren't we? The constable will see you out when you're ready."

Conway turned to go but Baz blocked his way.

"Is anything going to be done about this, or are you just going to file it in the bin?" he asked.

Conway seemed to be finding it impossible to meet his eye. "You'll understand, sir, we do have other priorities."

"So try killing two birds with one stone. Ask Gary Treddle where he was at midnight on Saturday night."

That got Conway's attention, all right.

"Sir, if you wish to make a change to your witness statement …"

Baz struggled with himself. If he changed his statement, told them he had definitely seen Gary, then they'd have to investigate. But Rebeccah's face interposed itself and he shook his head.

The sergeant's eyes narrowed. "I should remind you it's an offence to make false or malicious allegations."

His face grew hot. He had a choice now—either shut up before he got himself into trouble or take a leap and trust Conway.

"Look, I thought I saw him near the temple, five minutes before the fire bomb went off. But I'm not sure. It was just shadows. If he was there, maybe he saw something, though."

The sergeant's eyes seemed to drill into Baz's head. Baz held his gaze and, after a long moment, Conway nodded.

"Very well, sir. I'll keep it in mind."

Chapter 81

Rebeccah was waiting outside the station. Baz barely acknowledged her before brushing past her and disappearing into the underpass. I watched him go. On the other side of the road, a news vendor was calling, '*City Final! City Final!*'

Rebeccah rummaged in her pocket and pulled out her car key. "Don't worry," she said. "Sometimes he just needs to work these things out."

"I think he's angry with me."

She paused, her hand resting on the top of the car door.

"What makes you say that?"

"I kind of blindsided him. Told the police about one of Gary's mates who'd harassed me. Someone I'd never told him about."

"I should imagine he's mostly angry *for* you." A breeze caught a strand of her grey hair, ruffling it, and she tucked it behind her ear. "He can't take it out on the people he's really angry with, and so he stews. It's unsettling, but you mustn't take it personally."

"I guess you've been through this before?"

She smiled. "Oh, on and off for the past ten years or so. Not so often lately, but it still happens. To be honest, compared to the temper tantrums we had to begin with, this is quite restful."

I gave a shaky laugh. Oh, God—the guilty pleasure of taking the piss out of the male animal. That was one of the things I missed, not having Genny around.

"So how do you stop yourself worrying?" I asked.

She looked down at her hands where they rested on top of the car door. They had the sort of ingrained dirt in them that would only come out with a soak in the bath and a really savage scrubbing.

"I generally find working in my garden takes the edge off."

"Couldn't use any help, could you?"

She tilted her head on one side. "Now, is that a genuine offer, or the counsel of despair?"

I gave her an apologetic half shrug. "If I go back, I'm only going to fret. Occupational therapy could be just what I need."

"Then let's see if we can't keep you out of harm's way for an hour or two."

The smell of the Morris's worn leather interior jerked me back to the day I first met Gary, outside the shop his family had once owned.

"Do you think Gary is behind all this?" I asked Rebeccah, as we waited to pull out into the road.

"It's possible, yes. He's always had a bee in his bonnet about Bhajan. But it's also possible Bhajan is making too much of their shared history. Sadly, as you pointed out, Gary is far from the only racialist in this city."

"You fostered him, didn't you?"

"For about a year, yes."

I thought of my mother's dictum that once we start to make sense of something, it ceases to frighten us. If I could start to understand Gary, would it help me to unravel some of this mess? No harm in trying, anyway.

"How did he end up in care? Was it when the family lost their home?"

"Not immediately. They had a council flat for a time after that." The traffic lights changed and she eased the car forward.

"It was the father's fault they lost the shop. He was a gambler and an alcoholic, and he drove the business into the ground, then walked out on his family. The mother was left with four boys to look after. Gary was in the middle, old enough to see what was going on and too young to understand any of it. And he went off the rails. Stealing things at first, then setting fires. He would climb onto demolition sites, gather up all the old rubbish he could find and set it alight. Then sit and watch it burn until someone came along and fetched him home."

"How old was he?"

"Eight. Nearly nine when he came to me. I think the mother and the elder brothers between them decided that, if Gary stayed around, the younger one might go the same way. So they told Social Services he was out of control."

"God."

"I was supposed to be an emergency placement, a couple of weeks at most. But there was the usual bureaucratic mess up. They couldn't find anyone else to take Gary on, and so he just stayed."

"With Baz? Christ!" A fire starter with a boy who was afraid of fire. A mixed race kid with a boy who blamed all his problems on a bunch of Pakis. "No wonder they're both still hung up on each other."

"Indeed. It wasn't a happy association."

Rebeccah turned the Morris onto her drive. She sat with her hands on the wheel, staring at the pink and white blossom on an apple tree by the corner of the house.

"The sad thing, if you can bring yourself to feel sad for someone like Gary, was that he absolutely adored his little brother. Would have done anything for him. But the family decided that until Gary got his act together and stopped getting into trouble, he wouldn't be allowed to see him. As far as I know, they've kept them apart to this day."

I ducked underneath the branches of the apple tree and followed Rebeccah along the gravel path and up the sloping lawn to the back of the garden. She opened the greenhouse door and the sharp, earthy smell of tomatoes filled my nostrils.

"I have some seedlings to pot on. How would you like to sow these lettuce seeds for me?" She handed me some packets of seeds. "A little of each, scattered on the surface. You scarcely need to cover them."

The sun on my face warmed me and a soft breeze blew the scent of blossom over the garden. I drew circles with different sorts of seeds on the pots and covered them with a skim of chocolate-coloured compost. Rebeccah carried a tray of tomato seedlings onto a bench outside and started to transplant them into large pots.

"What about you, Maia?" she asked. "How are you doing?"

"Me?"

"Here we are, worrying about Bhajan, worrying about Gary. And yet you're the one who received a poison pen letter. That's not an easy thing to deal with, I should imagine."

I could tough it out, tell her I was fine. But something about Rebeccah commanded honesty.

"I think I could handle it, if it was just me. But I get so frightened, sometimes, thinking how all this could affect the baby."

Her soft face wrinkled into a frown. "Have you thought at all what you're going to do once the baby arrives?"

"Oh, heck. You're one of the Skipper's trustees, aren't you? Look, I do realise I can't stay on at Paradise Road."

"Oh dear, that makes it sound as if we can't wait to turn you out. We're supposed to be a charity for preventing homelessness, not creating it."

"But I'm not exactly Cathy Come Home, am I? My parents would have me, if I went back there. It's just that …"

"You don't want to go back to being their little girl, just when you're taking on responsibilities of your own?"

"Yes. That's it precisely."

She gave a Mary Poppins-like sniff. She held a tomato seedling between her thumb and forefinger and pressed it into a pot. "I don't imagine I'd have wanted to go back to living at home, not once I'd grown accustomed to making my own decisions." She contemplated me for a little longer, head on one side, looking, in her earth-brown gardening clothes, not unlike one of the birds that followed her round the garden. "Would you object if I made a few enquiries on your behalf? I can't promise miracles, mind. But I could keep my eyes and my ears open, and pass on anything I find out."

Too late, I saw the potential for misunderstanding. If Rebeccah was assuming Baz was the father, this baby would seem like a grandchild to her.

"You do know, don't you …? I mean, that Baz isn't …"

She sat down on the step next to me, hands clasped in her tweed lap.

"My dear, I may be an old biddy, but even I can see that Baz would have to be a jolly fast operator to have anything to do with your baby."

"Oh. Yes."

I stared at the ground between my feet, my face burning. Rebeccah placed her hand over mine. It felt cool, and a little rough, against my skin.

"Maia, I wouldn't dream of judging you. So long as you're not deceiving Bhajan—"

"I'm not."

"Then it's nothing to do with me. And any advice offered is entirely disinterested."

I turned to look at her and she smiled in a way that made it easy to understand why Baz still turned to her, after all these years. "In that case, thank you. You're very kind."

"I think perhaps you're owed a little kindness just now, don't you?" She squeezed my hand. "And you can stop crying on my lettuces, young lady—the salt isn't good for them."

Chapter 82

It was well into Sunday afternoon before Jaswant Bal's long-heralded march got under way.

Coach after coach parked outside Edgwick Park; more and more people poured through the gates. Stewards marshalled them into a rough line that snaked round the park. Five thousand people or more, Baz estimated, standing four or five abreast. Exuberant, noisy, colourful. The wind snatched at flags: Sikh gold, Muslim green and triangular red Hindu *jhandas* all snapping in the breeze. Men unfurled banners from the Indian Workers' Association, the Asian Youth Movement.

On the other side of the park, Rebeccah and some other Quakers were with an interfaith group that included Paras and Noordin. Simon and his CovARA mob, carrying a banner that read 'An Injury to One is an Injury to All', had linked up with a mixed bag of anarchists and socialists. Libby and Robyn were with a women's group near the front of the march. But the vast majority of the marchers were Asian.

Vik and Mohan, behind them, had joined a group that included Sona and a group of rival musicians from Handsworth. As they started to move, they raised a banner and kicked off a chant.

Come What May, We Are Here To Stay.

Their drums picked up the rhythm and played with it, and it oscillated back and forth down the line, dhol calling to tabla, tabla calling to dhol. Maia gasped and hugged her arms around her stomach.

"I think someone likes drums. That was quite a kick."

The thin white cotton of her dungarees stretched over her bump and gave her an air of sexy vulnerability. If it were up to him, she wouldn't be here at all. Except, as she had pointed out, her other choice was to stay home alone in Paradise Road. Which—given there was an unidentified psycho out there who knew where she lived—was an even less attractive prospect.

"Just promise me one thing," he said to Iain and Tom. "First sign of trouble—"

"I know, I know. First sign of trouble and we get Maia out." Tom threw an arm across her shoulders. "Don't fret. We'll not let anything happen to our girl."

At least the authorities were taking no chances this time. Every five rows or so, a pair of policemen marched beside them. A police motorcycle led off. Police vans followed behind, steel mesh over their windscreens. Mounted officers trotted back and forth. All along the Foleshill Road, people stopped and smiled as the march went by. A few raised a cheer, or clapped along to the beat of the drums. But as the road swung south, and the twin spires of St Michael's and Holy Trinity came into view, a new mood rippled down the line, raw and nervous. Long before they began the climb towards Broadgate, Baz heard it. Over the drumming. Over the chants. Hundreds of male voices in unison.

Sieg Heil! Sieg Heil! Sieg Heil!

They lined Broadgate on both sides: baying skinheads in the front lines and, behind them, a phalanx of grey men like the Weasel. The roadway was reduced to a corridor between two solid ranks of Nazi salutes.

Sieg Heil! Sieg Heil! Sieg Heil!

For fuck's sake, my father fought in the War. And you bastards think you can decide who's British?

He pulled away from Maia and sidestepped out of the march. A policeman put a hand on his chest to bar his way, but he held up the camera. The officer shrugged.

"One picture, then you get back in line."

He took his shot and then scanned the crowd, hunting for two faces. The policeman was growing edgy. Baz turned on his motor wind and kept recording until he saw the cop reach for his night-stick, then he ducked back into the march. He pushed his way through the ranks of demonstrators till he found Maia and clasped her hand, and together they passed underneath the arch of outstretched arms.

"Are they there?" she asked.

"I couldn't spot them."

Tom threw a glance over his shoulder. "There's some big buggers in that front row. That little nowt Gary'll be skulking behind them, take my word for it."

"I hope so. I'd rather have him under our noses than off someplace where I don't know what he's up to."

Iain pushed his glasses back up his nose. "Keep your friends close and your enemies closer," he said.

"Something like tha— Jesus Christ!"

A brick whistled through the air. Baz ducked, pulling Maia with him, and it sailed over their heads. Behind them, a group of Punjabi youth scattered, then scrambled to grab the brick and hurl it back at the skinheads. The police closed in, moving them on. When he moved his feet, his shoes stuck to something tacky. Looking down, he saw the road surface spattered with broken eggs.

"Maia—" he began.

She shook her head, her jaw taut. "Not yet."

He glanced at Tom and Iain and they closed round her,

forming a protective triangle. As the last protestors entered the narrow neck of the High Street, the skinheads broke ranks and streamed after them, looking for a way to break through the police lines. If they succeeded, it'd be carnage.

On the steps of the museum, a cluster of men looked on. They were immaculately dressed in grey suits, and they watched without emotion. Two steps below, the Weasel sleeked down his comb-over and smirked.

Fury shook through him. A piece of paper fluttered across his memory. *We are soldiers in a war,* it said, *and the colours of our uniforms are the colours of our skins.* You bastards. You fucking bastards, he thought. You tell those kids that and they believe you ...

They were hemmed in on every side now. From the steps of the Cathedral, a group of about twenty skinheads, hurling empty aerosol cans, sang, *Burn, burn, burn a Paki early in the morning.* Through the gaps between the buildings of the Poly, he could see more skinheads running parallel to them, trying to head them off. Further down the hill, beyond the concrete arches of the Halls of Residence, the rest of the turgid flood had found its level. Vik ran by, shouting *"Here to Stay! Here to Fight!"* Mohan and Saeed followed.

Behind him, Tom let out a shout. Baz struggled round and saw blood spurting from Tom's cheek where a stray can had nicked him. Baz seized hold of Iain and thrust him towards Maia.

"That's it," he yelled. "Get them both out of here."

Then he grabbed his camera and ran.

The protestors came to a halt at the edge of the road, fists raised. Over their heads Baz could see the skinheads ranged across the entrance to the bus station. In between, two double lines of police, linked arm to arm, were trying to hold them apart by sheer weight of numbers. Dissonant shouts reverberated off the concrete walls of the surrounding buildings.

A little to the left, a lamppost stood on an island in the middle of the road. Baz elbowed his way out of the crowd and scrambled up, his feet balanced on the widest part, one arm wrapped round the upright, the other holding his camera. Bricks and bottles flew in both directions. A skinhead sat on the kerb, holding his arm. A young Asian stumbled away, blood running down his face. All the while, the thin blue line holding the two groups apart was washed this way and that, like seaweed on the tide.

This was no longer his city. The buildings were the same, but nothing else was familiar. It was as if the ground had opened up and spewed out a special kind of hell. Even the *desi* kids he'd marched with were barely recognisable.

As he thought this, the roar from the crowd reached a new pitch. Part of the Asian line stormed forward, arms linked, heads down. Baz spotted Vik at the apex of the charge, Saeed next to him. Across the road, the skinheads saw what was happening and stampeded towards them. They ripped through the police line and suddenly the opposing groups were head to head.

Baz zoomed in on the vortex of the action, and a face flashed across his lens. A broad face, reddened with acne. A face Maia had picked out in a photograph.

Startled, he pulled back, then struggled to locate him again. Anger, thickened with helplessness, seethed through him. No way to reach the bastard through that press of people, even if he tried. Nothing to do but keep the camera running.

And suddenly he saw him, in a space carved out of the mob, like a fighting ring without ropes. He had Vik in a headlock, but he must have been thrown off balance because Vik was driving forward, using his shoulder in the bastard's gut. Then the two of them went down and all Baz could see was a shifting space in the roiling movement of the crowd.

He'd been praying that Vik didn't have the knife on him but now, for a sick moment, he willed him to pull it out and plunge the blade into that bull neck. Then a police van came down Priory Street and more officers spilled out. They waded into the crowd, wielding truncheons, and heaved out Bull Neck. He had blood on his face. A few moments later, four more officers staggered out, carrying Vik by the arms and legs. They'd dragged his jeans and jacket half off him and several skinheads spat at his bare flesh as they passed.

Baz's knees buckled and he almost lost his perch on the lamppost. But before he had time to think what might happen to Vik, he heard a pounding in the road. A line of mounted police officers galloped towards him, spread across the width of the road, their long batons raised high. Others had seen them too. People were screaming. Shoving frantically for the edge of the roadway. A young woman in a *shalwar kameez* tripped and those nearest to her yanked her to her feet.

If he stayed where he was, he was a sitting target. He managed one shot of the charge then let go of the lamppost and ran, heading for the protection of the arches. The road vibrated from the impact of the hooves. As they swept by, a baton caught him a glancing blow to his shoulder and pain shot up his arm. He lost control of his feet and stumbled over the kerb. His arms instinctively wrapped round his camera and his face hit the pavement. More pain, in his jaw this time. He curled into a ball as others scrambled over him, fleeing the charge. He got to his feet, spitting road grit.

His left shoulder ached from where the baton had struck him, as did most of his right side from where he had hit the road. But he seemed to be more or less in one piece, and the camera was undamaged. He took out a handkerchief and blotted blood from the graze down the side of his chin.

The horses wheeled for a second charge. At the same time, a phalanx of police moved down Priory Street, escorting a group of community leaders from the rally. Three or four of them were helped onto the roof of a police van. At the front of the group, Gurinder-ji stooped and took a loud hailer that one of the officers held out to him. He had egg splattered across the front of his jacket and his hand shook at little. A beer bottle sailed past the van and crashed in the road beyond. Gurinder-ji flinched, but stood firm. The loudspeaker squawked, then his voice came through, clear and steady.

"… remain calm and disperse quietly. I repeat, we ask you to remain calm and disperse quietly …"

You're too late, Baz thought. They've got Vikram.

Chapter 83

Most of the marchers in front of us had climbed down the steps into Cathedral Square to join the official rally. Those behind ran on, towards the sound of battle, taking Baz with them. Beside me, Tom cursed and tried to staunch the blood from the gash on his cheek.

"Come on," Iain said. "Let's get the pair of you home before you give me any more grief."

I clenched my fists behind me and shook my head. "We've come all this way. One of us should make it to the rally."

"No chance, hen. Baz'll mollocate me if anything happens to you."

I picked a random point in the crowd and pointed. "Look, there's Libby and Robyn. I'll join them. You take Tom home and get that cut sorted out."

Before Iain could answer, I ran the steps and let myself to merge into the crowd. I gave them two minutes to give up and head for home, then I slipped back out and crept up the steps.

I knew I was probably being stupid. Iain wasn't the only one Baz would mollocate if anything happened. But it wasn't like I was going to walk straight into the battle. I'd keep out of the way. I just had to see for myself that he was okay.

I crept down the hill as far as the concrete arches spanning the end of Priory Street and peered out from behind them. Below me, two angry mobs strained to reach the other. One side giving Nazi salutes. The other with their fists raised, thumbs sticking out between their index and middle fingers. My mom catalogued gestures like that—how they were used, their half-forgotten meanings. This one I knew. It meant 'cunt.'

I searched the crowd, looking for one head taller than all the others. At first I couldn't find him and my heart juddered, picturing him knocked to the ground, trampled in the crowd.

Then I saw him. A long thin streak of black clinging to a street light, camera to his eye. And memory ambushed me.

… I was about six. Was this the first time my mother took me to Africa with her? I guess we must have been caught up in one of those ethnic conflicts that periodically threatened to rip old colonial boundaries apart. I could see women in bright skirts and headwraps running down the road, babies in their arms. I was holding my mother's hand, being pulled along. But I couldn't keep up and I kept falling. Then someone with dark skin bent down, lifted me up, placed me on his shoulders. My mother gasped. We were bundled into a car that smelt of mildewed leather. My mother, in the front seat, laughing, the edge of hysteria to her voice.

I knelt on the back seat and looked through the small window. Something dark swung from a solitary street light. A human being, stripped naked …

Baz still clung to the street light, but I couldn't watch any more. I turned and forced myself up the hill, lactic acid building in my muscles till cramp knotted them. On the wall of the Cathedral, Epstein's statue of St Michael, arms and wings outstretched, was trampling a Devil in chains. Lucky old St Michael—he had his Devil just where he wanted him.

My eye caught a movement below St Michael's upraised spear. A handful of onlookers remained on the Cathedral steps. Among them, one man I knew.

I recognised the blast pattern first, that weird mark on the back of his jacket. Then the grubby bandage on his hand. His beanie was pulled down low over his head and his hair stuck out long and lank. He turned and, just for a second, I thought he looked straight at me. Then the eyes glazed over. And I saw who he was with.

Gary stood one step higher up, thumbs in his braces, swaggering. The extra step brought him eye-level with the older man. Derek had his head tucked down and he looked as if he were mumbling in response to whatever Gary was saying. What was he doing here? Where had he been? And why the hell was he talking to Gary?

I'd almost made up my mind to walk straight up there and ask, when Derek's demeanour changed. He reared up and thrust his face towards Gary's. Gary put up an arm to block him and Derek grabbed his wrist and bent it back. Gary's face twisted up and his knees buckled. Derek said something into his ear, Gary nodded, then Derek let him go and started down the steps, looking from left and right as if he thought someone might be watching him.

As the noise from the battle raging in Pool Meadow rose to a crescendo, I shrank back into the shadows of the Old Cathedral. Derek walked away, back along the route the march had taken. Mick the Boxer's voice echoed in my head.

The look in your man's eyes, that day, it put the heart crossways in me.

Chapter 84

The hail of missiles slowed to a drizzle, and then stopped. The crowd fizzled away, slipping into back streets, dodging away from the hungry maws of police vans.

Baz leaned against one of the arches under the halls of residence. He felt as if he had been awake for days on end. The graze on his chin stung and sweat ran into his eyes. Dull hopelessness was replacing anger. Maia's tormentor had been arrested, but so had Vikram. He thought about going to the police station, asking after Vik. But that could mean facing Gurinder-ji, knowing he should have stopped Vik carrying that knife. And he hadn't the courage for that yet.

As he stared at the churned up grass at his feet, a pair of scuffed Green Flash appeared in front of him.

"*Kiddan*, mate? You okay?"

Mohan's shirt was ripped and he had the beginnings of a black eye. Baz slumped back down.

"The police took Vikram."

"I know." Mohan wagged his head from side to side, grinning. "Took four of them to hold him though."

"For fuck's sake! This isn't some game of tag. Did he have that sodding knife on him or not?"

The grin slid from Mohan's face. "Bollocks. I don't know …"

They stared at each other, numb.

"Hey, look, come to my place," Mohan said. "He's bound to

call me there, sooner or later."

"He may not be able to, if he's under arrest."

"Then leave it to the *desi* telegraph. One way or another, we'll get news."

By the time they reached Mohan's house, his eye had swollen till it looked as if an engorged black slug had taken up residence under the socket. His mother took one look and pulled them inside, scolding volubly in Punjabi. Ignoring their protests, she sat them at the kitchen table and applied a bag of frozen peas to her son's eye. Then she turned her attention to Baz. Clamping his jaw between her finger and thumb, she tilted his head up and inspected his grazed chin. Still scolding, she daubed it with something that looked suspiciously like turmeric.

"Ow, fuck!" he said, as the sting brought tears to his eyes. Then, "Ow!" again, when a small, heavily ringed hand clipped him round the ear.

Mohan winced an apology. "Mummy-ji barely speaks a word of English, but she can always tell if you swear."

"You could have warned me."

Ministrations complete, she ushered the two of them into the front room and had to be dissuaded from turning on all three bars of the electric fire. Even if he hadn't glimpsed the surprise on Mohan's face, Baz would have guessed that this was a room put aside for guests and special occasions. Everything in it looked untouched. Even the furniture was still plastic wrapped, as if to use it was to miss the point. He sat down gingerly. Mohan turned on the black and white television and searched for a channel.

"ATV news, man. We might be on it."

Ann Diamond's face appeared on the tiny screen. Sure enough, the violent end to the march was the lead news item. The screen showed shots from behind the lines of demonstrators, with bricks and bottles flying towards police lines.

'… seventy-four people were arrested when two hundred young whites and Asians, said to be members of the Communist Revolutionary Party, attacked police after an anti-racist march …'

Mohan was on his feet, yelling at the screen. "Who are they calling communist? I'm no communist." He pointed at the grainy images on the screen. "And it wasn't the police we attacked, anyway. It was the bloody National Front. Can't see that, though, can you? Or the way the police charged their fucking horses at us."

Baz felt in his pocket. His film would tell a different story—if anyone cared to look.

"It's always the same. Look what happened after Brixton. Easier to blame outside agitators than to admit ordinary people are so pissed off they'll take the law into their own hands."

"I'd like to see them be so fucking law abiding if one of us had murdered one of them."

The door opened, a smell of spice wafted in, and his mother entered, bearing a tray of fresh samosas. She looked suspiciously at Mohan and let fly with another burst of Punjabi. He ducked his head and said something that sounded like an apology. She scowled, then put the tray down on the table.

"Eat now," she said to Baz. As she left the room, she pulled the door to instead of closing it. Mohan rolled his eyes.

"I tell you, it's a kind of radar. All *desi* mothers have it. I think it's implanted in them when they get married or something."

The younger man popped a samosa, whole, into his mouth, flung himself down on the shrink-wrapped sofa, and almost slid straight back off again. He stared despondently at the ceiling and groaned.

"Communist bleeding Revolutionaries. They're going to throw the book at him, *haan*?"

Chapter 85

Baz must have taken my last bollocking to heart because, not that long after the six o'clock news, he phoned me from Mohan's house.

"I'm going to stay until we hear from Vik," he said.

"But you're all right?" I was too relieved to hear from him to worry overmuch about Vik.

"A few bumps and bruises. I've scraged my chin and Mohan's mum has put something on it that makes my face look like I'm ready for the tandoori oven. Other than that, I'm fine."

"Really?"

I heard a soft chuckle and his voice dropped to a purr. "You can check for yourself when I get home, if you like."

"You should be so lucky, mister." I tilted back on the chair, twisting my finger through the telephone cord.

"How's Tom?" he asked.

"Lying on the sofa with a gauze bandage on his cheek, letting Libby ply him with cups of tea. Simon says he'd have got himself injured too if he thought waitress service was going to be laid on. I think he's quite put out that it looks like Tom was more in the thick of it than he was. He'll be mortified if he finds out Vik got himself arrested."

I heard a pause, not much more than a catch in his voice, then Baz said, "I reckon one idiot at a time is more than enough."

I rocked forward in the chair, catching the anguish in this

voice. "You're really worried, aren't you?"

"I think the stupid bugger could have landed himself in big trouble this time."

"Oh, Baz, I'm sorry." Vik might be a belligerent sod, but I knew if anything happened to him, Baz would be devastated.

"Look," he said. "I've got to go. The Chands are paying for this call."

I was going to tell him about Gary and Derek, but we'd run out of time. Baz rang off and I went out into the yard. What I really wanted right now was a soak in the bath to ease my aching limbs. And sleep. God, how I wanted sleep. But last night, Dr Kheraj had dropped off an entire pharmacy of Frank's pills, and tonight I'd promised to go down to the Skipper and persuade him to take them. It shouldn't take more than an hour but, right now, I wished I hadn't been so precious about doing it myself.

As soon as Frank saw me, he folded me in a big hug.

"They've discharged me, wee girl. Old Frank's a free man again."

The Skipper was quiet. With the warm weather and long evenings, a lot of men drifted in, had their food and drifted out again. Far fewer bothered to pay up for a night's sleep when they could bed down comfortably enough outside. So only a small band of regulars greeted the returning hero. Frank was in his element, though, surrounded by mates and telling scurrilous tales of nurses ministering to his every wish. I had my work cut out to extricate him and frog-march him into the office.

"You're as bad as those nurses, so you are," he said. "Always after me to be taking pills and that. I thought I was out of hospital now?"

I held out a paper cup containing the three different pills he had to take each day.

"Frank, you do understand how important it is that you go

on taking these?"

"I know, I know. Dr Ker-ash has told me. But it's ..." he gave a furtive look round, then leaned across to whisper, "... it's making me piss red. They say it's perfectly normal, but that can't be right, can it?

He looked so indignant I struggled to keep a straight face.

"Never mind what colour you piss. The important thing is, this medicine's keeping you alive."

"Fair enough. I'm feeling grand now anyway. You don't have to worry about Frank."

It was like talking to a logical and self-possessed child. I took a deep breath and tried again.

"You're feeling okay because you're taking the medicine, but you're not cured yet. That's what you have to understand. If you stop taking the medicine, the TB will come back. And it will be harder to fight off a second time."

"Okay. Fair play."

He beamed at me, heedless and happy. I wanted to shake some sense into him.

"Promise me, Frank. You come in every night, and you keep taking the medication, right?"

"Feck, where else would I be going?" He took the pills from me, swallowed them, and patted my hand. "You worry too much, lovely girl. All this fretting's no good for that babby of yours."

It was a miracle those nurses hadn't strangled the old bugger weeks ago. He sauntered off to rejoin his mates. I sat for a minute with my head in my hands. Then I locked the pills away with the petty cash and went back out.

Jerzy was sitting, as usual, a little aside from the main group of regulars. As I passed, he held out a hand to me for me to shake. The air of profound Slavic pessimism was heavy on him tonight.

"You have badge," he said, pointing a finger at my chest. "*Solidarność.*"

"I do, yes." I'd pinned it to the front of my dungarees before the march, along with my collection of anti-Apartheid badges.

"Is good. Is good. Maybe we have new battle to fight."

"Don't tell me you've been having more problems with Social Services?"

He shook his head and beckoned for me to sit down.

"That man who come here before, making speeches. The one gaffer throw out, you know who I mean?"

I knew all right. The man who'd led the protest outside the gallery. The one we'd seen on the steps of the museum with the Fascist high-ups, like a hyena waiting for scraps from the lions' table. I shuddered as Jerzy went on.

"He not dare come here again, I think, but I see him. He talk to some of the men, make trouble for you."

That bastard would make trouble for us, all right. Any bloody chance he got. That was no surprise. But the thought of a new front opening up in this bloody war …

"Men like that," Jerzy said, "when I first come in England after War, they put sign in window. No Irish. No Poles. I have to live in camp, like prisoner of war. Now they here again. Say only English may live in England." He turned his head and spat on the floor. "And today, boys fighting in street, like dogs. Is what happens when men say these things, no?"

"Yes. Yes, it is. Thanks, Jerzy. Thanks for telling me."

He patted my arm, blue eyes sparkling. Nothing, it seemed, brought Jerzy to life like the prospect of a lost cause.

"You and me, we catch God by the arm again, yes?"

"Oh, Jerzy!" I felt so tired even catching a low-flying angel seemed too much of a stretch. "We can try. But this one might be a harder nut to crack even than Social Services."

"Pah! Not possible." He winked at me. "Woman who crack Social Services crack any nut she like."

Chapter 86

By the time Vik called, every nerve in Baz's body had been stretched on a rack. He and Mohan squeezed together in the hallway, ears pressed to the receiver, trying to keep their voices down so as not to disturb the rest of the house. Vik sounded exhausted and chastened.

"I haven't got long, *yaar*. My *pyo* is letting me make one phone call."

"What happened?" Baz asked. "Have they charged you with anything?"

"Yeah." He gulped some air. "Violent disorder. Resisting arrest. Carrying a concealed weapon."

Baz had told himself to expect something like this. But he must have still hoped Vik would get away with a caution, because this was like a punch in the kidneys.

"Fuck me," Mohan said. "You're lucky they let you out at all."

Vik lowered his voice. "*Papa-ji* had to ask Mr Bal for help to raise the bail. He's furious. Says I've single-handedly destroyed the family's *izzat* for three generations at least." He made a noise somewhere between a laugh and a groan. "*Phenchod*. It's not going to make much difference if I go to gaol or not. *Papa-ji* is going to have me under house arrest for the rest of my life."

"You know what?" Baz said. "Serves you fucking well right. What did you think was going happen if you carried a knife into the middle of a riot?"

Silence. He thought Vik had hung up on him, then his voice sounded, tight and bitter.

"Maybe you're right, *yaar*. But that big fucker was looking for me. I never drew my knife, never had the chance. But he had his blade out right from the start. When the police came, he dropped it and his mates kicked it away. Made it look like I had a weapon on me and he didn't. So the pigs let him off with a caution and charged me."

"They let him out?" Anger leeched from him, to be replaced with a cold wave of despair. What about the fingerprints on the envelope? Did the police not make the connection? Did that bastard detective block it? Why hadn't they held him?

"That's British justice for you." Vik didn't seem overly interested in the fate of his attacker. When he spoke again, something of the old spark was back in his voice. "Hell of a day though, *haan*? Small price to pay for teaching those *gora* fascists they can't walk all over us."

He was too wired for sleep. Better to do something with his restless energy than waste it tossing and turning in bed all night. He called Maia from a call box down the road and headed for the darkroom. He souped the day's film, then dozed for a few hours on the couch in the studio before getting up to develop the contact prints and make enlargements of a few of the best. In the morning, he went straight to the offices of the *Coventry Evening Telegraph* and asked to see the picture editor. Yes, this time, they were planning to publish photographs of the events. But no, sorry, they had their own staff photographers there. No need for any freelance pictures.

"I was right in the thick of it. I've got some pictures your people aren't likely to have."

"Sorry, mate. We've got it covered."

Not much trace left of yesterday's clashes. A bit more litter blowing along the streets. The odd missile left lying in the road. The congealed remains of egg on the pavement. Half the people on the streets today probably had no clue their city had tried to tear itself apart less than twenty-four hours earlier.

He passed the spot outside the museum where the men in suits had stood. The puppet masters. It must have seemed like a good day to them: the opening skirmish en route to all-out war. As for Vik—son of one of the march's organisers, arrested for an 'unprovoked' attack on a white youth? They must be wetting themselves over that one.

Weariness threatened to swamp him. The bastards had to be stopped, but what could he do? The police couldn't help—or wouldn't. The papers had their own story to tell. What did that leave him?

He was halfway down the hill, almost to the onion dome of the Odeon cinema, when an idea struck him. He stood in the middle of the pavement, exploring it, testing it for weaknesses. Then before doubt could set in, he turned and bounded up the steps of the museum.

Standing in front of the curator's desk, he laid out the prints, one by one, like tarot cards.

"This stuff is happening right here, right now, in our city," Baz said. "People need to see it. They need to have a choice about what sort of city they want to live in."

"Mr Lister, I would love to exhibit your photographs, really I would."

The name plaque on the desk read James Almond, M.A. He was their new man, brought in with a big fanfare a few months back to bring the museum up to date. He certainly looked like something new. Expensive suit, trendily narrow silk tie. He tugged at his cuffs, showing off over-sized cufflinks.

"You have to understand, what you ask is impossible. Perhaps in three months' time—"

"Three months is too late."

"Then there's nothing I can do for you."

Baz loomed over him, conscious the scabs on his chin made him look more like Knoxie on Friday night than an aspiring artist. "Look. I've got my own easels. All I need is a few feet of space—"

"And I keep trying to explain that all our exhibition space is committed."

"—in your vestibule, so people see it as they come in."

He sensed a hesitation and pushed on, driving home the advantage.

"Mr Almond, you're new here. I understand that. But in three months, this city could have torn itself apart. I want to stop that happening."

The curator got up and crossed to the window. He stood with his hands folded behind him. The window looked out on the steps from where the puppet masters watched their plans unfold. But what could that possibly mean to a man like this? A man with a silk tie and an MA? An incomer?

"As a matter of fact, I grew up down the road from you, Mister Lister," Almond said.

Baz stared at the nape of his neck, wrong-footed.

"I read all about you when I took this job," the curator said. "Part of getting myself up to date with the Coventry Arts scene. Rumour has it, last time you exhibited one of your photographs in public, someone threw a brick through the window and set fire to it."

Something in Almond's voice made Baz's fingers tingle, as if he'd felt the hum in the line that tells a fisherman when he's hooked a fish.

"So, what do you want your time here to be remembered for? How safe your exhibitions were? Or how brave?"

When Almond turned round, he had the look of a man who

was about to place a large bet on a rank outsider.

"You can have one week," he said. "In the lobby."

For a second night running, Baz snatched a couple of hours sleep in the studio, in between making full-sized enlargements of the prints he'd selected and mounting them for display. In the morning, Mohan helped deliver them to the museum and set them up on the easels. The curator, his cufflinks now so large they looked like talismans against evil, grasped Baz's hand and pumped it up and down.

"We can't offer you any publicity," he said. "Not at this short notice."

"Just let people see for themselves. That's all I ask."

But within hours, Mercia Sound called Baz. They'd heard about the exhibition (James Almond's doing, maybe?) and wanted an interview with him. No, not on the Asian language programme. What they had in mind was tomorrow's regular morning talk show.

This was serious exposure. Half the population of Coventry tuned in at some point in the morning. For a heartbeat he considered telling them he couldn't do it. But that would be missing the point of the exhibition.

Time to break cover and come out fighting.

By the time the production staff at the radio station had fitted him with headphones and adjusted the microphone on its anglepoise to the right height, Baz's mouth was as dry as the Thar Desert.

The interviewer was a cheerful disc jockey called Kenny. Like the rest of Coventry, Baz knew his voice. He hadn't expected him to look so young, though. And he'd never pictured glasses.

Kenny gave Baz an airy wave, faded out the music and leaned

into the microphone. "Let me introduce you to my guest for this morning, Bhajan Singh," he said. A garrotte tightened round Baz's throat. "Bhajan Singh is the photographer who was at the heart of the controversy over the *Desi Art* exhibition in the city earlier this year. But since the murder of the young Sikh student in the city at Easter, and the violence that erupted at this weekend's Peace March, Bhajan has put on an impromptu exhibition of his photographs at the Herbert Museum in Jordan Well. Bhajan, you called this exhibition, *Which City?* Why's that?"

The interviewer glanced at the clock and swung back in his chair. Baz swallowed hard several times, took a sip from the glass of water helpfully pointed out by Kenny, and heard his own voice sounding like a stranger's, loud in the little studio.

"The photographs I'm exhibiting, they're in pairs. I-I've twinned pictures of ordinary city life with images of violence. Images from over the past few weeks, taken in the same location."

The images flickered through his mind. The firebombed temple paired with the punks at the wedding. The *sieg-heiling* punks in Broadgate next to an image of two sisters in *shalwar kameez*, carrying Owen Owen bags and giggling as they wait for the bus. The mounted-police charge in Fairfax Street paired with a Sikh couple emerging from Fishy Moore's.

"I'm asking people to think about which city they want to live in—the one where all of us can live together or the one where we go to war over the colours of our skins."

Kenny frowned. "Go to war? That's a pretty strong term to use, isn't it?"

Baz took a deep breath, aware of what consequences his next word could reap, feeling the air hot and burning.

"I have no doubt there are people who want to seed the conditions for a race war. And I have no doubt their actions fed the violence we saw on Sunday."

"Wow. Challenging views there from Bhajan Singh." Kenny moved a few sliders on the panel in front of him, and music faded in before they went to a commercial break. Far too soon, he heard Kenny say, "that was The Specials, with 'Concrete Jungle'. You a fan of The Specials, Bhajan?"

"Very much so."

"And of course the boys have just announced that they will be holding a Concert for Racial Harmony, right here in the city. Will you be going along to support them?"

He rubbed his damp palms against his jeans. "If I can, I'm sure I will."

"Of course, many of the Asian community here in Coventry are from India or Pakistan, or more recently from Uganda and Kenya. But, Bhajan, you are not an immigrant, are you?"

"No, I was born in the West Midlands."

"To an Asian father and an English mother, is that right? Do you think that's why you've attracted all this attention from the Far Right? For them, the mixing of races is the ultimate taboo, isn't it?"

"So I'm told. But I've never understood what they think they have to lose. The English are a mongrel race to begin with. There is no pure English blood to protect."

"But would you say you identify yourself as Asian?"

Too Paki to be White. Too *gora* to be *desi*. Vik, if you're listening to this you must be laughing your arse off.

"I identify myself as what I am," he said. "A person of mixed race."

Kenny swung in his chair, keeping a practised distance from the mic.

"So can you tell our listeners what it is like to come from a mixed family? Most people might imagine it's like being torn between two worlds."

A familiar buzz of irritation made him twitch.

"That's a massive oversimplification. Look at the language we use about mixed race. 'Half-caste'. Why should I be half of anything? Gardeners know that mixing two strains make a plant stronger, not weaker. Two Tone music isn't diluted by the blending two sorts of sounds—"

"And that sounds like a cue to play some music," said Kenny, busy with his sliders again. "Here's The Selecter with 'Three Minute Hero.'"

Baz unclenched his hand from around the glass of water. Why had he agreed to this? It was like volunteering to have his skin flayed off. He focused his mind on Pauline Black's quirky soprano and let it carry him through the short break until he heard Kenny say, "I'm talking this morning to Bhajan Singh, whose new exhibition, *Which City?* has just opened at the Herbert Museum and Art Gallery. Bhajan, you yourself were attacked by racists when you were still a child, weren't you? Your house was firebombed and, in fact, your mother was killed?"

Another layer of skin stripped. How come these days everyone seemed to know everything?

"It wasn't a firebomb." It seemed important to be clear about that.

"But your mother was killed?"

"Yes."

"And you escaped. How old were you then?"

"Thirteen."

"Your father was already dead. Any other family?"

"No."

"So, an orphan at thirteen. What happened to you?"

The tightness in his chest eased a little.

"I was placed in a foster home. With a woman called Rebeccah who probably saved me from becoming a basket case."

"A lucky break at last, then?"

"Yeah, I guess."

Kenny picked up a pen and doodled something on the pad in front of him.

"So, just out of interest, if it wasn't a firebomb, how was the fire started?"

He closed his eyes, seeing himself in the old cathedral, camera pointed towards the East Window.

"They nailed a burning cross to our door," he said.

For the first time, Kenny seemed floored by one of his answers.

"A burning cross? Like the Ku Klux Klan, type of thing?"

Baz wiped a handkerchief across his face. "Something similar happened a few weeks later, to a black family in Handsworth. That time, someone saw it early enough and the fire was put out. In our case, no one saw it. Or some bloke coming off a late shift, he thought he might have seen something, but he figured someone was messing about with fireworks and he drove on by. By the time my mother woke up, it was too late. We were trapped."

"But you got out? Clearly."

"Yes."

"How was that?"

He could see Kenny digging for the story that was going to tug his listeners' heart strings. The brave little boy, climbing to safety against all the odds. A chill settled over his skin. There was a long stretch of dead air. The DJ's face slid towards unease. Baz closed his eyes.

"I … don't know," he said.

Chapter 87

When Baz returned from the radio studios, he looked as if he'd unravelled. He stared at me with unfocused eyes, pulled his tie from his collar and headed straight up stairs. When I followed him, a few minutes later, he was already fast asleep.

I sat on the end of the bed, watching the lines of tension disappear as he sank deeper into sleep. He must know what he'd just done. God, he might just as well have stood on a rooftop waving a flag and yelling, 'Come on you bastards, come and get me!' And I loved him for it. I loved him for doing the right thing and to hell with the consequences.

But it terrified me that they might hear him and heed the call.

He was still asleep, sprawled face down across our bed, when his Rasta friend phoned. I ran to answer it and when I called him, he came downstairs barefoot, rubbing sleep from his eyes.

"It's Jah Green," I said. "He says he and Emmett will come to the exhibition tomorrow, and will you meet them there?"

Baz's face split into a grin of pure happiness. "Well, tell him not to bring his damn spliffs into the museum," he said, projecting his voice towards the phone.

Jah Green chuckled. "Babylon should not be so facety. There's no harm in a likkle herb," he said.

I was about to hand the phone over but the Rasta forestalled me. "You tell Bhajan he a brave mon," he said. "And you take care of him, y'hear? He need someone looking out for him right now."

"I know."

"Okay, then. Let me chat to the bwai."

Baz went off the next day, walking as if the lead jacket he'd been carrying had been lifted from his shoulders. The reprieve might be only temporary, but it was just what he needed.

He was still out when I left for work. The weather had cooled and a fine drizzle filled the air, yet the Skipper was still abnormally quiet.

"Where is everyone?" I asked Pongo, as he put his ironing board away. "It's getting like the Marie Celeste in here."

The old soldier glanced round the half-empty room and shrugged. "Some of them have started going down the Sally Ann. Or that Cyrenian place." He turned away from me, folding his shirt. "Don't know how much longer I'll be coming here, if I'm honest."

"Pongo, why?"

He put one foot up on the bench and bent over it, applying polish to the shoe with a practised action.

"I've nothing against the gaffer," he said. "He's always been good to me."

"Of course, I know that. What is this, Pongo?"

He glanced in my direction and away again. "Folk have started calling us Paki-lovers, just 'cos we come up here. Hard enough on the streets without that sort of cack."

Pongo swapped feet and began applying polish with equal vigour to the other shoe, while I tried to absorb the shock of his words.

"You don't believe any of that garbage, though, do you? Couldn't you say something? People'd listen to you."

He fitted the brushes back into their little case, still avoiding my eye. "Learnt in the army: keep your head down and get on with the job. Only way to get through." He spread the pages of the *Evening Telegraph* out in front of him and sat down. "Men like the gaffer, them that stick their necks out—they're either heroes or mutineers. And both'll get themselves shot in the end."

Across the other side of the bench, Jerzy raised his head. "Do not be angry, Maia. They are good men, mostly. But they do not know how to fight."

Pongo half rose in his seat. "Who're you saying doesn't know how to fight?" he growled.

Jerzy stared back, his face impassive. "You say yourself. You keep head down. You want easy life."

Pongo glared at him, then shrugged. "I'm past all that," he said.

Jerzy dismissed him with a wave of his hand and beckoned me over. "I have idea how to fight them," he said, in a guttural whisper. "We put sign on door, say: No Fascists. Is good idea, no?" He slapped his thigh and gave a wheezing laugh that turned his face red.

"You're an old fool, Polish," Pongo snapped. "You'll get yourself in trouble along with the rest of the fools."

But Jerzy just went on laughing.

When I got home, Baz was sitting up on the bed, headphones on, a smile on his face and the smell of dope clinging to his clothes. I sat on the bed and lifted the phone off one ear.

"Take it you had a good time then?"

He smiled a benign smile, wrapped an arm around me and drew me between his legs.

"Fuck, Maia. They get what I'm trying to do. They really understand. And James Almond says visitor numbers are way up. He showed me some of the comments. I mean, I know the people who go to the museum will be a self-selecting bunch but, they were so supportive …"

Enthusiasm bubbled up out of him, as if Jah Green's presence had chased away the shadows and he had been able to stand in the sun for a day. He lay down and pulled me on top of him, and I could feel him horny underneath me.

"Emmett and Jah Green loved the demo tape the *Sona* guys gave me," he said. "And I have to remember to phone Mohan. They know someone who owns a machine shop. It's got workspace, welding facilities. Everything he'd need."

Jah Green, the wizard, putting everything to rights. If only he could.

"Mohan'll be chuffed to bits," I said.

He stretched out, his fingers locked behind his neck. "Emmett Bailey brought a portfolio of his photographs for me to look at. God, his stuff is incredible. The way he gets under the skin of his subjects, like he's more than just an observer. Yet his dark room is nothing but a blacked out bathroom! Can you imagine? Mind you, his camera makes up for it. He's got a Leica Rangefinder. That's the camera I've always wanted."

I trapped a finger in a lock of his hair and tugged gently. "I love it when you talk dirty."

He rolled us both over, his weight pinning me to the bed. "I'm boring the crap out of you, aren't I?"

"No, you're not. It's lovely to see you so happy. I just couldn't resist."

He kissed me back, his tip of his tongue touching mine. Then he pulled back.

"Something's wrong though, isn't it?"

I shook my head. "Not tonight."

He put a finger to my lips. "Tell me."

Chapter 88

Baz was almost expecting it when it came. A plain brown envelope dropped through the door. A sheet of coarse paper.

He slid it out and unfolded it. No glued-on words this time. Just the outline of a burnt cross, singed onto the page.

He held it by its edges, a smouldering fury gathering inside him. It seemed as if this one image—a cross, in flames—had been the backdrop of his whole life. How many times could an image be recast before it became impossible to unpick all its meanings? Impossible already to unravel what it meant to him—the fear and hatred and disgust, shot through with a glimmering thread of hope.

And now they *dared* use it again to threaten people's lives? People he cared about?

"There!" he said, in the police station, thrusting envelope and contents at Conway. "No one else has handled it and I've barely touched it."

The sergeant took it, half reluctantly, it seemed to Baz. "We'll see what we can do Mr Lister. But I doubt it will take us much further forward."

"Six other people live in that house," Baz said. "I'd like to be able to tell them you'll do something to protect them."

Conway looked tired. "Mr Lister, if we put a police officer outside every home where there's a chance of a racist attack, we'd run out of police officers and the slags would have a field day." He took off his glasses and rubbed the bridge of his nose. "If it's any consolation, it's rare for anonymous letters like this to be followed up with any actual violence. And as far as we know, no one who's been attacked has had any kind of threat or warning beforehand."

"Yeah, well. It's one thing to take that chance myself. It's a bit different asking other people to take it for me."

As the sergeant was showing him out, Baz stopped and turned back.

"You had the guy Maia pointed out. Did you know that? He was arrested on the day of the Peace March. But you let him go."

"We did, sir, yes."

Conway's stolidity kicked off a surge of anger. "If you knew you had him, why wasn't he held?" he said.

"We checked the fingerprints. No match."

"And the other stuff? Threatening Miss Hassett?"

"Frankly, that's his word against hers, sir. No witnesses. Or no witnesses that'd ever be persuaded to say anything."

Like it was Vik's word against his that the bastard was carrying a knife.

"What about Treddle, then?"

"No match on his fingerprints, either."

"Pound to a penny the racists are trying to put the wind up me," he told the others at tea time. "Get me to shut up. That's what the police think anyway. What with this and the state of the roof, I've asked the council about finding another place for us. But don't expect it to happen any time soon. In the meantime, if any of you want to leave, you're free to go, of course."

Nobody moved. He looked at them all. His volunteers. His responsibility. If his actions had put them in danger, it was up to him to set things right.

"There is another way," he said. "None of this has anything to do with you, or with the Skipper. If I left, the problem would go with me. I could hand in my resignation in to Rebeccah and be gone tomorrow."

They stared at him, frozen in various attitudes stunned silence. Libby stood up.

"I don't know about anybody else, but I don't see why I should be frightened off by a bunch of oiks with over-zealous haircuts. No more should you, Baz."

"The police are right," Tom said. "Poison pens don't follow through. They're cowards, and they think everyone else is a coward too."

"My bedroom's at the front of the house," said Simon. "I can help keep watch. And CovARA will keep an eye out and all."

"We should fit some smoke alarms," Robyn said. "My parents have one."

"I can do that," said Iain. "If we put one in each room at the front, that should keep us safe enough."

God, they were amazing, every one of them. He felt a rush of gratitude for their loyalty, for their confidence in them. For their sheer fucking ballsiness.

Please God they wouldn't pay the price.

"If they'd said yes, would you have gone?" Maia asked later.

"I don't know. Probably. I'm glad I don't have to, though." He circled his arms round her, the firm little bulge in her belly keeping him ever so slightly at a distance. "I'd have taken you with me, if you'd wanted."

She dug a sharp little finger between his ribs. "Didn't bloody ask me first, though, did you?"

He could sense the rippling movement in her abdomen as her baby twisted and tumbled inside her, buoyant and acrobatic.

She wound her arms around him and ran her fingers up his back, and he knew he was forgiven.

"You still reckon Gary is behind all this?" she said, a while later.

He called up an image of the burnt cross, singed into paper. It could have been done with a lighter, though whoever did it would have needed some kind of template to make the shape so precise. Did Gary remember the hours he'd spent in the old Cathedral, the photographs he'd taken, even back then? And if he did, he might put two and two together and understand how much this particular image would get to him.

"There's something clever about it, isn't there?" Maia said. "Nastily clever. It's not the same sort of mindless thuggery that throws firebombs … or attacks kids."

"No. And up until now I'd have put Gary squarely in the mindless thug camp."

He had an elemental need to separate the random violence of the past few weeks and the calculated spite of the letters. But the thought came to him that the same minds that stoked the skinheads' testosterone-laced hatred could also play off Gary's knowledge of his foster brother to get at him.

Chapter 89

The headline blared across the *Evening Telegraph:*

```
    THREE MORE ATTACKS
  ON ASIANS THIS WEEKEND
```

By far the most serious attack, I read, involved an Asian doctor who not long before had joined a practice in the city centre. He was popular and dedicated and he lived on his own. On Saturday night, he went to pick up some chips. As he came out of the chip shop, he was stabbed, apparently by a teenager with a grudge against Asians. He staggered as far as his car and locked himself in, where he continued to bleed until he was found slumped over the wheel, barely alive …

Dear God. This was no kid caught up in a turf war. This was a grown man—a professional.

A picture came into my head of my bedroom at the top of the house, back in safe, leafy Hampstead. The narrow white bed. The sloping ceiling. The Pierrot doll I'd had since I was fourteen. When I'd gone back at Easter, the room had suffocated me. But right now, I wanted to run there and hide. Hide from all this.

Maybe Baz was right. Maybe it would be better if the two of us just left. Then Tom and the others would no longer be putting themselves at risk for our sake. The Skipper would return to normal.

And my baby would be out of danger.

Except that wasn't true, was it? The scars on Baz's back proved that. Sooner or later, they'd find you out. Sooner or later, you had to stand and fight.

After all, this was Ossie's child. Perhaps it was fitting that he should be born fighting.

That night, Frank didn't come in for his pills. Dr Kheraj told me not to worry; one day without the medication wasn't the end of the world. The important thing was to ensure Frank finished the whole course. Sure enough, the next day, he was back, full of apologies and hazy excuses. But the day after that, he went missing.

Just before I went to work that evening, we had a spring downpour that sent the water pouring down the gutters. It overflowed the storm drains and sent brown water running through the streets. The Skipper should have been packed to the gills, but it was still only half full. By now I was worried that, despite everything Frank had said at the hospital, the campaign against the Skipper had got to him too. With a sick feeling in my stomach, I phoned the Sally Ann and the Cyrenians, but no one had seen him. I explained about the medication and they promised to call, should he show up. But I heard nothing.

In the morning, now desperately anxious, I swung by the Bird Street Day Centre and left another message about Frank's medication. Then I went searching for him.

The rain had stopped but the pavements were still wet and the sky was covered in a grey blanket, trapping the chill, damp air over the city. I wanted to believe Frank had found somewhere warm and dry to wait this out, but in my head I kept hearing the terrible hacking cough that had wracked him before he went into hospital, and it drove me to keep looking.

After a couple of hours, I came across a group of homeless

men in one of the underpasses off Greyfriars Green. They were smoking rollups and passing round a bottle of Woodpecker, their voices echoing off the tiled walls. I recognised Knoxie and his pal Joey. The fellow with a rainbow belt that I'd seen on my first night. Walter, rocking himself as he mumbling the words of the Morning Prayer. And Charlie Singer.

I hadn't been scared of anyone at the Skipper in a long time. But I was a lot more vulnerable out here. Charlie's presence gave me confidence, though. Not all the guys from the Skipper liked you to acknowledge them if you met them outside, but our resident minstrel could be relied upon to produce a cheery wave and a few bars of a song to greet you.

"Hi, Charlie, how's it going?" I said. "Haven't seen you for a few days."

The busker's eyes slid away and he stared at a patch of graffiti on the wall. It crossed my mind that no one knew where I was.

"Listen, guys, I'm looking for Frank. Frank Duffy? Any of you seen him?"

A stretch of sullen silence was broken only by dripping water further along the tunnel and Walter's singsong recitation. Then the man with the rainbow belt spat at my shoes.

"Going to report him to the Social, are you?"

"I'm nothing to do with the Social. Frank's been ill, that's all. I have medicine he needs to take."

"Why should we trust you, anyway?" Rainbow Belt said. "You're from that Skipper, aren't you?"

"So?"

"The Skipper's got a Paki gaffer and a Paki doctor. Feeding us a pack of lies they are, so they can look after their own—"

"You know what? This is bollocks. Charlie, how many times has Baz stood up for you in court when you've been done for begging? Knoxie, you wouldn't even be alive if it wasn't for Baz and Dr Kheraj—"

Joey got to his feet. He stood eighteen inches in front of me, his cider-laden breath in my face.

"This one doesn't just work at the Skipper, though, does she? She's the Paki's bint, she is."

My stomach knotted and my hands and feet went cold. I remembered the relish with which Joey had joined in baiting Baz, the night the story of his mother's death came out. But I stood my ground.

"You should be ashamed of yourself, bitch," he said. "Call yourself an Englishwoman? Where's your fucking pride? Now get out of my sight before I thrape some respect into you."

Most of the men looked uneasy. It was no part of their code to threaten a woman, yet I wasn't sure that would stop them joining in if Joey started something. The walls of the tunnel swam.

I didn't run till I was out of sight of the underpass.

Four nights later, I found Frank slumped on the doorstep as I went to put the milk bottles out. He was badly bruised, with several cuts to his head, and his breathing was once again laboured and rattling. Baz and Tom carried him in and laid him on our bunk in the office, and I called Dr Kheraj.

"I gather our friend's not been taking his medicine?" the doctor asked, when he arrived.

"He's not been in for days," I told him.

He worked gently, absorbed in his task, treating poor Frank's body as reverently as though he were royalty. When he held Frank's wrist to take his pulse, I noticed how beautifully manicured the doctor's hands were, though their skin was papery and covered in liver spots. Frank's hands, by contrast, were big, with broad fingers, blackened nails, scars, and a couple of open sores. The doctor felt his brow and put his ear to Frank's chest. Frank coughed, but the doctor didn't flinch. He showed no revulsion as he opened his dirty, sweat-stained shirt and put his stethoscope against his skin, or touched the purplish bruises on his chest.

"The disease is taking hold again. And it looks as though he has taken a beating too, poor fellow."

Fragments of conversation ran through my mind. Had Frank gone and stood up to the wrong people? Stood up for us? Was that how this had happened?

"He needs to be readmitted to hospital," the doctor said. "Tonight if possible. I'll call an ambulance. He can travel more comfortably than in my car, and it will focus their attention."

"He's very ill, isn't he?" I said.

"Yes, Miss Hassett. He is."

"Worse than last time?"

It seemed unbearable that we should come so close to losing the old bugger again. Dr Kheraj took my hands and held them.

"Miss Hassett, we have learnt from this how hard it is for someone like Mr Duffy to go on taking his medication once he is out of hospital. He has been shown how important it is that he does. If we both take those lessons to heart, then he has perhaps one more chance at life. Beyond that, it is in the hands of Allah."

He squeezed my hands and I nodded. He made his call and I heard the calm, professional manner with which he stressed the urgency of the situation.

"I'll wait for them outside," Baz said. "They never know how to find this place."

"You stay here," Dr Kheraj told him. "I need some things from my car. I will fetch them and wait there for the ambulance."

I knelt on the floor, holding Frank's hand. Outside, Tom was left serving tea single-handed. After what seemed an eternity, Baz erupted from his seat.

"Those bastards hear our address and they think they needn't bother to hurry. I'm going out—see if I can see them."

Frank's cough was losing strength, his breath fading. Alone, I let a tear trickle down my face and onto Frank's hand.

Chapter 90

It was so near to the longest day that an afterglow still lit the western sky as Baz left the Skipper. The streetlight at the end of Fob Watch Lane blinked orangey-red, lighting the entry in a series of freeze-frames. He called the doctor's name, but heard no answer.

As he reached the end of the entry, his eye caught a movement away to his right. He peered down the lane towards Spon Street, but could make nothing out. He turned back towards the doctor's car, parked further up the lane.

The fitful streetlight flashed on, and in the brief flare of reddish light, he saw a pair of legs jutting from the back seat. He ran towards them and stopped, one hand on the open door. Inside, Noordin Kheraj lay sprawled against the old tartan blanket on the back seat, his arms flung awkwardly out like a mannequin upended in a shop window. Baz's first thought was that he must have had a heart attack. Then the light flashed on again and he saw, almost black against the doctor's pale suit, a spreading stain of blood.

A howl of rage and pity ripped through him, answered by a siren racing along Spon Street. He heard footsteps running down the entry and, in seconds, Maia was at his side. She whipped round, towards the ambulance men.

"Over here. Please. This man needs your help."

Maia's voice was steady and efficient. His own seemed to have been swallowed up in a yawning sense of loss that threatened to consume him. He had to lean against the wall to stop himself falling. He was trapped inside a bubble that let in light, but no sound or feeling. Somewhere outside the bubble, ambulance men were fitting an oxygen mask, attaching a drip, applying pressure around the wound.

"What about the other man?" Maia asked, as Noordin was lifted on a stretcher into the back of the ambulance.

"He's wounded too?"

"No. But he is seriously ill."

The driver glanced at his mate. "We'll call another ambulance for you. But if we don't get this one to hospital …" He let the words hang.

Baz pulled himself away from the wall. "You'll stay and wait with Frank?" he asked Maia. "Please? I have to go with him."

The ambulance screamed along the road, lights flashing, siren blaring. Onto the Ring Road and off again, up Stoney Stanton Road, past Swanswell Park—moonlight glinting on the murky surface of the duck pond. Baz sat beside Dr Kheraj, holding his hand, a numbness spreading through his body.

"This your father?" the ambulance man asked.

He shook his head. "A colleague. And a friend …"

"What's his name?"

"Noordin Kheraj. Dr Noordin Kheraj. He's a GP."

The ambulance man's bristling eyebrows shot up.

"Poor sod in the papers, he was a GP, wasn't he? Hanging by a thread, they say he is." He bent over some dials, checking pulse and respiration. "Don't know what this city is coming to. Never used to have anything like this when I first joined the service. A few drunks on a Saturday night and, apart from that, falls and heart attacks and kids with broken this or that. What I call nice clean emergencies. None of these knives and stabbings and that."

The hospital floor kept disappearing from underneath his feet and there was nothing to stop him falling into the abyss. His brain refused to yield up Noordin's address and he started babbling his childhood address from Leamington. A nurse in a white cap sat him down with a cup of hot, sugary tea. The taste made him think of the milky *chai* he and Noordin had drunk at Abdul Saleem's house, the night some bastard nailed a pig's head to his door.

"When can I see him?" he asked, again and again.

The woman went away and came back with the news that Dr Kheraj was in emergency surgery.

"Would you like to wait in the relatives' room?" she asked.

She led him into a side room. His eyes kept focusing inconsequential details, like the nurse's faint scar that began above her right eyebrow and ran down the inner edge of her eye socket.

"Does Dr Kheraj have any family?" the nurse asked.

He shook his head, trying to clear it. "His wife died a while ago." He struggled to remember. "I think he has a daughter in Canada and a son somewhere—Dubai, I think. I-I don't have addresses or anything."

"It's okay. Don't distress yourself."

She left him alone. In the corner, between the two settees, was a small, square table, covered in Formica. In his mind's eye, he could see another table, just like it, in the corner of Auntie Harjit's sitting room, where the household shrine stood. A picture of Guru Nanak, the first Sikh guru, at the back. A statue of Lakshmi, the Hindu goddess of good fortune. An incense holder. A little brass *jyot* shaped like the bottom half of an

Aladdin's lamp.

Every day, she lit the incense and, on special occasions, the ghee in the *jyot*. And there was a prayer she used to say, standing in front of it with her hands folded. The words had snagged in his brain, their meaning lost or never known.

Ek Onkar Satnam. Waheguru.

Chapter 91

The two doctors both died on 18th June. That was the day that The Specials released 'Ghost Town'. For days it keened from every radio, every jukebox, every stereo. Those stabbing horns and that eerie, wailing chorus became the soundtrack of their deaths. Each time I heard it, tears welled up.

Baz walked round the house as if cut off from the world. He didn't rage, or cry. Whole conversations took place in front of him without his seeming to hear a word. I wanted so much to comfort him, but at night when I tried to put my arms around him, he lay like a felled tree.

"It's not your fault. None of it is your fault."

He pushed his face into the pillow, fists pressing into his temples as if the pain inside was unbearable. "It should have been me. I should have been the one out there waiting for the ambulance."

It was a riff he'd played over and over since the night of the stabbing, as if he were determined to drag the weight of guilt onto his own shoulders. Rebeccah said he just needed time, but it seemed to me that something deep-rooted had hold of him and wouldn't let go.

Saturday morning, a miserable little group gathered for The Specials' concert. Tom had got us tickets weeks before, but if it hadn't been for the desperate need to keep up the protests, none of us would have felt like going. Only Simon held onto his enthusiasm, but he was spoiling for a bit of aggro and convinced the skinheads would show up to provide it.

Shortly before we were due to leave, Baz came in, avoiding the looks that turned his way.

"I'm going to the studio. Rebeccah needs a photograph for the obituary."

I could tell the others thought he was making an excuse. In his present state of mind, why would he want to spend the day in a crowd of concert-goers, half of whom knew little and cared less about the purpose of the gig? But I didn't like the idea of his spending the day alone.

"Shall I come with you? Keep you company for a bit?"

I half expected him to tell me to get lost, but he shrugged and headed outside. I followed him into the yard and grabbed a bike. He didn't look round as he set off, but he did slow down a little.

As we crossed the main road, the wind blew a fine mizzle in my face. I spotted a few small groups making their way towards the stadium in the Butts, ready-prepared with blankets and umbrellas. A couple of weeks ago, the NF had threatened to organise a march past the stadium. The Council got nervous and toyed with the idea of banning the concert. They settled in the end for just banning the march, but jitters remained. Simon wasn't the only one expecting trouble.

We propped our bikes against Rebeccah's garden wall and Baz let us into the studio. He went straight to the cabinets where he kept his books of contact prints and started rifling through the drawers. I tucked myself away on the chaise longue overlooking the garden.

I'd never been much good at sitting and doing nothing, but pregnancy was teaching me to appreciate stillness. I closed my eyes, slowed my breathing and waited. After a minute or two, the baby responded with a kick and a tumbling roll, as though telling me how good it felt to be alive, and safe. My breasts tightened painfully, releasing a storm of love.

For a moment I was back on the couch in the surgery, gentle hands pressing the foetal monitor to my side. I heard the whooshing sound of my own blood, and then the galloping beat of my baby's heart. I couldn't remember if I'd ever told Dr Kheraj how much it had meant to me.

I was crying now. I didn't want Baz to hear, but the tears wouldn't let up. We'd none of us had a chance to say goodbye, not even Baz or Rebeccah. For all the ten days the doctor clung to life, only his son and daughter were allowed by his bedside. With each day that passed, we told ourselves, if he survives today then his chances of surviving tomorrow are that much better. But it hadn't worked out like that.

We had the full attention of the police now. The obnoxious DI turned up to question everyone who'd been at the Skipper that night. Officers combed the alleyway and Fob Watch Lane for signs of a weapon. But whoever attacked Dr Kheraj had left no more trace than a gust of wind. Unless someone at the Skipper knew something and was keeping quiet—and I didn't want to think about that.

After all the bad feeling, I was surprised how many of the men came and told us how they remembered Doctor Kheraj being good to them—dressing this wound or that or giving them their sick lines—and they wished him well. One or two who had stopped coming to the Skipper drifted back, looking shamefaced. But Joey stayed away. And so did Charlie Singer.

One of the worst moments was when someone scrawled graffiti on the wall along by where Dr Kheraj had been stabbed. Blood red letters that read:

```
GET YOUR FRESH-SKEWERED PAKI HERE!
```

I thought Baz was going to tear down the wall with his bare hands. Simon managed, with the help of a couple of pots of paint, to convert it to:

GET YOUR FRESH SKIPPER TEA HERE!

But we never found a culprit for that, either.

A sound outside punctured my thoughts, and I opened my eyes, scrubbing tears away on my sleeve. Over to my right, Baz was bent over a drawing table, examining contact prints through a loupe. I caught a movement, somewhere out in the garden, and figured it was Rebeccah. Then a few moments later, Mrs Peel shot through the cat flap. Her fur, dew-dropped with rain, stood out like a puffball. She shook herself, sneezed and made for a warm patch near the heater.

"Hello, old girl," Baz murmured. "I'll get you some dinner in a minute."

She was a striking cat but no beauty queen. Easy to see why Baz called her Mrs Peel. All over, her fur bore evidence that the lady was a fighter. A rather fat fighter, though, it had to be said.

I half closed my eyes, feeling the baby flip and twist as my muscles relaxed. I had the same fleeting sensation of a movement half seen, and opened them, expecting to see Rebeccah in the garden.

A man stood at the foot of the steps, his back to us. He wore a stained donkey jacket and a bobble hat pulled low over his ears. He bent over, reaching for something in the garden. As he straightened up, I saw a mark on his back. A mark like a blast pattern.

Chapter 92

At the first sound of breaking glass, Mrs Peel gave a yowl and disappeared under a pile of easels.

The stone left a hole in the glass, and a spider's web of cracks radiating outwards. It seemed to Baz he had time to study the crazing of the glass before the stone hit the table and bounced off, knocking him backwards off the stool, winded and half stunned.

He scrambled to his feet, the stone in his hands. It was the rose-coloured coral limestone, the one that Noordin gave Rebeccah. Baz stared at it, uncomprehending, then from missile to assailant, trying to decipher the face under the dark woollen hat. But Maia got there first.

"Derek—?"

"Paterson? What the fuck—?"

Then Baz saw what the Geordie was holding in his still-bandaged hand. A milk bottle, three quarters full of cloudy liquid, a rag sticking out the top.

"Get out of here. Get the fuck out!" he yelled at Maia.

Her eyes widened in understanding. She ran for the door and rattled it, but it wouldn't budge.

"Baz, he's blocked it."

He started towards her, but Paterson raised the milk bottle in one hand and a gold lighter in the other. The Geordie was sweating, his hands shaking.

"One more step, you Paki cunt, and I'll throw it."

Baz couldn't take his eyes off the liquid sloshing in the bottle. The smell of petrol was everywhere. His mind was relaying scenes from the Brixton riots, fast-forwarding them through his head. Policemen covered in flames as the petrol ran down the inside of their shields. The pub ablaze, burning out of control …

"Baz!"

Maia's voice anchored him. He had to keep his head, for her sake. If he let the fear take over now, they were both done for.

"You got a beef with me? Okay. Let Maia go."

Paterson's eyes darted over his shoulder towards Maia.

"Her? Dirty slag deserves it more than you."

"For God's sake, Paterson, she's pregnant."

"Aye. I noticed. Yours, is it?" His lips curled back in a horrible imitation of a smile. "I'd be doing it a favour."

Maia took a step towards the glass. *Don't*, he pleaded silently. *Don't draw attention to yourself…*

"Derek—"

"Shut up, bitch!" Paterson brought his hands closer together. They were trembling violently now. Baz found himself riveted by the gap between the lighter and the wick. "I thought you were different. I trusted you. But you betrayed us. Set us up with that bastard Paki landlord—"

"I didn't set you up, Derek. That was a decent room—"

"When I was down on my luck," he carried on, as if she hadn't spoken, "you let this piece of shit kick us out on the streets."

"I had no choice," Baz said.

Paterson's thumb spun the wheel of the lighter and a tiny flame flickered and died. "I was the one as had no fucking choice. You? You could have said, well, Derek, you've got nowhere to go, your hand's cut to ribbons—why don't you stay here tonight? But no. I got drunk. I lost my temper. And that was it. You kicked us out. Like the bastard bosses at the steel works. Like that bastard Paki landlord. No one. Ever. Gives. Derek Paterson a choice."

Baz's vision closed around the single point of a man holding a lighter and a petrol bomb. *Look at me, you bastard. Forget her. Just look at me ...* "Derek, you do have a choice. Right now."

"You don't think I've got the guts, do you? Just like them. You think I'm a useless prick that can't even get this right?"

"Who thinks that, Derek?"

The Geordie shook his head, as if a bee was buzzing round it.

"They want you dead, you know that?" He flicked again at the wheel of the lighter and this time, the flame held. "I do this, and I'll be a hero. They'll have to show us a bit of respect then, won't they?"

"Derek—!"

It seemed to take hours for Paterson's hands to close the gap. Baz threw himself towards Maia, but she was too far away. His limbs moved as if the air had grown thick. The petrol soaked rag in the mouth of the bottle ignited and Paterson stood holding it, as if he might turn himself into a human torch. Then his arm came back in a bowler's arc, and the bottle pitched through the air, wick blazing.

As it struck the glass, a cloud of flaming droplets fanned out. A thousand points of hungry flame seeking food to nourish their fire. They landed on books, on dustsheets, on frames, on easels, on the reprinted picture of the punks at the wedding. In seconds, the studio was choked with smoke and heat.

Baz's gut liquefied. His whole being was shrinking back into the shell of a terrified thirteen year old. He was a coward, a miserable fucking coward, that was the truth of it. He'd found the key. No one knew that. Not even Rebeccah. He'd saved his own skin and left his mother to burn. He was a coward and a killer and he deserved to die.

"Baz!"

Not Maia, though. She didn't deserve it. He could save her and her baby.

The thought unlocked his paralysed limbs.

"Get down!"

He saw her drop on all fours and ran back through the smoke—praying he wasn't disoriented, praying he'd remember where to find it. Eyes smarting, body scorching, he groped until his hands closed round the heavy tripod that was part of his disused studio equipment.

"Baz!"

He heard Maia's voice and moved towards the sound till he could see the outline of the door. He swung the heavy tripod and the glass shattered. Reaching through it, he found the rake Paterson had wedged under the handle. He yanked it free and flung himself at the door.

"Get out. Get out now."

He grabbed her and shoved her in front of him. She went, arms wrapped round the baby in her womb. As she made it to safety, he heard a cracking sound overhead, like metal screaming in agony. A blink of an iris later, pain struck the middle of his back.

Chapter 93

I staggered out, through clouds of smoke. Eyes stinging. Throat burning. Stumbling in what I hoped was the direction of the front of the house. If I could get out onto the street, if I could rouse Rebeccah, then I could raise the alarm.

I heard the sickening sound of a crash, as the beams holding up the conservatory buckled in the heat. Thank God, Baz was right behind me. I stumbled forward a few more steps and beyond the smoke, hands reached for mine.

"Help, please. Someone needs to call the fire brigade—"

Then I saw the hands that were holding me. They were tattooed with LOVE and HATE. Attached to them were arms marbled blue with Celtic knots and the branches of the tree of life. Gary's arms.

I screamed and pulled away, but he gripped my wrists tight.

"Don't be fucking stupid."

He dragged me towards the front of the house and propped me up against the apple tree, my chest wracked with coughing.

"Where's that Paki?"

I wanted to lie, but my voice froze in my throat. Another crash reverberated over the noise of the flames, and my eyes flicked towards the back of the house.

"In there?"

Gary let my wrists go and ripped at his shirt. Tied it over his mouth and nose. Sprinted through the wall of thick smoke that rolled up the side of the house. I tried to move after him but I doubled over, coughing up blackened sputum. By the time I could see again, he was gone.

I lay on a trolley in the ambulance, an oxygen mask over my face. I'd seen Rebeccah as I'd been lifted in. It must have been she who called 999.

"I'm fine," I kept telling the uniformed figures fussing over me. I pulled at the mask. "You have to help Baz."

"Hey, behave yourself," the ambulance attendant said. "You need to take care of that baby. We don't want to risk carbon monoxide poisoning. Just lie still and breathe through the mask."

Oh God. Could I lose both? Baz and the baby? When was the last time I felt a kick? Panic threatened to take hold and I forced myself to lie quiet, breathing through the mask. *Hang in there*, I thought. *Just you bloody well hang in there.*

I turned my head at the sound of another trolley being lifted into the ambulance, my heart racing. But the figure with an oxygen mask over his face wasn't Baz. It was Gary. I moaned and scrabbled at the mask.

"Where's Baz? What's happened to him?"

"Hush now," the ambulance man said. "Your friend's going in his own ambulance."

"That's one brave young man," his mate said, nodding at Gary. "Without him, your friend would've been dead for sure. Pulled him clear, he did. Burnt his hands something terrible."

Gary lay rigid at the other side of the ambulance. He had plastic bags over his hands, reddened patches on his chest and arms. After a moment, I lifted the mask.

"Why?"

"Put the mask back on. The babby. They said."

"I thought you hated Baz?"

He stared at the roof of the ambulance, arms held awkwardly at either side. The ambulance man had fitted a morphine drip, but it wouldn't have had time yet to take full effect.

"It all went too far. When the killing started." The attendant clambered back on board and Gary turned his face to the wall. "It all went too far, that's all."

So many hours, these past few months, spent in the waiting room of the Casualty department. With Derek. With Frank. With Dr Kheraj. And now Baz. They'd rushed him in ahead of Gary and me, and left the two of us lying in a corridor, so I knew it was bad. But I also knew things would have been a hell of a lot worse if Gary hadn't turned up when he did.

"What were you doing there?" I asked him. "How did you know …?"

I thought he wouldn't answer. When he spoke, his voice was hoarse and so low I could hardly hear it.

"Stupid ponce was boasting, wasn't he? Telling everyone what he was going to do. How he was going to prove himself, be a hero to the movement. No one else believed him…"

"But you did?"

He shrugged. His fine blond hair had grown over the tattoo, almost covering it.

"I'm glad," I told him.

"Didn't do it for you."

"I know."

He tried to shift on the trolley, his face contorted with the effort.

"For the babby, maybe. When I saw you were pregnant. Babby's got nothing to do with all this."

I stared up at the strip lights in the ceiling. "Actually, I think it's got everything to do with it."

A nurse came past, clipboard in hand, shoes squeaking on the vinyl floor. A doctor in a white coat shouldered his way through a pair of double-swing doors. Where was Baz? Why did nobody come to tell us how he was?

"Said in the paper someone tried to kill that stupid bastard before," Gary said. "Got me thinking. I don't want this country filling up with Pakis. I'd send 'em all back where they came from if I could. But where'd you send Baz?"

I turned my head to look at him. He lay very still, his voice drowsy, as if the morphine were taking effect. "Then that Geordie twat started saying he'd do it all over again. Make a better job of it this time."

"So was it Derek who was sending those anonymous letters?"

He made a face of disgust, as if I were too stupid to live. "Nah. That was them at the top. The people he'd upset with his exhibitions and that. They wanted to put the frighteners on him, stop him throwing his weight about. Paterson just had the notion of making it real."

He came so bloody close to succeeding too. And might still. God, where was Baz? Why wouldn't they tell us anything?

I shifted on the hard trolley. "Gary, would you tell any of this to the police?"

"Fuck off. I'm not fucking suicidal. The police want to know anything, I was walking down the road and saw the smoke. Went to see if I could help like any concerned citizen." He raised his head off the pillow and scowled at me. "You tell them any different and I'll—"

"Okay, okay. I get the message."

I lay back on the trolley and counted ceiling tiles. So many across. So many along.

God, I'd been wrong about so many things. Hero or villain—you never know which someone's going to turn out to be till they're put under pressure.

You don't even know how you'll turn out yourself.

Chapter 94

Baz opened his eyes. He was in a narrow bed with side rails. A mask was pressed to his face and a needle dug into his arm. As he started to test parts of his body out, he discovered his ribs were strapped up and large parts of him were swathed in gauze bandages.

But his mind was clear.

He knew what happened after he found the key.

Later that day, Maia sat, holding his hand, while he coughed until tears ran down his face from the pain in his broken ribs and he brought up sputum the colour of charcoal. Bit by bit, as he could get the words out, he started to tell her.

He crouched on the floor, wet towel over his face, heat bellying under the thick pall of black smoke over his head. He crawled forward, his face close to the bottom of the door, trying to catch a breath of fresh air from the draught that always blew underneath. Then he felt it, pressed into his bare sole. The key.

His fingers curled around the metal shaft and held on tight. He groped towards the door, half blinded with smoke. Hands all over the place as he fumbled for the lock. Shouting and shouting.

"Mum. Mum. I've found the key. We can get out. Come *on*,

mum."

His voice was hoarse and he kept coughing. He didn't know if she'd heard him. If he could get the door open and get some air, maybe he could clear his lungs and shout properly.

Maybe something had distorted in the heat, because the key wouldn't turn. Then the chambers of the lock clicked into place. He grabbed the handle and tugged. The door, too, resisted, before flying open. Clean, fresh air rushed into the oxygen-starved room. Baz looked back for his mother and saw the flames by the front door surge forward and up the stairs like a Yuletide blaze up a chimney. Then something thumped him in the middle of his back with the force of a charging bull and flung him into the garden …

"You see?" he said. "I didn't abandon her. I opened the door and the backdraught threw me out into the garden. That's why I was unconscious. That's why I didn't remember."

Maia smiled at him fondly, like a teacher whose pupil has finally grasped her lesson "I knew you hadn't. You couldn't."

"I burnt her photograph. I was so angry with her. I cut her out of her wedding photograph and burnt it in the bin. I wanted her to burn and she did, and I thought it was because of me."

"Baz, if every teenager that wished their parents dead …"

"I know. But not every teenager has my opportunities."

He coughed again and she took a cloth and wiped his face. It seemed like a miracle that she was there, safe and sound. A small act of redemption.

"And the baby is okay?" he asked, again.

"Yes. Absolutely. They're letting me out this afternoon."

"I'd never have forgiven myself if—"

She put a finger to his lips. "Shush, you. Enough guilt trips."

Slowly, his horizons were expanding. People and events came into mind that lay beyond the two fires bracketing his life.

"And everyone else? Did they go to the concert?" he asked.
"Yes, they all went."
"Was it a good gig? What happened? Was there any trouble"?
"Yeah, it was a good gig. A bit quiet. And nope, no trouble."
"Bloody miracle."
"Of course they were all worried sick about you. Especially yesterday, when they were doing tests to see if your spinal cord was damaged."

He wriggled his toes.

"Still in working order, so they tell me. It's these sodding ribs—which hurt like hell, let me tell you. Coughing with broken ribs is not to be recommended." He poked her tummy. "Childbirth, ha!"

"We'll see if you still say that in three months' time."

Baz started to laugh then grimaced. "Shit. Laughing's no picnic either. I'm not going to be much fun for a while."

Maia stooped and kissed his forehead. Her eyelashes brushed against his skin. "I should let you get some rest."

When she came back the next day, conversation was a little easier. She sat beside him on the armchair by the bed, her legs tucked underneath her.

"The police, have they been to see you?"

He nodded.

"Baz, I didn't want to say anything yesterday, but—"

Something in her tone alerted him. He lifted his head from the pillow, then let it back down again, grimacing. "What?"

"I think there's a connection."

"What do you mean?" His brain was still moving too slowly to keep up. She threaded her fingers through his.

"Think about it," she said. "The firebombing at Mr Arain's house. Dr Kheraj being stabbed. Us. What's the linking factor?"

"… Paterson …" he said.

She turned her face away, but not quite enough to hide the flush that rose in her cheeks.

"Right now, I wish I'd kicked the bastard out the first night he came," she said. "If he killed Dr Kheraj—"

He touched her cheek. "Hey, what were you saying about guilt trips?" He smoothed away a strand of hair. "Rebeccah would tell you, helping people is never the wrong thing to do. Another time, it might have been just enough to make a difference."

She looked away, towards the hospital-green wall.

"I've told the police. About what I suspect."

"That's all you can do."

The fire had claimed one other casualty. Rebeccah broke the news later that day.

"Mrs Peel. She was trapped when the conservatory collapsed. The firemen found her body." Rebeccah laid her hand on his forehead the way she would when he was young and in need of comfort. "I've buried her in the garden, underneath her favourite patch of catmint."

At last, the tears came. All the tears he'd held back, for Noordin, for his mother. They flowed now, while Rebeccah cradled his head and let him sob himself into exhaustion.

Chapter 95

The circular mosaic on the floor at my feet represented Africa. The continent that linked Ossie, me and Noordin Kheraj.

Dr Kheraj's children had asked us to say a prayer for their father forty days after his death. Today Baz and I had come to the Chapel of Unity in the new Cathedral to keep that promise. For a long time, I stared at the mosaic, not knowing what to say. Then the baby, growing impatient perhaps, did a somersault inside me, and I remembered how I'd longed to tell the doctor how he'd connected me with my child, helped me find a way to fall in love with this tiny being. A rush of gratitude poured out of me—too incoherent for prayer, but I figured he'd understand.

I felt for the letter in the back pocket of my dungarees. It had come two days ago from South Africa, via a tortuous route of safe houses to the old flat in Leamington Spa, and hence on to Paradise Road.

I've heard from him at last, I told the doctor. I've heard from Ossie. I've got an address. Only a *post restante*, but he promises anything I send there will reach him eventually. So I can do the right thing—tell him that he's going to be a father. I don't know how he'll feel about it, but he has the right know, doesn't he?

I glanced at Baz and saw the tear glimmering at the corner of his eye.

Insha'Allah, that's what you say, isn't it, doctor? I stroked my bump and felt an answering kick. *Insha'Allah*, this one will have a chance to meet his father one day.

I looked once more at the mosaic at my feet, as Baz unclasped his hands and craned his neck towards where the long narrow windows appeared to converge in a ten-pointed star.

Khuda hafiz, doctor.

The tower of the old Cathedral was open for the day and we headed up the spiral stairs. Baz had only just started walking without a stick and sweat soon beaded on his upper lip. My body, too, was slow and heavy. But we had promised each other we would do this.

As we came out at the top, blinking in the bright sunlight, we could hear bells across the city ringing for the Royal Wedding. I'd spoken to my dad that morning: apparently, Mom's proud American republicanism had crumbled at the first glimpse of a golden carriage. In Brixton, Abena told us, the bunting was not red, white and blue but red, gold and green; people were turning the day into a Rasta holiday. Jah Green and Emmett Bailey were knocking in tent pegs for the marquees at the *Healing of Nations* festival. Back at Paradise Road, Libby had planted herself in front of the television with a bottle of Cava and a large box of tissues. Robyn was with her, armed with a homemade 'Don't Do It, Di' placard. And Tom, Simon and Iain had cracked open a polypin of Tom's most lethal homebrew and were laying into it while they prepared the meal we were giving at the Skipper that night, in honour of the *ex gratia* Public Holiday.

I leaned against the parapet of the tower. The sun was on my face and the breeze ruffled my hair. Looking down, I could see the slope of the Upper Precinct where the skinheads drove off the Asian kids. The square of green by Lady Godiva where Beefy grabbed me and Gary held a lighter to my face. Broadgate, where we marched between two walls of Nazi salutes. Behind me were the steps of the Cathedral where I'd seen Gary and Derek argue.

Just before Dr Kheraj's body was released for burial, the police found Derek, holed up in a derry near some old topshops, surrounded by milk bottles and a half-empty jerry can of petrol. Conway told us he'd confessed to our attempted murder, and to the firebomb attack on Abdul Saleem Arain and his family. But he denied murdering Dr Kheraj. Even though he'd tried to kill us, I wanted, I really wanted, to believe that was the truth.

A couple of days after that, a riot broke out in Southall, when a skinhead band tried to play a gig at the Hanborough Tavern. The next day, the riots erupted in Toxteth and then Brixton, Handsworth and a dozen other towns and cities across England. But whether because of The Specials' concert or Baz's exhibition or just because Coventry had shocked itself to its senses, the riots never came here. Like Gary, the city stepped back from the brink.

Today, everything looked tranquil.

"Has anything really changed?" I asked.

The warmth of Baz's body pressed against my back.

"Maybe we've made grain of difference. Enough to buy us a little time. No such thing as a fairytale ending, though."

"What? Not even for a Prince and Princess?"

I leaned back and he folded his arms around me and pressed his chin on the top of my head.

"Yeah, well. Maybe for them. Us ordinary mortals have to settle for the real world, *jaan*."

"I can cope with that."

As Pinda used to say, better to walk than to complain about the road.

Acknowledgements

I am indebted to the archive of the *Coventry Evening Telegraph* at Coventry City Library for providing details of the events that unfolded in Coventry between January and July 1981.

For my account of events during the Brixton riots, I have drawn on the *The Scarman Report: The Brixton Disorders 10-12 April 1981: Report of an Inquiry* (Penguin 1982, supplemented by fictional accounts, especially Alex Wheatle's *East of Acre Lane* (Harper Collins, 2001), and the numerous eye-witness accounts that can be found online.

Other sources of information about the Black and Asian communities in Britain include:

Mike and Trevor Philip's *Windrush: the Irresistible Rise of Multi-Racial Britain*; HarperCollins Publishers Ltd, 1998

Roger Ballard's *Desh Pradesh: South Asian Experience in Britain*; C. Hurst & Co. Publishers, 1994

Yasmin Alibhai-Brown's *Mixed Feelings, the Complex Lives of Mixed Race Britons;* Women's Press Ltd, 2001

Dervla Murphy's *Tales from Two Cities;* John Murray, 1987

Ziauddin Sardar's *Balti Britain: A Provocative Journey Through Asian Britain*; Granta, 2008

Moving Here: Two Hundred Years of Migration to Britain (http://www.movinghere.org.uk/)

The Skipper in Fob Watch Lane is based loosely on the Cyrenian Shelter in nearby Spon Street, where I worked for a summer after leaving university. To fill in the gaps in my memories of the conditions for the homeless, I drew on Tony Wilkinson's *Down and Out* [Quartet, 1981] and Jeremy Sandford's *Down and Out in Britain* [Peter Owen, 1971].

Sudha Buchar, co-director of Tamasha Theatre, kindly read the manuscript and helped me avoid the pitfalls inherent in writing about a culture not one's own. Any mistakes that remain are mine, not hers.

Accuracy in some medical detail has been provided by the unfailingly helpful Writers' Forensic Expert, D. P. Lyle, MD [http://www.dplylemd.com/].

Finally, my thanks, as always, go to Jane Dixon-Smith, my brilliant designer, to Perry Iles, my sharp-eyed and adverb-phobic proofreader, and to my fellow members of the Triskele Books author collective, who have supported me in more ways than I can count.

GLOSSARY

South Asian words and phrases (Punjabi unless otherwise stated)

Aaiie:	exclamation of surprise, disgust etc
Abu (Arabic):	father
Achcha:	Yes; colloquially, 'okay, then'
Achcha?:	really?
Alhamdulillah (Arabic):	Praise God
Arré:	hey (can express a wide range of emotions)
Asalaam alaikum:	Muslim greeting, literally 'Peace be upon you'
Badmaash :	criminals, miscreants. Or affectionately, of children: rascal, scamp
Barfi:	sweets made from condensed milk and nuts
Bara changa:	excellent, very good
Beta:	term of affection for son or daughter; literally, 'son'

Beti:	daughter
Bhangra:	traditional Punjabi dance, originally a harvest celebration
Bhangra music:	traditional or modern music for the Bhangra (dance)
Bhai:	literally 'brother' but used also to refer to male cousins one's own age
Biraderi:	brotherhood
Bismallah (Arabic):	In the name of God
Chak de phatte:	'raise the floorboards,' used as a rousing call to get people dancing the Bhangra
Churha:	sweepers, untouchables
Desi:	meaning 'of our country,' general term used by South Asians to refer to one another
Dhoti:	long cloth wrapped round the waist and legs, worn by men
Dhol:	double headed drum
Dupatta:	scarf loosely covering a woman's hair
Ek Onkar Satnam:	a line of a Sikh prayer, 'God is One, His Name is True'
Five Ks:	the five symbols of Sikhism
Gora (gori/gorey):	white man (woman/people), mildly derogatory
Gurmukhi:	Punjabi script
Gurdwara:	Sikh temple
Haan:	yes

Halal (Arabic):	Pure, permissible
Haram (Arabic):	sinful, impure, not permitted
Haramzada (haramzadey):	bastard(s)
Insha'Allah (Arabic):	God willing
Izzat:	honour
Jaan:	term of endearment between lovers; literally 'life'
Jalebi:	a type of syrupy sweetmeat in the shape of a coil
Jhanda:	flag
ji:	used on its own or as a suffix, indicates respect and affection
Jyot:	small oil lamp used in household shrines
Kala Bandar (plural, kaale):	black monkey, insulting term for a black person
Khota:	donkey, term of insult
Khuda Hafiz (Arabic):	Goodbye used by Muslims; roughly, 'I leave you in the hands of God'
Kiddan:	informal greeting, roughly 'how's it going?'
Kirpan:	ceremonial dagger carried by all baptised Sikhs
Kofta:	curry with spicy balls of meat or vegetables
Kurta:	long shirt
Kurta-pyjama:	long shirt worn over loose trousers (for men)

Laddu:	round sweetmeat
Langar:	a shared meal served after a service in a Gurdwara
Ma-ji:	mum, mummy
Mahabharata:	ancient Hindu epic
Masala chai:	milky black tea brewed with spices like cardamom
Mona Sikh:	secular, unbaptised Sikh; one who cuts his hair and beard
Mudra:	hand positions used in meditation
Murti:	holy statues kept in Hindu temples
Namaste ji:	formal Hindu greeting
Nishan Sahib:	Sikh flag
Papa-ji:	dad, daddy
Pyo:	literally, 'father,' used colloquially as 'the old man'
Phenchod:	Punjabi profanity (literally sister fucker)
Rab da shukar hai:	Thank God for that
Rishi:	scribe or sage
Rishi Knot:	long hair tied into a knot on the top of the head
Roti:	flat bread
Sadhu:	an ascetic, a wandering monk
Sala (saley):	literally, 'brother(s) in law', used insultingly to mean bastard(s) or idiot(s)

Sarson ka saag:	traditional Punjabi dish with spinach and mustard leaves
Sat sri akaal:	formal Sikh greeting
Shalwar kameez:	long blouse and loose trousers worn by women
Sona:	Gold (also beautiful)
Tabla:	pair of hand drums
Tumba:	single stringed instrument
Wehegeru:	Wonderful teacher, referring to God
Yaar:	friend, mate, dude
Zat:	caste, clan

Jamaican/Rasta slang

Babylon:	refers to institutions of authority, especially the police
Beastman:	policeman
Bwai:	boy, youth
Cha:	expression of surprise or annoyance
Coolie:	someone of South Asian extraction (derogatory)
Cyan:	can't
Dub poetry:	performance poetry delivered over Reggae rhythms
Facety:	fussy
Haffe:	have to

Herb:	marijuana
Irie:	Rasta Greeting
Kiss [his/her] teeth:	expression of annoyance or disapproval
Likkle:	Little
Limin':	hanging around on the streets, socialising
Maga:	skinny
Man and man:	everyone
Mon:	man
My yard:	my place
Raas claat:	swear word (literally, arse cloth)
Raatid:	mild swear word
Tallawah:	strong, mighty
The Gong:	nickname for Bob Marley

Other

Bach (Welsh):	endearment ('little one')
Beefheads:	another term for skinheads
Bint (Midlands):	woman (insulting)
British Bulldog:	tag-based and sometimes violent playground game
Butty (South Wales):	friend, mate
Cack (Midlands):	shit
Cock (North Midlands):	mate

Cherryknockers (West Midlands):	kids who bang on a door and run away
Chuffed:	pleased
Cludgie (Scots):	toilet
Chiv:	stab
Deid (Scots):	dead
Derry (homeless slang):	a derelict building used as a shelter
Feck (Irish):	swear word (comparatively mild)
Gadgie (Northeast):	a working man
Gaffer:	boss
Ganja:	marijuana
Have a bun in the oven:	to be pregnant
Lummed up (Scots):	drunk
Mayibuye iAfrika (Xhosa):	Come back, Africa
Mucker (Irish):	friend, mate
My gaff:	my place, my home
Neb (Northeast):	nose
Nosisi (Xhosa):	endearment ('little sister')
On the lash (Irish):	drunk
Poke:	a paper bag (especially for holding chips [fries])
Sais (Welsh):	Englishman
Scrage (Midlands):	scrape or graze
Scran (Irish):	food

Shanachies (Irish):	traditional story-tellers
Shook (Irish):	looking unwell
Skank:	dance style associated with Ska (not unlike running on the spot)
Slag:	sexually loose woman
Solidarność (Polish):	Solidarity (the union that led opposition to communist rule in Poland)
Skelp (Northeast):	beat
Skipper (homeless slang):	a place to sleep
Taff:	insulting way to refer to a Welsh person
Tanner:	slang term for sixpence, occasionally used, post-decimalisation, to refer to any small coin
Thrape (Midlands):	Beat
Toubab (Senegalese):	a white person
Tidy (South Wales):	good
Ubuntu (Xhosa):	Southern African philosophy; 'human kindness'
Up the duff:	pregnant

Thank you for reading a Triskele Book.

Enjoyed *Ghost Town?* Here's what you can do next.

You can explore the locations in Ghost Town on http://pinterest.com/triskelebooks/ghost-town/

Or find out more about the real-life events behind the novel on www.catrionatroth.com.

You can follow Catriona Troth on her blog www.catrionatroth.blogspot.com or on Twitter on https://twitter.com/L1bCat

If you'd like to help other readers find Triskele Books, please write a short review on the website where you bought the book. Your help in spreading the word is much appreciated and reviews make a huge difference to helping new readers find good books.

More novels from Triskele Books coming soon. You can sign up to be notified of the next release and other news here:

www.triskelebooks.co.uk

If you are a writer and would like more information on writing and publishing, visit www.triskelebooks.blogspot.com and www.wordswithjam.co.uk, which are packed with author and industry professional interviews, links to articles on writing, reading, libraries, the publishing industry and indie-publishing.

Connect with us:
Email admin@triskelebooks.co.uk
Twitter @triskelebooks
Facebook www.facebook.com/triskelebooks

Also by Catriona Troth
Gift of the Raven

The people of the Haida Gwaii tell the legend of the raven—the trickster who brings the gift of light into the world.

Canada. 1971.

Terry always believed his father would return one day and rescue him from his dark and violent childhood. That's what Indian warriors were supposed to do. But he's thirteen now and doesn't believe in anything much.

Yet his father is alive. Someone has tracked him down. And Terry is about to come face to face with the truth about his own past and about the real nature of the gift of the raven.

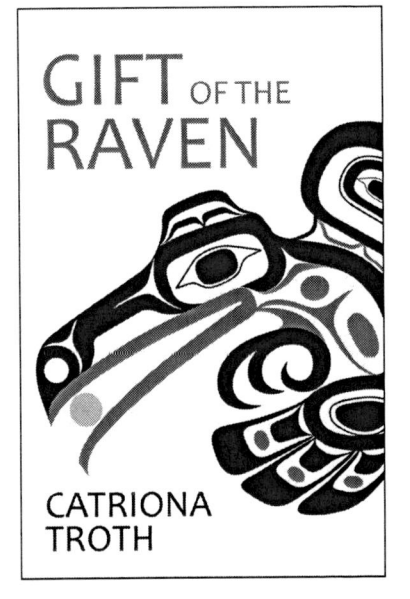

"Don't be fooled into thinking that, because this is an easy read, the novella is light on content. Far from it: there is an underlying richness and a profound sense of compassion pervading through the narrative, and the spirit of the story stays with you for a long time." Jo Barton at jaffareadstoo

You can read the full text of Jo Barton's review at: http://jaffareadstoo.blogspot.co.uk/2013/06/review-gift-of-raven-by-catriona-troth_27.html

Also from Triskele Books
Wolfsangel by Liza Perrat

Seven decades after German troops march into her village, Céleste Roussel still cannot assuage her guilt.

1943. German soldiers occupy provincial Lucie-sur-Vionne, and whilst the villagers pursue treacherous schemes to deceive and swindle the enemy, Céleste embarks on her own perilous mission when her passion for a Reich officer flourishes.

Her loved ones deported to concentration camps, Céleste is drawn into the vortex of this monumental conflict, and the adventure and danger of French Resistance collaboration.

As she confronts the harrowing truths of the Second World War's darkest years, Céleste is forced to choose which battle to pursue: illicit *rendez-vous* with her German lover, or General de Gaulle's call to banish the enemy.

Her fate suspended on the fraying thread of her will, Celeste gains strength from the angel talisman bequeathed to her through her lineage of healer kinswomen. But the decisions she makes will haunt her forever.

A woman's unforgettable journey to help liberate Occupied France, *Wolfsangel* is a stirring portrayal of the courage and resilience of the human mind, body and spirit.

Coming Soon from Triskele Books
Overlord by JD Smith

My name is Zabdas: once a slave; now a warrior, grandfather and servant. I call Syria home. I shall tell you the story of my Zenobia: Warrior Queen of Palmyra, Protector of the East, Conqueror of Desert Lands ...

The Roman Empire is close to collapse. Odenathus of Palmyra holds the Syrian frontier and its vital trade routes against Persian invasion. A client king in a forgotten land, starved of reinforcements, Odenathus calls upon an old friend, Julius, to face an older enemy: the Tanukh.

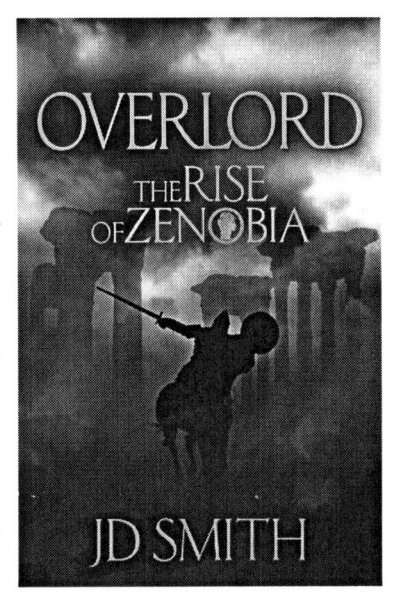

Julius believes Syria should break free of Rome and declare independence. But his daughter's beliefs are stronger still. Zenobia is determined to realise her father's dream.

And turn traitor to Rome ...

Also from Triskele Books

The Open Arms of the Sea by Jasper Dorgan
The Charter by Gillian Hamer
Closure by Gillian E Hamer
Complicit by Gillian E Hamer
Behind Closed Doors by JJ Marsh
Raw Material by JJ Marsh
Tread Softly by JJ Marsh
Spirit of Lost Angels by Liza Perrat
Wolfsangel by Liza Perrat
Tristan and Iseult by JD Smith
Gift of the Raven by Catriona Troth
Overlord – COMING SOON